The Unravelling of Thomas Malone

The Unravelling
of
Thomas Malone

Elly Grant

Books by the Author

Death in the Pyrenees series:

- Palm Trees in the Pyrenees
- Grass Grows in the Pyrenees
- Red Light in the Pyrenees
- Dead End in the Pyrenees
- Deadly Degrees in the Pyrenees

Angela Murphy series:

- The Unravelling of Thomas Malone
- The Coming of the Lord

Also by Elly Grant

- Never Ever Leave Me
- Death at Presley Park
- But Billy Can't Fly
- Twists and Turns

To my husband and children

Prologue

Thomas Malone remembered very clearly the first time he heard the voice. He was twelve years, five months and three days old. He knew that for a fact because it was January 15th, the same day his mother died.

Thomas lived with his mother Clare in the south side of Glasgow. Their home was a main door apartment in a Victorian terrace. The area had never been grand, but in its time, it housed many incomers to the city. First the Irish, then Jews escaping from Eastern Europe, Italians, Polish, Greeks, Pakistanis, they'd all lived there and built communities. Many of these families became the backbone of Glasgow society. However situations changed and governments came and went and now the same terraces were the dumping ground for economic migrants who had no intention of working legally, but sought an easy existence within the soft welfare state system.

A large number of the properties were in the hands of unscrupulous landlords who were only interested in making money. They didn't care who they housed as long as the rent was paid. So as well as the people fleecing the system, there were also the vulnerable who they exploited. Drug addicts, alcoholics, prostitutes, young single mothers with no support, they were easy pickings for the gangsters. The whole area and the people living within it smacked of decay. It had become a no-go district for decent folk, but to Thomas Malone, it was simply home.

Thomas and his mother moved to their apartment on Westmoreland Street when Clare fell out with her parents. The truth was they really didn't want their wayward daughter living with them any more. They were embarrassed by her friends and hated their drinking and loud music. When Clare became pregnant, it was the last straw. Thomas's grandparents were honest, hard-working, middle-class people who had two other children living at home to consider. So when Clare stormed out one day after yet another row with her mother, they let her go. She waited in a hostel for homeless women for three weeks before she realised they weren't coming to fetch her home and that's when Clare finally grew up and took charge of her life in the only way she knew how.

When Thomas walked home from school along Westmoreland Street, he didn't see that the building's façades were weather worn and blackened with grime from traffic fumes. To outsiders they looked shabby and were reminiscent of a mouth full of rotting teeth, but to Thomas they were familiar and comforting. He didn't notice the litter strewn on the road, the odd discarded shoe, rags snagged on railings, or graffiti declaring 'Joe's a wanker' or 'Mags a slag'. He functioned, each day like the one before, never asking for anything because there was never any money to spare.

He was used to the many 'uncles' who visited his mother. Some were kind to him and gave him money to go to the cinema, but many were drunken and violent. Thomas knew to keep away from them. Sometimes he slept on the stairs in the close rather than in his bed so he could avoid any conflict. He kept a blanket and a cushion in a cardboard box by the door for such occasions. Many a time, when he returned from school, he found his mother with her face battered and bruised crying because the latest 'uncle' had left, never to return. It was far from being an ideal life, but it was all he knew so he had no other expectations.

It was a very cold day and, as he hurried home from school, Thomas's breath froze in great puffs in front of him. He was a skinny boy, small for his age with pixie features common to children of alcoholics. His school shirt and thin blazer did little to keep him warm and he rubbed his bare hands together in an attempt to stop them from hurting. He was glad his school bag was a rucksack because he could sling it over his shoulder to protect his back from the icy wind. As his home drew near his fast walk became a jog, then a run, his lungs were sore from inhaling the cold air, but he didn't care, he would soon be indoors. He would soon be able to open and heat a tin of soup for his dinner and it would fill him up and warm him through. He hoped his mother had remembered to buy some bread to dunk.

As Thomas approached the front door something didn't seem right, he could see that it was slightly ajar and the door was usually kept locked. There was a shoe shaped imprint on the front step, it was red and sticky and Thomas thought it might be blood. There was a red smear on the cream paint of the door frame, he was sure it was blood. Thomas pushed the door and it opened with a creak, there were more bloody prints in the hallway.

Thomas took in a great breath and held it as he made his way down the hall towards the kitchen. He could hear the radio playing softly. Someone was singing 'When I fall in love'. He could smell his mother's perfume it was strong as if the whole bottle had been spilled. The kitchen looked like a bomb had hit it. His mother wasn't much of a housekeeper and the house was usually untidy, but not like this. There was broken crockery and glassware everywhere and the radio, which was plugged in, was hanging by its wire from the socket on the wall, dangling down in front of the kitchen base unit. A large knife was sticking up from the table where it was embedded in the wood. The floor was sticky with blood a great pool of it spread from the sink to the door, in the middle of the pool lay the body of Thomas's mother. She was on her side with one arm outstretched as if she were trying to reach for the door. Her lips were twisted into a grimace, her eyes were wide open and her throat was sliced with a jagged cut from ear to ear. Clare's long brown hair was stuck to her head and to the floor with blood and her cotton housecoat was parted slightly to expose one blood-smeared breast.

Thomas felt his skinny legs give from under him, he sank to his knees and his mother's blood smeared his trousers and shoes. He could hear a terrible sound filling the room, a guttural, animal keening which reached a crescendo into a shrieking howl. Over and over the noise came, filling his ears and his mind with terror. Then he heard the voice in his head.

"It's all right, Son," it said. *"Everything will be all right. I'm with you now and I'll help you."*

He felt strong arms lift him from the floor and a policeman wrapped him in a blanket.

"Don't be frightened," the voice told him. *"Just go with the policeman. Someone else will sort out this mess. It's not your problem. Forget about it."*

"Thank you," he mouthed, but no sound came out.

The policeman gathered Thomas in his arms and carried him from the room. It was the last time he ever saw his mother and he cannot remember now how she looked before she was murdered. The voice in his head, the voice that helped him then, remains with him today guiding and instructing him, often bullying, it rules his every thought. Sometimes Thomas gets angry with it but he always obeys it.

Chapter 1

It was ten to six on Tuesday morning and Angela Murphy was already showered and dressed. Her charcoal-grey coloured, 'Next' suit was well cut and a perfect fit, it clung to her long, lean frame in all the right places. You could get the wrong impression about Angela when she was dressed in that suit if it wasn't for the austere white shirt, the no-nonsense opaque black tights and the sensible black leather shoes she wore with it. But in fact, today was Angela's second day as a detective and she was excited and edgy because she'd been assigned to a murder case. Some detectives work their whole career without being involved with anything as meaty, but because Angela was to work with Frank Martin, she went where he went, and he was heading up this investigation.

She sensibly made herself a substantial breakfast and, although she had little appetite because of her anticipation and excitement about the day ahead, she forced herself to eat it all. Who knew when she'd get the chance to stop and eat again? Standing in front of the hall mirror for the umpteenth time, she checked her hair and makeup. Her face had the fresh, healthy look of someone who enjoyed an outdoor life, her skin glowed and her blue eyes sparkled even at this early hour of the morning. Rich, thick, black hair framed her pretty, heart-shaped face and she couldn't help smiling at the image reflected back at her.

"You're smart, you're strong and you're ready," she said to her reflection.

"And you're very hot," a voice behind her said, startling her.

She turned to see her husband Bobby. He was still half asleep but he'd thrown on last night's shirt and a pair of jeans so he could rush downstairs and see her before she left for work. His sandy coloured hair had a tousled look that Angela found particularly attractive and his cheeky smile melted her heart. Bobby was a teacher, head of Maths at his school in fact, and today was a school holiday so he could have stayed in bed. He was tall and strong and very handsome and he looked more like a professional sportsman than a maths teacher. Angela had fallen in love with him the first time they met. On that occasion, she'd been nine years old and the new girl in class and he was the class clown, the daring boy who made everyone laugh, and he was kind to her. Once they finished primary school they lost touch until years later when, as a young police cadet, she gave a talk to the pupils at the school where he worked. After that chance encounter they began dating and two years later they were married.

"You didn't need to get up this early. You're on holiday."

"I wanted to see you off, Darling. Have you had enough to eat? Do you want me to make you a cup of tea?" Bobby asked.

"Thanks, but no thanks, if I have any more tea I'll be peeing all day and I can't use the loo at the murder scene. I've already been to the toilet twice in the last half hour with nerves."

"Don't be nervous, Darling, remember, you're smart, you're strong and you're ready," he replied with a wink.

"Yes I am, I'm all these things, but I'm also scared shitless."

"And you need to leave now," Bobby observed as he glanced at the clock on the kitchen wall. He reluctantly steered her towards the front door, she looked so sexy that he would much rather have steered her back to bed.

After a last hug and a quick peck on the cheek Angela made for her car. She had everything she needed with her but obsessively checked her bag once again before driving off to work.

When Angela arrived at the office there were two detectives at their desks, Jack Dobson and Gordon McKay. Their shift was coming to an end, they looked really tired and their clothes were crumpled. The office was artificially warm and the air was fuggy. Being the middle of winter, the two men had left the heating on full blast all night. Angela couldn't imagine what it would've been like had they been allowed to smoke indoors. As it was, both men reeked of stale tobacco.

"Is the Boss not in yet?" she asked innocently by way of a greeting.

"Been and gone," Jack replied without lifting his head from his 'Classic Cars' magazine.

"Forensics is still at the scene and the body's not been shifted yet. The Boss wants you to meet the corpse in situ. He said you've to grab a driver and make your way over to the scene when you've finally decided to grace us with your company," Gordon added with a smirk.

"But he told me to meet him here at seven o'clock, it's barely gone six thirty," Angela protested.

Gordon gave a shrug and Jack didn't even acknowledge her. Bristling with annoyance at the injustice Angela made her way towards the front desk to try to commandeer a car and driver. As she walked down the corridor she heard Jack and Gordon laughing in her wake and she realised they'd been winding up the new girl. She was angry at herself for being so naïve and rising to the bait. Bastards, she thought, that wouldn't happen again.

It took only a few minutes for Angela to locate a driver in the shape of a fresh faced young constable whose enthusiasm about going to a murder scene was actually rather disturbing. He chattered on and on all the way to Govanhill and by the time they reached their destination Angela had been treated to most of his life story. It was a relief to finally get out of the car and into the creepy stillness of the murder apartment.

Frank Martin was standing in the narrow hallway of the red-sandstone, tenement flat.

"You took your time," he said grumpily. "What've you done with your driver, have you sent him back to the job?"

"And good morning to you too," Angela replied stroppily. "We had arranged to meet at the office at seven and I was there at six-thirty, so please don't talk to me like that. I might be new but I still deserve your respect."

"Feisty, I like it. I see you're going to keep me on my toes Missy."

He smiled at Angela and she calmed down and managed to return a grimace. "And don't call me Missy. I'm Detective Murphy or Angela if we're on our own."

"Yes, Mam," Frank replied, laughing. "That's put me firmly in my place. As long as you remember that my place is superior to you. As long as you don't forget that I'm the boss."

"Yes Boss," Angela replied determined to have the last word.

"Send the boy away," he said, now noticing the young policeman hovering by the doorway. I've got my car outside. Then come back in here and for goodness sake suit up and cover your shoes. Although forensics is finished, this place is covered in blood."

Angela went back out of the front door, she told the young constable that he was no longer needed and he reluctantly left. She wiped her shoes with a tissue before covering them because they were smeared with blood. In her rush to get inside she hadn't noticed just how much of it there was on the floor of the hallway. It was lucky she wasn't squeamish.

When she returned Frank had entered the kitchen and he was kneeling beside the body of a young woman. Frank was a big man. He was tall and broad with a large, square shaped head and enormous meaty looking hands. No one would describe him as handsome in truth he was rather ugly. He had a fat face with little piggy eyes and a squashed nose which had been broken more than once. His skin reminded Angela of a greasy, pork sausage. However, incongruously, Frank was a fastidious dresser and Angela knew that under his protective suit, his clothes would be immaculate and expensive. His hair was perfectly groomed, not a strand out of place and his fingernails were manicured and spotlessly clean.

"Something's not right here," Frank muttered. "I'm having a de-ja-vu moment. I've seen this crime scene before. That knife embedded in the table and the radio hanging from the socket, I've seen all this before."

Angela didn't comment. She stood transfixed beside the corpse. She didn't sicken easily but nothing could have prepared her for the brutality of what she saw.

"You see the way the body is draped in that dressing gown with one boob hanging out? And the way she is reaching towards the door? I've seen this same layout before. It was about ten years ago. Just round the corner in Westmoreland Street. I was new to the job, just like you, and there was a child involved, a wee skinny boy about twelve years old. He came home from school to find his mother dead, with her throat cut, just like this poor cow. This is really weird it's the same scene all over again. I think someone staged this. I think there might be a connection."

After two more hours of Frank's mutterings and copious note taking by Angela, they'd gathered all the information there was to be had from the apartment. As they stepped outside onto the pavement Angela found herself blinking at the brightness of the morning sun. She felt rather dazed by the contrast between it and the dim, dingy, artificial light of the flat and she reached out to steady herself by grabbing onto the railings at the side of the building.

"Your not going to faint on me, are you?" Frank asked as he grabbed her by the elbow. "You look a bit peaky, are you okay?"

"I'm all right. It's just the brightness of the sun after the darkness in there. I don't faint but thanks for caring."

Angela drew her elbow from Frank's grasp. The big man gave her a sheepish look and cleared his throat.

"We have months of summer without a hint of blue sky just grey and rain every day and now, in the middle of winter, would you just look at that." He pointed upwards with his thumb. "Bloody cold though, it must be minus something. After the damp in that apartment I need something to heat me up. The mobile incident room's arrived at the end of the street we'll walk down to it and see if they've got the coffee on yet."

Angela was delighted to be out of the oppressive apartment and she inhaled deeply to try to clear her head. She hadn't realised just how bad it smelled in there until she'd stepped outside. It had been a cloying mixture of dirty cooking oil and cheap perfume mixed with deprivation and despair. Angela thought it unlikely that the dead girl could even imagine how the other half lived, she'd probably never seen inside a clean, suburban home.

Frank and Angela made their way down the street to the mobile unit and, when they entered it, they were immediately handed polystyrene cups of boiling coffee by a young policewoman. Frank commandeered the only two chairs and the small desk and, as they sat in the tiny space sipping their coffees, he planned the rest of the morning's work. He suggested that Angela go and interview the neighbour who'd made the first emergency call.

"You'll have to see if you can take a uniformed officer with you," Frank said. "I've nobody to spare. We're stretched to the limit because some people are off sick with the bloody flu. It should be quite easy to get what you need from the woman," Frank added. "I've been told that Mrs Ali is the neighbourhood busy-body so she'll have plenty to tell you. Just try and sift through the dross until you get to what she actually saw and heard. It'll probably take you the rest of the morning. I'm going back to the office."

"But you have the car," Angela protested. "How am I supposed to get back when I'm finished with Mrs Ali? You told me to send the other car away."

"For a clever girl you can be really dumb sometimes. I do hope you're not going to be one of these moaning minnies, whining all the time," Frank answered quietly so as not to be overheard. "When I leave this incident room you are the most senior officer here. You are in charge. Just call for a car when you need it and someone will come and fetch you. For God's sake don't let anyone here think you're not up to the job or they'll fall on you like a pack of dogs. Remember, you're in charge, right?"

"Yes Boss," Angela replied embarrassed by her faux-pas. She'd never been in charge before and she was thrilled by the prospect. When Frank left Angela made a quick telephone call to Bobby.

"Guess what, Pet," she began. "I'm in charge. Isn't that so cool?"

"Fantastic," he replied enthusiastically. "I knew you'd be okay. You're smart, you're strong and you're ready, right?"

She laughed softly unable to hide her delight.

"I've been to the twenty-four hour ASDA in Toryglen and I'm cooking my special pasta for dinner. There's a bottle of Rose chilling in the fridge to wash it down. Is that okay?"

"Perfect, it sounds perfect. I'm so glad you didn't buy steak because after what I've just seen, I couldn't have stomached it."

Angela noticed that the young policewoman who'd made the coffees was waiting patiently for her to end the call.

"Gotta go now, we'll liaise later," she said into the phone, trying to sound businesslike.

"I'll liaise with you any time you like," Bobby replied suggestively.

Angela smiled to herself, "Bye now," she said ending the call.

"I've been assigned to you," the policewoman said when Angela returned the phone to her pocket. "I'm Constable Brown, Liz Brown."

"Pleased to meet you Liz," Angela replied proffering her hand. "I'm Detective Murphy, Angela Murphy."

Liz took Angela's outstretched hand and shook it vigorously. The two women couldn't have looked more different. Liz was short whilst Angela was tall. Liz was sporty looking and had better muscles than most of her male colleagues where Angela was slim and elegant. Angela could pass for a model but Liz looked more like an athlete. Both had naturally pretty faces. The two women sat at the table for a few minutes and discussed how they were going to handle the interview with Mrs Ali then they left the confines of the mobile unit and made their way down the street towards her home.

Chapter 2

Stupid, stupid, bitch. Look what you made me do. He was right. I knew he would be, all the signs were there, cheap booze, cheap perfume and that filthy kitchen. I tried to ignore it. I almost convinced myself you were my friend but he knew you were just a whore. Why did you do it? I don't understand. If you needed money I would have given it to you, that's what friends do, they help each other. You only had to ask me.

Stupid, stupid, bitch. Now look at you, lying in the dirt. I could have been your friend. But no, you had to offer me your disgusting body for money to buy drugs. As if I would want you that way. I'm not a loser. Dirty, dirty, whore. It's all your fault. Everything is your fault. Look what you made me do.

* * *

Angela found it difficult to get the image of the dead girl out of her head. It was just so shocking. She thought that once she was out of the apartment she could push it all from her mind, but instead everything seemed more vivid as she walked along the street in the fresh air. If Frank Martin was right about the death scene being staged and linked to a previous murder, what kind of monster would they be dealing with she wondered?

"Are you all right, you're very quiet and rather pale. Are you not feeling well?"

Liz's words broke Angela's train of thought. "I'm sorry Liz, I was miles away. I'm okay, just a bit dazed from being in that apartment. It was pretty awful in there."

"We could take a walk around the block before we go to interview Mrs Ali, if you'd like," Liz offered.

"Thanks, Liz, but we'd better not. Time is important and she might know something that will help us nail the bastard who did this."

The terrazzo steps leading to Mrs Ali's main-door apartment were scrubbed and gleaming and the brass surround of the front doorbell was polished to within an inch of its life. When Angela rang the bell the door was opened by a short, plump woman aged about forty. She had a clear, pale complexion and she was dressed in a two piece suit made from burnt-orange coloured chiffon fabric. The sound of children's squeals and laughter drifted from behind her.

"Mrs Ali?" Angela asked. "I'm Detective Murphy and this is Constable Brown."

"School holidays," the woman said by way of a greeting. "Doesn't it drive you mad?" It was more of a statement than a question.

They were ushered into the large, front room and offered a seat on the leather, cream-coloured suite. Mrs Ali disappeared for a couple of minutes to chase her curious and noisy children into another room leaving Angela and Liz to take in their surroundings. The room was an odd mix of style and colours. The carpet was a patterned blue and, at the window, heavy curtains of plum and gold brocade hung from a pelmet to the floor. Wine-coloured, Regency striped wallpaper adorned the walls. From the ceiling hung a magnificent crystal chandelier and gold-coloured, glass-topped, occasional tables were placed at various parts of the room. Everything was spotlessly clean and smelled of polish. Angela was very impressed, although not to her own taste, there was no doubt that a lot of money, time and effort had been spent creating and maintaining this room.

"Would you like tea?" Mrs Ali asked in a broad Glasgow accent when she re-entered the room. Angela glanced at Liz who smiled and shook her head.

"Thank you, no, I'd like to get started on my notes if you don't mind," Angela replied and Liz took her notebook and pen from her pocket.

"I'm sorry for that poor lassie's mother. Imagine finding out your daughter was a prostitute. Imagine the shame of it," Mrs Ali began. "Her name was Magrit you know, everyone knew what she was."

"Margaret as in M.A.R.G.A.R.E.T.?" Liz spelled.

"Aye, that's right, Magrit, Magrit Deacon. When she first moved here she said she was a nursery nurse and she asked me if there was any baby-sitting work about. As if anyone would leave their children in the care of a junkie prostitute. We all knew what type of girl she was. Men visiting day and night, she couldn't fool anyone. This used to be a decent community you know. Then the Council began renting flats to all and sundry and now we have a dead prostitute on our doorstep. I've told my man we'll have to move. I'm not having my children exposed to that sort of rubbish."

"Could you tell us what you saw and heard last night that made you think something was wrong?" Angela interrupted.

"Aye, aye, let me think now. I was standing in the street outside Mrs Rehman's house speaking to Mrs Rehman. She lives next door to Magrit. It was about six o'clock and I had just been to the fruit shop to buy onions when Magrit and a tall, slim, man in a hoodie went into the house. I just thought it was another of her customers. At eight o'clock I was walking past again because I was collecting my daughter, Nusrat, from her friend's house where they'd been studying together. She is such a good student my daughter, my man and I are expecting her to get five 'A's' in her 'Highers' you know. He says she can go to University if she gets good grades. In my day girls rarely went to University because you got married young and had a family so there was no time for further education. But it's different now, girls have much more opportunity."

"What happened at eight o'clock?" Angela prompted trying to get Mrs Ali back to the question.

"I was passing Magrit's house and the door was open. I could hear shouting coming from inside." She hesitated and looked uncomfortable. "I'm sorry, but I don't swear I can't say the words I heard."

"Could you write it down for us Mrs Ali?" Liz asked. "I have some paper here."

"It's so embarrassing, I hate bad language, but as it's just us here, I'll tell you if one of you stands at the door to make sure that none of my children overhear."

Liz handed Angela the notebook and walked over to the door then she nodded and mouthed an okay to Mrs Ali.

"He shouted 'stupid bitch', stupid bitch, over and over again. Then he shouted the 'F' word over and over again. I thought I heard Magrit shout, 'get out' then there was a scream. To tell you the truth, I was a bit frightened so I didn't stop. I went to pick up my Nusrat, I thought it was just Magrit and one of her customers. Mrs Rehman told me there was often a lot of noise coming from that house. I didn't know the lassie was being murdered."

Liz returned to her seat retrieving her notebook from Angela. They gave Mrs Ali a moment to blow her nose and regain her composure. She was obviously much more upset than she'd first let on.

"What happened that prompted you to call the police?" Angela asked.

Mrs Ali concentrated she touched her forehead with the fingertips of her right hand then said, "I was walking along the street at about twenty past eight with Nusrat. We were talking about making her a new three piece suit with some pretty fabric she'd seen in the sari shop. We were just passing Magrit's house when a man ran out and he bumped into my Nusrat. If I hadn't caught hold of her arm she would have been knocked to the pavement. Her schoolbag fell and her books were all over the place. It was the same man I saw earlier, the tall man in the hoodie. He didn't stop to apologise, he didn't stop, period. He just ran down the street towards the main road. As he passed us I'm sure I saw blood on him. His hoodie was light grey and it was covered in dark red patches."

She stopped to blow her nose again. "Please go on," Angela said.

"I saw that Magrit's door was still open, but I didn't want to go in because I was frightened and besides, I had Nusrat with me. So I rang the bell at Mrs Rehman's. There was no answer because Mrs Rehman and her family were visiting her son round the corner. Her daughter-in-law just had a baby, a boy, eight pounds ten ounces and they'd gone to see the baby."

"So you came home with Nusrat then you phoned the police from here?"

"Aye, that's right. I telephoned Govanhill police station and told them what I'd heard and seen."

"You didn't call 999?"

"No, I didn't want to waste police time. I didn't know she was murdered. How could I know?"

"Would you recognise this man if you saw him again, could you give us a description?"

"Not really, I didn't see his face, he was tall and he was wearing a hoodie that's all I know. Are you sure you won't have tea?"

"No, thank you Mrs Ali, I think we're about finished now," Angela said and stood up. "I'll prepare your statement then, if you don't mind, would you come into the station to sign it?"

"I'm not going to the police station. I don't want the neighbours to think I'm complaining about them. These Albanians are dangerous, you know. They could stick you with a knife as soon as look at you. I don't mind going to the incident room on the street because they'll know then it's about Magrit and not them."

"That's fine Mrs Ali, I'll be in touch."

Angela and Liz left the house and made their way back down the street.

"She saw the murderer, didn't she?" Liz asked.

"Yes, I'm sure she did. I just hope he didn't see her. He's a very dangerous man and by the sound of things he's got a short fuse. According to Mrs Ali there wasn't much time between his shouting and Margaret's scream."

"And Magrit sounded delightful, a junkie prostitute. Her mother will be so ashamed." Liz said mimicking Mrs Ali's voice with comical accuracy.

"You're terrible Liz. How can you poke fun at a time like this?" Angela asked unable to stop smiling at her.

Chapter 3

He sat in the steaming hot bath and scrubbed at his hands and arms with a nail brush but he couldn't get rid of her stink.

'*I told you she was a slut. I told you she was a dirty whore but you wouldn't listen. You just wouldn't listen*'. The man's voice pounded his brain. '*All the signs were there, you saw them, the cheap perfume and that filthy kitchen. But you knew better, didn't you? You stupid little shite*.'

He began to sob, great, loud, painful gasps. "I thought she was my friend. I just wanted her to be my friend. Please leave me alone," he begged.

'*Friend, hah, you don't have any friends, just me and I don't like you very much, you useless piece of crud, I don't like you at all, but I'm stuck with you and you're stuck with me. Remember that the next time you ignore me. I'm inside your head and you're stuck with me until I choose to leave*.'

"Choose to leave? What do you mean choose to leave?" His voice sounded thin and reedy like a frightened child. "I can't manage without you. You know that. Why are you threatening me? Please don't leave me. Please don't leave me again. I'll be good, I'll listen to you, I promise I will."

Thomas Malone ran more scalding water into the tub and scrubbed and scrubbed at his skin with the nail brush until it bled.

* * *

Thomas liked his job, it empowered him. After his mother died his life was one rejection after another. His Grandparents didn't want to take him in. His Grandfather told the authorities that he could barely cope with his wife, who'd been disabled by a stroke, so a traumatised and disturbed twelve year old would probably finish him off. Thomas didn't even get to meet his family because his Grandfather insisted on no contact. He said it was kinder not to give Thomas any false hopes. Kinder for who?

He hated the children's home because being an introverted, slightly-built child, placed him well down the pecking order and being bullied by the older, more street-wise children became an almost daily ritual. Even the younger children stole his meagre belongings then challenged him to take them back which he, of course, didn't. Thomas was too unhappy and frightened to even try.

The authorities did try to place him in foster care but it wasn't successful. The first foster mother complained and said he upset her own children with behaviour that 'creeped them out', whatever that meant. She also said he had an inappropriate affinity to knives and she was rather frightened of him. So Thomas was removed and returned to the local authority's care. The second home might have worked out because the couple were kind to him, but unfortunately they were not kind to each other and they separated, so once again, Thomas was returned to the home. After that the social workers stopped trying. It was a relief when he could finally leave the place and move into his own bed-sit because, for the first time in a long time, he felt safe.

At the beginning it was a real struggle for him trying to live within the benefit system, but Thomas was smart and he soon learned how to make some extra money on the side. He also attended college where he made sure to always conduct himself in an appropriate way. He was well-mannered and polite and his landlord and lecturers respected him. Thomas's life changed completely when his college principal helped him to get a job as a traffic warden. Mr Barker, 'barking mad', as he was called by the other students, wrote Thomas a wonderful reference which won him the post.

Suddenly Thomas found himself in a position of power. He was in charge and he had a uniform to prove it. It didn't matter if the recipients of the tickets he wrote were nasty or nice, polite or rude because his word was law. He was less lonely at work because people spoke to him and not just the public asking for directions. The police spoke to him and treated him like a colleague, bus drivers and taxi drivers passed the time of day with him cracking jokes and telling stories. The manageress of 'Tasty Bakers' in Victoria Road gave him free coffee when he went in to buy his lunch.

Thomas liked his job very much and most of the time, when he was working, he functioned normally. It was the rest of the time that gave him grief, the times when his mind was not fully occupied. It was then that the voice sneaked in and took over his thoughts. At first, he didn't know who the voice belonged to, but after a while he believed it to be his father. His mother always said his father was dead and they were better off without him. She never told Thomas anything about him she just said he was gone and he was never coming back. Thomas believed her and he was sad because he'd never known what it felt like to have a 'Dad'. He often wondered how and when he'd died.

Before his mother died Thomas's life was much different. He was introduced to many 'uncles' who drifted in and out of their lives. Every time a new one arrived he hoped that this man would become his Dad. They came and went like the changing seasons and mostly he only remembered the cruel ones, but Uncle Mal was different from the rest because he stayed for almost two years. His Mum didn't bring men home when he lived with them, instead she went out to work in the evenings and brought her pay back to Mal. Clare seemed happy with Mal and Thomas really liked him because he bought all the latest computer games. He stayed home and played 'Super Mario' with Thomas while Clare went out at work. He called Thomas, 'wee man' in a chummy sort of way that made him feel like part of a family. In fact Mal was the closest thing he'd ever had to a father.

20

Then, like all the others before him, Mal suddenly left. Thomas's mother was bereft. She couldn't understand how he could just go without a word. She searched every pub and every bookie's for three weeks before she discovered he was dead. Clare eventually found out that he'd been killed by a bus in Argyle Street when he fell off the pavement while blind drunk. One of Mal's cronies came round to see her and he told her that Mal had been married and his widow had already held the funeral. She also discovered that he'd had other 'second families' and, in the words of his friend, 'Mal got around a bit'. This news threw Clare into a deep depression that went on for months. During this time she developed a very expensive drug habit. Thomas was upset when the computer console and games were sold as it was his only tangible connection to Mal, but they needed the money so, as usual, he accepted his lot without complaint.

When he thought back on his life it made him angry because it was a rotten life. His mother was a junkie and she was a whore and he'd deserved better. He knew that now because the voice in his head told him. When he heard the voice it upset him because it told him things he didn't want to hear and it made him do things he didn't want to do. But a boy must obey his father so Thomas always did as he was told.

Chapter 4

On Liz's advice Angela had some lunch before heading back to the office. Liz was the third generation of her family to be a cop and both her brothers were policemen.

"Trust me," she said, "Eat whenever you can when you're on a job because the high heed yins think you're a machine. They think you can run on hard work and air."

When Angela got back to the office it was practically empty. There was just one typist clicking away on her computer keyboard and a detective called Paul Costello in the room. The office was overdue for refurbishment and nothing had been upgraded since the nineteen-sixties. The grey, metal desks and filing cabinets, strip lighting and vinyl floor covering, had seen better days and the whole place looked dingy and depressing. Angela had just laid her bag on a desk when a voice boomed out from the small room at the end of the main office.

"Murphy," Frank Martin roared. "Get your arse in here and bring coffee with you, milk, no sugar."

Paul Costello chuckled and shook his head.

"Is he always that polite, or have I been singled out for special attention?" Angela asked.

"Naw, it's not you, Hen, he's always a grumpy old bastard. You'll get used to it."

"I don't think so," Angela said, setting her jaw in a determined way that made Paul chuckle again.

"What are you doing Murphy? I'm dying of caffeine deficiency here. Get a bloody move on."

Paul winked and smiled. "You'd better get going before he blows a gasket. The coffee will calm him down. I'm sure he'd rather have a Scotch, but he doesn't drink on the job, well not much, not like some of them."

Angela picked up two polystyrene cups and filled them with coffee then headed for Frank's room.

"You took your time," he said as she placed the cups on his desk. "Typical, you wait for ages then two turn up at once," he added eyeing the coffees.

"One's for me," Angela said stating the obvious. "I don't appreciate being bellowed at across the office. I know you're the Boss, but your manners are atrocious and it's against all policy to speak to me like that. Would you please try to remember I'm a professional," she added primly.

"Oh, for fucks sake, Angela, this isn't some namby pamby girl's finishing school. If you're going to survive in this job you'll hear a lot worse than me. Get over yourself girl. Now pull up a chair, sit down and shut up."

Angela bristled with indignation, but rather than create a fuss, she did as she was told and sat down on the ripped leather chair facing Frank. It surprised her that, although he was fastidious about his person, his office was a mess. The bin was overflowing with rubbish and pieces of screwed up paper lay around it on the floor. His wooden desk was pitted and marked with rings and the cork message board behind it had aged notes, curled and brown, attached haphazardly with drawing pins.

"What did you find out from the witness?" Frank asked.

"Not a lot, I'm afraid. She saw a tall, slim, man wearing a grey hoodie, but as Mrs Ali is very short, to her, a tall person might be anything over five foot six. The timing was right though and she was close enough to see what she thought were blood stains on the hoodie. Are these the photos from the scene?" She asked nodding at the images strewn on the desk.

"No, these are the photos from the other murder, ten years ago. It could be the same apartment. You thought they were from this morning's job. I told you it looked staged."

"Oh my God, you're absolutely right, it looks the same. The radio plugged into the socket and hanging off the worktop, the way she's lying with the robe slightly open and her hair stuck to the floor with blood, it's identical."

"Aye, the only thing missing from the scene, as I remember it, is the victim's son."

"I didn't realise you were actually at the first scene. It must have been quite disturbing to witness today's murder with it being so alike."

"It freaked me out. I don't mind telling you. It really freaked me out."

"Do you think we're dealing with the same killer?"

"I just don't know. If it is, where's he been for ten years? The original killer was never caught, so it's not like he was in jail. In fact, when I read the case file, I was shocked at how little we'd had to go on. There were no witnesses and hardly any evidence. The woman was a prossie, dozens of men visited the house. It could have been anyone."

"You said she had a son, didn't he see anything? Couldn't he give the names of any of the men?"

"No, the lad was traumatised. The only men he mentioned were his Uncle Mal, who was dead, and his father, who he'd never met, and who was also dead."

"What happened to the boy?"

Angela, it's been ten years, who the hell cares what happened to a dead prossie's son? Let's concentrate on the job in hand. We need to get out on the street and talk to people. If Mrs Ali saw something then maybe other people have information too."

"So you want me to go back to Govanhill? I've just got into the office. Could you not have phoned me and told me to stay put?"

"What's your problem? You're being paid. Are you worried about missing your lunch?"

"No problem, Boss, I've already had my lunch," Angela replied smugly. So that's his game, she thought. Keep the junior on her toes. Give her a hard time and toughen her up. Nice try.

"I'm requesting a uniformed officer to assist me. Have you any objections?"

Frank smiled slowly, "I take it you have someone in mind for the job?"

"I don't care who it is," Angela replied, not wanting to give anything away. "As long as they're smart and don't get under my feet."

"Choose who you like, it makes no difference to me as long as their boss is okay with it. Just get you're arse back out there and come up with some answers before the press remember the previous case and crucify us. Now fuck off back to work and give me some space."

As soon as Angela got back to her desk she put in a request for Liz Brown. Although she was a junior officer she had a lifetime of experience dealing with cops and that was just what Angela needed. With a bit of luck Liz might be able to help her understand what made Frank tick.

Chapter 5

By the time Angela got home she was exhausted. She found a space at the side of the house to park her car, although it was more abandoned than parked. She didn't have the energy to negotiate the garage and she knew that Bobby would take care of it later for her. As soon as she entered the hall he was there to greet her.

"How was your day, Darling?" he asked. Before she could answer Bobby noticed her drawn look. "I'll run you a hot bath, you look beat," he said. "There's a bottle of wine in the kitchen, it's open, pour yourself a glass."

Bobby briefly embraced her, kissed her forehead then disappeared upstairs. After getting herself some wine, Angela went into the lounge and flopped into the recliner. The chair was an extravagant purchase they'd made to celebrate her new job and, as she sank into the luxurious, plush leather, she felt it had been worth every penny. Angela gulped at the wine swallowing but hardly tasting it and, by the time Bobby returned to usher her upstairs, the glass was empty and she was practically asleep.

When Angela returned after her bath she felt revived, Bobby had dinner ready and she was now able to discuss her day. She quickly ran through the events leaving out the more gory details, not just to spare Bobby, but also to avoid having to remember them herself.

"Your Boss sounds like a bit of a prick," Bobby said. "Will you manage to work with him?"

"He's actually okay, just a bit rough round the edges. He's let me have an assistant which I'm pleased about. I'll have to use my own car though, all the work vehicles have been signed out, but I'll get a mileage allowance. I prefer my car anyway, it'll be fine, and I'm not likely to be doing any high speed chases," she replied, smiling.

"John Kerr phoned me today," Bobby said changing the subject. "Do you remember him?"

"Yes, he was a physics teacher, wasn't he? Nice guy but a bit of a geek. You haven't heard from him for ages, didn't he move to the Borders?"

"Yes, that's right he went to teach at a private school. Anyway, he's done rather well for himself. The school's great, there are only about twenty pupils in each class and the kids are keen to learn. He said the head of Maths is about to retire and he immediately thought of me for the job."

"Nice of him to think of you," Angela replied, "But surely he knows our life is here in Glasgow. You can't just drop everything and move to the Borders."

"I know, I know, but I can dream, can't I?"

Angela looked at Bobby's face. He seemed sad and rather defeated. She was so caught up in her own job recently she hadn't noticed this before. "I didn't know you were unhappy. I thought you loved your job," she said.

"I do love my job, Darling, I love teaching, but the school I'm in is a shit hole. The classes are huge, thirty kids at least. Half of them don't want to be there, they're disruptive and bored and the other half struggle to concentrate because of the constant disturbances."

"But didn't one of your pupils win the National Maths Challenge last year?"

"Yes, Keiran Bedi, she was my star pupil. She got five 'Highers', each one a high band 'A'. I was all set for her sixth year, she was practically guaranteed a place at a top university, but she didn't come back after the holidays."

"Why ever not?"

"She was married off. Her husband owns a fruit shop and he's nearly twice her age. Instead of becoming a doctor or a lawyer she's the wife of a shopkeeper who's old enough to be her father. All her hopes and aspirations have been swept aside. In ten years time she'll have five kids, her husband will be middle-aged and she'll still be in her twenties."

"But maybe that's the sort of life she wants, maybe she wants to be a wife and mother," Angela argued.

"Not a chance. After her 'Highers' last year she was planning which universities to apply for. She was excited about learning. Her life's been thrown away. She's the oldest of three daughters. Her parents have fulfilled their duty then wiped their hands of her."

"Is that why you're looking at other jobs? Why don't you apply for a post in a private school nearer home?"

"I plan to," Bobby replied. "It's just that they don't come up very often."

"I'm so sorry you're unhappy, I had no idea," Angela said. "I interviewed a woman called Mrs Ali, today. Her daughter Nusrat is doing very well at school and she told me her husband wants the girl to go to university, so not every Asian parent chooses marriage as a first option for their daughters."

"Ignore me Darling, school holidays give me too much time to think. I'll get over it tomorrow when I'm back at work. We've got a great life, I'm sorry I moaned, and my job's a pushover compared to what you've been through today."

Angela was unsettled by the conversation and although they began to watch a film on television, she couldn't get into the plot. She relied on Bobby to be her rock and hadn't considered his needs. What if he became more and more disillusioned? She'd heard about teachers who'd had complete breakdowns because of the pressures of the job. Angela realised she'd have to pay more attention to Bobby. He'd been supporting her and she'd let him, without thanks or even acknowledgement. She'd acted like a selfish child. Her earlier conversations with Frank Martin came flooding back to her and she realised how prim and foolish she must have sounded. 'Time to grow up', she thought.

Chapter 6

"Just another half hour Tommy then we can go home. We should get a few bookings in this street. Everyone thinks they'll be okay in the last half hour so they don't pay the meter. Which side of the street do you want, Mate, the one with the Merc or the one with the BMW? Tommy, Tommy. Are you listening?"

Thomas was staring at two women who were standing on the street corner. They were both scantily clad for the time of year. It was obvious to anyone who observed them that they were prostitutes. His colleague, Alan, followed Thomas's gaze in time to see the two women kiss each other on the lips.

"Ugh!" Alan said in disgust. "Can you imagine kissing one of them on the mouth knowing where their mouths have been? They make me sick. I wish we could ticket them for being illegally parked."

Thomas shuddered at the image Alan's words conjured up.

'*Dirty whores,*' the voice said. '*They should be put down, done away with. They're poison.*'

"See that pair, they're lesbians, you know," Alan continued. "They don't even like men. They just use them for money. What kind of sad bastard would want a dirty, scabby lesbian sucking on his dick? He would have to be desperate."

Thomas didn't reply. He continued staring at the women and listened to the voice in his head.

"You're too late Tommy," Alan shouted, as he ran across the street. "I'm having the BMW."

When he reached the car he smiled at Thomas, gave him a 'thumbs up' sign then began to write a ticket. At the end of their shift Alan invited Thomas for a beer, but he declined. Although he liked spending time with Alan he was shy and didn't feel ready to socialise with him yet.

"See you tomorrow then," Alan said. "We'll be back at our usual patch in Govanhill, home ground for you."

Thomas continued watching the women. The voice in his head was relentless, describing things Thomas didn't want to hear. After a while the women finished their conversation, said their goodbyes, and set off in different directions.

'*Follow that skinny bitch,*' the voice said. '*See where she lives.*'

Thomas was tired and he just wanted to go home. He didn't want to follow the woman. The very sight of her made him feel squeamish. But how could he ignore the voice? How could he defy his father? Thomas was pleased when she stopped at the same bus stop he normally used. He hoped that she too was going to Govanhill then he wouldn't have to travel out of his way.

The bus stop was surprisingly busy for the time of day and it was difficult to keep track of the woman in the milling crowd but when his bus, the number sixty-six arrived, Thomas was delighted to see her get on.

'*Go and sit beside her,*' the voice said. '*Get a good look at the dirty bitch. Does she remind you of your mother? She was a skinny whore too.*'

"Shut up, shut up, she's not a bit like my Mum," Thomas hissed. "My Mum was beautiful. People liked her."

The woman getting onto the bus alongside Thomas gave him a sympathetic look and he realised that he'd spoken aloud.

"I'm not sitting beside her," he said. "I'll sit in the seat behind."

'*Wimp,*' the voice said contemptuously, '*Scared of a dirty whore.*'

Thomas fidgeted nervously in his seat and as the bus neared Victoria Road he began to worry. What if she didn't get off, he could end up anywhere. He started to rock slightly in his seat.

'*Sit still, idiot,*' the voice bellowed. '*You're drawing attention to yourself. I know you're a useless piece of shit, no need to prove it to the whole bus.*'

Thomas took a deep breath and clasped his hands tightly together, they were cold and clammy. Then he exhaled slowly. The bus approached Alison Street, his stop. He couldn't sit still. Nearly at the stop, what should he do? He didn't know. Should he get off? The bus stopped, the woman stood up and joined the line of departing passengers, relief swept over him.

"Hah," he said and jumped to his feet, once again drawing curious looks from the other passengers as he pushed his way to the door and alighted. He followed the woman as she turned into Alison Street. She scurried along it with a quick, jerky walk. Thomas practically had to run to keep up with her. When she reached the corner with Garturk Street she suddenly wheeled round.

"Are you following me?" she shouted. "Are you looking for a girl-friend?"

"N-no," Thomas stammered.

The voice in his head was screaming, '*Fucking bitch. As if you'd want a diseased whore. She's got pock marks on her face, for Christ's sake.*'

"Are you sure?" the girl asked. "I'm good with virgins. I won't bite," she added smiling, revealing a mouth full of brown, rotting teeth.

Thomas stared in horror at her, he felt nauseated and shied away. The woman was annoyed.

"Well fuck off then and stop following me. You probably couldn't get it up anyway," she added maliciously and took off across the road.

Thomas continued to watch her as she turned into a close and disappeared. Number twenty-two he noted. After a couple of minutes a light came on at a first floor window and he could see her as she closed the curtains.

'*Now you've got her,*' the voice said. '*Apartment one up right, 22 Garturk Street. Go home for your tea, Boy. Get a rest. Her time will come. You'll know when the time is right.*'

"Yes," repeated Thomas. "I'll know and I'll be ready."

Chapter 7

The streets of Govanhill consisted of vast Victorian terraces of tenement buildings and these constructions were built of the sandstone that Glasgow is famous for. Many areas of the city had tenements and in some locations, like Muirend and Shawlands, the apartments had become desirable first homes for young, high flyers and children of the rich, but not Govanhill. The hotch-potch of incomers which included economic immigrants, both legal and illegal, together with many Housing Benefit tenants who'd never worked and didn't ever intend to, diluted the quality of life in the area. Throw in a quantity of drug pushers, alcoholics and prostitutes and the area was lost. Although Govanhill had well constructed housing, decent people were moving away.

Angela and Bobby Murphy were fortunate to live in a substantial house in a desirable suburb. Although they had good earnings, it was a generous legacy from Bobby's great-aunt that allowed them to move into Netherlee. They laughingly called the area Nether-twee because it traditionally housed the genteel and the rich, but even though they made jokes about it, they loved living there. Their home was a six roomed, end of terrace, stone built house with a double garage and well-stocked, large gardens. There was a lot of space for just two people but Angela and Bobby managed to fill it.

Netherlee was in the catchment area for some of the best schools in Scotland and Bobby would've loved a job teaching in any one of them. By contrast, the school where he actually worked was in a difficult area where there was constant conflict between the children of the large, mainly Asian community and the offspring of the so-called white majority. The situation was so bad that often police were called to break up fights between teenage trouble makers which spilled out from the playground and onto the street. Bobby had to stop driving to work because the only parking was in the school playground and cars were constantly being vandalised. So instead he struggled, in all weather, with two large, heavy bags stuffed with papers, on and off the bus each day. No wonder he was fed up Angela thought. It must be soul destroying to work under those conditions. Having to travel to Govanhill to interview people was enough to make her feel depressed and she would only have to be there for a few days.

Angela made sure that Liz was insured to drive her car in case it was required then she arranged to meet her at the incident room in Govanhill. Angela suggested she wear smart, plain clothes and Liz was delighted to be out of uniform. This secondment would look great on her record and she was grateful to Angela for choosing her and giving her the opportunity.

When she arrived at the incident room, Angela arranged for two uniformed officers to begin the door to door enquiry with strict instructions to call her if they found anything interesting to report. She and Liz were going to interview local shop keepers in case they'd seen the victim with a man fitting the description Mrs Ali had supplied. However, by four o'clock, no information had materialised and they seemed to be wasting their time. Everyone they met wanted to talk about the murder but nobody saw anything and no one even admitted to knowing Margaret Deacon. Then, when they had just about given up, out of the blue a man called Mr Anwar was ushered into the incident room. He was very rotund and he reminded Angela of a child's drawing of a man. His round moon face had cushioned cheeks, a small nose and eyebrows that looked permanently surprised. This was topped off by a head full of unruly hair. His body was equally spherical and his generous middle had no waist. As he spoke he held his pudgy little hands in front of him almost apologetically.

"I have something to say about Margaret Deacon," he began. "I knew the girl. I was sorry for her and I gave her 'Irn bru' and sweeties when she was ill and had no money. She was a drug addict you know. I wasn't around when you came to my shop earlier."

"Please sit down, Mr Anwar," Liz said offering him a chair. "Which shop do you work in, Sir?"

"I own Anwar's General Store," he said proudly. "I've owned my shop for over twenty years. When you came to ask questions I was at the cash and carry so you spoke to my wife. She speaks just a little English and she only works in the shop when I have to go out. I knew Margaret because she was a customer. She told me things and talked to me about this and that. I think she was lonely. She said she had no family and her Mum and Dad were dead but I didn't believe her. I think maybe they were only dead to her."

Angela produced her written description of the slim man in the hoodie and read it to Mr Anwar. "Do you remember seeing Margaret in the company of such a man?" she asked.

"I saw her once or twice with a tall, slim man who she said was her friend. It could be the same man, but why would her friend hurt her? She was just a little girl, very slightly built and very gentle, why would anyone do her harm?"

"I don't know Mr Anwar. All we do know is that Margaret had a drug problem and she had a lot of male acquaintances."

"I knew Margaret was a prostitute. My wife said I shouldn't have anything to do with her, but I felt sorry for her. Someone should've been looking after her because she was a very sick girl. My wife said I shouldn't get involved, but Margaret was very vulnerable. Somebody had to care, didn't they? I couldn't just ignore her."

Mr Anwar was obviously a kind man but Angela doubted he had any information that could help.

"Is there anything else you can tell us about Margaret or her friend? Did you see her the day she died?"

"I'm sorry, but no, I didn't see either of them that day."

Angela and Liz exchanged disappointed glances as once again they'd come up with nothing.

"There was just one more thing, but I don't know if it will help you," Mr Anwar said as he stood to leave. "Margaret's friend sometimes wore a dark coloured uniform. I think maybe he was a security guard. I never saw him wear a hat, but he might have been some sort of official worker, like a policeman or a community warden. It wasn't a bus driver's uniform. I would have recognised that because I used to work on the buses before I opened my shop."

Angela felt her spirits soar. At last something to go on. "That's a great piece of information," she said reaching out and grasping Mr Anwar's fat little hand which she shook enthusiastically. "Constable Brown will sit down at the desk with you and go over once again what you've told us. She'll write out a statement for you to sign. Can you please spare us a bit more of your time?"

Mr Anwar's head nodded as he answered, "I am in no hurry," he said. "My wife can manage the shop without me for a while."

Liz sat down at the desk and began transcribing the statement while Angela paced the floor. She was restless with nervous energy. Exasperated with her constant too-ing and fro-ing as it broke her concentration and also disturbed Mr Anwar, Liz threw Angela a dirty look and signalled for her to leave the incident room. Angela smiled sheepishly and took her pacing outside onto the pavement. She was excited to have a little success so quickly in the investigation, but she wasn't sure what to do next. Having the lead was one thing, but knowing how to follow it was an entirely different matter and she was determined to prove to Frank Martin that she was worthy of her job.

When Angela telephoned Frank to update him on the day's progress, she told him about the statement from Mr Anwar. She also said that there was little else to report. His reaction was not what she expected.

"Fucking Hell, Angela, Oh for fucks sake, that's all we need."

Angela didn't reply she couldn't understand why he was so upset.

"You've got to make sure that no one leaks that information, understand? Not one word. Where's your witness now? Is he still there with you at the incident room?"

"He's just this minute left," Angela replied. "I can send Constable Brown to fetch him back if you like."

"No need to bring him back, just send her to talk to him. She's to make him understand that it's vital he talks to no one. Tell him it'll harm the case if he blabs."

Angela kept Frank waiting on the phone while she asked Liz to go after Mr Anwar. "I've sent her, Boss," she said still mystified why such a small amount of information should have to be kept secret.

"If the press get hold of this they'll have a field day. Can you see the headlines? Cop kills prostitute. Panic in Govanhill," Frank explained. "As soon as they hear 'uniform' they'll think one of us is the murderer."

The enormity of what he said finally dawned on Angela.

"I'm counting on you girl, not to fuck up."

"Don't worry, Frank, I'll make sure everybody knows the score."

"Okay, okay. Oh, and don't you go talking to any reporters. If they come sniffing around refer them to me and only me."

"Yes, Boss, I understand."

"Good girl. By the way, that was an excellent piece of work. At least we've got something to show for the day," he added encouragingly. "Tomorrow I want you and Constable Brown working in the office. You'll have to compile a list of all the working girls living in the area. We'll need to interview every one of them in case they know who this man is. You'll also have to get in touch with a woman called Jackie Cosgrove. She's a former tart who discovered Jesus and converted to Christianity. She's now some sort of preacher who helps working girls to get off the game. She's a bit of a pain in the arse and a real holy-moly but the girls trust her. If you can get her on your side the tarts will talk to us and they might tell us something useful."

"Will I keep a couple of officers on the streets talking to the local community?" Angela asked.

"You might as well, we've got precious little else to go on. Good choice of assistant by the way. I know the lassie's Dad, Jack. He's a great cop, old school. If she turns out to be half the officer he is, she'll be very useful. Her whole family are cops you know. You could learn a lot about police life from that girl. She grew up with it."

Angela was about to agree with him when the line went dead. It seemed that their conversation was over. She must remember to always treat him as one of her male colleagues would and not expect small talk.

Angela was completely shattered as it had been another long day. She arranged to meet Liz at the office in the morning then both girls left for their homes. It was Angela's turn to cook the dinner tonight but she was too exhausted to even think about food, so it would have to be the 'Joy Bowl Chinese Takeaway' or the 'Turban Tandoori' because either would deliver. If Bobby didn't like it, then too bad, he could cook. All Angela wanted to do was make it home before she became too tired to drive.

Chapter 8

It was a cold, bright Saturday and Thomas felt really happy at his work because today was a 'Farmer's Market' day in Queens Park. Although he worked all over the south side of Glasgow, whenever he worked on a Saturday, it was always at this location. He and Alan had already booked several cars and it was only eleven-thirty. It was always the same people thought they would only be a couple of minutes at the market so why bother paying for parking. For the sake of a ten pence ticket they ended up paying a hefty fine. Thomas loved his job. He particularly liked it when some stuck-up rich bitch challenged him or a cocky thirty-something lost his temper. On the down side, he'd been spat at more times than he could count and he often had a slap or punch aimed at him. Last week a woman threw a fit of hysterics and he had to call for assistance from the police when she lay in the road and refused to move.

He liked his workmate Alan because he always had tales to tell and he could be very funny. Alan was short and plump and his round face always had a smile on it. He wore small, round, 'Benny Hill' style glasses and his facial expressions often made Thomas laugh out loud. Jokes rolled off Alan's tongue and that day was no exception.

"I've got a story to tell you Mate," he began, "It's a true story, not a word of a lie."

Thomas had heard this opening line several times before and it was never even close to the truth.

"A policeman was driving his car when he spotted a woman driver weaving about all over the road so he pulled alongside her." Alan began. "He was shocked to see that she was knitting. Pull over, the cop shouted. No, she yelled back, it's a scarf." Alan was doubled up with laughter. "Get it, he said pull over, she said scarf, do you get it?"

"I get it, I get it," Thomas replied. "Your jokes are getting worse Alan, much worse. I need a cup of tea after that one."

Alan looked at his watch, it was nearly lunch time. "I think we've done enough work for now. A couple more tickets near the end of the day so the Boss doesn't think we've skived off, and we're done. Shall we get a sausage roll and a cake in Tasty Bakers then have a wee rest in the park?"

"That sounds like a good plan," Thomas agreed.

As they crossed the road to the bakery Alan told him another joke. "My Missus asked me what was on the telly last night," he began. "Dust, I told her. She wasn't happy."

"Are you going to be like this all day?" Thomas asked laughing.

"I'll do my best," Alan replied.

"Then I'd better buy ear plugs in the chemist," Thomas said.

"Oh, my God, Mr Serious has cracked a joke. Good on you son!"

Yes, Thomas loved his job and he liked working with Alan because most of the time the voice in his head stayed quiet and he felt like an ordinary person, like one of the boys. When he was with Alan he felt safe.

* * *

Angela had tried for several days to make an appointment with Jackie Cosgrove but the woman was never available. Finally she managed to arrange to meet Jackie at her home. She could think of a million other places she'd rather be on a sunny Saturday and so could Liz, but here they were ringing the doorbell of a cottage flat in Kingspark, so they could talk to a reformed prostitute.

"Hallo, Girls, come in," a hard faced woman with pock-marked skin greeted them. They followed her up a narrow stairway to the upper apartment. "Excuse the bags of clothes, but I've got a wee lassie from Eastern Europe staying with me just now. She's just got away from a violent gang and those bags contain all her possessions." Jackie opened a door and showed them into the living room. "I'm trying to contact her family in the Czech Republic so I can send her home," she continued. "They thought she was coming here to work in a hotel, they had no idea she was being trafficked as a prostitute. Poor wee lassie is only seventeen. It's criminal. Sit down and I'll make us a brew."

Without waiting for a reply Jackie disappeared into the hallway leaving Angela and Liz to find a seat. Every surface was covered with stuff but they managed to clear some bags off the sofa then sat down.

"I don't know what I expected but it certainly wasn't this," Angela said and Liz agreed with her. The lounge suite consisted of a brown, velvet sofa and two mismatched leather armchairs, there was also a small dining table with three odd chairs. At one end of the room was a television on a stand and in the centre of the floor there was a coffee table where three overflowing ashtrays, an empty Vodka bottle and piles of papers were strewn. The room had a fast food smell about it and, in particular, there was the strong aroma of chip shop vinegar.

"And you say she's a minister?" Liz said incredulously. "She's not like any minister I've ever met."

"She's a preacher not a minister. Ministers have to be ordained, a preacher can be anyone." Angela explained.

"Well someone should preach to her about cleanliness being next to godliness. Look at the state of this place. It's a disaster, it's filthy and it smells awful, she should open a window."

"I hate being here too," Angela said. "So let's get what we can from her as quickly as possible then we can leave."

"Here we are, girls, help yourselves," Jackie said as she re-entered the room and plonked a tray on the dirty table balancing it on a pile of papers. Three odd chipped mugs of stewed tea, a bag of sugar and a carton of milk sat on the tray. There was also a small plate of digestive biscuits.

"Come on girls, don't be shy," Jackie said lifting the least chipped mug and offering it to Angela.

"I'm sorry, but I don't drink tea or coffee," Liz lied before one was handed to her. "I didn't get a chance to tell you before you went to make it."

"Never mind, Pet, would you like a cold drink? Some ginger or maybe a beer?"

"No thanks, I'm fine just now, I'm not really thirsty," Liz replied.

Angela wished she'd thought of that, she didn't fancy eating or drinking anything and she hoped they could get out quickly before one of them needed to use the toilet. The very idea of it made her feel sick. Jackie poured some milk into her tea and gave it a stir. When she was satisfied with the colour of it she plunged the wet spoon into the sugar bag then shovelled three spoonfuls of lumpy, discoloured sugar into her mug.

"Well now girls, shall we get started, what do you want to know?"

"We're trying to trace working girls living in the Govanhill area to see if they can help us with our enquiries into the Margaret Deacon murder. So far we have only come up with three names. Can you help us?"

"As far as I know, there are only three Scottish girls working in Govanhill now. All the rest are foreigners like the wee lassie I've got staying with me. The gangs from Eastern Europe have moved into the Southside, they bring the girls over and keep them locked up. They drug them and rape them repeatedly until they lose all hope. Then they're worked day and night until they become ill or die. You might find a corpse floating in the Clyde from time to time, but you've got no chance of talking to one of those girls."

"How do these gangs get away with it? Don't the neighbours complain to the police, surely they must know what's going on?" Angela said.

"Maybe they do and maybe they don't," Jackie replied and reached for her cigarettes. "Smoke?" she offered.

"No thanks," both girls replied simultaneously. Jackie lit her cigarette and inhaled deeply.

"Would you risk upsetting one of these men? I don't think so. The neighbours move out and the gangs rent more flats in the close until they've taken over the whole building. Then there is no one left to complain and that's why your people don't hear about it. I know of two whole buildings and several more individual flats that these gangs use."

"If you know about this why don't you inform the police? You're obviously not afraid or you wouldn't have one of these girls here, now."

"Two years ago I went to the police but nothing was followed up. You see at the moment the problem is contained. Everyone knows it's going on, but either they're too scared to complain or it doesn't affect them. Either way it suits the police and the social workers to ignore it because their resources are already stretched to the limit." She took another long drag on her cigarette then exhaled slowly. "And, by the way, I am scared," she continued. "Only a fool wouldn't be and I'm no fool. As for the girl who's staying here, I paid for her, five thousand pounds. She's HIV positive and she's ill, the gangsters want shot of her before she gets really sick. I buy these girls their freedom with donations I receive from good, caring, Christian people. Even when I have the money to help them only a handful will let me. They're ashamed, you see. They don't want their families to know what's happened to them."

Angela was shocked, "I had no idea," she admitted. "I don't know what to say."

"There's nothing you can say. It's life, and life isn't always nice," Jackie replied. "Anyway, I'll try and help you with the Scottish girls although one of them, Megan Reece, is actually Welsh. She and her girlfriend, Anne-Marie Connor, are lesbians and they live together in one apartment. Then there's Kelly Jamieson, her Mum's an alcoholic and she lives with her. Kelly only gives sex in the punter's cars or in doorways because her Mum is always at home, drunk. I'll speak to these girls and ask them to talk to you if you think it'll help. Maybe one of them will know the punter you're looking for, but to be honest your description could fit a quarter of the men in Glasgow. It's so vague. Is that all you've got to go on?"

"I'm afraid so," Angela replied. "Will you call me once you've spoken to the girls?" she continued and handed Jackie her card. "Here's my number, it's got my mobile as well as the office."

Angela and Liz stood up they were both desperate to leave. "You've not touched your tea," Jackie observed. "Would you like me to heat it in the microwave for you?"

"Thank you, but no thank you. We really must get on."

"Yes," agreed Liz. "We're late for another appointment."

"Oh, well, maybe next time," Jackie replied and showed them to the door.

When they left the house and the door closed behind them Liz turned to Angela and said, "Did you drink any of that tea? I hope you didn't because that place was filthy."

"Not a drop," Angela replied. "I see you got out of having any. Frank Martin said I could learn a lot from you and he's obviously right, the first lesson being how to avoid e-coli or salmonella."

Liz looked at her watch. "Five minutes till our shift's over. I don't know about you but I'm going home for a shower. Then I'm going for a swim. With a bit of luck the chlorine in the pool will disinfect me."

"That house could do with being disinfected," Angela replied. "What a way to live and yet Jackie's one of the success stories. It's like another world and these people are like another species. I didn't realise how sheltered my life was."

The two girls parted company and Angela headed for the suburbs. As she drove away from Govanhill she could almost feel the air becoming cleaner and the streets more welcoming. It was a relief when she reached the sanctuary of her home.

Chapter 9

It was late afternoon on an uneventful day and Thomas and Alan were finishing their shift. Thomas had managed to overcome his shyness and he accepted Alan's offer of a beer because he had exciting news he wanted to share. He'd just passed his driving test and he was proud of his achievement. When Thomas finished college his lecturer had continued to mentor him and it was he who encouraged him to learn to drive. With his help Thomas was able to get lessons at a reduced rate and Mr Barker told him that once he'd passed the test many more job opportunities would be available to him. Thomas was particularly proud of himself because he'd passed first time with no faults. They were on their way to the pub, deep in conversation, when a woman's voice shouted after them.

"With your boyfriend, are you? No wonder you didn't want me. Do you do him or does he do you, or maybe you do each other?"

Thomas turned to see a rather drunk woman reeling towards them. It took him only a moment to recognise her as the prostitute he'd followed the other day.

"He tried to buy my time, you know," she said to Alan. "He said he'd never had a woman before and he didn't know what to do." She stared at Thomas and grinned maliciously. "But his dick was so small, I couldn't find it." She started to laugh and coughed until she choked.

"It's not true, none of it is true," Thomas said helplessly. He looked so upset that Alan thought he might cry.

"Of course it's not true," Alan replied kindly, "As if you'd touch a scabby old whore."

Alan was angry with the girl and he couldn't understand why she was being such a bitch. It was probably the drink he reasoned. He and Thomas had worked together for a long time yet this was the first occasion they'd arranged to socialise after work. Alan didn't have any children, but if he had, he would have wanted a son like Thomas. He liked the shy, young man.

"I'm going home," Thomas said. "I'm sorry Alan, I'm sorry." Thomas took off. His disjointed run was reminiscent of Dustin Hoffman's portrayal of Raymond Babbit in the film 'Rain Man'. His legs looked as if they were trying to go in different directions and his arms were held stiffly, sticking out from his sides with his hands flapping. As he sped away he could still hear the girl and Alan shouting at each other.

"Now look what you've done, you've upset my friend," Alan bellowed. "Why don't you just shut the fuck up, you dirty slag."

"Ha, ha serves him right," the girl said laughing. "Run rabbit, run rabbit, run, run, run," she shouted after Thomas in a sing-song voice then she laughed until she had another coughing fit.

Thomas did run. He ran and ran and ran. '*Kill her,*' the voice in his head screamed. '*Kill her.*'

When Thomas got home he sat in his armchair with his elbows on his knees and his head in his hands. He was sobbing and rocking back and forth. He didn't know who'd made him most angry, the girl for ridiculing him in front of his friend, the voice for screaming at him and making him nervous or himself for being scared and running away. He'd been having such a nice day and now it was ruined. He couldn't get the voice to stop and his head was so sore that he thought it might explode.

Thomas didn't know how long he'd sat in his chair but through the window he could see dark sky. It was a very black night with no moon or stars visible and his home felt very cold.

"I hate her," he said aloud. "I hate her, I hate her, I hate her, he chanted over and over again. "I'll kill the bitch. I'll shut her dirty mouth."

'*Don't be so fucking stupid, it's not time yet,*' the voice said. '*You need to plan your next move. You need to know more. Who does she live with? When is she home? Does she carry a weapon like mace or a knife?*'

"I'll find out everything about her, Thomas said aloud. "I'm smart, but she thinks I'm stupid. She won't expect me. I'll show the bitch. I'll show her. You'll be proud of me, Dad. I'll make you proud."

Chapter 10

Angela was coming out from the shower when she heard the phone ringing. Who would call this early she wondered? She strained to listen, but although she could hear Bobby talking she couldn't make out what he was saying. Angela rushed to get dried and dressed, she was worried that something might be wrong, but when she ran down the stairs, Bobby was just hanging up and he was grinning.

"I've had great news," he said. "There's a vacancy coming up at Jamieson's Grammar School. The chap who's in the job is going to Australia. My Mum's friend Peggy is the school secretary. The Headmaster and her husband are best friends. I think I've got a real chance."

"That's fantastic news. You were just telling me how hard it is to get a placement in a private school. It's really spooky to get that call now? What do you have to do next? Do you need an application form or is there someone you've to contact?"

"Peggy wants me to go to the school at five-thirty. She's going to introduce me to the Head. If we get on all right he'll give me the application form. Peggy said the job will be advertised and all applications will be put to the school board, but the Headmaster has the final say. If he likes me, I'm in. I'm easily qualified for the job."

"It would be so good for you to get a change. At least there shouldn't be any discipline problems at Jamieson's Grammar. The fees cost a fortune," Angela said. "I'd better iron you a white shirt and you'll need to wear a suit and tie."

"Good idea," Bobby replied. "But I'd better change after work because if I go into my school dressed like that I'll be massacred. You've got to look tougher than the kids or they walk all over you."

"I've got a suit bag," Angela offered. "Bring me your stuff and I'll pack it for you then I've got to run because I'm interviewing three prostitutes today and I've to go into the office first."

"I'm going for a job interview at one of the most prestigious schools in the country and you're going to interview hookers. I fancy my day more than yours," Bobby replied grinning.

"Me too," Angela agreed.

She arrived at the office at eight because she'd had to collect papers from another office on her way in. Frank was pacing the floor and everyone was sitting at their desks keeping their heads down.

"Nice of you to join us," he grumbled at Angela while continuing to pace.

She sat at her desk and took some interview forms from a drawer then leaned over towards Paul, who was sitting at the next desk, and asked, "What's up with the Boss today? He seems grumpier but less vocal than usual."

"He's scared shitless. He's to make a statement to the press today about the murder. Orders from above and he's got nothing to tell them. All he can say is that we're continuing with our enquiries."

"But it's only been a week. What do they expect?"

"More than we've got, obviously." Paul answered. "The Govanhill Community Council is up in arms. They think we're just not interested because it's a mostly immigrant community."

"But that's ridiculous. We're following procedure. It doesn't matter who lives there."

"Oh, you poor, naïve girl," Paul said. "Of course it makes a difference. If this was Muirend or Newlands do you think the Boss would have left you in charge of the incident room? Every senior cop in Glasgow would be in on it. No offence, Angi, but you're a bit green and inexperienced for a murder investigation."

Angela hadn't thought about it that way before, but now that she did, she realised Paul was absolutely right. There was no urgency about the investigation and she supposed if it wasn't for the Community Council this case would probably have gone the same way as the previous murder, ten years before. She felt sad that who you were or where you lived made a difference to the justice you received.

"Penny for them," Paul's voice broke her chain of thought. "Hadn't you better get going?" he continued.

"Yes, Paul, I'm on my way. To tell you the truth, I'll be glad to get out of this place. I don't fancy your day stuck here with Hitler."

"Now Angi, that's a bit harsh, not Hitler, surely, I'd say more like Ivan the Terrible or Vlad the Impaler."

"Gotta go, bye bye," she said grabbing her bag and the interview forms. "Good luck. My day doesn't seem so bad now."

Angela was relieved to get out of the office without having any further contact with Frank. She met up with Liz in reception and she was delighted when Liz showed her a bag containing six cans of coca cola and a packet of chocolate biscuits.

"This will save us from the tea and digestives and it makes us look generous and well-mannered," Liz explained.

"Bless you, Liz. You've probably saved our lives. Put your receipt through as an expense and I'll authorise it. If you don't mind I'd like you to drive so you get used to my car." She threw the car keys to Liz and who caught them easily.

"Fabulous, I love your car. I'll try and resist the urge to speed."

"You'd better my girl. That car is my baby. One dent or scratch and your life won't be worth living."

"Oooh, I'm scared," Liz replied laughing.

When the two women got into the car Liz started the engine and sped out of the car park with a screech of tyres. Angela gripped the seat. She was beginning to wonder if she'd done the right thing in letting her drive. Ten minutes later they reached Jackie's house.

"Come on in," Jackie said. "I'm sorry but there are just two of the girls here to speak to you. Megan and Anne-Marie have fallen out with Kelly, so she's not coming. I'll have to get you back another day to speak to her."

Angela's heart sank at the thought of returning to this horrible house for a third time. When they entered the living room Liz plonked the carrier bag of cans and biscuits on the coffee table. The two prostitutes were seated side by side on the couch.

"Is that a wee carry-out, a wee bevy at this time of the day? Good on you girls and I thought pigs were boring," the skinny woman with bad teeth said, grinning.

"Behave yourself, Anne-Marie," Jackie scolded.

"It's just cola and chocky bics," Liz answered. "I don't like visiting empty handed.

"That was very thoughtful of you, Hen. That pair never bring anything and they eat me out of house and home. Anyway, time for introductions. The one with the big mouth," she pointed to Anne-Marie, "You now know is called Anne-Marie. Her friend here is Megan. She's the quieter one, but not by much."

They shook hands formally which seemed rather incongruous under the circumstances. Angela and Liz sat on dining room chairs opposite Anne-Marie and Megan and Jackie sat in an armchair. Angela noticed that the two women held hands. Megan was very feminine with a soft curvaceous figure, a sweet smile and short curls framing her face. They were about to begin the interview when a willowy figure appeared at the doorway. A young girl with large sunken eyes and gaunt cheeks peered at the group.

"What is it, Anya?" Jackie enquired. "Do you want something to eat?"

The girl shook her head, "No, thank you," she said and disappeared as quietly as she had come.

"Sorry about that. She's Anya, the girl I'm trying to repatriate. "Poor wee soul is scared of her own shadow."

"They should all bugger off home, bloody foreigners, they're stealing our jobs," Anne-Marie said.

"Stealing our jobs," Jackie repeated incredulously. "You've never worked a day in your life. Shut up with your prejudices. These girls are in real jobs and their time is valuable," she added nodding towards the two police women.

"Aye and we're paying for their time," Anne-Marie said, determined to have the last word.

What a vicious wee woman she is, Angela thought, then she said. "First of all I'd like to ask if either of you knew Margaret Deacon?"

"We both knew her," Megan replied speaking for the first time. "She kept herself to herself. She used drugs, you know. We prefer to keep away from junkies because they usually end up begging or stealing from you."

"So neither of you use drugs then?"

Megan rolled up her sleeves, "We're clean, see," she said exposing her arms.

"We're just a couple trying to get by the best way we know," Anne-Marie added. "I have a daughter, Victoria, she lives with her Dad. I haven't seen her since she was born. I was in a mess then with drink, so the Social took her away from me. I put money away every week for her and she'll get it when she's eighteen. I want her to know her Mum loves her even though she doesn't know me."

"She's saved four thousand pounds," Megan said proudly and she squeezed Anne-Marie's arm with encouragement. "That's why we do the men, so we can save money for Vicky."

"Do you think the men who visit you also go to the Eastern European girls like Anya?" Angela asked.

"Maybe, but I doubt it, the men who come to us are scared of the foreign pimps. Most of the girls like Anya are much younger and prettier than us, but their bosses are evil fucks who wouldn't think twice about knifing you. We get the poor sods who just want a plain, ordinary, hand job or suck. Neither of us does fuck. The men who want other stuff will go to the pimps. As long as they have the money they can do want they want to these girls."

"Have you come across anyone who has frightened you recently, anyone weird?"

"They're all weird, life's losers, that's why we get them in the first place. We get men who are too scared or too boring to have a girl-friend."

"Some of them are too dirty and stinky," Megan added.

"I won't put a smelly cock in my mouth even if it's got two condoms on it," Anne-Marie said. The very thought made Angela feel sick and Liz shuddered noticeably.

"So you can't think of anyone that Margaret Deacon might have come in contact with who could be violent?"

"There are one or two men who talk about hurting you when they're fired up, but none of them would actually touch a hair on your head. It's the talk that gets them excited," Anne-Marie said.

"I've got one who likes me to hurt him," Megan added, "Nothing serious mind you, just pinching and slapping. You might try asking Kelly Jamieson, she's a druggie like Margaret was, so she might have rougher customers. A junkie will do anything if they're desperate for a fix."

Angela was disappointed that the girls were of no help. She didn't know exactly what she'd expected of them, but she'd hoped for something. She supposed it would've been just too easy if they'd given her the name of a violent man, who might be the killer, but it would've been nice.

"Is there anything else you can tell me?" she asked making a last ditch attempt.

"Sorry, but no, there's nothing more we can say. We live a simple life. We have a few customers each, just to boost our income, and we keep ourselves to ourselves," Megan said.

"Is there a reward for information?" Anne-Marie asked slyly. "If there is we could keep our ear to the ground."

"There's no reward at the moment," Liz answered. "But you never know what might materialise if you find out something useful. Angela will give you her card so you can phone her with anything relevant. But don't waste our time, or trust me, I'll waste yours, understand?"

"Aye, aye, we get it," Anne-Marie answered for them both.

With the interview over, Jackie showed the policewomen to the door. "I'm sorry they couldn't help you," she said. "I'll try and speak to Kelly later today and I'll phone you if she'll meet you. It's all very strange. I could understand if it was one of the foreign girls who was attacked and murdered but not Margaret Deacon. I think it might be a regular bloke who did this. I just have a feeling it wasn't a punter."

"What makes you say that?" Angela asked.

"I don't know. It's just a hunch. Remember I used to be a working girl just like them. You get to know if there's a bad man doing the rounds but nobody's heard a word. I think you could be barking up the wrong tree. Your murderer might be an ordinary working man. Maybe even a local. It might have nothing to do with Margaret's line of work."

Angela and Liz said goodbye to Jackie then made their way to the car. As they walked they talked about what Jackie had said.

"Where do we go from here?" Liz asked.

"I wish I knew. If the murder had nothing to do with Margaret's working life, then what the hell had it to do with?"

Chapter 11

Angela arrived at the office half an hour early for her shift and she was no sooner in the door than Frank bellowed for her from his office.

"Glad you're on time today, Murphy. Come to my office and bring coffee."

Paul Costello, who sat at the next desk to Angela, began to chuckle. Paul, like Angela, was in his early thirties. He had a very cheeky smile and a glint in his eye that melted every woman's heart irrespective of their age. His colleagues used to joke that it was because of his talent for attracting the ladies that he had four children, but the truth was, Paul and his wife Gemma were childhood sweethearts and he would never look at another woman. In fact, that was another reason for his popularity with the ladies. They felt safe teasing him knowing it would go no further than gentle flirting.

"What is wrong with that man?" Angela asked in exasperation. "I'm really early, but he's still in the office before me. Does he ever go home or is this where he lives?"

Paul shook his head and laughed all the more. She didn't even get the chance to unpack her bag of files, but instead she went to the drinks machine, fetched two coffees then walked over to Frank's office. When she sat down he looked up and she could see he was very tired. His normally immaculate suit was crumpled and he was unshaven.

"Yeah, yeah, I know I look a mess," he said. "It was Mike Smith's leaving do last night, we went on a pub crawl and before you ask,

I didn't go home. We all stayed in a hotel because we were too rat arsed to face our wives. I'll warn you now, if you smirk, you're fired," he added.

Angela tried but failed to suppress her smile. "Did you want me for something or did you just want coffee?" she asked cheekily.

"Margaret Deacon's parents have turned up," he replied.

"What? She's been dead for over a week and they've just got in touch now. Where the hell have they been?"

"China, they've been walking the Great Wall for charity, so they didn't see a paper."

"Didn't a friend or a relative see the papers? Surely someone could have contacted them."

"It seems that their friends didn't know Margaret existed. They're 'Christians for Jesus' and Margaret didn't conform so she was banished from their lives. The husband is not the girl's father, her father's dead. The mother married him when Margaret was a teenager."

"So why get in touch now?"

"The mother wants to give her a proper burial, albeit not a religious one. I want you to go and see them. Talk to them about Margaret. See if they know anything at all about how she lived. Ask if any of their friends or family might have had contact with her. Find out about their religion and their church but don't let them preach to you. I don't trust these very religious types. See if you can dig up any dirt about the stepfather."

"If she was banished, isn't this a complete waste of time?"

"Probably, but they're still the girl's parents. We have to show them some respect because when the press get hold of this, and trust me they will get hold of it, we want to come up smelling of roses, okay?"

"I understand Boss, leave it to me. I don't fancy going on my own though, I'll take Liz Brown with me."

"Do what you like, just get the job done. Now get lost and shut the door behind you. Tell everyone I don't want to be disturbed. If anyone bangs on this door, there'll be hell to pay."

Angela was quite glad to leave the office. She was sure that before very long someone would be on the receiving end of Frank's temper and at least it wouldn't be her. She put in a call for Liz and arranged to meet her at the incident room. Margaret's parents lived in the village of Eaglesham so she could easily collect Liz on route. The address she'd been given suggested the couple must be comfortably off because the houses that were in the heart of the old village were very expensive. Angela had always wanted to see inside one of these houses but they rarely came up for sale.

When she picked up Liz, the younger girl was in uniform, but on this occasion, Angela felt it was appropriate attire. She wanted to keep the interview very formal.

"When we finish we could have lunch at the 'Wishing Well' Liz suggested. "It's in the village and my Auntie Vy works there, she'll look after us. That's if we have the time, of course."

"That's a marvellous idea, Liz, I'd love to. It would break up our day and besides I think we'll need some sustenance after this interview. I hate visiting victim's relatives, don't you?"

"This will be my first time. I'm a bad news virgin," she replied. "But from what you've told me, they're not too upset."

"Don't be fooled, the girl's mother will be very upset, Margaret was her only child."

"But I thought they'd sent her away."

"Yes, that's true, but I think the mother would've always thought there'd be time to reconcile their differences. There's no chance of that now. Besides, the death of a relative or friend is always a shock. The truth is I don't have a clue how she'll react, but we have to be prepared for anything."

"What do I say? Do I tell them I'm sorry for their loss? Or do I say nothing?" Liz asked.

"Let me do the talking. I've had to give this sort of news to families of road accident victims, so it's not new to me."

Liz sat quietly for the rest of the journey. She seemed rather subdued and Angela could see she was nervous. Before very long they turned into the village and parked outside a white cottage which had a deep blue coloured, painted front door and matching window frames. The house was very well kept and the stone façade had a freshly white-washed look about it. There was no garden so the front door opened onto the pavement. Angela rang the doorbell and it was quickly answered by a smartly dressed woman of about fifty. She glanced at the girls and, on seeing Liz in uniform, ushered them into a narrow dark hallway. Angela had expected the house to be very austere but that couldn't have been further from the truth. They were shown into a very spacious room with large windows to the rear through which the sun shone brightly, flooding the room with light. The décor was simple and it was furnished in an almost minimalist style that created a comfortable, airy space.

"Sit down, please," the woman said. "I'm Jean Glen it's me you're here to see. My husband George will be joining us shortly."

"Shall we wait for him before we begin?" Angela asked.

"No need," Jean replied. "Margaret was nothing to do with my husband, he wasn't her father. They didn't get on. Margaret was always rebellious and often in trouble. She never accepted our Lord as her saviour. George always said she would come to a bad end and he was right."

Jean showed no emotion. There was no wringing of hands or biting of lips. Angela was shocked at how cold and matter of fact her attitude was towards Margaret. This woman's daughter had just been murdered for God's sake. Was she made of stone? If this was how religion affected a person then Angela was glad not to be a follower.

The door opened with a slight creak and they all turned to see a tall, stooped man enter. He had a thin face with a prominent pointed nose and a weak chin. His pale, bald head had a skeletal look, and when he smiled, he looked like a grimacing death's head. Jean quickly introduced everyone. George crept across the room to sit on an armchair which was obviously kept for him and him alone. He was a very strange man, creepily quiet, he made Angela feel most uncomfortable. Before she could speak George addressed the room.

"We are so disappointed that Margaret could not be saved. The Lord is very forgiving but she was beyond redemption. I am sorry for my poor wife because she will never see her daughter again. There is no place in heaven for an unrepentant sinner. Please be kind to Jean, Officers, she has done nothing wrong. The devil had Margaret as soon as she was born. My wife is innocent."

Bloody Hell, Angela thought, how on earth do I follow that?

"I am very sorry for your loss," she began aware of Liz's grimace as she tried to contain a smirk. "It must be hard to come to terms with Margaret's death."

"If only she was in a better place, I could bear it, but to know that she is lost is very painful to me," Jean replied.

"Can you tell me anything about Margaret? Did any of your family or friends keep in touch with her?"

"We've had no contact with her for ten years," George responded. "My wife wrote to her every so often and invited her to pray with us but she received no reply. The girl didn't want to know."

"George is right, we tried over and over again, but she was lost to us."

"She was a drug addict and a whore," George continued and Jean winced as if she'd been struck. "No decent person would give her the time of day. We prayed day and night for her, but she fought God at every turn."

Jean looked sad, no matter what George preached, she had still suffered a terrible loss. She rested her head on her hand and shut her eyes.

"There is nothing more to say," George said. "My wife is tired and I would like you to leave now, please."

"Of course," Angela replied and she and Liz stood. "Do you have any children, George?" she asked as she headed for the door. It seemed to throw him off his guard.

"Nnno, no," he stammered.

Jean opened her eyes and looked up. "George's daughter, Carol, from his first marriage is dead, she drowned," Jean offered. "They were on holiday when it happened. That's what broke up the marriage. It was the strain of losing a beloved child." Her voice caught in her throat. "Now we have both lost a daughter," she added.

"It's not the same, my daughter is in heaven. My daughter was a good, God-fearing girl." He practically spat the words.

Jean hung her head and turned away. George led Angela and Liz down the hallway to the front door and when they exited he shut it quickly without saying goodbye.

"That was very strange," Liz commented. "Do you think he had something to do with his daughter's death?"

"I have no idea, but you're right, he's a very odd character, very creepy. Their home felt so nice and welcoming before he came into the room. It must have been hell for Margaret when he moved in. No wonder she rebelled. It just goes to show, you really don't know what goes on behind closed doors."

"I'm starving," Liz said, "Time for lunch with Auntie Vy. She'll cheer us up, she's very funny and she might have some gossip about Jean and George."

"Don't say a word about them and don't ask any questions," Angela warned. "George would be the first one to complain about us and my Boss is already in a bad mood. It's bad enough that we got nothing from them without incurring the wrath of Frank as well."

"The wrath of Frank," Liz repeated, laughing. "That sounds like a bad comic book. My Dad thinks the world of Frank, you know."

"Maybe so, but trust me, it's different when you work for him. We're getting absolutely nowhere with this case," Angela continued. "I think we need to sit down and go back over what we know. Mr Anwar was sure he saw Margaret with a man dressed in a uniform. We need to identify that man. I think he might be the key to solving this case. First we need a list of all police officers and community wardens who live in the area. It would do no harm to include any security company workers as well. Once we eliminate them we'll be in a better position to see who we're left with."

"Angela Murphy in the Wrath of Frank," Liz said dramatically. "Follow this intrepid crime fighter as she solves the case."

"Oh, shut up you idiot," Angela replied laughing. Let's go and meet your Auntie Vy."

Chapter 12

Thomas loved watching the young Asian girls because they looked like butterflies dressed in their colourful clothes. The fabrics they wore were pretty and flimsy but they covered their bodies modestly and Thomas liked that. These girls looked wholesome and healthy, untouched and unharmed by the world that surrounded them. The contrast between these girls and the sluttishly dressed teenagers who scorned them was stark. The Asian girls were demure and polite. They never shouted abuse at Thomas or called him names.

"I see you eyeing up the girls," Alan's voice broke his chain of thought. "Can't say I blame you though, they're gorgeous. Have you got a girlfriend, Thomas?"

Thomas wasn't used to answering personal questions and he hesitated.

"I take it that's a 'no' then," Alan continued. "You're better off without women. All they do is cost you money and give you grief. Anyway, enough chit-chat, we'd better get a move on and write some tickets or we won't be able to skive off to the park this afternoon."

Thomas was nervous about coming into contact with the foul-mouthed, skinny prostitute who gave him a hard time the previous week. She lived in this area and he could bump into her at any time. He imagined her in every doorway waiting to pounce on him. He glimpsed her reflection in every shop window. The voice in his head, berated him. *Stupid boy* it said, *you're a weakling, you're a fucking worthless piece of shit, frightened baby,*' it shouted. His head was bursting, he couldn't shut it up. The voice was relentless, demanding and he couldn't go on like this, frightened of his own shadow. He had to get rid of the problem but he was so scared. '*Scaredy cat, scaredy cat,*' the voice chanted. '*Run rabbit, run rabbit, run, run, run.*

* * *

Bobby had been very quiet, the application form for the job was sitting on the desk in the study but he hadn't begun to complete it. Angela was worried by his silence and eventually she could stand it no longer.

"Is there anything wrong, Bobby?" she asked. "Has something upset you? You've not said very much since you visited the school. I thought you loved the place. I know you've had a meeting with the Head of Maths, is there a problem with him?"

"I'm sorry, Darling," he replied. "I'm just a bit disappointed that's all. The reality is never quite like the dream. When I met with Bill Meecham, the head of Maths, I realised just how much I'd be giving up. I'm the Head in my school and the drop in position and salary is massive."

"But you hate the school you're in. Some things are worth more than money, peace of mind for example."

"It's not just the money, it's everything. I thought the school was this idyllic place where everyone got on with each other and everyone found learning exciting, but I was so wrong. There's rarely the sort of running battles that I get in my school, but there's this underlying bullying of both pupils and teachers and it's very nasty."

"I don't understand Bobby, what do you mean?"

"The school favours the academically brilliant children who are also good at sports. Then next in line are the ones who are academic but not sporty. Then the outstanding sportsmen who are okay academically, there's a hierarchy you see and the same goes for the teachers. As an ordinary teacher and the new boy, I'd be the bottom of the pecking order for everything and I'd be the one who's dumped on for all the crappy extra-curricular work."

"So are you saying that you don't want the job? You can let it go and wait for something better, you don't have to apply."

"I'm stuck between a rock and a hard place. I hate where I am, but what I've been offered is no good either. I just don't know what to do. I'd love a complete change, but I don't know how to get it."

Angela felt very sorry for Bobby. He was so miserable and she realised it was time for her to step up and be the strong one. They could just about manage on her salary alone if they had no extras or luxuries. They knew that if one of them ever lost their job, they could survive.

"What else interests you other than teaching? Maybe it's time for a new career. You can't keep on day after day doing something that stresses you out."

Bobby sat up and he stared hard at Angela, "But I can't just quit. How would we manage? At least my job is well paid, even if I do hate it."

"You're friend Jake is always asking you to go and work with him. He's desperate to grow his internet trading company and you said yourself, he's making a fortune. He wants to branch out into electronics and you know all about that stuff whereas Jake hasn't a clue about it."

"But it might mean a large drop in salary until the electronics side is established. It could take six months or more to get back to where I am now. We couldn't have any extras like nights out or holidays, it might be quite a struggle."

"Look on the positive side, Bobby. You wouldn't have to travel to work because you'd be working from your computer here or at Jake's house, which is just around the corner, and we would never need to buy carry-out food at the last minute because you'd be able to shop and cook for us. So that would save a lot of money for a start. More importantly, you'd be in charge of your own destiny."

"And you'd be okay with this? You're not scared? What if it doesn't work out?"

"It will work out. I know it will," Angela replied taking Bobby's hand in hers and kissing the back of it. "Get on that phone to Jake right now and if the job offer is still there, grab it. Sometimes you just have to take chances in life and this is one of those times."

"I can't believe I'm even considering this," Bobby said reaching for the telephone. "You're fantastic you know, unbelievable. We must both be mad."

"I love you Bobby and perhaps we are mad, but don't you feel a thrill at the prospect of being your own boss? If this goes well, I might be able to give up my job and become a lady who lunches. I might become an old fashioned housewife who cooks and looks after her man. Then again I might get a cleaner and a cook and a gardener and shop all day and party all night. There are endless possibilities."

"Don't get carried away, Darling. I haven't got the job yet. But I will try and phone Jake right now. Keep your fingers crossed and wish me luck."

Bobby went into the study to telephone Jake. Angela felt excited but terrified, her hands were shaking and her stomach was churning. Had she just prompted Bobby into making the biggest mistake of his working life? Only time would tell.

Chapter 13

Megan Reece loved the flat she shared with Anne-Marie because they'd made it such a cosy home and she felt safe in it. Her strict Catholic parents had thrown her out when she told them she was a lesbian. She was sixteen and completely alone. If it hadn't been for Anne-Marie she would have been in real danger because she didn't know how to survive on the streets. When the older woman found her in Central Station, Megan was cold and tearful. She'd come to Glasgow because her aunt, who she was named after, lived there. She'd rashly used the last of her money to travel north in the hope of finding her, the plan being to beg her aunt to take her in, but of course with only a first name and no address, it was an impossible task.

Anne-Marie saw the girl crying and approached her, giving her the hamburger and coffee she'd just purchased in Burger King. Megan was so relieved to be offered company and kindness that she spent the next half hour blurting out her story. When Anne-Marie said that she too, was a lesbian and offered her a room for the night with no strings attached, Megan jumped at the chance. That was six years ago and they'd been together ever since. Their friendship grew into a relationship and now they were partners.

Although Anne-Marie was fifteen years older than Megan and she'd had numerous problems with alcohol, Megan loved her with all her heart. She'd have done anything for Anne-Marie. The older woman groomed her and taught her how to handle men and relieve them of their money, and Megan did exactly what Anne-Marie said. She trusted her and she was grateful to have her make all the decisions because she felt safe within their relationship. Anne-Marie was wife, mother, sister and friend all rolled into one.

It was six o'clock on a dreary, cold day and being winter, it was already dark. Megan was carrying two heavy bags of shopping and she was anxious to get home and start making dinner before her friend returned. As it was Anne-Marie's birthday she'd planned a special treat, she'd bought two sirloin steaks at Morrison's and potatoes, onions, mushrooms and tomatoes from the corner fruit shop. She'd also picked up the birthday cake she'd ordered from Tasty Bakers the day before and a six pack of Carlsberg Special Brew. Anne-Marie was at Jackie's house collecting the present which Jackie had bought her. Megan planned, that by the time she got home, dinner would be well under way and the flat decorated with balloons and banners.

Hurrying along the dimly lit street and struggling under the weight of the bags, Megan felt uneasy. She had the distinct feeling that someone was following her. She'd whirled round several times but couldn't see anyone. Being on the game, her instincts were sharp and she was careful when she worked the streets. As she reached the close entrance she once again swung round, but apart from a traffic warden who was checking cars and two giggling Asian schoolgirls, the street was empty. You're imagining things, she told herself, get a grip girl.

Observing her enter the close, Thomas carefully took a note of the time in his notebook. He watched from the street as the girl drew the curtains of the first floor flat and he began to formulate his plan. Thomas was a meticulous man and he liked everything to be just so. There was no room for errors. He couldn't have any loose ends. Even the writing in Thomas's notebook was neat and tidy. There was no scoring out of spelling errors and if he did make a mistake, which was rare, the whole page had to go. His mother had been an untidy, dirty whore and Thomas's father hated her for that. His father was demanding and it was difficult for Thomas to concentrate when the voice shouted in his head, but Thomas knew it was because he cared about him and wanted him to turn out right.

Thomas walked to the end of the street to wait for the skinny prostitute to come home knowing she'd never notice him waiting in the dimly lit doorway. From his observations, he knew that the younger girl always arrived home at least half an hour before her friend because she did the shopping and presumably cooked their meal. He had nothing against the younger girl, but she was in the way and she would probably need to be dealt with as well.

Thomas enjoyed his surveillance work, now he knew how spies felt. His father told him that vermin must be eradicated or they'd take over the world. Rat catchers kill rats, mole catchers kill moles and Thomas killed whores. It's a job that had to be done and, although Thomas was scared, he knew he was the right man for the job. A satisfied smile crossed his lips because the voice in his head was silent. Finally he'd managed to please his father. At last he could have some peace.

Megan could hear Anne-Marie singing before she entered their apartment.

"Happy Birthday to me, Happy Birthday to me, Happy Birthday, Happy Birthday, Happy Birthday to me."

When Anne-Marie threw open the door Megan could see she was rather merry from alcohol. Her eyes were watery and bright and her cheeks were red and shiny.

"Hi Darlin'," Anne-Marie slurred and she looked around the room. "This place is brilliant," she continued noting the balloons and banners. "And dinner smells great. I've had a wee drink or two at Jackie's, just a wee swally to celebrate my birthday, but I'm not drunk, just happy. At least I'm not drunk yet," she added spying the cans of beer and laughing. "Come here you sexy woman and give your old girlfriend a hug."

Megan allowed herself to be held by her intoxicated partner and they both swayed to the cd that was playing on the machine.

"By the way, I'm having a fantastic day, Darlin'," Anne-Marie said, "All the better for sharing it with you. You won't ever leave me will you? You'd never trade me in for a younger model, would you?"

It was at times like this that Megan realised Anne-Marie was vulnerable and needed her as much as she needed Anne-Marie. They drew strength from each other.

"Don't be daft, I love you. We'll be together until we die," Megan replied kissing her drunken friend and giving her a squeeze, "Happy Birthday you silly old bag."

Chapter 14

It had been nearly four weeks since Margaret Deacon's death and, apart from the first week, nobody had come forward with information. Plenty of people had called in at the incident room with complaints ranging from the condition of the roads to noisy neighbours, but nothing about the murder. The police, who were on duty at the mobile unit, were the target for all kinds of abuse and the unit itself had been egged and scored with graffiti.

Frank was pacing the floor which was not a good sign. Angela and Paul Costello, who were on duty that day, kept their heads down and avoided making eye contact with him.

One of us is in trouble," Paul commented. "There's a large group of Govanhill residents in the outer office demanding to see someone about the prossie's murder. All six members of the Community Council are there and they've brought a press photographer with them."

"Why is one of us in trouble? Surely Frank will have to talk to them. He's in charge."

"Never going to happen," Paul said. "Why keep a dog and bark yourself? It'll be down to one of us, you'll see."

Frank stopped his pacing and looked over at his junior officers. Paul immediately picked up a file from his desk and scurried into the typists section of the office.

"Murphy, I need you in my office, don't bring coffee," Frank shouted.

"Damn," Angela said under her breath. Caught out again she thought, I'll swing for that Paul he's left me in the shit.

When she entered Frank's office her hands were clammy and shaking because she was genuinely terrified of having to face the rabble in the outer office, particularly as they had a photographer with them. It's bad enough having your inadequacies on full public view without having a record of it as well.

"I want you to go and talk to the fuckers at the front desk," Frank ordered. "Just make a brief statement then leave, don't answer any questions and don't stand amongst them, stay on our side of the desk."

"What exactly can I say to them? Should I tell them about Mr Anwar seeing a man in uniform?"

"Not on you bloody life. It's too late for that now. If we were going to give out that information it should have been in the first couple of days."

"But I've checked all the police, fire brigade and community wardens living in the area and all of them are accounted for at the time of the murder."

"You say nothing, understand? Not one word. We're getting nowhere with this case and we're spending a fortune maintaining the incident room. This is going to disappear into obscurity just like the case ten years ago. I can feel it in my bones, so we can't give these fuckers anything that's smacks of our incompetence. You'll make a statement, but tell them nothing."

"What on earth do I say, then? Have you any suggestions, because I don't have a clue?" Angela answered with anger replacing fear in her voice. She didn't want to be the sacrificial lamb.

"Look girl, you're much prettier than me and you look like a kid, they'll be easier on you. I'll give you a statement to read along the lines of, 'we are very disappointed with the response from the public and feel we are being denied vital information. Someone somewhere must know this killer. Did a relative or friend arrive home with blood on their clothes that day? We are asking whoever is protecting this man to come forward. The murder of a young woman is a terrible burden to carry. We beseech the killer to give himself up. If any further developments occur, an announcement will be made.' After you make that statement wait for a few seconds until the photographer takes your picture. The rabble will all be shouting questions at once, ignore them. Hold up your hands in front of you and say, 'sorry, but that's all I can tell you at the moment,' then leave. Don't look back. The desk Sergeant will handle it from there, okay?" Frank didn't expect a reply he walked over to his office door and opened it for Angela to leave. "When you've scribbled down that statement run it by me then get out front before any more of them arrive. You've got ten minutes."

When she got back to her desk Paul placed a Mars bar in front of her, "A Mars a day, helps you work, rest and play," he said smirking. "I think you'll need it."

"You're a bastard Paul. You're a cowardly, snivelling bastard."

"Yes Angela, you're absolutely right," he agreed. "But I'm the cowardly, snivelling bastard who gets to stay at his desk while you get thrown to the wolves."

"I hate you Paul. I hope you know that. I hate you," she said vehemently.

Angela felt sick to her stomach, her first big case and it was at risk of slipping into obscurity and now she had to face the baying crowd. She had to redouble her efforts. Surely someone must have seen something that she could use.

Frank felt guilty sending a junior officer to do the dirty work but what else could he do? There was absolutely nothing to report. On reflection, he probably should have released the information about the uniform but it was too late now. He'd made the judgement call and only time would tell if it was the right decision. He admired Angela Murphy, because although she was inexperienced, she was carrying out the investigation like a professional. She was young and her career could stand one or two dead ends. It wouldn't stop her from being the high flyer she was destined to be. He hoped her enthusiasm for the job wouldn't be dented if this case went nowhere. He still remembered what it felt like because that's exactly what happened to him ten years before.

Chapter 15

Angela finally had an appointment to interview Kelly Jamieson but Kelly didn't want to meet her at Jackie's house. Jackie disapproved of her drug use and she couldn't face another lecture on top of talking to the police. Margaret Deacon had been a close acquaintance of Kelly's. They were both drug users and they helped each other out more than once. Angela didn't want to go anywhere near the incident room at Govanhill after being forced to give the statement this morning, so they arranged to meet in a small tearoom in Cumming Drive in Cathcart which bordered the area of Govanhill. Whilst Angela appreciated having Liz Brown to assist her she was annoyed that she had to rely on the uniformed officer. Angela's department was so stretched there simply wasn't another detective available to work with her on interviews. At any time Liz's boss could pull her off the job and there'd be nothing Angela could do about it.

"You're awfully quiet today," Liz observed as she drove Angela's car to the meeting place. "Have I done something to upset you?"

"Oh no, Liz, it's not you, I've had a horrible morning. I had to give a statement to the Govanhill Community Council and they had a photographer with them. I felt really guilty because there was nothing positive I could tell them. I think our case is slowly dying from lack of information and there's nothing I can do. I so much wanted to be a success because it's my first big job." She held her head in her hand and her expression was sorrowful.

If Angela was hoping for sympathy, she was disappointed as Liz replied. "Stop being such a wimp and stop feeling sorry for yourself, this isn't about you it's about Margaret Deacon. Poor cow is relying on us to get her justice. So perk yourself up before we meet Kelly Jamieson because she might just have the lead we're waiting for."

Angela felt ashamed, Liz was absolutely right, it wasn't about her.

"I'm sorry Liz, your right, please forgive me and thank you for pointing out that I'm a selfish wimp."

"Don't mention it," Liz replied chuckling. "And by the way, did I mention that when we solve this case I want plenty of recognition. Remember there's no such thing as a free lunch."

Angela shook her head and laughed, she really liked this tough young woman and she felt they could become friends outside of work.

"My Bobby's going for a job interview this evening," Angela said changing the subject. "His friend Jake has an internet business and he wants to expand it. Bobby really fancies a change of career because he's sick of dealing with horrible children and their equally horrible parents."

"I suppose his job is even worse than ours, at least we can beat the criminals when they annoy us," Liz replied.

"No we can't," Angela answered with a shocked expression on her face.

"Yes, we can," Liz replied turning the car into Cathcart Road and swerving to avoid a jaywalker. "We just mustn't get caught. So if you arrest someone who deserves a kicking, call me, I'm your girl."

Angela stared at the younger woman and frowned, she wasn't sure what to say next.

"Got ya," Liz said winking and laughing at Angela's expression, "You really are very gullible you know Murphy."

She pulled in to the side of the road and parked the car beside Cumming Drive. The kerbside was piled high with boxes and rubbish.

"Are you in a better mood now? Are you ready to interview this junkie prostitute? She said mimicking Mrs Ali's voice."

"Give me a break," Angela said. "Please stop mimicking Mrs Ali because I can't carry out a serious interview if I'm laughing."

"Her mother would be so ashamed," Liz added.

The two women arrived at the tearoom before Kelly and sat at a table beside the window so they could look out for her coming. After twenty minutes of waiting they began to think she wasn't going to show up then, through the window, Liz spotted a very fragile looking young woman walking towards the shop. She was rail thin with greasy, straggly hair and she was clothed in a black mini skirt, an anorak that had seen better days and over the knee black boots. The girl had the same quick, nervous walk that was common to junkies and she hugged herself as if she was cold.

"I bet that's our girl," Liz said and Angela nodded in agreement.

The girl stopped outside the door and lit up a stub of cigarette. "Should I go out and get her?" Angela asked.

"No, just sit tight, she knows we're here, I'm sure she's seen us," Liz replied. "Just give her a minute to have her cigarette because she can't smoke indoors and she looks like she'll be due a fix soon. We don't want to scare her off."

After only three or four puffs Kelly Jamieson stubbed out her cigarette on the wall of the building and entered the tearoom. She walked directly over to the girls' table and slid into the vacant chair.

"I can only give you a few minutes," she said. "I've got to meet my friend."

It was patently obvious by the way she bit her lips and squeezed her arms that her friend was a pusher and she was indeed, needing drugs.

"Thank for meeting with us," Angela said and she asked Liz to fetch a coffee with plenty of sugar for Kelly. When Liz returned Angela began, "I'll try and make this brief. What can you tell us about Margaret Deacon?"

With shaking hands the girl lifted the cup, it rattled against the saucer, she took a sip. "Margaret was my friend. She was my only friend, now I have no one," Kelly answered matter-of-factly. Then she sipped more of her coffee cradling the cup in her hands for warmth.

"Do you know of anyone who wanted to hurt her?"

"Everyone liked Margaret, she even had a boyfriend. She told me he was a quiet lad, tall and skinny, she said he was shy and kind and he bought her food."

Angela's heart skipped a beat because the description was the same as Mrs Ali's. "Did you ever meet her boyfriend, would you know him if you met him in the street?"

"No, I never met him, when you've got a good thing going you keep it to yourself because you never know when someone will steal it away from you."

"But I thought you two were friends?" Angela said.

"Aye, we were," she agreed. "But not in that way. We didn't share punters and we didn't share boyfriends, not that I've got a boyfriend mind you."

Angela didn't know what else to say she looked at Liz for inspiration but the younger woman just shrugged.

"Is that it? Can I go now?" Kelly asked shifting nervously in her seat.

"Just one more question if you don't mind," Angela said.

"Do you have any punters who hurt you? Are there any who get off on your pain?"

"Look at me," Kelly replied pulling her anorak and sweater off her shoulder to reveal a mass of bruises. "Off course I get hurt, but I'm usually too out of it to notice. It's the next day I feel it. I couldn't even tell you who I go with because I don't remember them. When you're desperate for money you'll do anything with anyone. I've been fucked and beaten more times than I can remember, I've been hospitalised twice and one punter cut off my hair. Margaret and I were alike. The only difference is that I'm still alive and I don't mind telling you, I'm fucking scared. The killer might come after me next and there's nothing I can do about it."

Angela and Liz sat in stunned silence. Kelly stood up to leave.

"Can you give me any money?" she asked nervously moving her weight from one foot to the other, she was unable to keep still. "Just a fiver for fags, I'm absolutely broke."

Against her better judgement, Angela reached into her bag and took out a ten pound note which she held out to the girl. Kelly snatched the note from her hand and without a backward glance, bolted out of the tearoom before she could change her mind.

"That might stop her working tonight," Angela said almost apologetically to Liz.

"That's only a drop in the ocean," Liz replied sadly.

Angela was in a hurry to get home because Bobby was seeing Jake today and she was anxious to find out how he had got on, although she had mixed feelings about him changing his career. At first she'd felt absolutely sure she could embrace any change in a positive and constructive way, but after today, her confidence had taken a battering and she wasn't so certain about coping as the main breadwinner. She'd planned to get home early, but the day ran away with her and it was nearly seven o'clock by the time she put her key in the front door. She'd worked a twelve hour shift. As soon as Angela entered the house she could smell the mouth watering aroma of Bobby's cooking. The click of the front door closing brought Bobby into the hallway to greet her.

"Hello Darling, I've got great news," he said helping her off with her coat. He held her face in his hands and kissed her on both cheeks. "Jake is not only going to give me a job but he's going to take me in as a junior partner. Isn't that great? I can start right away while I'm working my notice at the school." He stopped to draw breath and his face was flushed with excitement. "Jake has so much work that he can't handle it. He's desperate for help. So you see I'll be an asset from the start not a liability and I'll be making almost the same money."

"The same money, really, Angela exclaimed, "That's fantastic news. And you're absolutely sure that you and Jake can work together?"

"Absolutely, we'll hardly see each other because each of us will be working from our own computers, but we've always got on okay anyway."

Bobby poured them each a glass of red wine. "To success," he toasted.

"To my wonderful, clever husband," Angela said smiling, but secretly she was overwhelmed by the speed her life was changing. Angela didn't know whether or not she could cope, but circumstances had overtaken her, so she accepted that she just had to get on with it and hope for the best.

That night Bobby made love to Angela with a new found passion. They hadn't actually had sex for some weeks and she knew now that it was because he'd been so miserable. How blind she'd been. Bobby was always a confident and considerate lover but tonight something had subtly changed, he was full of raw energy and their lovemaking was daring and exciting. As she lay in his strong arms she felt satisfied and safe. She listened to his steady breathing and Angela knew then that Bobby would always look after her, she needn't have worried. As she drifted off to sleep she thought once again about the contrast between her life and the lives of the women she'd interviewed and she was selfishly pleased that her life was the better one.

Chapter 16

Megan and Anne-Marie shared a passionate kiss in the doorway of their close before Anne-Marie set off to work. They'd spent a typical Thursday together beginning with them rising late and eating a large cooked brunch. They'd stuffed themselves with Lorne sausage, bacon, fried eggs, beans and black pudding accompanied by hot buttered toast and mugs of strong sweet tea, heart attack food but a diet that most Scots enjoyed. Then, as was the norm, they headed off into town for a day's shopping. Not that they actually bought anything but they enjoyed trying on shoes with impossible heels and evening dresses they'd never wear. No Thursday trip was complete without a stroll through the Argyle Arcade, a long, narrow, covered shopping area, in the city centre, that stretched from Argyle Street to Buchanan Street and housed most of the city's jewellery shops. Megan loved to look at the sparkling diamonds in the windows and she particularly liked the pre-loved pieces that McGowans often had on display.

Thomas watched from the end of the street, the skinny girl actually walked past him but she didn't see him hidden in the shadowy entrance of a close. He took the latex gloves from his jacket pocket and slowly pushed his hands into them being especially careful not to tear them. Then Thomas did a last minute check of his bag to make sure he had all the stuff he needed. This is it, he thought and a jag of fear stabbed at his chest. 'Do it, do it, do it,' the voice chanted in time to his steps as he made his way towards the girls' flat.

The sound of his footsteps echoed in his ears and he looked around nervously because he was sure that someone would hear him, but he needn't have worried as the street was empty. When Thomas reached number twenty-two he pushed the security door and it swung open. Thomas had followed the postman into the close earlier in the day and disabled the lock. He softly climbed the stairs and rang the bell of the first floor flat.

Don't tell me you've forgotten your keys again, Megan said to herself. She walked to the door and looked through the spy hole. It wasn't Anne-Marie. A man in a dark uniform was at the door. Oh my God, what's happened, Megan wondered? Thinking the man outside was a cop, she turned the handle and wrenched open the door.

Thomas threw his punch as soon as the door swung open. It hit Megan square in the face and she staggered back two or three paces before hitting the deck. As she lay on the floor stunned by the blow, Thomas entered the apartment and shut the door behind him. He pounced on the dazed girl and quickly bound her hands behind her back with the duct tape from his bag. Then he stuffed a clean dishcloth into her mouth and ran the duct tape round and round her head sealing her mouth shut. He dragged the near comatose girl into the kitchen before surveying the room.

As Megan began to come round she realised she'd been restrained and, on seeing Thomas, a look of absolute terror passed across her eyes. She watched him as he took a large kitchen knife from his bag, it was brand new and still in its packaging. He placed it on the kitchen table. There was no radio in the room but a cd player was on the worktop and Thomas switched it on. Then he carefully plugged in the toaster and suspended it by the wire over the worktop near the sink. It wasn't exactly right but it would have to do.

Megan began to moan and she tried to move her body towards the door. Thomas laughed at her, oh no you don't, he thought. He looked up and saw the pulley, used for drying clothes, suspended from the ceiling and it gave him an idea. He lowered it and untied the rope that held it in place leaving the wooden slats on the floor. Then he pulled over a kitchen chair and lifted Megan onto it. Thomas bound Megan to the chair with duct tape then carefully taped each of her legs to the legs of the chair. Her short skirt rode up exposing her crotch and her pink, satin panties. The sight of the soft fabric barely covering silky hair filled Thomas with feelings of both disgust and excitement and he felt himself grow hard.

'*Dirty boy,*' the voice shouted. '*Dirty boy wants the dirty whore. Why don't you touch her? You know you want to. Go on, do it, do it, do it,*' the voice goaded.

"Nooo," Thomas croaked, "No." He wrenched at Megan's skirt and tried to straighten it but it still didn't cover her, so he took a towel from beside the sink and draped it over her legs. He dragged the chair and the girl through a beaded curtain and into a large walk in cupboard, then, using the pulley rope, he tied the chair to the fridge freezer which stood against the back wall. "That'll stop you moving around and making a noise."

Large tears ran from Megan's eyes and snot dripped from her nose in long streams, she watched as Thomas arranged the room in a ritualistic fashion. She was petrified that he was going to cut her with the knife and she prayed for Anne-Marie to come home and save her. Once Thomas was finished with what he was doing he surveyed the room and gave a satisfied sigh then he entered the cupboard and spoke to Megan.

"I just want you to know," he began, "It's not you I'm here to kill. It's just a shame that you were home, bad luck eh? We'll wait for your friend now, don't worry it'll soon be over."

He stepped out of the cupboard and took a packet of decorator's disposable overalls from his bag, stripped off his uniform and carefully folded it laying it on the floor in the far corner of the kitchen. Then he dressed in the white plastic suit. Megan watched from the cupboard, she was paralysed with terror, a stream of hot urine ran down her legs. She realised that Anne-Marie would soon be home and she was helpless. They were going to die.

Thomas looked at his watch, it's time, he thought. The other girl would return any minute. He knew from his surveillance that she only serviced two men in their cars on Thursdays. Then she went to the pub for a beer before returning home. He reached into his bag and took out a clear plastic carrier then headed for the cupboard.

"If you believe in God, then you'd better pray for your soul now," he told Megan.

Panic stricken, she thrashed about in a last desperate attempt to escape. Thomas forced the bag over her head and tied it in a knot behind her neck. The terrified girl struggled fighting for air and for her life. The polythene sucked in and out with every breath she took and, as it began to fog up, she heard Anne-Marie's key in the lock.

"Where are you, Megan?" she heard her call.

Thomas ran from the cupboard. He grabbed a hammer wrapped in cling film from the table where he'd carefully placed it and hit Anne-Marie several times as she entered the kitchen. She was taken completely by surprise and, unable to defend herself, she fell like a stone.

Thomas took his time with his work. He was in no hurry because he knew that people rarely visited this house. It was important for everything to look just right. If made him feel sick when he slashed the girl's throat and her blood spurted out over his overalls but it had to be done. He carefully arranged her body on the floor with one arm outstretched then stuck her hair down with the blood. When he was satisfied that the scene was set he carefully peeled off his bloody overalls and packed them, together with all the other things that he'd brought, into his bag. He washed his gloved hands at the sink before drying them on a dishtowel then once again he donned his uniform. The only thing left to do was to check that the other girl was dead.

He entered the cupboard and prodded Megan with his gloved hand, she didn't move. Thomas could see through the bag, her terrified eyes were wide open and staring. He poked at one eyeball with his outstretched finger, she didn't blink. Good job, well done, he thought to himself. He looked at Megan for a few moments considering the girl.

'*You've never seen a cunt before,*' the voice in his head growled. '*Go on have a wee look, she's dead, she'll never know.*' Thomas hesitated, '*What kind of a man are you? Are you a gay boy?*' The voice goaded, '*Gay boy, gay boy,*' it chanted.

"I'm not gay, I'm not."

'*Well what are you waiting for then, Christmas? Go on gay boy get on with it. Do it now.*'

Thomas drew a deep breath perspiration ran down his forehead and ran into his eyes making them sting. With trembling hand he reached out and gingerly lifted the towel covering Megan's lap. He pushed back her skirt and his whole body shook with excitement. The sight of her urine soaked panties made him groan. Hooking his fingers under the elastic he slowly pulled it down letting the back of his gloved hand brush against the hair and skin of her crotch. He felt faint. His whole body throbbed and he slid his other hand inside his trousers and rubbed himself. Thomas felt disgusted but he couldn't help it and when he climaxed he cried out sinking to his knees on the floor, his shaking legs were unable to support him.

'*You're disgusting, dirty and disgusting,*' the voice said full of revulsion.

"But you told me to do it, you told me," Thomas whimpered.

'*Stop snivelling, you disgust me, I hate you when you're weak,*' the voice replied.

"Don't talk to me don't call me that. Shut up, shut up."

Thomas covered his ears with his hands and rocked back and forth.

'*You're a pathetic pile of shit, no self control,*' the voice said spitefully. '*And you're just like your mother.*'

Chapter 17

It was almost six weeks after Margaret Deacon's murder and the incident room in Govanihill was shut down. No one was coming forward with information and all it did was serve as a constant reminder to Frank of his shortcomings. Jean Glen had buried her daughter and moved on, and even the Community Council had lost interest. Like the similar case ten years before, it was consigned to an evidence box in a store room.

Liz Brown was back doing her usual work and Angela was stuck in the office which she hated. Angela was working on a case of armed robbery at a bookie's in Shawlands. The thief had been apprehended by two brave but foolhardy young men who'd set upon him and overpowered him. They thought his handgun was a replica, it wasn't. All that remained for Angela to work on was the paperwork and she was bogged down by it.

The phone on her desk rang, "There's someone at the front desk to see you Angela," the duty constable said. "She said her name's Jackie and you'd know who she is."

"Is she a hard faced woman with pock-marked skin?" Angela asked.

"Aye, that would be right," was the reply.

"It's Jackie Cosgrove, I wonder what she wants. Show her into the interview room please, and if it's not too much bother, offer her tea and tell her I'll be with her shortly."

Angela re-applied her lipstick after checking her face in her compact mirror then she poured herself a coffee from the machine, picked up a notebook and pen and made her way to the interview room. When she arrived a young constable was placing a cup of tea on the desk in front of Jackie. The interview room was stark, just a desk and four chairs with no window.

"I've been in this room more times than I care to remember," Jackie said, with a wry smile passing over her lips. "But that was when I had a different life."

"What can I help you with? Is there a problem with one of your girls?" Angela asked cutting the formalities.

"Not exactly," Jackie answered. "At least I'm not sure."

Angela stared at Jackie and with her head slightly tilted to one side, she frowned, "Why don't you start at the beginning," she prompted.

"It's Megan and Anne-Marie, they're missing. No one's seen them in over a week."

"Have you tried their house," Angela asked stating the obvious.

"I've rung the bell twice but there's no answer. I'm really worried because I usually see at least one of them every couple of days. I've asked around but it's as if they've disappeared off the planet. I even spoke to one of Anne-Marie's punters, an old boy, who she sees every Thursday night, but she didn't turn up yesterday. He saw her last week and they'd arranged to meet at seven o'clock. I just don't know what to do."

Jackie sipped her tea, she was near to tears.

"I know Anne-Marie can be a pain in the neck but they're basically good girls and they don't do drugs," she continued. "Can you help me find them?"

"The first thing to do is file a missing person's report." Angela advised. "Do you know the name and phone number of their landlord?"

"Aye, it's Govanhill Housing Association."

"Good, I'll send someone round and get them to open up the apartment, just in case they've done a moonlight flit."

"They wouldn't have done that," Jackie said vehemently. "I told you, they're basically good girls. I have this really bad feeling that something's happened to them." She stopped to wipe a stray tear from her cheek. "Please find them. I'm worried sick. I don't have many friends and that pair always looked out for me."

"I'll do my best," Angela replied, smiling sympathetically. "Don't worry, most people turn up. They go on holiday or visit friends and forget to tell the people who care about them. It's teenagers who run away and they're not teenagers."

"Sometimes they act like teenagers," Jackie said regaining her composure. She stood to leave. "Thank you for seeing me, please call me as soon as you hear anything." She held out her hand and Angela shook it then showed her out of the interview room. "Why don't you and Liz come round for a wee cup of tea sometime soon? You know you're always welcome," Jackie said as she left.

"Thanks," Angela replied weakly. She took Jackie to the front desk and arranged for her to fill out the missing person paperwork then she returned to her office. As the door shut behind her she muttered, "That's all I need."

* * *

After killing Anne-Marie and Megan, Thomas felt a mixture of relief and revulsion. He was pleased to be able to walk the streets of Govanhill without the risk of bumping into the skinny whore. He'd been nervous when he was working with Alan in case the girl ridiculed him again. Losing his self control with Megan terrified him. The voice in his head had likened him to his mother, but he wasn't like her, was he? Thomas was unravelling, his well ordered life felt frightening and chaotic.

He couldn't leave his house for four days after the killings because he no longer felt safe and he didn't trust himself not to fall apart. When he phoned in sick to his work, Alan, thinking he was ill, texted him with offers of help. If only his friend knew that he was simply hiding from the world. When he did emerge from his solitude, Thomas had regained his self control and could now separate himself from his crime. In his mind someone else was responsible for the killings. In his mind he would be just as surprised as the next man when the bodies were finally discovered.

* * *

"Oh Jesus Christ no, not again," Frank's voice boomed across the office. "Murphy," he called.

Everyone stopped working and looked up. Angela jumped out of her chair and practically ran to Frank's room, the fact that 'Murphy' hadn't been followed by 'bring coffee' let her know that something was seriously wrong.

"Uniform is just off the phone," he said when she entered his room. "They've found your two prossies. They're dead, murdered."

Angela sank into a chair her legs felt wobbly, she was completely stunned.

"Where? How?" was all she could manage to say.

Frank looked at her pale face and sickly expression. He took a bottle of whisky from his desk drawer and poured a small amount into a paper cup.

"Sip this," he said handing Angela the cup. "Just a couple of wee sips will steady you."

For once Angela didn't argue with him and after a couple of swallows of the burning liquid the faint feeling passed.

"Thanks Boss, I needed that."

"Now you're feeling better I'll fill you in on what's happened. You asked uniform to check out the apartment. They called Govanhill Housing and this morning a man from the Association let them in. The bodies of both girls were there. They've been dead for some time. One of them has been murdered in a similar way to Margaret Deacon and the other girl was suffocated."

Frank paused to let the information sink in. Angela took a tissue from her pocket and blew her nose, she felt quite emotional because she'd known these girls.

"There's so much work to do that I hardly know where to start," Frank continued. "Forensics is already there and we'll have to visit the scene of course. That will take until late afternoon, but before we go you'll need to telephone Jackie Cosgrove because, although she's not a relative, she reported the girls missing. She lives practically on the doorstep so you'll want to tell her before someone else does. This will be all over the lunch-time news. We'll need to get her in tomorrow to identify the girls. Do you think she'll be up to it?"

"She'll be devastated, Frank. Those girls were like family to her. I think I should go round to her house. I don't think it's right to simply telephone. If it's okay with you I'll ask uniform if they can let me have Liz Brown again because I can't go alone and we're going to be too stretched here for anyone to accompany me."

"Do whatever you have to. Just get the job done. Do you know if either of the girls have family?"

"I know Anne-Marie has an ex-husband and a child but Megan's a complete mystery to me. Perhaps Jackie Cosgrove will know more."

"Try to get all the information you can and when you're finished join me at 22 Garturk Street. Now fuck off and get started, we've no time to waste."

Angela was pleased to have the normal, foul mouthed Frank back as the polite version made her cry. She returned to her desk and put in a call for Liz Brown.

The news spread around the office like wildfire and the words 'serial killer' were being bandied about. It was a shocking prospect, one murder was bad enough, but if this was just the beginning, it didn't bear thinking about. Angela felt sick to her stomach as if she were somehow to blame for not solving Margaret Deacon's murder. If only they'd caught her killer then Anne-Marie and Megan might still be alive. But life was full of 'if onlys'. Within half an hour Angela had picked up Liz and the two women were on their way to Jackie Cosgrove's house.

"This is horrible," Liz said and Angela nodded in agreement. "And once we tell her the news I'll have to make her a cup of tea in that disgusting house. I hate to think what her kitchen is like, a mixture of e-coli and salmonella probably. I suppose I could put on latex gloves."

"For goodness sake, Liz, she's just lost her two best friends and you're worried about a dirty kitchen."

"Let's get one thing straight, Angela," Liz said sternly. "The death of these two girls does not affect me. I hardly knew them and the truth is, I didn't even like them. After I went home from the job I didn't think about them at all. However, catching something nasty from that house would hurt me personally. You've got to toughen up if you're going to survive in this job. You can't take on everyone's misery. If you can't detach your outside life from your working life then quit now."

"But surely you feel compassion for someone else's pain," Angela protested.

"Feeling compassion is one thing, taking on their pain is something else," Liz replied.

Much as she hated to admit it, Angela knew in her heart that Liz was right. When she was a teenager she liked nothing better than to have a good cry at a sad movie and, as she was growing up, she brought every waif and stray home to be rescued by her long suffering mother.

"My advice is," Liz began, "Once we break the news, you go and make the tea and I'll sit with her. By the time you join us she'll have calmed down and we'll both be able to ask her questions. Most gain least pain, don't you think? You won't have to cry with her and I won't have to risk poisoning."

"No Liz," Angela said taking charge once again. "You make the tea and I'll talk to Jackie. Thanks for your advice, but this is my case and I have to deal with it."

Liz pursed her lips with annoyance and Angela realised that this tough young woman was used to getting her own way. They drew up outside Jackie's house and Angela noticed the curtain being pulled back slightly and a face at the window.

"At least she's in," Angela said. "We'd best get on with it."

The two women climbed out of the car and walked towards the house. As they reached the threshold the door was pulled open. Jackie stood in the entranceway, she looked distraught.

"I guess you're not here for the tea," she said with a catch in her voice.

"I'm so sorry," Angela began, "Its bad news."

Jackie's eyes fluttered, Liz stepped forward, grabbed her by the arm and steadied the older woman.

"Let's go into the living room and get a seat, shall we?" she said as she steered Jackie through the doorway and into a chair. "I'll make a wee cup of tea, shall I? Two sugars isn't it?"

Jackie nodded, tears now streaming down her face. "Are they both dead?" she asked.

"I'm afraid so," Angela replied.

"What happened to them? Was it an accident? Were they drunk?"

There was a moment's pause before Angela took a deep breath and said, "It wasn't an accident, I'm sorry Jackie but they were murdered."

"Murdered, both of them, how?"

"I wish I could tell you more but we've only just found them. They were killed in their apartment."

"So all the time I was phoning and going round there, they were lying dead inside? Oh my God, and to think I was cursing them for not getting in touch, those poor girls, those poor, poor girls."

Jackie rested her elbows on her knees, held her face in her hands and cried. The silence of the room was punctuated by great gasping sobs. Angela sat quietly. She felt awkward and didn't know what to do. Thankfully Liz arrived with a mug of tea and managed to get Jackie to take some sips from it. Having to hold the cup and drink from it made Jackie steady her hands and calm down.

"There's only Kelly left now," Jackie said. "Do you think she's in danger? Do you think the killer will target her next? Someone should warn her."

Angela and Liz exchanged glances, neither of them had thought about that. They simply hadn't made a connection, but of course there was a risk, anything was possible. After about twenty minutes and with a fresh mug of tea clasped between her hands, Jackie began to talk about the murdered women.

"Anne-Marie has an ex-husband called Graham and a daughter, Victoria, they live in Edinburgh. I have their address. Anne-Marie and Graham divorced because her drinking became so bad she was out of control. She hasn't seen her daughter for years but she's saved over four thousand pounds in a Post Office Savings account for her. I have the account book. She gave it to me for safe keeping, together with a copy of her will."

"I'm surprised that she'd made a will, she just didn't seem the type," Angela said.

"Both girls made a will each leaving everything to the other apart from Victoria's money. Neither of them wanted their families to benefit in any way from their deaths. Not that they had much. I doubt if there's even enough to cover their funerals."

Jackie mopped at her eyes with a sodden tissue. Angela reached into her bag and took out a packet of paper hankies which she handed to her. Jackie took them gratefully and mouthed a thank you.

"Do you know anything about Megan's parents?" Liz asked.

"Only that her parents live in a small seaside town in Wales called Abergelly. Megan told me that they're very religious. She said they've lived in the same house all their married life. She's also got an aunt somewhere in Glasgow, Bearsden, I think. Megan said her aunt didn't want any contact with her because she didn't want to fall out with her sister, Megan's mother. As far as I know Anne-Marie and I were the closest thing to a family that Megan had."

Jackie was now much calmer but she was exhausted. "I'm sorry girls," she said, "But I'll have to go and lie down for a while, I'm beat. I don't think I've anything else to tell you at the moment."

"There's just one more thing, if you don't mind," Angela began. "Do you think you could identify the girls for us? Liz and I would pick you up in the car and we'd stay with you the whole time. It wouldn't be until tomorrow morning at the earliest because their bodies haven't been moved from the crime scene yet."

Jackie mopped at fresh tears. "I don't suppose there's anyone else, so it will have to be me. If you don't mind I'll ask someone from my church to come with me. It would help to have some spiritual support."

"Of course, that's not a problem, would you like us to call someone for you, it's no bother. Liz could telephone now if you like."

"No thanks, not just now, I'll get a wee rest first, then I'll make the call. Would you girls mind seeing yourselves out and I'll just sit in my chair and shut my eyes for a few minutes."

Angela and Liz said their goodbyes and left the house shutting the door behind them.

"Do you think she'll be okay?" Liz asked. "She looked ghastly and we don't want her carking it before she identifies the corpses."

Angela was shocked at Liz's cold attitude, "You really are all heart," she said.

"And you're a soppy old Granny," was her immediate reply.

Chapter 18

Angela and Liz travelled to the crime scene in silence. They felt annoyed with each other because nobody likes their weaknesses to be pointed out. As they turned into Alison Street they could see a crowd had gathered at the junction with Garturk Street.

"Great, now what do we do," Angela said aloud. "We'll never be able to drive into the street and there's nowhere to park round here."

Liz edged the car forward and, as they neared Garturk Street, they could see that a BBC outside broadcast van was parked at the corner and, within the crowd of onlookers, press photographers were snapping away with their cameras.

Liz said, "Don't worry we'll get through. I'm going to lock the doors, get out your warrant card because we'll need to identify ourselves or we won't be allowed into the street."

She drove very slowly manoeuvring the car expertly round the swarms of people who had spilled out onto the road. Every few yards Liz revved the engine, this action made people aware of the car and they moved to let it pass. Angela felt claustrophobic, the crowd surrounded the car like a swarm of ants and she couldn't make out the road ahead. As she looked at Liz she could see the young woman's teeth were gritted and her expression was one of steely determination. Angela's joints ached as her body tensed with nerves. Eventually Liz eased the car to the police barriers that blocked the road at the front of

Garturk Street. Angela flashed her warrant card at the policeman on duty and he pulled the barrier aside to allow their car to pass through.

"I'm sorry I implied that you were hard and unfeeling," Angela said to Liz by way of an apology. "You're a fantastic driver and you've got nerves of steel, I could never have driven through that crowd," she added with admiration. "I admit that at times, I can be soppy, but I'm not old and I'm not a Granny. All right?"

"Okay, apology accepted and I have to agree with you," Liz replied laughing, I'm fantastic and you're soppy. I'm sorry I called you an old Granny."

"Friends again?" Angela asked.

"Friends again," Liz agreed.

Liz parked the car immediately across the road from number 22 then the policewomen made their way to the close entrance. Paul Costello was standing outside smoking a strong, foul smelling cigar. He was wearing a crumpled raincoat and his stance was slightly stooped reminding Angela of the TV detective, Colombo.

"You took your time," he said to Angela and he nodded an acknowledgement to Liz, "The Boss wants you inside. It's not a pretty sight. I'm going to Tasty Bakers for a sausage roll. Do you girls want anything?"

"I'd like a steak pie if you don't mind," Liz responded.

"How can you two eat at a time like this?" Angela asked incredulously, "Especially you Paul, because you've just been inside looking at corpses."

"I've had no breakfast," Paul answered as if that explained everything.

"And I'm starving," Liz added.

"I bet you two would be knitting as the guillotine blade fell," Angela said shaking her head.

"And we'd probably have packed some sandwiches," Liz added making Paul laugh.

"Anyway off you pop, Angela. I'll take care of this delightful young officer and I'll personally look after her till you return," Paul said placing a protective arm around Liz's shoulder.

"You watch out for him," Angela said to Liz, "He's married and he's got four kids."

"Don't you worry," Liz replied shrugging off Paul's embrace. "I've met his type before they're all talk and no action. You just take care of yourself."

Angela left the pair to their banter and donning protective gear she made her way up the stairs to the first floor. As she reached the front door the sweet, cloying smell of death reached her nostrils and she gagged. A forensic assistant who was kneeling in the hallway packing a kit bag handed her a mask impregnated with menthol.

"Wear this," he said, "It will cut through the smell. And don't worry everyone is wearing them. They're all the rage."

Everyone's a comedian today Angela thought as she gratefully placed the mask over her nose and mouth. She entered the room and cautiously stepped over to Frank being extra careful not to stand in the sticky pool of black blood that had gathered round the corpse. When she looked down it took her a moment to realise that she was looking at the body of Anne-Marie Connor because decomposition had dramatically changed her appearance. Her body was completely discoloured and blood-tinged blisters covered the surface of her skin which looked loose as if it could fall off her bones. The smell in the room was foul.

"The stench is caused by the internal organs and fatty tissue decaying," Frank said, "She's been like this for at least a week. I'm sorry but Paul came with me for this one. You saw the vultures at the end of the street. I couldn't wait for you. He's just stepped out for a smoke and to get us some lunch. How did you get on with Jackie?"

"She's got a name and address for Anne-Marie's ex and a town in Wales for Megan's family. She said she'd identify the girls."

"Good, that's fine. We've got to inform the relatives as soon as possible, although the press know not to release the names until the family are told."

"Do you think she'll recognise this as Anne-Marie? I couldn't identify her and I've seen her recently," Angela said nodding at the body on the floor.

"If you think this one's bad just wait till you see the other one. She's had a plastic bag over her head and her eyes and tongue are bloated and bulging. The top skin of her hands has fallen off in one big sheet because someone tried to bag them so I expect the same thing will happen to her face when that bag's removed. If anything she smells worse than this one because she's in that wee space," Frank said pointing to the cupboard.

"Do you want me to look at Megan?" Angela asked feeling sick at the thought.

"Naw, no point both of us having to stomach it, besides it's this one who was the intended victim the other girl is just incidental. Look at the room Angela, see anything familiar about it?"

Angela noticed the minute she entered the kitchen that this scene, whilst not identical to the previous one, was laid out in a very similar fashion to Margaret Deacon's. The way the body was positioned, the toaster hanging from the worktop, a knife embedded in the kitchen table and the broken crockery strewn about the room had obviously been staged. The only real differences were that this room had started off clean and of course this scene had an extra corpse.

"Do you think we're dealing with a serial killer, Boss?"

"Two murders scenes don't make a serial killer but there are certainly enough similarities to link these deaths. Let's just hope we catch the bastard before he strikes again. If another corpse turns up murdered in the same way, then yes, we will be dealing with a serial killer."

"Something that Jackie said got me wondering. Do you think Kelly Jamieson might be at risk? She's the only home grown hooker known to be living in the immediate area who's still alive. Shouldn't we be keeping an eye on her?"

"The short answer is, I don't know. We can warn her to stop picking up punters, but you and I both know that's not going to happen. We don't have the resources to follow her around and we don't have a good enough reason to justify it even if we had. Paul and I are going to be here for most of the day. I'd like you to call Jack Dobson. He's in the office today, working on the paperwork for that drive past shooting case. Give him the addresses for the next of kin and ask him to get them traced. Tell him the press are hovering like vultures and we need the relatives informed ASAP. Then you start banging on doors in this street and see if anyone saw or heard anything. We could really do with a break here, if we don't come up with something this time, the media will crucify us. Now fuck off out of here while you can."

Angela was relieved to be out of the humid, stinking flat. She inhaled deeply when she reached the cool air of the street.

"How was it?" Liz enquired. "Is it as bad as Paul said it was?"

"Whatever he's told you, it's ten times worse," Angela replied. "Even though I had on protective gear, I feel as if my clothes and hair smell of the place."

"You smell okay to me," Paul said with a leer. "I certainly wouldn't turf you out of bed," he added.

"That's because you wouldn't have the balls to get her into bed in the first place," Liz chipped in.

"Paul pulled an expression of mock hurt."

"You can forget that look for a start," Liz said. "It might work with your wife and four kids but it won't work with me. I've got the measure of you, my lad."

"So you're saying I've no chance with you, either?" Paul asked winking at Liz.

"Paul, my dear, you've more chance with one of the girls in there. At least they can't say no."

Paul and Liz laughed at her retort but Angela just didn't understand their gallows humour and she wondered if she ever would.

Chapter 19

"Aye, aye, what's going on here?" Alan asked as he and Thomas walked along Alison Street. "The place is teeming with photographers. Something's happened in Garturk Street. Come on Tommy let's go and have a look."

For an instant Thomas felt a stab of anxiety, but it was only for an instant.

"I wonder what it is," Alan said as he speeded up his pace. "That's the street where the two lesbians live. Maybe something's happened to them."

Thomas had to practically run to keep up with Alan and, as they hurried past the shops, they had to dodge the boxes of fruit and bags of rubbish that littered the pavement. When they arrived at the junction with Garturk Street they couldn't see anything through the crowd of people.

Alan took his ID card from his pocket. "Official business let me through," he said loudly holding the card in front of him. "Follow me Tommy, stick close behind me and we'll see what's going on."

Miraculously, on seeing the uniformed men, the crowd parted and let them pass. When they reached the barrier Alan spoke to the policeman on duty for a few moments then he turned to Thomas.

"I was right Tommy, it's them, the two prossies and they're both dead, murdered. The police aren't releasing their names until the families are informed but it's their house. Three dead prossies in a couple of months, someone's cleaning up this part of town. If it carries on like this Govanhill will soon be as posh as Newton Mearns." Alan laughed at his joke. Thomas smiled uncomfortably. '*You're a hero*' the voice said sarcastically.

* * *

At the end of their working day Angela and Liz went to a nearby pub for a beer. Angela didn't usually drink anything if she was driving but one beer would be okay and she really needed it. The pub was very old fashioned and dark inside, it smelled of alcohol and cigarettes even though smoking was banned. There was also an underlying odour of urine and fried food, not an inviting setting for a relaxing drink. The pub was completely empty except for two traffic wardens who were sitting at a table near the bar. When Angela went to buy the beers the older man spoke to her.

"Terrible business in Garturk Street, I knew the girls you know, I used to see them all the time because, like them, I work these streets," he laughed at his own little joke.

Angela didn't want to talk about work she just wanted a beer to unwind before going home. "Yes, it's awful," she agreed to be polite then she lifted the beers and carried them over to where Liz was seated.

"What did he want?" Liz asked when Angela placed the glasses on the table.

"He wanted to chat about the murders I think, but he's out of luck. I don't want to think about it anymore and I certainly don't want to talk about it. What a day, what a crappy day."

"It could be worse," Liz said, "We could be traffic wardens."

Angela chuckled, "I suppose so," she said. "At least we don't have a quota to fill."

"If we did have to, we'd be well ahead this month," Liz said with a wry grin.

The girls supped their beers quickly and almost in silence then they left the pub and Angela drove Liz home. Now Thomas and Alan were the only customers. Although Thomas would normally rush away after one beer he lingered on for a second one because he was particularly interested in what Alan was telling him.

"I've had the caravan for four years," Alan said. "My wife hates it because she says there's nothing to do there but that's why I like it. I love the peace and quiet. It's just me and the fishing, no people no noise, just the occasional bird song. My friend Jimmy owns the field and he's given me permission to park the caravan on it."

"You'd think that vandals would break in and damage it," Thomas said. "It's a miracle nothing's happened to it."

"Well, you see Thomas, the way it's parked behind a line of trees you can't see it from the road. So no one knows it's there."

"And what do you do all day? Surely you don't spend hours just sitting and fishing."

"Actually I do. Sometimes I make a cup of tea but most of the time I just enjoy the solitude. After working and living in a city all week, there's nothing I like better than going into the country. The air is cleaner and everything is green and beautiful. I tell you what, Thomas, why don't I take you down to see it on Sunday, it's not far we could be there in just over an hour. The winter will soon be over and I'll have to get the caravan ready for the better weather. You could help me with the tidy up then we could go to the local hotel for a bite of lunch, what do you say, are we on?"

Thomas thought for a moment, he'd never gone anywhere for a day trip because he didn't have any friends to go with.

"What would I need to wear and what would I have to take with me?" he asked tentatively.

"A pair of good strong walking shoes or boots, a warm, waterproof jacket and you'd better also have a knitted hat and gloves because it can get mighty cold and windy there in winter. Does that mean you're coming?" Alan asked smiling.

"Yes, thanks, I would like to see it," Thomas replied. "Will we be doing any fishing? I've never fished before."

"We could drop a line or two, I've never tried at this time of year but who knows, we might be lucky. I'll bring a few sandwiches just in case the hotel is shut. If it is open for lunch we'll eat the sandwiches anyway."

"Where is your caravan? Is it easy to get to?"

"Past Cumbernauld, through Kilsyth and keep going, down the Tak-Ma-Doon road to the Carron Bridge and we're there. Dead easy if you know the way. I'll pick you up at nine o'clock at the corner of Victoria Road and Alison Street. That'll save me from manoeuvring around parked cars. Is that okay with you?"

"Aye, that's fine, I'll be there on time, don't worry."

The two men chatted about their trip for a while longer before Alan headed home for his dinner. Thomas was excited, not just to be going on an excursion, but also to be doing something that normal men do. Thanks to Alan he was learning how to fit in and behave appropriately. It made him feel in control and the voice in his head couldn't spoil it.

Chapter 20

When Angela arrived home she felt grubby and tired. Bobby was working at the computer and the house was untidy. He hadn't begun to prepare dinner even though he'd been home for two hours. When Angela went into the kitchen there was no food in the fridge.

"Why is this place so untidy and why is there nothing to eat? I'm absolutely shattered. You said you'd do a shopping today," she said accusingly.

"Is that the time?" Bobby asked looking at his watch. "I'm sorry, Darling, but I'm working two jobs at the moment and I lost track of time. I'll just finish what I'm doing then I'll fetch something in," Bobby said without raising his head from the screen.

"Don't bother I'm too tired and too hungry to wait. I'll just make some toast," Angela replied expecting Bobby to do a bit of grovelling for his misdemeanour.

"Okay, then I'll just continue what I'm doing, I should be finished in about an hour and we can order in a carry-out."

Angela was raging. She left the room and slammed the door behind her. Selfish bastard, she thought. He might well be working two jobs but his day is no longer than mine. She went to the bedroom and sat on the unmade bed and for some reason she found herself weeping helplessly. Maybe it was tiredness or disappointment at Bobby but probably it was the stress of her day. The sight of the dead girls in their clean kitchen with all their personal items like little ornaments on display revealed a lot about Anne-Marie and Megan. The girls had had a close, happy relationship and they'd built a home together. Some man had destroyed all of that when he came into their place. A maniac was walking the same streets and breathing the same air as normal people like Mr Anwar and Mrs Ali and Angela had to find him before he struck again. She was now surer than ever that he would strike again and she was scared, very scared.

* * *

Thomas walked home from the pub with a spring in his step. He didn't bat an eyelid when he passed Garturk Street on his way. It was over, nothing to do with him, he wasn't interested. He had other, more important things, to think about now.

When he walked towards the sweet shop in Allison Street two teenage girls were standing outside. One was tall and elegant and the other short and plump, both had beautiful faces. They were dressed demurely in suits of brightly coloured silk and each girl wore an anorak over her outfit. Thomas found himself unable to stop staring at them. As he neared them he saw them looking at him. Feeling confident, he said, "Hello." The shorter girl covered her mouth with her hand and giggled but the other girl returned the 'hello,' shyly.

"Are you the traffic warden who booked my Dad's van?" the taller girl asked. "He has to park outside the shop to deliver the stuff to my uncle. He's only ever parked for ten or fifteen minutes. The boxes are heavy so he can't carry them any distance, he's got a bad back. It doesn't seem fair."

"It might have been me," Thomas admitted. "What day was it?"

"Saturday, he always brings the delivery on a Saturday."

"Well if it was Saturday then it would have been me or my colleague. Sorry, but it's our job."

"I don't think it's fair. How's my Dad meant to manage with his bad back?"

Thomas found himself smiling, he liked this young woman. He liked the way she was trying to protect her father. A tall slim man stepped out from the shop.

"What's going on here? Who are you talking to Nadia? You know better than to talk to strange men."

"He's not a strange man Uncle Safdar, he's a traffic warden. I'm asking him about parking the van for the deliveries on Saturdays."

Her uncle glared at Nadia and looked sceptically at Thomas, "I think you girls should come inside," he said.

"Sir," Thomas began, "If you give me the van registration number and promise to park for no longer than fifteen minutes, my colleague and I won't book the vehicle. Although, If the police come along and write you a ticket, then there's nothing I can do, okay. You can thank your niece here for pleading your case so well," he added smiling broadly at the young woman.

Nadia looked down at her feet modestly and a shy smile passed across her lips.

"My name is Thomas by the way and I live just round the corner, I've been in your shop, I'm actually a customer."

"Thank you very much Thomas," Safdar said offering his hand. "You can stay at the doorway, girls," he conceded.

Thomas shook the outstretched hand and when Safdar returned indoors he stood and chatted to Nadia for a couple of minutes more. He asked her if she was at college or university and she told him that both she and her cousin were in their final year of High School and they were sixteen. Thomas was surprised because he thought they looked older. When he left the girls to walk home he couldn't get the image of Nadia out of his head. She was beautiful and he found her modesty particularly attractive. Thomas was determined to see her and talk to her again. Perhaps, he thought, in time, she would become his girlfriend.

Nadia and her cousin Susan lived in Newlands. Their father's, brothers called Zaffer and Safdar, had bought a large Victorian villa ten years before then spent a further six months changing the layout to make two homes, an upper and a lower conversion. Nadia's family of father, mother, and five children, lived in the upper part which consisted of six bedrooms, three public rooms, three bathrooms and a large family kitchen, while Susan's family lived in the lower apartment. The free-standing property had two double garages, a tennis court and substantial gardens.

Both families were wealthy because the brothers had made a fortune owning and operating an import/export business. The sweet shop was not dependant on profit it was there simply to provide a meeting place for the other more sinister activities they were involved in.

To the residents of Govanhill who didn't really know the families, the brothers were seen as hardworking, rather ordinary men, who were trying to scrape a living from their little shop. They carefully guarded their privacy. Even their wives had no knowledge of their business activities.

Nadia and Susan enjoyed a fair bit of freedom as they were allowed to attend the local secondary school. Their fathers believed that each girl would make a better marriage if they could bring culture and education to the relationship because modern men didn't want ignorant wives.

The girls had a carefree, simple life. They enjoyed each other's company and they were occasionally allowed to socialise out with the family with their father's approval. Neither girl had any idea of what the future held for them. They didn't know that their fathers felt a heavy weight of responsibility towards them or that a double wedding had already been arranged for two years ahead, when they both turned eighteen. With several daughters in the family managing to arrange good marriages for the two eldest girls was a great relief to Zaffer and Safdar. The brothers loved their daughters and they believed that they knew best how to give them a good and fulfilling life.

It was planned that Nadia and Susan would leave High School at the end of the school year and they would both attend college to complete sixth year studies. After that a family holiday to Pakistan would take the girls to be married. Nadia would marry Bashir, a twenty-eight year old lawyer who lived in New York and Susan would marry his twin brother, Arif, an accountant working in London. Their fathers thought it best to say nothing to the girls because they didn't want to give them the opportunity to complain or run away. Many young women were afraid of marriage and afraid of leaving their family but every woman had to have a husband to provide for her.

After the weddings Nadia and Susan would live with their in-laws so they could be trained to be obedient wives. When the family were satisfied with them, they would be sent to live with their respective husbands. With no knowledge of what the future held, the girls sat in the living room of Nadia's family home and chatted happily about their day.

"You were really cheeky to that traffic warden," Susan said. "I thought my Dad was going to explode when he saw you talking to him. You know how he feels about us talking to strangers, especially men."

"He was happy when Thomas said he wasn't going to book the van," Nadia replied.

"Oh, its Thomas now, is it? That's a bit familiar, next thing you'll be dating him."

"Don't be stupid Susan, he's too old and besides, my father wouldn't allow me to date a man who wasn't Moslem and who had limited education. I shouldn't imagine traffic wardens have degrees."

"My father wouldn't let me marry a man with no money," Susan said. "He doesn't want to have to support me and a husband."

"Anyway enough talk about men. We're far too young to date. After college let's see if we can attend university together," Nadia said changing the subject. "I want to do business studies and you want to be an optician. Strathclyde Uni for me and Caledonian Uni for you would be the best choice and they're practically next door to each other. Let's make a pact here and now to stick together for ever."

"For ever," Susan agreed.

Chapter 21

Three days after the discovery of the bodies of Anne-Marie Connor and Megan Reece their families had been informed and their stories were still front page news. Every paper had pictures of the girls and their relatives. Every headline linked their deaths to that of Margaret Deacon. Women were frightened to walk alone in Govanhill and a vigilante group of local men was formed to keep the streets policed.

Over the next few days the forensic team came up with very little. They were sure that the murderer wore latex gloves and they suspected that he also covered himself in some sort of protective clothing. They did, however, find a hair on Megan's skirt that didn't belong to either her or Anne-Marie, but given that both girls were prostitutes, it could have belonged to anyone.

Frank was like a bear with a sore head. He now had three unsolved murders on his hands and a vigilante group walking the streets that was full of loose cannons. Once again the door to door was turning up nothing and no one had come forward with information. With little else to go on, and with the press hounding him, Frank decided to give the media the information about a man wearing a hoodie being seen near Margaret Deacon's flat at the time of her murder. He also mentioned the possibility of the same man wearing a uniform, stressing that all police, fire and ambulance staff living in the immediate area had already been ruled out. All that succeeded in doing was to stir up more suspicion. Every security guard, every nightclub bouncer, in fact, every owner of a black jacket was suspected and, whenever a man wearing a hoodie walked along the street, women crossed the road to avoid him.

The newspapers were relentless in their criticism of the police and Angela was bad tempered and irritable. This wasn't helped by Bobby continually not pulling his weight at home, even though he had now finished his teaching job. The one thing that they expected to cause stress, lack of money, wasn't a problem. Bobby earned almost as much as he did before and if business continued the same way, within a few months, he would actually earn more. Things that wouldn't have bothered Angela before, like papers left strewn on the dining table or unwashed cups in the sink became the centre point of spectacular rows. The truth was she needed a break, but Bobby was reluctant to take time off from his new business at such an early stage and that was understandable.

When Angela arrived at her desk on Monday morning a list of names and file numbers was waiting for her.

"What's all this?" she asked Paul who was sitting at the next desk doodling on a piece of paper.

"Ah," he replied. "You were last in this morning so you got the booby prize."

Angela frowned, "What do you mean, what is this?"

"It's a list of every prostitute who's been murdered or assaulted with a knife in the last ten years. It covers the whole of the South of Scotland. The Boss wants you to go through it and look for any similarities."

"What kind of similarities? Did he give any clue about what he's looking for?"

"Nope, he just said look for details. So far we've got nothing, nada, zilch, and he's under a lot of pressure."

"And what are you doing while I'm doing this?" Angela asked.

"I'm having tea with the Community Council and assuring them of my best attention at all times," Paul replied smugly.

"Are you sure you weren't meant to have this list and me the Community Council?" Angela asked suspiciously.

"As I said, you arrived last. Last in gets the crappy job." Paul rose from his desk. "Bye now, I'll make sure to eat an extra biscuit for you," he said and he headed for the door and freedom, leaving Angela scowling in his wake.

By mid-afternoon Angela was bogged down with detail but couldn't make any tangible connections. Her head was pounding and she felt sick. The unnatural stuffy atmosphere in the office had drained all her strength and she felt that if she didn't get outside and breathe in some fresh air she might faint. With shaky hands she took a coffee from the machine and made for the front door.

It was a dreary, grey day, the sky was the colour of gun metal and a smur of rain made the air feel damp. As she stood sipping the bitter coffee Angela's mobile bleeped, a message had been received. She opened the text, 'in metin wit Jak- ples get dinr- luv B'. It was the final straw. She threw the last of her coffee onto the pavement, crumpled up the paper cup and tossed it into a bin, then strode back into the office. As she passed Frank's room he came out of his door and she almost bumped into him.

"Look where you're going, you nearly cut me in two," Frank said.

Angela stopped in her tracks, stared hard at Frank then burst into tears.

"My office now," he said pushing the door open for her.

She took a seat at the desk, accepted the tissue that Frank offered her and blew her nose loudly.

"Can I get you anything?" he asked kindly.

Angela shook her head. "I'm sorry," she said. "I don't know what came over me there."

Once she calmed down Frank asked. "Is it work or home that's the problem?"

"Everything, but mostly home," Angela replied.

Frank was relieved because he didn't want to be blamed for overworking or upsetting his new detective.

"Do you want to talk about it? Can I help?"

"My husband Bobby's changed his job and he's not pulling his weight at home," Angela sobbed. "When I get in after a long day there's no food and the house is a mess. I'm just so tired. It wasn't meant to be like this."

"Well thank Christ for that," Frank said sighing with relief. "I thought you were going to tell me he was having an affair. So you need a housekeeper to come in and clean once a week and collect the shopping for you. You're not short of money are you, with Bobby changing work?"

"No, we're okay for money. I never thought of paying for help."

"My wife has a girl who does for us. Not that my Katy is short of time it's just that there's other things she'd rather be doing. Would you like me to get the girl's phone number for you? It would leave you and your husband with a bit more time for the important things, like each other."

"Thanks Boss, that would be great," Angela replied mopping the last of her tears from her face.

"Are you feeling better now?" Frank asked.

"Yes thanks, much better, I'm sorry to be a pain."

"Good, now fuck off back to work the Social Work Department's closed."

Angela thanked her boss again then returned to her desk. She realised that she'd allowed herself to get into a state over nothing. Frank was absolutely right at least Bobby wasn't having an affair. His work had become his mistress and she could deal with that.

Frank had been wondering how long it would take Angela to crack. The last couple of months had been an absolute bugger. Angela was a smart girl and tough with it, but Frank couldn't remember another time when a young officer had to deal with a murder in their first few weeks in the job, let alone three. The pressure was tremendous and everyone in the office was feeling the strain. These killings were particularly gruesome and bloody, they sickened Frank, so he could understand that Angela would be upset by them. Nevertheless, he was very impressed with her because she handled everything that came her way with little or no complaint. She had initiative and worked doggedly to get the best results. Frank had seen grown men throw up at crime scenes such as these, but not Angela, she faced every horror every ghastly, stinking detail with grim determination and true grit. She left lazy cops like Gordon McKay and Jack Dobson on the starting blocks and Frank was convinced that one day she would take over his job or perhaps his boss's, if he could just get her through the next few weeks and keep her from throwing in the towel.

Angela found it soul destroying, checking through the list of prostitutes who'd been attacked. None of the information she examined seemed to link any of the girls to the recent murders. The details were shocking and after reading through several of the files Angela began to think that there were no normal people left in Glasgow. One girl was raped and murdered by her grandfather, another was stabbed while pregnant by the father of the baby, and one young prostitute was slashed and beaten by a man she picked up outside a church. Tired and sickened by what she'd read, Angela was just about to close down her computer and give up for the day, when a name caught her eye. She didn't know what made her notice the name Katherine Kelly, but when Angela got the file up on screen, she realised from the photograph, that she was looking at Kelly Jamieson.

The most recent entry in the file was an incident that occurred eleven months before when Kelly had been slashed by a man who'd raped her. There were photographs of defensive wounds to her arms and hands, caused as she'd shielded her face and throat from her attacker. The man had picked her up in his car and taken her to a flat in Govanhill near to her home. She'd gone with him willingly expecting to be paid for sex, but after she entered the apartment he pounced on her punching her several times in the face before cutting her clothing with a knife. Her statement read that she was dazed from the blows to her face and terrified of being killed, so in her words, she 'let him do what he wanted' in order to survive. When the man was finished with her he became very agitated and angry and he attacked her again slashing at her with the knife before running off. Kelly managed to stagger into the street where a local shopkeeper saw her covered in blood and phoned for the police and an ambulance. The apartment where she was attacked had been owned by the local Housing Association and was listed as uninhabited awaiting renovation.

Reading the file Jackie's words of concern came back to Angela and she began to think that Kelly Jamieson might indeed be at risk. There was also the chance that she was the killer's first victim. It was certainly worth looking into although, given the circumstances, it was doubtful if she'd be able to give Angela any further information because it was noted, that at the time of the attack, she was very drunk. Further reading of the file showed that Kelly had been assaulted by men several times before and the first sexual assault was by her own father when she was eight years old.

It made very sad reading and Angela felt drained. She decided to phone Liz to see if she would like to meet her for dinner at the pub as she didn't really want to spend the whole evening at home. Angela was hungry and she wasn't ready to face the disappointment of another day with no meal prepared and no food in the house. Bobby could sort himself out. It was time for self preservation. When she dialled Liz's number the phone was answered right away.

"Thank God, Angela," Liz said. "Now I've got an excuse to be out of the house when my aunt and uncle come round to visit my parents. They visit every Friday and I couldn't stand another night of reminiscing about the good old days. You're a life saver. If you'd like we could make an evening of it because 'The Black Bull's' got a quiz on tonight. The first prize is a crate of beer."

"Fantastic," Angela replied. "I could use a crate of beer."

"You're pretty sure we're going to win then?"

"We have to. The way I feel at the moment, I could drink a lake of booze."

"Good day then?" Liz asked.

"Don't ask," Was the reply.

Angela decided to go home and change then leave her car and call for a taxi. She didn't phone Bobby to tell him her plans because she didn't think he deserved advance warning. Even though she had a possible solution for the housework and chores she was still annoyed at his selfishness and his blatant flaunting of the schedule they'd agreed on. Let him see how it feels to be ignored and not considered, she thought. It's his turn to feel upset and annoyed.

Liz was pleased to hear from Angela, she was always ready for a night out. It was difficult being an adult woman in a responsible job still living with Mum and Dad but the current economic climate made it nearly impossible to get on the property ladder. Liz, being a canny Scot, didn't want to waste money on rent that could be saved for a deposit on her own home. As much as she was delighted to establish a friendship with Angela who she admired enormously, Liz wondered why she'd been called at such short notice. From what she'd heard about Angela's husband, Bobby, he would have been her obvious first choice of company. Perhaps everything was no longer perfect in paradise.

Chapter 22

Thomas was very excited about his day out with Alan and he'd been up since the crack of dawn packing and re-packing his bag. Now he was anxiously pacing the floor waiting for the numbers of the digital clock to click on to eight-fifty so he could lock up and leave his flat. He always enjoyed being with Alan because the older man had so much life experience and he was interesting.

Thomas looked at the clock impatiently, eight-forty seven, that would have to do. He couldn't wait any longer. He lifted his rucksack packed with his knitted hat and gloves, spare socks, in case his feet got wet in the river, a sharp knife for gutting any fish they caught, a flask of tea and two packs of sandwiches that he'd bought at Tasty Bakers the day before. At the last minute, just before he left, he grabbed a couple of chocolate biscuits from the biscuit tin and shoved them into his bag because he knew that Alan had a sweet tooth. As he walked to the corner Thomas began to fret, maybe tea and sandwiches weren't the right things to bring on a fishing trip, maybe beer and cooked chicken legs were more appropriate for a lad's day out. Never having been on a lad's day out, he hadn't a clue. Mind you, he thought, Alan's driving so tea was better than beer.

Thomas was at the corner at eight-fifty-two and started worrying. What if Alan changed his mind, what if he didn't turn up? He fidgeted nervously and, as he waited, Nadia and Susan came walking along the street towards him, he felt his heart thudding in his chest at the sight of them. He had the hood of his jerkin pulled up over his head to keep out the early morning cold but he pushed it down as the girls approached.

"Hi Nadia, Susan," he said as they came level with him on the pavement, "How are you today? I'm just waiting here for a lift because I'm going fishing with my friend."

The girls looked at him suspiciously because they didn't recognise him out of uniform.

"How do you know our names, do we know you?" Nadia asked tentatively.

"Of course you do," Thomas replied grinning awkwardly. "I'm Thomas, the traffic warden, remember? We met the other day outside your family's shop."

"Oh yes, I do remember," Nadia replied. "Sorry, but we've got to go, our Dads will kill us if they see us talking to a man in the street and we're already late. We're going to our friend's house, she lives on Westmoreland Street, you know where the girl was murdered a couple of months back."

Colour flushed Thomas's face. "That's not an appropriate subject for young women to talk about," he said staring at the ground.

"Because she was a prostitute," Nadia asked laughing. "You're just like my Dad he says exactly the same thing. Talking about my Dad, we'd better get going before he sees us. He's just along the road at the shop. Come on Susan."

Just as the girls were about to walk away Alan's car pulled up beside them, "That's my friend," Thomas said pointing his thumb at the car. "I've got to go too. We're heading off for a day's fishing," he added trying to sound like one of the boys.

"Bye Thomas," Nadia said. "Bye Thomas," Susan mimicked and both girls headed off down the street giggling.

Thomas opened the car door and climbed in, "Hi Alan," he said to his friend.

"Chatting up the girls I see," Alan replied. "I always said it's the quiet ones you have to watch."

Thomas felt his cheeks burn with embarrassment, "it's not like that," he said. "Nadia is going to be my girlfriend we've just got to get her dad's approval."

"Isn't she a bit young for you, Son? What is she, fifteen or sixteen maybe?"

"She's sixteen and she's going to leave school soon. She's never had a boyfriend and she's modest and decent. You said yourself that these Asian girls are the best because they're not allowed to run around dressed like whores."

"Aye and they also marry other Moslems who their families choose. Not older men who happen to fancy them. Don't put yourself through the misery, Son, it's never going to happen."

Thomas didn't answer he sat quietly and contemplated what Alan had said. He decided that Alan was wrong. One day Nadia would be his girlfriend and he would keep her pure and safe and away from the seedy world outside. He would love her and she would love him and no one and nothing would interfere.

The journey didn't take long and once they were past Cumbernauld they were quickly surrounded by fields and pretty scenery.

"We've arrived," Alan declared pulling off the road and onto a wide track between two fields. He parked the car, "Come on, Thomas, grab your bag and the box from the backseat and follow me."

"But where's your caravan?" Thomas asked as he climbed out of the car. "I don't see it anywhere."

"Remember you asked about security and whether or not my caravan would be safe from vandals, well there's your answer," Alan said with a sweep of his hand. "If you can't see it then the vandals can't either." He smiled smugly. "Do you see that clump of trees and bushes to your left?" he asked pointing. "Look closely because my caravan's behind them."

Thomas stared and stared but he still couldn't make it out. It was only when they walked towards the trees, and had practically reached them, that it became visible.

"See Tommy, by painting it green, it's camouflaged. You just can't see it unless you know it's there. That's why I never have any bother."

Alan unlocked the door and showed Thomas inside. It was like the TARDIS from Doctor Who because it was much bigger inside than it looked from the outside. There was everything you would need for day to day living and it even had a chemical toilet. Thomas was impressed.

"This is fantastic, Alan," he said.

"Aye, if I fall out with the wife I could live here for quite a while and be very comfortable. Anyway, Tommy my boy, let's get this show on the road. I've brought cleaning things with me, once we get this old lady spick and span, I'll show you how to bait a hook."

Thomas was in his element. He was so happy to be there helping Alan and he worked hard at cleaning and preparing the caravan. This is how it should have been with my father, he thought.

'*Yes, if that bitch hadn't kept me from you*', the voice added.

Chapter 23

When Angela went for her evening out to the pub with Liz she'd planned exactly what she would say to Bobby before leaving the house. As she drove home from work that night she rehearsed it over and over in her head, but when she did arrive at the house there was a no sign of Bobby. Instead, on the fridge door, was a post-it note, 'At Jakes back soon food in fridge', it read. No explanation no 'love Bobby'. She opened the fridge door to see a ready meal packet of lasagne, only fifteen minutes in the oven for authentic Italian food it declared.

"I don't think so," Angela said aloud. She was absolutely raging. Not only had she not had the opportunity to say what she'd planned before casually leaving for her night out, to cap it all, Bobby obviously thought it acceptable to leave a box of processed muck for her to eat after a heavy day at work. She angrily wrote a note for him, 'out with Liz back later', it read.

That night Angela drank too much and ended up crying.

She'd hardly spoken to Bobby the whole weekend, no small talk and definitely none of their usual banter. Now it was Monday morning and she'd left for work without saying goodbye. Bobby too was annoyed. He'd worked his socks off these last few weeks to establish his part of the company as quickly as possible. It wasn't easy being self-employed because if you don't create the business yourself there's no one else to pay your wages. Angela had agreed to him giving up his teaching job. He'd thought she'd be supportive and understand how hard it was for him, but now she'd stormed out of the house without a word and he assumed it was because he'd been forced to work the weekend. She was spoilt and selfish and he was disappointed in her, but he was too busy to worry about that now.

When Angela reached the office she resumed her work on the files but the information on Kelly Jamieson was the only possible lead so far. Paul Costello arrived twenty minutes late for work. He thought he'd managed to slip in past the Boss's room without being caught, but as he slunk past the door it suddenly opened.

"What time do you call this," Frank bellowed. "You should have been here on time to work on those files I gave you."

Paul looked sheepish, "Sorry I'm late, Boss, don't worry about the files, Angela's reviewing them."

"I gave them to you," Frank replied dryly. "Angela's got enough to do without wiping your lazy arse. No wonder the poor lassie's under such a strain. Go and see what you can do to help her, and just so you know, you're the tea boy today and you can start by bringing me a coffee and getting one for Angela. I've got my eye on you Paul so you'd better pull your weight, right?"

"Yes Boss, absolutely."

"And by the way, you're working for Angela today, you'll be her gopher and I better not see you slacking."

A sick expression passed over Paul's face but he knew better than to complain. He fetched the coffees as instructed then placed one cup meekly on Angela's desk.

"You're a bastard, Paul," she said. "I heard what the Boss said. I hope the Community Council gave you a hard time on Friday."

"It was Hell," he replied, "Lots of smelly old women knitting."

"Serves you right, bring me a biscuit I need the glucose, then pull your chair over, there's something in these files I want to discuss with you."

Paul and Angela pored over the details in Kelly Jamieson's file, it made shocking reading.

"Good grief," Paul said. "Did you see this, Angela? Her own father raped her when she was eight, then her mother's boyfriend assaulted her when she was eleven. She became a drug addict at sixteen and, as if that wasn't enough, her mother's an alcoholic. What a life, what a terrible life. I can't help thinking of my own children when I read this. My kids have got such a happy, carefree life, how could a father hurt his own child like that? I can't get my head round it."

"It is very disturbing," Angela agreed, "But I'd like us to concentrate on the incident that happened eleven months ago because some aspects are similar to the killings of Anne-Marie Connor and Megan Reece. Kelly was taken to a house in Govanhill and assaulted whereas the other girls were murdered in their own home, but Megan was punched in the face as was Kelly and both Anne-Marie and Kelly were attacked with a knife."

"But Anne-Marie was slashed across the throat while Kelly's wounds were to her arms and hands."

"Kelly was injured while trying to protect her throat. Read the notes Paul."

"Oh yes, I see, and you think there's a connection. Do you think Kelly's an earlier victim of the murderer?"

"I just don't know. I'm not sure. I might be making something over nothing. What do you think?"

Paul sat with his elbow leaning on the desk and his chin resting on his hand, he pursed his lips and frowned as he considered his reply.

"I think it's a long shot," he replied. "But there's nothing to lose by talking to Kelly and we daren't ignore the possibility when we've nothing else to go on. There is another way to look at it of course, what if this man's intent on killing all the prostitutes in Govanhill? He might be a crazy, on some sort of crusade."

"Funny you should say that, Jackie Cosgrove said something similar, she thought that Kelly might be at risk. What do you think we should do?"

Paul scratched his head. "We can't turn our backs on this, much as I'd like to. I think we should pull her in for an official interview and warn her of the risks. We have to be seen to care, but the truth is, there's nothing much we can do. We can't stop her from going with men because she's desperate for money for her drugs."

"Can we not get her off the streets maybe into a rehab programme?"

"Not a snowball's chance in Hell, there's a waiting list a mile long and besides, she probably wouldn't want to go. The only life she knows is drugs and, even with the terrible things her mother's exposed her to, she still stays with the bitch and looks after her. She lives closely with death every day so I don't think she'll consider our killer to be a big deal. It's just one more risk that she has to put up with."

"I think we should try and get her in for a chat ASAP," Angela suggested. "Given her lifestyle she's probably at home in the mornings. Should we go round just now?"

"Your word is my command," Paul replied saluting. "Grab your stuff we'll take my car. I don't trust women drivers," he added laughing.

"Just when you were beginning to grow on me, you have to go and spoil it," Angela replied. "I don't know how your poor wife puts up with you."

"Neither do I," Paul replied, "It's one of life's great mysteries."

When they arrived at Kelly Jamieson's address they weren't surprised at the condition of the close entrance. It was strewn with all manner of litter and used condoms and syringes lay amongst the debris. From the street they could see that the windows of the ground floor apartment were filthy and someone had even written the word 'fuck' in the dirt. A blanket hung over the glass as a makeshift curtain.

"What a state," Paul said. "This is one of those places where you wipe your feet on the way out."

Angela pressed the doorbell but heard no sound.

"I think it's broken," Paul said and he banged on the door. "Open up, police," he called, still nothing. "Kelly Jamieson, open the door, it's the police." There was some discernable movement from inside.

"Go back to sleep, Mother, it's for me." They heard what they assumed was Kelly saying.

"Tell them to fuck off, it's the middle of the night," another voice replied.

There was a fumbling sound as a bolt was slid open then a jingling of keys, the door moved a crack and a face appeared, the security chain was still in place.

"What do you want, I've done nothing wrong," Kelly said defensively.

The face at the door was pale and gaunt, the hair thin and patchy, Kelly was sporting a black eye and the skin on her cheek was red and puffy.

"We're here to help you, not to arrest you," Paul said, "Would you open the door please because we don't want to discuss your business on the doorstep."

The door closed over to allow the chain to be unclipped then it swung open and Kelly turned and walked towards the front room leaving Angela and Paul to follow in her wake. Paul looked at Angela and shook his head in disgust, the inside of the flat was worse than the outside. Clothes and empty cans covered every surface, the place was filthy. At the front window was a sink which was piled high with dirty crockery and rubbish, this room doubled as kitchen and Kelly's bedroom Incongruously, on the unmade filthy bed, sat a pink poodle pyjama case. Kelly threw herself down on the only chair in the room, a heavy armchair which was covered in a ripped and stained fabric.

"Talk quietly 'cause my Mum's asleep, she was out last night," Kelly said.

"We want to talk to you about the attack you sustained last year," Angela began. "We'd like to know more about the man who assaulted you."

"No one was very interested when it happened, what's changed now?"

Paul and Angela exchanged glances neither was sure how much to say. Kelly noticed the look.

"Is it to do with Margaret's murder?" she asked, "Because it's not the same man. The man who attacked me was short and stocky and he was old, at least forty. Margaret's boyfriend was tall and skinny and he was young, in his twenties."

"We don't know that Margaret's young man had anything to do with her death, he might be completely innocent," Paul answered. "The man who attacked you obviously knew the area and he used a knife. We have to follow every possible lead before someone else is hurt."

"With three young women dead, all prostitutes and all living in Govanhill, we're worried about your safety, Kelly," Angela added. "Do you think you could come into the station and go through mug shots just in case someone stirs your memory? It wouldn't take long and we can drive you there and back."

"I already looked at the photos last year and I didn't recognise any of them, it's a waste of time."

"Last year you were traumatised and frightened, it's different now and there are more pictures so you never know. You want the man to be caught, don't you?"

"Actually, I don't give a fuck and neither do you, you're only interested in solving your case. What's happened to me or any of the working girls doesn't affect you so don't pretend you care. I'm not coming to the station and I'm not looking at any photos I'm tired and I haven't got the time. Get to fuck and shut the door on your way out. You're off the hook now, I'm refusing police help."

Kelly pulled an old cardigan off the back of the chair and held it to her face like a comfort blanket, she shut her eyes. Angela and Paul were being dismissed, the conversation was over. They had underestimated Kelly, she was much tougher than they gave her credit for and she was right, with her refusal of help, they were off the hook.

"I'm giving you a formal warning Kelly," Angela said. "You know that there's a dangerous individual out there and if you continue to prostitute yourself you could be at risk. I'm leaving you my card so if you change your mind, call me and I'll come and talk to you again."

Kelly didn't answer her only response was to pull the cardigan over her face and pretend to snore. Angela laid the card on the arm of the chair.

"Come on," Paul said, "We're wasting our time here. This girl's too stupid and lazy to help herself so why should we care?"

Frustrated, they left the dirty flat and Paul did wipe his feet on the way out.

Chapter 24

Thomas made a point of walking past the sweet shop at every opportunity because he was desperate to see Nadia again. Every time he passed by, his walking slowed and he stared into the shop hoping she'd be inside, but he was out of luck. On two occasions he entered the shop and bought some pieces of the sweet milk confectionery even though they were too rich for his taste. He gave them to Alan who was delighted because he had a very sweet tooth.

Nearly a week had gone by since he'd seen Nadia and he was getting desperate. He'd almost convinced himself that something must be wrong, maybe she was ill or maybe she was being kept indoors to protect her from unsavoury types. He decided that if he didn't see her soon he would have to speak to her uncle. It was important that Safdar understood how Thomas felt about Nadia. He wanted to tell him that he was respectable and he had a good job and that he'd never do anything to harm her.

As he walked along the street on Saturday morning to meet Alan for work, he stopped at the shop, but he was disappointed as none of the family was about. A young man who was working at the counter told him they'd all gone to Pakistan to attend a wedding and they'd be away for three weeks. Thomas was bereft. He'd been rehearsing what he was going to say to Nadia's uncle and he wouldn't have the opportunity now for weeks. Miserably he bought a small bag of sweets for Alan and left the shop with his head bowed and his back stooped.

He was so upset he could hardly summon the energy to walk along the street. He was worried too because Nadia was used to Scotland. Who knew what dangers she might be exposed to in Pakistan? The thought prayed on his mind.

'*They're all the same, bitches on heat,*' the voice said. '*Some brown skinned man will be rubbing his hands all over her. He'll be shoving his dick deep into her and she'll be begging for more, more, more. And you think she's good and pure and waiting for you. Idiot, you're a fucking idiot.*'

"Shut up," Thomas said aloud. "Shut your dirty mouth, it's not true, none of it is true."

Thomas was aware of people staring at him curiously. "I'm rehearsing for a play," he shouted, "I'm practicing my lines."

'*What do you know about plays,*' the voice said spitefully. '*That was a stupid excuse from a stupid, fucking idiot.*'

Thomas walked quickly along Allison Street, his shoes slapping the pavement as he dodged round people coming towards him. He wanted to get out of this street, he had to get away. He'd arranged to meet Alan at the usual place outside Queen's Park and he was already five minutes late. He really wanted to speak to Alan about Nadia but the older man had already expressed his opinion and it wasn't encouraging. It was very difficult for him and Nadia, Thomas thought. Their story was so romantic, two young people in love against a sea of disapproval. But one day they'd be together, Thomas was sure of that, he would just have to be patient.

When he met up with Alan the older man was very quiet, there was none of the usual banter and he didn't comment on Thomas being late. After ten minutes of virtually no conversation Thomas could stand it no longer.

"Have I upset you in some way, Alan? You're unusually quiet."

Alan looked at Thomas, "I'm sorry, Son," he said. "It's nothing to do with you, honest. It's my wife, she's not so well. The truth is I'm worried sick, she's to go for tests because they think it might be MS. I just don't know how I'll cope if it is. Ann is my rock."

Alan looked as if he might cry. Thomas felt uncomfortable he didn't know how to react or what to say.

"Can I help you?" he asked finally.

"There is one thing you could do for me Son. You could look after my caravan. I won't be able to disappear down there at weekends this year because I'll need to support Ann. Would you do that for me?"

"I'd love to," Thomas replied. The very thought of being able to escape to the country thrilled him. "I've just got one problem, how will I get there? Although I've passed my driving test I don't have a car."

Alan considered the problem. "Well," he said, "Ann doesn't want to drive at the moment, she's lost her confidence. I could lend you her wee van if you like. Driving a van isn't much different from driving a car, if Ann can manage it, so could you. She used to compete in shows with the dogs, so the van was ideal for her and, as I said, it's not big. You'd only have to pay for the extra insurance and petrol. What do you think?"

"That would be amazing," Thomas replied excitedly. "I could go down to the caravan every weekend and perhaps I could take my girlfriend if you didn't mind."

"Of course you can take your girlfriend she'd probably love it. I didn't know you had a girlfriend what's her name?"

Thomas hesitated, he didn't want to say Nadia because technically she wasn't his girlfriend yet so he lied and said the first name that came into his head. "Mary, her name's Mary."

"Mary, eh, and is she a virgin? Get it, virgin Mary." Alan attempted a joke.

"I get it, and yes of course she's a virgin. I wouldn't go out with a slag."

"Well, well, Thomas has a girlfriend and a good girl at that. Where did you meet her, in church?"

"I'm not talking about her any more. Leave me alone. No wonder I don't tell you things."

"Don't fret, Son, it's just my bit of fun. I'm really happy for you. It's about time you had a sweetheart. Just ignore this silly old man."

"You're not silly and you're not old and I'm very sorry about your wife." Thomas stared at his feet, he felt uncomfortable sharing his feelings. "You know you're like a father to me Alan," he finally managed to say.

"Aye and you're like the son I never had," Alan replied. "But enough soppy talk we're like a pair of old women. Come on, Tommy, we've got cars to book and people to frustrate. Do you want the side with the Hyundai Tucson or the one with the Range Rover?"

Thomas hesitated. "Too late," Alan said in his usual jocular style, "I'm having the Range Rover. Eat my dust Tommy my boy, eat my dust."

Chapter 25

The newspapers had lurid headlines with dire warnings about the murderer. They'd tried several names for him before finally settling on the 'Southside Slasher'. Today's papers were still carrying their messages. One read,' Southside Slasher still at large'. Another demanded, 'Who is harbouring the Southside Slasher'? Angela found it sickening, how dare they sensationalise something so awful.

"Who writes this rubbish?" she asked throwing down her copy of The Mail. All this is doing is terrifying people who are already vulnerable. It's not keeping prostitutes off the streets and it's not helping our case.

"Sorry, were you talking to me?" Paul asked lifting his head from his 'Motor Sport' magazine.

"Oh, never mind," Angela replied. "I'm just moaning again. We're getting nowhere and I'm fed up."

"You shouldn't have believed everything you saw on TV. The world isn't like 'CSI' or 'Law and Order', in the first place this isn't America and in the second place, they're not real. Welcome to Scotland where we do our best, but even with sterling work, we aren't always lucky. You see Angela most of our work depends on luck, we need people to come forward with the right information at the right time. So don't stress yourself about something you've got no control over."

"It's just so frustrating, I feel so helpless and I'm constantly waiting for the call to tell us he's killed again. I've run out of things to investigate and I'm pushing these crimes further and further away, at this rate they'll become cold cases."

"Then so be it, torturing yourself isn't going to make a jot of difference. Just imagine how the Boss feels because he's being hounded by everyone to get a result and the press keep mentioning him and pointing the finger. He's been stuck in that wee room of his for days, I think he's hiding and I don't blame him." Paul lifted his magazine from the desk and resumed reading. "There's five minutes till our shift starts, fetch us a coffee will you?" he asked.

Normally Angela would protest and make Paul collect the coffees but today she meekly walked to the machine. Her heart wasn't in the fight, in fact her heart wasn't in anything at the moment. She and Bobby were still not communicating although she had hired Frank's cleaner and Jean was proving to be a godsend. She resented the fact that Bobby could stay at home and work and she was convinced that his work wasn't as demanding as hers. Bobby made out that he sat at the computer all day, but dirty coffee cups left all over the house proved different. Angela wouldn't have wanted him to stay in the old job and be miserable, but this new arrangement was hard to live with and it was damaging their relationship.

"Are you going to stand there daydreaming all day?" Paul called. "My five minutes are up and my coffee will be getting cold."

"I'm coming, keep your hair on," Angela replied, she hadn't realised that she'd been distracted for so long.

The morning dragged on and on, not that there wasn't jobs to be done, on the contrary, there was lots of work, but it was dead boring. On more than one occasion Angela saw Paul's eyes straying from his computer screen to his Motor Sport magazine. She, on the other hand, stared at her screen continuously, but took nothing in because her head was full of her own problems. Suddenly, the phone on her desk rang and pulled her from her stupor. Paul visibly jumped.

"There's a woman here to see you, I think she's a bit of a nutcase," the constable at the desk said. "She's stomping around and shouting, demanding police protection." He paused then Angela heard him say.

"Shut up and sit down or I'll put you out that door." The constable returned to their conversation. "Sorry about that she's a junkie and she's strung out. Her name is Kelly Jamieson and she came in waving your card. Do you want to see her or will I send her packing."

"Don't send her away she could be a witness in the 'Slasher' murders." Angela felt a surge of excitement, "Please make sure she doesn't leave, in fact, would you show her into an interview room and if possible give her a cup of tea with lots of sugar and a biscuit if you can rustle one up. I'll just get my colleague and we'll be right there."

"Paul, Paul," Angela said interrupting his magazine perusal.

"What's up doc?" he replied in a 'Bugs Bunny' voice.

"I need you, Kelly Jamieson's just come into the front desk demanding police protection and we'll have to talk to her."

"Why do you need me? Why don't you talk to her yourself? I can't stand the bitch."

"I don't particularly like her either, but I want this to be a formal interview so move your arse and come with me."

Paul slapped his magazine on the desk then stood and stretched his arms. "Okay let's get this show on the road are you going to be good cop or bad cop?"

"You've just been telling me that true life isn't like the movies," Angela protested.

"Ah, but Kelly Jamieson doesn't know that," Paul replied with a grin.

When they entered the interview room Kelly was standing at the table and, as soon as she saw Angela, she walked right up to her invading her personal space.

"You said you'd protect me from that maniac," she said her finger jabbing the air inches from Angela's face. "You said you'd keep me safe, you're a liar, you're a fucking liar," she yelled accusingly.

Angela was stunned by the verbal assault. Paul stepped forward and grabbed Kelly by the arm and forced her down onto a chair. "Stay in that seat and behave yourself or your next move will be out the door," he said glaring at the girl. He gave Angela a smile and a wink. "Are you okay?" he mouthed. Angela nodded her reply but she was still shaking when she sat on one of the chairs opposite Kelly. Paul led the conversation.

"You've got a short memory, Kelly," he began. "You refused to speak to us and you asked us to leave your home, don't you remember?"

She gave a shrug that a Frenchman would have been proud of then sat chewing at her already bitten down nails.

"Now would you like to calm down and tell us what this is all about?" Angela asked regaining her composure.

Kelly shuffled nervously on her chair. She drew in her breath, brushed her hair out of her eyes with her hand then exhaled noisily. "It's him, the maniac who attacked me I think I saw him in the park. It was late at night and I was cutting through the park heading for home when I saw him. I'm sure he recognised me because I started to run and he ran after me. A woman walking her dog heard me screaming and she came to help me and when the man saw her he ran away. He's going to kill me he knows I can identify him. I don't want him to get me like he got Margaret. You've got to help me." Kelly was so edgy she couldn't sit still so she stood up and paced the room. She was muttering to herself and Angela was afraid that she was losing it. Angela wasn't sure how much of what Kelly said was true and how much was imagined.

"And you're sure it was the same man? Last time we spoke you said you didn't see him properly."

"It was him, I know it was him. He's going to kill me he'll cut me like last time." Kelly was very agitated she slapped her forehead with her hands several times, the sounds echoed in the sparsely furnished room.

"Will you look at our photographs now and help us to identify the man?" Angela asked.

"Yes, I'll look at them, but I have to come back later I've got an appointment now, I'll come back later. Let me go, I've got to meet my friend, I'll be back later, I promise."

Paul and Angela glanced at each other, "drug run," Paul mouthed. Paul stood and opened the door and Kelly bolted out like a startled deer. He walked her to the front door. "We'll see you later then," he said and he watched her as she walked away with the disjointed, quick pace which was familiar of drug addicts. Bet we won't see you today, he thought wryly, you'll be off the planet with heroin in half an hour.

Paul was quite right Kelly didn't return later that day or, for that matter, the next. Angela searched the computer files each day for any sign of her, both under the name Kelly Jamieson and her real name, Katherine Kelly. On day three she came up trumps as there was a file note from a police station in Govan reporting that they lifted Katherine Kelly off a city street for her own protection. It seems that she was drunk and paranoid, accusing strangers in the street of helping the murderer and shouting at imaginary people before running into the heavy traffic of a main road.

"I've found Kelly," Angela called over to Paul. "She's been at Govan but they released her when she sobered up."

"Oh aye, and what did the little princess do?"

"Drunk and paranoid, taken in for her own protection," Angela answered.

"Brilliant," Paul said sarcastically. "She's no damn use to us if she's paranoid. She might accuse Jesus Christ of being the murderer and, worse still, she might believe it. What a fucking waste of time."

"Can we really not get anything from her? What if she's sober and back to normal?"

"She's a spiteful, spoiled, junkie, whore, she'll never be normal, don't even think about it. Cut her loose or she'll just tell you what you want to hear, but mark my words, none of it will be true."

Angela knew Paul was right but she was bitterly disappointed as Kelly was the only lead she had. She could have cried with frustration.

The day was boring and tedious but for once Angela was looking forward to going home because Bobby had promised to stop work at a sensible time. The plan was that they would talk about their grievances and sort out some kind of timetable they could both live with. She felt sure, that once she showed him what a selfish pig he'd been, he'd see sense. After all, she'd made all the compromises and it was about time Bobby appreciated it. She was counting down the time till she could leave, when five minutes before the end of her shift, her phone rang. She hesitated for a moment wishing she could ignore it, but knowing it might be important, she picked up the receiver.

"I know you're about to knock off Angela," the constable from the front desk said. "But I've a Mrs Kelly on the phone. She sounds drunk and she's slurring her words, but I've managed to make out that she wants to report her daughter Katherine as a missing person. I think it is Kelly Jamieson's mother. She's insisting that her daughter's been abducted by the Southside Slasher. Do you want me to put her through?"

Angela's heart sank, she was desperate to get home but she felt that someone had to talk to Kelly's mother, just in case the woman was right. She would have passed the call to Paul, but as she lifted her head to look for him, she saw him heading out the door to freedom.

Angela sighed, leaned on the desk and rested her forehead on her hand. "You'd better patch her through," she said reluctantly.

"I'm really sorry Angela," the constable replied, "I'll put her through now."

The phone went silent for a minute then the constable came back on the line.

"Sorry to have wasted you're time," he said. "She's hung up. You might want to get out of here before she calls back."

Angela needed no encouragement she grabbed her handbag and ran.

Chapter 26

The conversation with Bobby was not as one-sided as Angela had expected because her resentment of him was equally matched by his resentment of her. Neither of them was satisfied with the sudden but inevitable change in their lifestyle and both longed for more time with each other. Gradually, after four hours of talking, they realised that they'd been pushing each other away while trying to cope with the strains of work. Bobby hadn't realised just how gruelling and depressing Angela's involvement with the 'Slasher' murders had been and Angela hadn't understood how difficult it was for Bobby to build his part of the business. She hadn't considered the pressure he was under, not only to earn money, but also to convince Jake that he was an asset to what was an already established business. By the time they went to bed they were drained and exhausted, but for the first time in weeks, Bobby put his arms round Angela and she didn't shrug him off. A tentative truce had been reached.

When Angela arrived at work the next day she found herself smiling and when people returned her smile, she realised what a miserable cow she must have been these last few weeks because it felt like a new experience.

"Have you won the lottery and not told us?" Paul asked, "Because you're grinning like a Cheshire cat."

"Am I not allowed to be happy? Is it a requirement of this job that we've all to be bloody miserable?"

"Well it's a miserable job dealing with rapists and murderers and all the other dregs of society. If you're happy, then all I can say is that you're weird, very, very weird. What's even more disturbing is that I like it. In a strange sort of way your weirdness turns me on."

"That's enough of that, Paul. Flattery will get you nowhere, remember…"

"I know," Paul interrupted, "Remember my wife and four kids. How could I forget with child number five on the way?"

There was a pause while Angela digested what he'd said then she responded excitedly, "Paul, that's wonderful news." She hesitated, "It is wonderful news isn't it?" she asked nervously.

"Yes, yes, I'm delighted, another patter of tiny feet and another little Costello to help make up my football team. We only found out a few days ago, so keep it to yourself would you, just till we get past the first three months then you can tell anyone you like."

"Is your wife happy? Will she manage all right? Has she someone to help her?"

"She's ecstatic because she loves being pregnant. It's probably an Irish Catholic thing. The priest loves her because she's single-handedly filling the chapel, he's always blessing her. As for help, she's got her mum who's never away from our door, three sisters and dozens of cousins and friends. The problem is that there'll be even less room for me now."

"Well you know what they say," Angela replied laughing, "If you can't do the time, don't do the crime."

Paul smiled, he gave Angela a leering look, "But I love the crime, Angela, I'm a very bad boy. Fancy a quickie?" he added cheekily.

"If that's code for a coffee then I'll have mine milky with no sugar," she replied.

"Spoilsport," Paul replied, but he went to fetch the coffees just the same.

It was mid-morning and Angela and Paul were on their second cups of coffee when Frank's door flew open.

"Costello, Murphy," he yelled.

"Oh, oh," Paul said. "He wants both of us, what have we done?"

Angela shrugged, "Nothing, I've done nothing."

"Me neither," Paul replied. "Maybe that's the problem, was there something we should've done?"

"Costello, Murphy, today would be good."

"Oh Christ," Paul said jumping to his feet, "Get a move on before he blows a gasket. I liked it better when he hid in that wee room, depressed."

They walked swiftly to Frank's office and when they entered they saw him sitting at his desk with his head in his hands. The telephone that normally sat on his desk was on the floor next to the wall and it looked as if it had been thrown there. The room was even more untidy than usual and there was a distinct smell of alcohol discernible through the fug.

"Sit," Frank said without lifting his head. Angela sat on the straight backed chair and Paul lifted a heap of papers onto the floor to make room on the leather office chair.

"What do you know about Kelly Jamieson?" Frank asked. "According to the press office her mother reported her missing."

Paul looked mystified and Angela shifted uncomfortably on her seat.

"She phoned late on yesterday, Boss," she said. "The desk constable put the call through to me, but when he tried to connect me she'd hung up. He said that Mrs Kelly was very drunk so I thought it would keep till today. I was planning to go round to their house this afternoon to give her time to sober up."

"And you knew nothing about this?" Frank asked Paul.

"No Boss, I must've been away when she phoned."

"It was the end of our shift Boss, another minute and I'd have been gone too."

"Well drunk or not she's gone to the papers and they've believed her. According to the press office the afternoon papers are going to be full of it. They're going to portray her as a grieving mother whose missing daughter might be the fourth victim of the 'Southside Slasher.' She's seemingly told them that her daughter begged for police protection but was turned away."

"That's absolutely not true," Paul said indignantly. "We interviewed Kelly here but she ran out to get a fix then never came back. We had no reason to hold her."

Frank looked at Angela. "Paul's right, we couldn't keep her here. She'd already been lifted by a city branch for being drunk and paranoid. I typed up a report about the interview, we were both in the room and everything was done by the book."

"I hope that's true because the press are going to hang us out to dry. Their reporting will create absolute panic and we're going to be inundated with calls. Every concerned citizen, every moaning Minnie and every freak with fried eggs for brains will want to speak to us so brace yourself, we're about to enter the snake pit. Just when I thought it couldn't get any worse, a fucking junkie's leading us a merry dance."

Frank took a bottle of whisky from his desk drawer and sucked hard on it swallowing several gulps of the golden liquid. Angela and Paul exchanged worried glances. They sat in silence.

"What do you want us to do, Boss?" Angela eventually asked.

Frank rubbed his eyes and sighed deeply. "Start by looking for Kelly Jamieson, circulate her description to every department in the Strathclyde region then get her wino mother in for an interview. We have to look as if we're taking her disappearance seriously, although according to the press office, the mother's being paid a pretty penny for her story. For all we know the pair of them could have concocted all of this for the money."

Another silence prevailed and Frank took another swig from the whisky bottle before replacing it in his desk drawer.

"Well what are you waiting for, Christmas?" he bellowed.

Angela and Paul jumped to their feet and practically fell over each other in their rush to leave the oppressive room.

"Bloody hell," Paul said when they were back at their desks. "And we thought today was going to be boring."

Chapter 27

Angela was finishing her breakfast when the letter box rattled and the newspaper thumped onto the floor. Munching on a piece of toast she walked into the hall and picked it up. The headlines emblazoned, 'Find my daughter, Police ignore plea for help'. Angela was shocked as she read the article that followed.

'Martha Kelly, mother of the missing prostitute, Katherine Kelly begs the public for their help. "My daughter went to the police when she realised she might have been the first victim of the Southside Slasher, but they didn't give her any protection. She was terrified in case the man came looking for her again and now she's disappeared. I've reported my daughter missing but no one has contacted me. The police don't care. I know Katherine works as a prostitute to finance her drug problem, but she's still a human being and she has rights. She's still my daughter"

Dramatic stuff but not factual, Angela thought as she scanned the rest of the front page. Martha Kelly was only interested in one thing, money for booze and, with her daughter gone, she must be desperate. The article continued, 'Today I interviewed the distraught mother of the missing prostitute Katherine Kelly,' the reporter wrote. Then a description followed, 'Katherine is twenty-four years old but looks younger. She has brown hair, hazel eyes and a slim build. She was last seen wearing a black skirt, a pale blue sweater and a faux-leather, black-coloured, bomber style jacket. If anyone has seen Katherine or knows of her whereabouts please contact the newspaper enquiry line where your call will be dealt with in strictest confidence. Please help us find this vulnerable young woman and save her mother from further anguish.'

An old photograph was also printed on the front page, Katherine couldn't have been more than twelve when it was taken and it showed a pretty, fresh faced girl smiling up at her mother. If the public think Kelly Jamieson looks like this, Angela thought wryly, then they'll never find her.

As Angela returned to the kitchen the phone began to ring and Bobby answered it. She saw him frown, he said, "Yes, this is Angela Murphy's husband. Who am I speaking to? No she doesn't have anything to say to you. How did you get this number? If you have any questions then go through the proper channels. Don't phone here again." He promptly hung up.

"What on earth was that all about?" Angela asked.

"That was Jessica Miller of the Southside Gazette. She wanted to ask you about Katherine Kelly. I sent her packing."

Angela felt a jag of fear, she didn't know how to handle the press and now they had her private, unlisted, phone number.

"I'd better call my boss," she said. "I don't like strangers phoning me at home and I don't know how she got my name or this number."

She got Frank's card from her purse and dialled his mobile. It was answered on the third ring.

"Hello."

"Hi Boss, Angela here, sorry to bother you this early but…"

"I know," he interrupted, "You've just had a call from a reporter. What did you say to them?"

"I didn't talk to them Bobby answered the phone."

"Good, don't talk to anyone, I want to see you and Paul in my office pronto. I want to read your interview report on Kelly Jamieson and I want a statement from the officer who took the call from her mother. I take it you've seen the papers."

"Yes Boss, I have and it's not a fair account of what happened."

"I certainly hope not because it makes damning reading. Anyway, we'll discuss it when I see you, get your arse into the office ASAP and talk to no one about this."

The phone went dead. What a bloody mess, Angela thought and she quickly got ready for work then said her goodbyes to Bobby. As she drove to the office, Angela felt nervous, she felt exposed and vulnerable especially when she was stopped at traffic lights. She avoided eye contact with other drivers and, although Angela knew it was highly unlikely, she locked the doors, in case anyone recognised her and tried to get into her car. She wondered if Paul had received a call and if he was feeling as freaked out as she was. When she arrived and entered the building the desk Sergeant gave her a sympathetic smile.

"Keep your chin up," he said, "it's never as bad as it seems."

The very fact that he'd mentioned it made Angela aware that it was as bad as it seemed. When she walked through the building to get to her office more sympathetic remarks came her way and, by the time she reached her desk, she felt sick with worry.

"I see by the look on your face that you've had a call from the vultures as well," Paul said.

"I didn't speak to them because Bobby answered the phone. What did you say to them?"

"I didn't speak to them either my daughter Poppy answered the phone and told them that Daddy was on the loo having a poo. She did offer to bring me the phone, but they declined."

Angela burst out laughing, "You certainly know how to cheer a girl up," she said.

"I'm glad you find this so funny," Frank's voice boomed across the room. "I'm still waiting for your notes," he added.

Angela and Paul gathered up the paperwork and made their way to Frank's room. As they entered it Angela noticed an almost full bottle of whisky standing on the floor beside his desk. She tapped Paul on the arm and drew his attention to the bottle. They exchanged worried glances.

"Sit," Frank ordered without raising his head from his computer screen. "Once I review your notes I've to contact the press office with a statement. We've got to look whiter than white so if your reports aren't absolutely pristine they'll need to be changed, comprende?"

"But these notes are the ones we took by hand. The full interview has already been typed up on the computer. It's already on the record, we couldn't alter it now," Angela protested.

"Then you better hope that these notes are good and they match up with the full report," Frank replied grimly. "Fuck off now and let me go over them. I'll call you back in when I'm finished and we can discuss the content then."

Angela and Paul went back to their desks. "If he thinks I'm going to change that interview report then he's got another think coming. He's the Boss and we've done everything that he's asked of us and more. If we've fucked up in any way then it's his fault," Angela said unable to contain her anger.

"Calm yourself down, Angela," Paul replied. "The Boss knows we've done our job right, he's just making doubly sure. He scared stiff because the press are trying to make this look like the Yorkshire Ripper case. Our boys fucked up more than once during that investigation and Frank doesn't want the same mistakes made here. But don't worry, we haven't done anything wrong."

"I'm worried about Frank's drinking on the job," Angela said. "It's so unlike him. Do you think he's losing it?" she asked.

"It's a very stressful time so let's see how things go shall we? Lots of cops like a drink or two. I don't think he's got an alcohol problem it's a just wee boost to steady his nerves that's all. The pressure on him is huge at the moment."

"We can't protect him. If someone from upstairs visits that stinking wee room of his it'll be obvious that he's drinking. He hasn't even tried to hide the bottle. We're meant to report colleagues who we think are having problems so they can get help."

"You can do what you like, Angela," Paul replied and he looked as if he had a bad taste in his mouth. "But my advice is mind your own business, the Boss will sort out his mess himself. When you've been in the job a bit longer you'll realise that we all go off the rails from time to time and we expect our colleagues to turn a blind eye until we get over it."

Once again Angela felt very much the new girl. She didn't really understand the inner workings of the job, but she was learning. She knew now that she had to ignore the rule book and play the game whatever the rights and wrongs of it were. More importantly she had to turn a blind eye to the misdemeanours and mistakes of her colleagues and protect them from exposure at any cost, or risk being shunned. The police force was like an exclusive club and she was still learning the ropes.

After about half an hour Paul and Angela were summoned back to Frank's office. He was sitting up in his chair and he actually had a smile on his face.

"You've done well, children," he said. "We've followed procedure at every turn and you've got the notes and reports to back it up. I've spoken to the press office and they're going to make an announcement on the telly. They're going to show an up to date photo of Kelly Jamieson from one of her mug shots and ask the public to keep a look out for her. We want to get rid of the image of a wholesome twelve year old and show her for what she is, a paranoid, junkie, whore who's probably not missing at all. The press officer agrees with me that she and her mother are probably trying to extract as much money as they can from the newspapers."

"What do you want us to do now, Boss?" Angela asked. "Should we go round to her house and see if she's there?"

"No, let her stew, I'm not wasting another minute looking for her, but I would like you to go back to Jackie Cosgrove and see if she's heard anything. That way we've absolutely dotted all the i's and crossed all the t's. What the media don't realise is that junkies go missing every day of the week, but like the proverbial bad penny, they usually turn up. In a few days time, once there's no more media money, Kelly

Jamieson will turn up and she'll probably come in here reading the riot act."

Angela hoped Frank was right but she was spooked by Kelly's disappearance. She didn't think that either Kelly or her mother was smart enough to dream up a scheme in order to get money from the press. So where the hell was she and, could she in fact, have put herself at risk?

Chapter 28

Alan went on and on about the missing girl. After an hour of the one-sided conversation the voice in Thomas' head had almost convinced him that he'd had something to do with her disappearance.

"What does your Mary think about all this? Does it make her feel scared to walk alone at night?" Alan asked.

It took Thomas a moment to remember who Mary was then it came back to him that he'd told Alan his girlfriend's name was Mary.

'*Mary, Mary, quite contrary,*' the voice sing-songed in his head. '*You haven't got a Mary, have you? And you'll never, ever, have a Nadia,*' it added spitefully.

Thomas's eyes filled with tears and he swiped them away with his hands. Alan looked concerned.

"Have I said something to upset you, Son?" he asked. "What's wrong, Thomas? Have you and Mary split up or something?"

Thomas regained his composure, "No, no, it's nothing like that," he said, "I'm just scared for her, that's all. What with all these murders and now a girl's missing. I can't be with her all the time to protect her." When he spoke about his girlfriend he envisaged Nadia alone in Pakistan.

"Now, now, Son, don't get into a state, your Mary's a good girl, so no harm will come to her. These junkies and prostitutes are always getting into trouble, it's just because there's a few of them from the same area involved that we're suddenly hearing about it."

"I'm sorry for her poor mother," Thomas said mimicking what he'd heard a woman on the bus say. "But this disappearance isn't a bit like the other girls, they were all killed in their own homes," he continued.

"Aye," agreed Alan. "This one's probably lying in someone's house out of her head with drugs and booze. She'll turn up when she's compos mentis enough to find her way home."

Thomas nodded in agreement.

"Would you and Mary like to come to my house on Sunday afternoon and have tea with me and Ann?" Alan asked changing the subject. "It would give Ann the chance to meet you and I could take you out in the wee van for a practice run."

Thomas blinked nervously he couldn't take Mary with him because she didn't exist and he frantically searched his mind for an excuse.

'*Now you've had it,*' the voice said. '*Liar, liar, pants on fire.*'

"I would love to come for tea," Thomas finally replied. "But I can't bring Mary because..."

'*Because she doesn't exist*', the voice persisted.

"Because she's visiting her old auntie in Bishopbriggs," Thomas lied. "Mary visits her auntie every Sunday and makes her tea and on Saturdays she does voluntary work in a charity shop."

The lie was developing a life of its own.

"She sounds like an absolute saint," Alan replied. "I knew you'd choose a good girl. You deserve the best, Son," he added kindly. "Will you be able to come by yourself? I could pick you up if you'd like, it would be no trouble. It's not far for me to come to Govanhill and if I bring the van you can drive us back in it."

"Thanks Alan, I'd like that. Are you absolutely sure your wife's okay about me borrowing the van because I don't want to upset her when she's not well."

"She's more than okay she's delighted because it takes the responsibility off of her."

"Have you heard any news about her tests?" Thomas enquired, not that he was particularly interested in Ann, but he knew it was the right thing to ask.

"No, nothing yet, it'll be another few days before we get the results. But I have noticed changes in Ann and I'm afraid the news is not going to be good," Alan replied sadly.

"I'm really sorry, Alan," Thomas said, he was truly concerned for his friend because he liked the older man and he didn't want anything or anyone to come in the way of their friendship. Thomas was relieved when they parted and each worked a different side of the street. He didn't want to talk to Alan any longer in case he said something wrong.

Every newsagent that he passed had headline boards outside and they all carried the story of Katherine Kelly's disappearance.

'*You must've known that whore,*' the voice said. '*She practically lived round the corner from you. What have you done with her?*'

"I don't know her and I don't know where she is."

The voice wouldn't give up. '*Did you touch her, was she hot, did she moan when you rubbed her cunt? You're too much of a loser to have fucked her. You couldn't even fuck a tart, could you?*'

Thomas remembered what it felt like to touch Megan, the smell of her and the softness of her skin, it aroused and excited him. His penis was painfully hard and he struggled to walk.

"I never touched her. I don't even know her. I've never met her. Leave me alone, leave me alone. I've done nothing wrong, do you hear me? Nothing."

Thomas stumbled along the street. He didn't notice the stares from people as he walked past them muttering. He wanted to run, to get away from the voice. As he passed the general store Thomas saw a picture of the missing girl displayed in the window. He stopped in his tracks because he recognised the girl from the photo. He couldn't be sure if she looked familiar because he'd seen the same picture in a newspaper, or if he did, indeed, know the girl. His hands began to flap, he was losing control. The voice was relentless, goading him and filling his mind with doubt. He came to a crossroads, turned into the street where he lived and ran to his home. His body felt leaden and he was sweating profusely. When he was safely inside he shut the door and breathed a sigh of relief.

Thomas knew he had to calm down and get back to work before Alan missed him, but before he could do that he checked every inch of his apartment. He even looked in the kitchen cabinets and under his bed to assure himself that the girl wasn't there. When he was satisfied he exhaled his bated breath, made a fist and knocked on the side of his head. "Hello, can you hear me?" he asked. The voice was silent. "I thought so," Thomas said. "You're not so smart now, are you? I told you I didn't have the girl."

'*Maybe you've just forgotten where you left her,*' the voice said and a niggling doubt wormed its way back into Thomas's brain.

Chapter 29

Over the next couple of days Thomas thought about Nadia and obsessed about her trip to Pakistan. He'd found out that the wedding was being held in Lahore and he searched the internet for information about the area. Whenever he pictured Nadia in his mind he always saw her standing still and calm with a serene look on her face, just like the statues he'd seen in church depicting the Virgin Mary. He found it easier now to picture Nadia but to call her Mary when speaking to Alan and he was less afraid of getting mixed up.

* * *

When Nadia and Susan arrived in Lahore it was unusually hot for the time of year. In the Punjab it was normally cooler during November to March but the first week of their trip had been made almost unbearable from the heat. They were living in their family's compound and the girls were sorting their outfits for the mehndi which was being celebrated jointly by the families of the bride and groom in order to save money. The girls were excited when they received their red, embossed invitations because they were looking forward to the socialising and partying that was to come.

"My shalwar kameez is orange," Nadia said. "What colour are you wearing, Susan?"

"Hot pink," was her reply.

"To match your eyes," Nadia replied cheekily.

"You'll soon have black eyes if you don't shut up," Susan answered smiling and holding up her fist.

"Don't you feel sorry for Khalid being rushed over here and forced to marry Rizwana. He always told me he didn't want to get married until he'd had a chance to visit America. Now he's stuck with a bride he doesn't even know and whose background is nothing like his," Nadia said sympathetically.

"He's doing it to please his family," Susan replied. "Besides if it was left up to Khalid he'd never marry."

"Why do you say that? Of course he'd get married. Everyone wants to get married eventually."

"Everyone except Khalid, he's gay and that's not acceptable in our family."

"Don't be stupid, he can't be gay, he's very religious," Nadia replied.

"Nadia, you can be so naïve sometimes. Don't you remember his friend Justin, who he hung out with at college, the slim guy with very long eyelashes? Well Justin was gay. He and Khalid were lovers."

"Shush," Nadia replied holding her forefinger to her lips. "Don't say such a thing someone might hear you."

"So I suppose marrying a girl from the sticks isn't such a bad plan. At least she'll be a model wife and do as she's told, but she might have a long wait if she wants children," Susan said laughing.

The two girls talked and made plans for a while longer then Nadia said she was going to find her cousin Khalid for a chat.

"Chat all you like," Susan said. "He'll still be gay."

Nadia found Khalid sitting under a tree in the garden of the compound smoking a joint.

"Who are you hiding from?" she asked flopping down on the ground beside him.

"Everyone," he replied miserably.

"Aren't you excited about your wedding?" Nadia asked probingly.

Khalid stared at her for a moment then replied, "You do know I'm gay, Nadia, don't you? You know this wedding's a sham to please my parents. If I don't marry Rizwana I'll be cast out and cut off without a penny."

"But what about Rizwana, does she know it's a sham wedding?" Nadia asked unable to hide the shock in her voice.

"Of course she does," Khalid replied. "But she's got secrets too, she was engaged and abandoned a month before her wedding because the groom to be got a better offer from another family. Her parents were very ashamed and it destroyed her chances of marriage. She and I are damaged goods but together we can save the honour of both of our families, besides, we'll have a good life. Our parents are paying the rent on a New York apartment for two years and, I'm sure in that time, I'll be able to establish an American base for the family business."

"But what about children, doesn't Rizwana want a family?"

"Of course she does and so do I and we'll have children, God willing, we don't have to have sex to make babies. Haven't you ever heard of a turkey baster?"

"But that's awful you'll be living a lie."

"Maybe, but it's not really any different from when you and Susan marry the chuckle brothers, Bashir and Arif. That won't be a love marriage either because you'll never have met them before the wedding day."

"What are you talking about?" Nadia asked. "Susan and I are going to university together we've no plans to marry and who are Bashir and Arif?"

"I'm sorry Nadia, I didn't realise that you didn't know. Your dad and your uncle Safdar agreed the marriages at the same time mine was arranged. That's why our fathers travelled to Pakistan together. You'd better not say anything to them or they'll be mad at me."

Nadia was completely shocked. She didn't know what to do. Suddenly she was desperate to get back to Glasgow because she felt trapped and helpless in Pakistan.

"Bye Khalid, I've got to go," she said jumping to her feet. "Don't worry, your secret is safe with me," she added and she raced indoors to find Susan.

When Nadia told Susan what Khalid had said, she was completely stunned. "How could they do that to us? How could they tell us lies and let us make plans for uni when they're going to throw us away."

Nadia was crying softly. "What will we do? What can we do?"

Susan sat silently she was deep in thought. "I have an idea," she finally said. "When we get home we'll apply for new passports. We'll fill in the forms as if the old ones are lost. Then we'll save all the money we can so we're solvent when the time comes to run away."

"But we'll need our birth certificates to get passports and our dads have all the family's paperwork. Why are you talking about running away? Where would we go? I don't want to lose my family."

"One way or another we will lose our family, but at least we won't lose each other."

"But what if Khalid's got it wrong? Maybe there's no plan to marry us off."

"Don't be a fool," Susan replied. "He's not going to make a mistake like that. He even knew the names of the men we're to marry. Do you want to be stuck with a man you don't know who might be as old as your father? He might turn out to be violent or smelly."

Nadia thought about what Susan had said and in spite of herself she began to smile. "I couldn't be married to a smelly man," she said, "Old and violent maybe, but not smelly, never smelly."

The girls continued talking while sorting their clothes for the wedding. They were upset by their fathers' betrayal but they had no choice for now. They had to continue as if nothing was wrong. Soon they'd be back in Glasgow then they could think about their futures and decide what to do.

* * *

Thomas was having disturbing dreams. Every night he woke up agitated and unnerved. The dreams were always sexual. Night after night he relived the high he got when he'd touched Megan and every dream carried him further and further into depravity. He would wake up sweaty and wet from climaxing, but that didn't really bother him. What disturbed him and frightened him was that every time he dreamed his behaviour became uglier and cruder. He did dirty, disgusting things, performed sordid, violent acts and when he climaxed the woman of his dreams was always Nadia. Although he respected her for her modesty and chastity he still wanted her sexually and the dirtier the sex the better the high. He cried with disgust at himself but he yearned for the next dream and the ecstasy it would bring.

Chapter 30

The media circus trundled on and Frank Martin found himself sitting next to Martha Kelly making a television appeal for information. Had it not been for the murders nobody would have had the slightest interest in Katherine Kelly aka Kelly Jamieson. The news desk's make-up department had cleaned up Martha and dressed her tastefully in a black skirt and white blouse but being off alcohol for several hours meant she couldn't function. Frank did all the talking while Martha twitched and shivered beside him. After only a few minutes it all became too much for her and she slumped forward onto the desk in front of her in a state of collapse. The press were delighted, wrongly interpreting her collapse as being from anguish and they fell on her with flashing cameras like vultures on a corpse.

Angela and Paul watched the scene unfold on a small television screen in the staff room.

Paul laughed loudly, "Good grief, look at the Boss's face, he's mortified. He hasn't a clue what to do. He's just standing there looking like a dick."

"It's lucky that newsman grabbed her before she slid onto the floor," Angela observed. She too couldn't stop laughing at the desperate struggle to lift Martha from her chair and away from the photographers."

"God, they've dropped her, look, she's sliding out of their grasp. What a performance. I'm glad I'm not there," Paul observed and he laughed even louder.

Suddenly the screen went blank and a sign appeared saying, 'We're sorry for the loss of programme, normal service will resume shortly.'

"The Boss is going to be livid," Angela said. "He didn't want to do the appeal in the first place. Anyway the phone lines will be busy soon so we'd better get back to our office. I'm sure lots of people will come forward with information after that charade. They'll all want to be part of the show."

As expected, the phone team received dozens of calls, mostly from people who lived in Govanhill. Some of them just wanted to talk about crime in the area but many were from nervous or frightened residents who wanted to be reassured. After several hours, none of them imparted any useful information.

"Did you see me on the box?" Frank asked Angela after he returned to the station, "What a commotion that was, eh? That bloody woman pee-ed her pants when she collapsed and I didn't want to touch her. Was it very obvious that I didn't give a shit about her? Did I look bad on screen?"

"Not at all, Boss," Angela lied. "I thought you did very well. I wouldn't have wanted to touch her either. We don't get paid enough for that kind of exposure."

"Have we received anything useful or is it the usual mixture of scared wee wifeys and perverts that are phoning in?"

"We've had nothing outstanding except one nutcase who said he killed her and fed her body to sharks in Australia. It's all been a waste of time so far, but you never know, we might still get lucky."

"I'm just so glad it's over," Frank said. "I hate that sort of thing. I don't like being in front of the media. They're like a pack of wild dogs the way they all shout questions at once. I really hate it."

"I can understand that, Boss, I'd hate it too, but you did really well, you were calm and in control. It was the best we could hope for given the circumstances."

"Thanks, Angela, I needed that, we'd both better get back to work now. Would you bring me a coffee please?"

Angela was stunned, the Boss said please, maybe he should do more media work it improved his manners. She and Paul spent the next three hours twiddling their thumbs waiting for useful calls to be patched through to them.

"This is a bloody waste of time, I'm bored stiff," Paul said. He had now made several paper aeroplanes from the contents of his bin and he was launching them at Angela's open handbag which was lying on the floor beside her chair.

"Would you please stop doing that," she said. "The Boss will have a fit if he sees you."

"I'm just so bored, Mum," he replied pouting like a spoiled child.

"Go out and buy us cakes then, don't sit around moping, you're doing my head in."

Paul stood and saluted, "Apple turnover or empire biscuit?" he asked. "Oh, and do you think I should get something for the Boss?"

"Iced doughnut please, and yes, you'd better bring him something, he likes Chelsea buns."

As Paul disappeared out of the office his phone rang and Angela answered it.

"This is the control line," a woman's voice said. "I've a Mrs Baxter holding, she's got information about Katherine Kelly. I think she's genuine, will I patch her through?"

Angela's heart pounded in her chest, a lead at last.

"Yes please, this is Detective Murphy, I'll take the call."

"Hello, hello, are you there?" Angela heard Mrs Baxter calling.

"Hello, Mrs Baxter?" she replied. "I'm Detective Murphy I believe you have some information for me."

"Oh, I thought I was speaking to another girl, she wasn't a detective. I don't want to waste your valuable time. What I have to say might not be important," Mrs Baxter replied hesitantly.

"Why don't you take your time and tell me what you know, don't worry about wasting my time, I'm here to listen, that's my job."

"Oh, well, if you're sure," she cleared her throat then began, "I am fairly certain I saw the missing girl, it was several days ago, the day she disappeared actually. I live in Cathcart and I was going to the Health Centre in Butterbiggins Road to pick up a prescription for my neighbour when I saw her. She was rushing along the road and she kept talking but nobody was there. She kept saying 'get away from me, get away.'"

Mrs Baxter paused and Angela spoke, "May I take down some details Mrs Baxter because I think your information could be very useful to us?"

Angela wrote down all Mrs Baxter's personal information then she filled in what she had already been told, she was exhilarated because the information sounded solid and truthful.

"Please continue Mrs Baxter," she said. "I'm up to speed with my notes now."

"I watched her for a few moments because she seemed so distressed but I was a bit scared to approach her. She went into a close on Butterbiggins Road, number 163, and she didn't come out again. The ground floor apartment of the building is empty and all boarded up so she could have got in there. I only remembered her when I saw her picture on the television and her poor mother fainting during the appeal. Is her mother all right now? My heart went out to the poor soul."

Dynamite, Angela thought this is pure dynamite.

"Hello, hello, are you still there?" Mrs Baxter called.

"Sorry, yes, I'm still here," Angela said. "Thank you so much for calling us Mrs Baxter your information is most helpful. The girl's mother is fully recovered, don't worry, she just fainted from the heat in the studio." All lies of course but what did it matter as long as the witness was happy.

"What should I do now?" Mrs Baxter asked. "Is that us finished, should I hang up?"

"Could you come into the police station and make a statement, I can send a car to pick you up and we'll drive you home afterwards," Angela offered unwilling to let her only tangible witness get away.

"I don't want a police car coming to my door thank you, I'll phone my son and he'll bring me, but it'll be about half an hour before I can get over to you, is that okay?"

"That's perfect Mrs Baxter, the statement will be prepared and you'll only have to read it and sign it so you won't be kept long."

"Right, I'll be there soon, goodbye."

"Goodbye Mrs Baxter."

As she hung up the phone Angela punched the air with her fist, "Yes," she said.

Paul, who'd returned with the cakes, gave her a mystified look, "What was all that about?" he asked.

"We've got a live one, she saw Kelly on the day she disappeared, and she watched her enter a close in Butterbiggins Road. The ground floor apartment is derelict and boarded up, we need to get over there and we'd better ask uniform to meet us because we might have to break a door down. Mrs Baxter's coming in to sign a statement so I'll have to pass my notes on to someone. Should I tell the Boss?"

"Whoa there, slow down," Paul said holding his hands up in front of him. "You can't just go off like a rocket because for all you know your Mrs Baxter might have told you a load of bollocks. Type up your statement and leave it at the front desk, then you and I will take a drive to the address and see how the land lies. The Boss told me he's going home early because he promised his wife he'd take her to the theatre to see a show, so he doesn't need to know anything unless there's something to report."

Angela knew Paul was right, she was overreacting so she took a deep breath and calmed down. She quickly typed up the statement from her notes then left it with Detective Jack Dobson who'd just started his shift. Paul and Angela each took their cars for the short journey as they intended to go straight home after they checked the building. As she drove along Butterbiggins Road Angela's heart started to thump with excitement, this is it she thought, if I find Kelly Jamieson hiding in that flat, paranoid and afraid, I'll be a hero.

Chapter 31

Angela arrived outside number 163 before Paul. Mrs Baxter was right. The ground floor apartment was boarded up and, by the look of the graffiti on the metal shutters covering the windows, had been that way for some time. There was no sign of Paul and Angela was anxious to look around. She climbed out of her car and tried to look in the side of the shutters but they were fixed tight. 'Where are you Paul?' she said to herself impatiently.

Unable to wait any longer Angela entered the close. She wasn't surprised to find the security entry system wasn't working and the outside door didn't even shut properly. The floor was covered in debris much of which was used syringes and condoms. 'God, what a place to live,' she thought. Angela banged on the door of the ground floor apartment but there was no reply.

"Kelly Jamieson, are you in there? Open the door, its Detective Murphy here. I've come to help you," still no response. "Kelly, Kelly, can you hear me?"

Angela went back to the street to look for Paul and she was pleased to see him parking his car behind hers.

"You took your time," she said accusingly. "Did you do your shopping first?"

"Actually, I had to stop for fuel or I wouldn't have made it at all, the tank was practically empty. Anyway, I'm here now, so let's get a move on."

"I've already tried knocking on the door but there was no reply," Angela admitted.

"Did you try opening the door?" Paul asked.

"Do you think there's any point? She probably just went into the close to shoot up, there are needles everywhere."

"Let's try it," Paul said, "We're here now so we might as well."

They entered the close and Paul banged on the door once again before trying the door handle. It turned easily in his hand.

"It doesn't seem to be locked," he said.

Paul gave the door a shove and it opened a crack, something behind it was holding it shut. The cloying sweet smell of death wafted out through the space and Paul drew back coughing.

"Something's dead in there, I hope it's not Kelly. Give me a hand to push this door because something's behind it stopping it from opening."

The two detectives put their shoulders to the door and they gradually managed to open up a space that they could squeeze through. When they got inside they could see that it had been blocked by an old broken sofa. The smell inside was awful and they both held their hands in front of their noses. It was almost pitch black because of the shuttered windows. Paul flipped the light switch but nothing happened. Angela took a penlight from her bag and switched it on.

"Be careful where you walk," Paul said. "This place is full of rubbish and it's a bit of a death trap."

They carefully searched the room. Angela edged her way to what seemed to be a heap of rags on a mattress in the corner. She wanted to see if any of them could be Kelly's belongings. As she approached she could just make out the shape of a person lying in a foetal position on the torn mattress.

"Oh no, oh my God, Paul come here, help me, I think I've found Kelly."

Stumbling over rubbish Paul joined Angela at the side of the mattress. "Oh Jesus Christ," he said. "Let's get outside and call this in, we can't do anything here. Oh Christ, she's covered in maggots and I can't stand the buggers. Move, Angela," he said grabbing her arm and pulling her along with him, "Let's go."

They pulled the door shut as they left and stood in the street dazed by the horror of what they'd witnessed. When they were sitting in Paul's car he phoned in the news of their discovery. Angela couldn't stop shaking.

"We've to stay put until forensics arrives and someone can get over here to relieve us," Paul said.

"Do you think it's Kelly?" Angela asked.

"Hard to tell in that light and with the body decomposed and crawling with maggots. But I'd say there's a fair chance of it, especially with what your witness reported."

"Do you think she's been murdered like the other girls?"

"Again, it's impossible to know at the moment, but I doubt it. When forensics check it out there's every chance they'll find a needle in her arm. I think it's more likely she went there to get high and injected bad shit."

"What a terrible place to die," Angela said and tears ran down her cheeks. "I'm sorry," she said mopping her eyes with a handkerchief. "I'm not upset it's just the shock of finding her like that."

"Don't apologise for being a caring, human being. It was a shock for me too," Paul said. "Just remember it might not be Kelly. We can't jump to any conclusions at this stage, so be guarded in what you say to anyone else, okay?"

The sound of sirens broke the quiet of the late afternoon. Angela and Paul got out of the car just as the cavalry arrived. Suddenly the street was full of vehicles and a theatre of players swung into action relieving Angela and Paul of their responsibilities. Although they were now free to go home they both hesitated because they wanted to see if the body could be identified as Kelly, but they were out of luck.

"We won't know anything until we get her out of there," one of the forensics people said. "But I can tell you the body is of a female and there's a needle still in her arm so there's a good chance it's your girl."

"We'd better tell Frank," Paul said.

"But he's at a show with his wife," Angela protested. "He's really stressed and needs the time out, besides he can't do anything that we haven't already done."

"Sorry, Angela, but you're wrong. We have to tell him because he's the Boss and he'd be much more stressed if we didn't let him know, besides, the show won't have started yet."

"I'll phone him then," she said dialling the number, "But I don't see that a few hours will make any difference."

"Trust me," Paul replied. "It'll be the difference between life and death and I'm too young to die."

Chapter 32

As Angela drove home her mobile started to ring but it was in her handbag on the back seat and she couldn't reach it. If it's important they'll leave a message or call back she reasoned and, sure enough, a couple of moments later she heard the familiar beep, beep, beep telling her one had been received. Once she'd pulled up outside her home she unlocked the phone and listened to the voicemail.

"Sorry I didn't answer my phone, but there was no signal because I was in a multi-storey car park. You and Paul did great work. I've sent uniformed officers round to Martha Kelly's house so they can prepare her for the worst before the press get hold of the story. Jack Dobson and Gordon McKay are at the scene and they'll remain there till we can close up the apartment. Gordon said he'd come in about lunchtime tomorrow to bring you up to speed. You've done a good job Angela, thanks for letting me know about it. See you tomorrow, 'The Phantom' awaits." The message ended without a goodbye.

Angela hadn't even considered Martha Kelly or the need for someone to wait at the scene, it's lucky she phoned the Boss or they'd have been in deep shit. Much as she hated to admit it, Paul was right.

When Angela opened the front door she was greeted by Bobby holding a bottle of Champagne.

"Hi, Darling," he said. "Have you had a good day, because I've had a fantastic one," Bobby was grinning unable to contain himself.

The delicious smell of warm bread and home cooking wafted out from the kitchen and the house looked very clean and tidy.

"I've had a good day too," Angela replied, "If you can call finding Kelly Jamieson's body, good."

"Oh no, and here's me greeting you with Champagne. I guess it's hardly a time for celebration."

"Actually it is," Angela replied, "At least we now know what's happened to her and we're almost positive it's a drug overdose that killed her. Anyway tell me your news, I'm intrigued."

"Jake phoned this afternoon to tell me that we've won a huge contract for electronics. I've been nurturing the company director for nearly a month and today he placed the order. Although I've been sending him all the information by email he wanted to speak to a person before placing the order so he phoned the company line and got Jake. It's worth forty thousand pounds to be supplied over four months and, get this, he's told us it's just a sample order. If he's happy with the way we handle it he'll increase it and make it regular. Our quote undercut everyone else even the big players in the market and we're still making a fortune."

"That's fantastic, Bobby, I'm so proud of you. I gather from the delicious smell coming from the kitchen and the bottle of Champagne in your hand you're mighty pleased with yourself too."

"You could say that," he replied grinning. "If only I'd known that I'd be good at this business, I'd have given up teaching years ago."

"I'm so proud of you, Pet," Angela said and she meant every word. "I'll just go and jump into the shower it'll only take me ten minutes. I'm so hungry I could eat a horse."

"Sorry, Darling, no horse on the menu, but I've made a Lamb Tagine, Nigella's recipe actually. I must admit I'm rather pleased with the way it's turned out. She is one sexy cook and you are one sexy lady," he said and he growled as he nuzzled Angela's neck.

"Patience tiger," she replied gently pushing him away, "I've been in a stinky, maggoty apartment let me get my shower before you get amorous."

On hearing that, Bobby pulled a face and held up his hands as if to ward off evil. He didn't protest as Angela disappeared upstairs.

When Angela came out of her shower she carefully dressed and re-applied her make-up. She felt that she too had to make an effort even though she was completely exhausted. The shock of discovering the decomposing body had drained her completely. She hoped that if the dinner didn't revive her then the alcohol would help to lift her spirits.

"You look beautiful, but absolutely knackered," Bobby observed when she entered the dining room.

"You're right, I am. It's been a gruelling day. I'm dying to hear your news though, it sounds marvellous. Does this mean we're rich?"

"It means we're doing pretty well," Bobby replied and he gave a thumbs-up sign. "In fact I think we can safely book a summer holiday, a decent one, not just a week in Millport."

"Fantastic, but I still don't understand how you're managing to undercut the competition."

"Sheer luck or maybe I should call it sheer genius. I have a contact in China who I met at university and he's the key to my success. Dan is half British and half Chinese and he's very well connected. After uni he went to work for a major electronics company and now he's one of their top men in China. As well as supplying us with the gizmos from his company, he's put me in touch with friends of his who work for other electronics firms. Jake and I are paying him a commission via his father who still lives in the UK and we're getting our supplies cheaper than everyone else in the business. It's a win, win, situation and it's going to make us very comfortable financially."

"And is it all legal? It sounds too good to be true. Won't the big boys in the business get wind of this and try to stop you?"

"No problem, because although we're making lots of dough, it's a drop in the ocean for them, we're too small for them to even notice us. The companies that we supply buy at most tens of thousands per order, not hundreds of thousands."

"I'm so proud of you Bobby, it's been hard for us adjusting to this business, but having the cleaner helps tremendously and I feel we're coping now."

"Yes, Darling, it has been quite a change for us both, but like you say, the worst is over now. Do you want to tell me about your day?"

"I'd rather not if you don't mind it was pretty awful. I'd rather forget about it."

They finished their meal talking about holiday destinations and figuring out the best time for a break. Then Bobby went to make coffees and Angela moved into the lounge and put on the television to catch the news. The last item of the headlines proclaimed 'Body discovered in Glasgow, is this missing prostitute Katherine Kelly and is she the fourth victim of the Southside Slasher?' Bobby came in with the coffees in time to hear the whole of the news report.

"Ken Jones reporting from Govanhill in Glasgow, where recently three young women have been murdered," the reporter said. "The decomposed body was discovered a few hours ago in the derelict building you see behind me. Police and forensic officers are still at the scene and all they can tell us at the moment is that the body is of a young female. The cause of death is not yet known."

The film cut to the scene outside the building and Angela could see Gordon McKay standing outside the apartment smoking and Jack Dobson chatting on his mobile phone. At least they haven't skived off, she thought.

Ken Jones continued, "The people of Govanhill are living in fear after the recent spate of murders. I have with me local resident Mrs Ali, who alerted the police to the first victim. Mrs Ali what can you tell us about Margaret Deacon, the first young woman to be murdered?"

"Magrit was a junkie prostitute, but a human being nevertheless. The foreign gangsters are ruining our neighbourhood. This used to be a good area before the Eastern Europeans moved in with their drugs. I just want to say…"

Realising that perhaps Mrs Ali wasn't the best person to give air time to Ken Jones quickly moved the microphone away from her,

"Thank you for that Mrs Ali," he said. This is Ken Jones in Butter-biggins Road, Glasgow."

The programme went back to the newsreader in the studio, "We'll bring you the breaking news on the situation in Glasgow as and when it happens," she said and she went on to the next item.

"Bloody Hell," Angela said. "I didn't expect the press to get hold of the story so quickly and I think they've got it all wrong. The forensic people said the body had a needle sticking out of its arm so it's probably an overdose not a murder."

"No wonder you didn't want to talk about it. I think we should turn off the telly because it's too depressing."

"I think we should take the rest of the Champagne and go to bed," Angela said. "We could both do with an early night, you to celebrate and me to take my mind off a horrible day."

"No need to ask me twice," Bobby said with a wink. "I'll just lock up. You go on up and warm the sheets."

As Angela climbed the stairs she felt relaxed, safe in the comfort of her home. She dreaded to think what tomorrow would bring, but for now at least, she could separate herself from the horrors of the outside world and in particular, Govanhill.

Chapter 33

Thomas sat in his armchair rocking and crying, he'd been awake all night after seeing the news. The voice in his head was cruel and it tortured him relentlessly.

"I didn't do it, shut up shut up shut up. Why can't you leave me alone?" he whined.

'*Of course you did it you little fucker. You punched her face and then you rubbed your hand between her legs. She had a plastic bag over her head and she pee-ed herself, you must remember the smell of pee and sweat. You do remember, don't you, you can practically taste it.*'

"No, no, that was the other girl not this one, I didn't touch this one."

'*They're all the same, they're all whores begging for a fuck, but you don't fuck them do you Boy? You just touch them and run away, you're pathetic. You're a pathetic little prick.*'

"I'm saving myself for Nadia. One day I'll make love to her and it will be beautiful and special."

"*Oh it'll be special all right you're so fucking special you're a fucking moron.*'

"I know Nadia will want me. She'll say 'no' at first but she'll mean 'yes' just like in the movies," Thomas spoke softly as he imagined himself with Nadia. "Afterwards she'll cry and I'll comfort her, but she'll love me for taking control and for being a man, her man. She'll love me for ever and ever."

'*For ever and ever,*' the voice mimicked. '*Life isn't a fucking fairytale. You'll never have Nadia so stop kidding yourself. The only way you'd ever get a girl like that is if you stole her from her family. Her father would never accept you. You're not Moslem and you're not rich, you're not even good looking. You're a useless little fucker who can't even fuck. Ha, ha, ha,*' the voice pounded and pounded in Thomas's head and he slapped his forehead with his open palm to try and make it stop.

"Leave me alone, leave me alone, I didn't touch that girl, I didn't even know her."

'*But you wanted to, didn't you? You still want her. You get hard just thinking about fucking a whore.*'

"I want Nadia, only Nadia. She'll be my girlfriend just you wait and see and when she's with me, she'll love me."

Thomas Malone was losing it, cog by cog his mind was slipping out of gear. Random exchanges between his mind and the voice found their way to his mouth and he could sometimes be heard arguing with himself. To most people he was just the same as always, invisible. When in uniform he was simply another hated symbol of authority and when he wasn't working he was a nondescript individual with few acquaintances and even less friends. Recently, some people had noticed Thomas muttering as he went about his business, but surprisingly, those who did give him more than a passing glance, assumed that he was talking on the phone, one of those little contraptions worn on the ear. They had no idea that little by little he was falling apart.

When Thomas was in the company of Alan he felt protected because the older man was like a father to him. Alan made him feel safe and he gave Thomas the confidence to push the voice to the back of his mind and force it to keep quiet.

To Alan, Thomas was the son he'd never had and he liked the naïve, shy, young man. When Alan was with Thomas he was no longer just an ordinary working class man with limited education and even less ambition. Instead Alan was a mentor, teacher and father, he felt strong and in control. It made Alan feel like a hero and to Thomas, he was.

As the two men walked down Butterbiggins Road ticketing cars they talked. Thomas would have preferred not to be drawn into a conversation about the dead girl because he was still unsure of whether or not he was somehow involved. Alan on the other hand loved a bit of drama.

"Four dead whores in a handful of weeks, the quality of residents living in this area will have to improve or at this rate only nuns will be able to stay here and survive," Alan said.

"The Asian girls will be okay," Thomas replied. He was trying to assure himself that Nadia in particular would be safe. "They don't dress like whores and they don't throw themselves at men."

"Aye, you're right there, Son. Their families keep them on a tight rein. Anyway about this latest tart, I spoke to one of the officers on duty and he said it wasn't a murder. He said it was a drug overdose."

"So she killed herself? Nobody murdered her."

"Well that's not exactly true, is it? Whoever sold her the bad drugs was responsible. Just the same as if they'd plunged a knife into her heart," Alan added dramatically.

'But it wasn't me,' Thomas thought to himself, 'it wasn't me.'

"Sorry Thomas, I missed that, what did you say?"

"N n nothing," Thomas stuttered, "I didn't say anything." He had to be careful because he hadn't realised he'd spoken aloud.

"I wonder when the killer will strike again," Alan said. "You mark my words Thomas he'll be back because he just can't help himself. According to the constable I spoke to, the police haven't got a clue. They're no further on now than they were weeks ago. What do you think about that Mrs Ali on the telly last night blaming the Eastern Europeans? Wasn't she hilarious? I bet that reporter was sorry he'd asked her."

Alan chattered on asking Thomas questions then answering them himself. He didn't really expect a reply. Thomas was lost, deep in his own thoughts. What if Alan was right, what if he did kill again. The voice in his head said he was weak, maybe it was true. He had to avoid going near another prostitute because they brought out the worst in him.

'*You know you can't help yourself, you need a whore to teach you, how else will you know how to do it? You can't expect 'N a d i a' to teach you*'. The voice said Nadia letter by letter in the sing song way that Thomas hated. '*Then again, maybe Nadia could show you what to do because she probably fucked lots of men in Pakistan. I bet she really liked it. I bet she begged for more.*'

"Alan to Thomas, is anybody there? Hello, hello earth to Thomas."

Thomas jumped, "Sorry Alan, I was miles away," he said.

"You can say that again, you've missed one Thomas and that's not like you. You've missed the Renault and it's on a double yellow line."

Chapter 34

Once it was proved that Kelly Jamieson died of a drug overdose and wasn't, as first thought, the fourth victim of the Slasher, the media lost interest. They no longer talked about the profile of the killer and they stopped berating the police for not catching him. There was speculation of a General Election being called which would probably lead to a new government and that was the story filling the headlines.

Angela rolled over in bed she was half asleep when she glanced at the clock. Seven-fifteen it read, she practically jumped out of bed, I'm late she thought then she realised it was Sunday and she had the day off. She tried to drop back to sleep, but it was too late, she was wide awake. Bobby was still in dreamland when she rose so she was careful not to disturb him. Angela quickly washed and dressed then went downstairs and put on a pot of coffee. The paper boy would deliver the morning paper, but the newsagent kept fresh rolls and croissants so Angela slipped out of the house to buy some for breakfast. It would be nice for Bobby to have breakfast in bed and she wanted to surprise him.

The morning was dry and fresh and Angela was in high spirits, she felt as if a burden had been lifted off her shoulders. Somehow all the pressure was gone and she actually was looking forward to going into work tomorrow. When she reached the newsagent's, Andy, the owner, was surprised to see her up and about so early on a Sunday.

"The paper boy's not left with your newspapers yet. Do you want to take them with you? It's the Mail and the Express isn't it?"

"Yes that's right," Angela replied. "I'll take them with me now. It'll save the paper boy a trip and can I also have four croissants please." She handed over a ten pound note.

"We've got something new in today," Andy said, "Mrs Goudie's home-made marmalade. It's really delicious if you like marmalade that is. I've got thick cut orange or thin cut mixed citrus, its two pounds a jar would you like some?"

"Sounds lovely I think I'll have a jar of the orange please, my husband loves marmalade."

"You'll be pleased to have the case closed on that missing girl. It's a shame she turned up dead but at least she wasn't murdered."

Andy passed Angela her purchases which he'd placed in a polythene bag, then he handed her the change.

"What do you think about this election then?" he asked changing the subject, and another customer, a man who was standing beside Angela, jumped in with a reply.

Small talk, she thought to herself, the world revolves around small talk. It doesn't matter if it's a murder or politics, it's all the same, give the public something or someone to talk about and they're happy.

By late morning Angela and Bobby had read most of their newspapers and were at a loose end.

"We could head down to the coast for a walk on the beach and some lunch if you'd like," Bobby offered. "Or if there's something you want to do I could plough through some of my paperwork. It would be good to get it cleared."

Angela was hoping to spend the whole day with Bobby but she knew what it felt like to be bogged down with work and how good it was to get clear of it.

"I see there's an antique fair on at the Kelvin Hall," she said pointing to her newspaper. "I could phone Liz Brown and see if she fancies going. I haven't seen her for a couple of weeks and it would be good to catch up."

"You do that and I'll take you out for dinner tonight to make up for me working. We could go to the new Italian place at Clarkston if you'd like."

"That's a great idea and we can have a bottle of wine because we can walk home from there. I'll go and phone Liz now."

Angela arranged to pick Liz up half an hour later and they decided to have a bite of lunch in the west end before going to the antique fair.

When they were seated in a pizza restaurant Liz said, "I've got some news. I've decided to go to university to study forensics, I'm getting support from work and they're giving me time off for study. I realised when I worked with you on the murder case that I was really interested in it."

"Wow, I didn't expect that, rather you than me. I hate working with maggoty, dead bodies it's the smell that gets to me. Are you really sure about it? What does your Dad think?"

"He's all for it, he thinks education is good, and he'd rather I worked with the dead than the living, less dangerous."

"I suppose you're right I never thought about it that way."

The two young woman chatted while they ate then they set off for the fair. Angela thought Liz was very brave to consider a career change. She couldn't imagine doing anything other than police work but then she'd never considered the alternatives. If Bobby's business continued to do well it might be worth looking at her options.

* * *

Thomas paced nervously waiting for Alan to pick him up. On a suggestion made by the lady in the grocer's he'd bought flowers for Alan's wife. He felt awkward holding the pink carnations as he'd never bought flowers before.

"Nice flowers, are they for me? You shouldn't have."

Thomas turned to see Nadia and Susan. "N n no, he stuttered, they're for my friend Alan's wife, she's ill. But I'll buy you flowers if you'd like," he added.

"I'm only teasing you," Nadia said. "I couldn't accept a gift from a stranger."

"But you know me," Thomas protested. "You're uncle knows me. I'm not a stranger."

"Don't be silly," Susan said. "Of course you're a stranger. You're not part of our community and you're not part of our family. We shouldn't even be speaking to you."

"But you like me Nadia, don't you? We could be friends. You never know when you'll need a friend."

Nadia thought about what Thomas said. With what she now knew about the arranged marriages, maybe someone like Thomas, who wasn't involved with her community, might prove useful after all.

"I'd like to be your friend," she said. "But my family must never find out. Can you keep a secret?"

Thomas exhaled his bated breath. "For you anything," he replied and he smiled a goofy smile.

Nadia laughed then fearful of being seen, she hastily said goodbye, grabbed a surprised Susan by the arm and marched off down the street.

"Are you mad," Susan said. "Why did you say that? Why would you want to have anything to do with him? He's weird and he's old, he's at least in his twenties. Your Dad will kill you if he finds out."

"He'd better not find out then," Nadia replied tartly. "Thomas could be very useful to us if we have to run away sooner rather than later. He is older but that's good because he's got a responsible job, an official job with a uniform, we'd be safe with him."

"I guess you're right," Susan said, but she didn't really know what to think. Suddenly running away seemed all too real and she wasn't as sure of herself as she had been before.

"Thomas will do whatever I ask because he fancies me," Nadia added. "But don't you worry about a thing, I can handle him."

"I hope you know what you're doing," Susan replied. "Because I have to tell you I'm feeling out of my comfort zone."

"You can't be feeling any more uncomfortable about befriending Thomas than being forced to marry a total stranger. Trust me, Susan, I do know what I'm doing."

Chapter 35

As Alan drew up in the van Thomas waved manically at him. He was in high spirits after talking to Nadia and he couldn't contain his excitement.

"You look happy," Alan observed. "I didn't think the prospect of driving this wee van was so special, but there you go, there's nowt as strange as folk." Alan got out of the van and went round to the passenger side.

"I'm happy because I've just been speaking to Nadia," Thomas replied climbing into the driver's seat.

"Nadia?" said Alan, "But I thought Mary was your girlfriend. What's happened to Mary?"

'*Yes,*' said the voice. '*What has happened to Mary? Have you killed her off?*'

"Nothing's happened to Mary," Thomas hissed. "She's perfectly all right. I'm allowed to have other friends who are girls aren't I?"

"Okay, okay, keep your hair on. Don't get annoyed I'm not criticising you."

"S s sorry, Alan, I'm not angry, I'm just a bit nervous about driving that's all." Thomas realised that he'd answered rather sharply.

"Don't be nervous, Son, I'll just show you where all the controls are then we'll be on our way."

The driving was a piece of cake. Thomas was methodical and confident and Alan was impressed. They soon arrived outside Alan's house in Cherrybank Road.

"This is a lovely street," Thomas observed. "It's very open and light not like the street where I live. It always seems dark even when the sun is shining."

"Yes, it is light and we have the ground floor apartment so we've got a garden. Ann likes pottering in the garden. She's got green fingers everything she plants grows. She's also a fabulous baker," Alan added patting his rotund belly.

They climbed out of the van and Thomas retrieved the flowers to give to Ann.

"That was a nice thing for you to do, Son," Alan said nodding at them. "The wife loves flowers especially carnations."

As they walked up the path the front door opened and Ann stood in the doorway. She was small and plump with bleached blonde hair which was arranged in a short, spiky style. She had a sweet smile and when Thomas arrived at the front door she put her arms around him and gave him a hug.

"I'm so pleased to meet you, Thomas," she said. "Alan speaks very highly of you. Do come in."

Thomas felt rather uncomfortable with the show of affection and he squeezed past Ann awkwardly as she remained at the door to greet Alan. Then almost as an afterthought he turned and pushed the carnations into her hands. "These are for you," he said stating the obvious.

"They're lovely, thank you," Ann replied.

When they entered the front room two little dogs ran up yapping and jumping about.

"Milly, Mopsy, leave Thomas alone. Sorry Thomas they get very excited when they meet new people," Alan said. "I'll just put them in the kitchen for the moment."

"It's all right, Alan, I don't mind them. Leave them here."

Ann beamed at him, "I knew you were a dog lover the minute I clapped eyes on you," she said. "You can tell a lot about people by the way they respond to animals."

"I've never had a pet," Thomas replied. "But I like dogs." He leaned down and petted Milly and Mopsy and after a few moments they settled down.

Ann went into the kitchen to make tea and Alan gave Thomas a print out of the insurance document showing him as a named driver.

"You keep that in your wallet," he said, "And when you leave take the wee van with you. Ann said you might as well hang onto it just now because there's no point in it lying outside here when you could be using it."

"But what if Ann needs to go somewhere? Wouldn't she prefer to have it outside the door? I can collect the van whenever I need it. I can come over on the bus it's not a problem."

Alan dropped his voice to a whisper, "The doctor has been in touch, Son, he's pretty sure that it's MS. She might never feel confident enough to drive again. But don't say anything, okay? She's trying to be brave to protect me."

The rattling of crockery on a tray heralded Ann's return to the room. "Let me get that," Alan said jumping to his feet. "Pull over that coffee table please, Thomas."

"I hear you've got a girlfriend, Thomas," Ann said when they were all seated having their tea. "Tell me about her."

Thomas's face twitched nervously. "She's at her aunt's house."

"So I believe," Ann said. "Maybe next time you come round I'll get to meet her."

'*Not on your Nellie,*' the voice said. '*Not fucking likely.*'

Thomas resisted answering the voice but it took great effort.

"Are you all right, Thomas?" Alan asked. "You've gone a bit pale and you're frowning."

Thomas's hands shook and his cup rattled in the saucer so he carefully placed it on the coffee table in front of him. "I'm fine," he said smiling the goofy smile that he'd mastered when he was at college.

It made him look friendly and benign and it never failed to endear people to him. "I'm just excited and thrilled to be able to borrow the van. You've no idea the difference having my own set of wheels will make to me."

Thomas was already thinking about Nadia and how great it would be to drive her places. A whole new world was opening up to him and it would be perfect if he could just stop the voice. If only his father was as kind to him as Alan, but the voice wasn't kind and Thomas hated it.

Chapter 36

The week dragged on and on and Angela was beginning to hate the office with its characterless décor and sixties style furniture. She was sick of pushing paper and staring at a computer screen.

"Murphy, my office," Frank yelled.

Angela sighed stood up and ambled to his office, "What can I do for you, Boss?" she asked and attempted a smile which was more of a grimace.

"Jack Dobson's been in an accident, he's in hospital. I want you to go home now and get some rest then come back in to cover his shift. You don't need to start bang on three but I'd appreciate it if you could try to get here as close to it."

"But Boss it's already ten o'clock, the best I can hope for is four hours sleep," Angela protested.

"Do you think I don't know that? I wouldn't ask you if I wasn't desperate. Gordon McKay's on holiday this week and Paul's wife is pregnant and needs him home. I'll have cover for tomorrow but for now you're all I've got."

Angela sighed and pursed her lips, "So I'm holding the fort alone?"

"There's a new boy doing his twelve month training, I've called him to come in."

"That's marvellous, it's worse than being on my own, I've got to run the office and baby sit a teenager at the same time. Thanks, Boss."

"Don't get stroppy with me, Missy. Change your attitude. Just remember I'm the boss and you work for me. I know I'm asking a lot but I've got no choice, besides, you've had it relatively easy these last weeks, so get over yourself. Now fuck off home and get some sleep and I'll see you later. I'll still be here when you get back because I'm working a twelve hour shift."

Angela stormed back to her desk. Trust the Boss to come out looking like a martyr while I look like a spoilt brat she thought. She lifted her bag from the floor, slammed it onto the desk then rooted around for her car keys.

"Who's rattled your chains?" Paul asked.

"I've to come in and work the back shift because Jack Dobson's been in an accident. You're off the hook because your wife's pregnant." Angela replied sulkily,

"But you're three hours into your shift," Paul said stating the obvious.

"I do know that. I'll be lucky to get four hours sleep," Angela replied. Paul started to laugh.

"It's not funny," Angela snapped.

"It is from where I'm sitting."

"You just wait till that baby is born and it keeps you up all night. Who'll be laughing then? Remember, he who laughs last, laughs best."

"Yeah, yeah, yadda, yadda, yadda."

"Well fuck you, Paul. Fuck you," Angela replied scowling. She stamped her way to the door with Paul's laughter ringing in her ears.

There wasn't much traffic so she got home quite quickly. When Angela put her key in the lock she could hear the sound of the vacuum. Oh bugger, she thought to herself, Jean the cleaner's in. Angela looked at her watch and saw that the girl had another two hours to go. She'll just have to clean quietly because I'll need to get a rest. The noise stopped as she shut the front door. Angela called out to Bobby so as not to give him a fright then headed upstairs to their bedroom. She was relieved to see upstairs had already been cleaned.

"What are you doing home?" Bobby said as he put his head round the bedroom door.

"I've to do overtime because we're short of people to cover. I've got to go back in for three."

"Oh, Darling, you'll be shattered. Will you be able to get something for your dinner? I could make you some roast beef sandwiches if you'd like."

"That would be great, thanks. I'm just going to get my head down for a couple of hours. I think it'll be a very long day. Wake me at two, would you please."

When Bobby went out and shut the bedroom door Angela took off her suit and climbed into bed. After what seemed like only minutes Bobby returned and knocked on the door.

"Angela, Angela," he called softly. "It's two o'clock. You said you wanted woken."

Angela woke more tired than when she'd gone to sleep. It took her half an hour to get ready and her head still felt like it was full of water. She had no idea how she was going to last till eleven let alone exchange small talk with a trainee. As she drove into work she realised she hadn't even asked what had happened to Jack Dobson. It better be something serious, she thought, otherwise it will be by the time I'm finished with him.

Angela got into the office at five past three. There was a man sitting at Paul's desk and Frank was talking to him. The Boss was half sitting half leaning on Angela's desk. As she approached them they stopped chatting and looked at her.

"There you are, Angela, I was just telling William all about you," Frank said.

"Hello," she said acknowledging the stranger.

"William here is your 'teenager'," Frank continued. He nodded and winked at William as if he were a long lost friend. Angela was annoyed.

"Perhaps we should be properly introduced," she said cutting in. "I believe you're working with me today. I'm Detective Murphy, Angela." She held out her hand to be shaken.

"I'm William Cruikshank and as you can see I'm not a teenager."

"If you'll excuse me I'll leave you to it, someone's got to do the work round here and I guess it'll have to be me," Frank said and he headed for his office.

When Frank departed Angela asked William about himself.

"As you'll realise from my age I'm not a new trainee," he began. I have a BSc in Applied Criminal Investigation. This twelve months traineeship is actually to give me the chance to decide which branch I want to build my career in. I was told your department was short staffed so I was happy to fill in."

William stood up and Angela was surprised by the size of the man. He was at least six foot four, his frame was broad and muscular and his hair was clipped very short almost skinhead style. If it hadn't been for his soft hazel-coloured eyes framed by sleepy looking lids he would more resemble a thug than a detective.

"We've investigated three murders and a death by drug overdose in the last three months plus the usual mixture of armed robbery, serious assault, etcetera, etcetera. We're getting nowhere with the murder en-quiries even though we've blitzed the area with posters and knocked on practically every door in Govanhill. I'm so fed up I could run away. To top it all, we're drowning under paperwork and we're short staffed. Welcome to my world, welcome to Hell," Angela painted rather a bleak picture for William, but every word was true.

"Thanks for your words of encouragement," William laughed. "Should I just run away now?"

"If you've any sense, the answer is yes, run, run like the wind and don't look back, but before you do, the coffee machine is over there and I'll have mine black."

"Yes Ma'am," William replied and he gave a mock salute. "What about Frank, should I make one for him?"

"A word of advice, William, if it ain't broke, don't fix it. Frank will let you know if he wants something, until then the less you interact with him the better. Unless you enjoy pain, that is."

"Message received and understood," William replied, "But he seemed like such a pussy cat," he added.

"So that's why you're here," Angela answered, "To curb your naivety. Now get a move on with the coffee Cruikshank, before I die of thirst and caffeine deficiency."

Angela and William worked steadily and silently until Frank left at seven o'clock. "Let's stop for some food now," Angela suggested. "I've got roast beef sandwiches, what've you got?"

"Two chicken legs, a bag of mixed lettuce and a large piece of quiche," William replied. "Want to share?"

"Sounds good to me," Angela answered. "Oh, and by the way, I've also got a huge piece of carrot cake."

"Now I would definitely like to share," William said.

Over the food they exchanged personal information and Angela found out that William was thirty-one, divorced and living in Giffnock. He also preferred to be called Bill.

"My ex-wife and I married far too young, we were only nineteen and we'd just started university. We're still good friends but we're both relieved that the marriage is over. Thank goodness we weren't stupid enough to bring children into the relationship."

They'd practically finished eating when the phone rang interrupting their conversation.

"What've you got for me?" Bill heard Angela ask. He watched her as she listened intently for a few minutes then she placed her elbow on the desk and dropped her forehead onto her hand. "Bloody Hell," she said. "Are you sure it's her?" there was a pause, "Tell them I'm on my way," she added then hung up.

William looked at her quizzically, "What's up?" he asked. "You look troubled."

"It's someone who's been involved with the murder investigations she's been beaten up and her house has been torched with her inside.

If it hadn't been for her neighbour, who risked his life to get her out, we'd be investigating another murder. She's been taken to the Victoria Infirmary. Grab your stuff we're going there now to talk to her."

During the car journey Angela told Bill about her involvement with Jackie Cosgrove.

"She sounds like a very tough lady," he commented. "And she's the one we're going to see in hospital? Who do you think would attack her and torch her house?"

"Someone who doesn't appreciate the work she does with working girls. She helps a lot of Eastern European girls escape from the gangsters who traffic them."

"So it's most likely gang related then," Bill said.

"If she's well enough to talk to us we'll know soon enough," Angela replied pulling up in the hospital car park.

The detectives made their way to intensive care where they were met by the staff nurse in charge of the ward. They quickly introduced themselves and showed her their identification.

"You're here for Miss Cosgrove," the nurse stated. "She's rather poorly, but she's been asking for you Detective Murphy. Just so you know what to expect, she's been badly beaten, her nose is broken, her eye socket is fractured, she has concussion and she's inhaled a lot of smoke. Her whole face is black and blue and her voice is little more than a whisper due to smoke inhalation. On top of that she's got broken ribs and severe tissue damage to her chest and abdomen."

"Thanks for warning us," Angela replied. "It sounds like she's in a terrible mess. Someone really worked her over."

"I hope you catch the people who did this," the nurse said. "From the state of her I believe they meant to kill her. It's a miracle she survived. God must have been looking out for her."

Angela and Bill followed the nurse as she led them to a bed in the corner of the small room. There seemed to be more machines than people in this ward and Jackie was attached to several by a system of wires and tubes. Even though she was prepared, Angela was shocked by the state of her. The nurse brought two chairs to the side of the bed and the detectives sat down with Angela placed closest to Jackie's head. When the nurse left them Angela spoke softly to Jackie and she stirred and opened her eyes.

"Hello, Angela," she whispered.

Angela could barely hear her.

Jackie slowly reached up and pulled down her oxygen mask. "It was the Albanians who did this to me." She took a gulp of oxygen then continued. "One of the wee girls escaped from them and came to me for help."

The effort of talking was a great strain on Jackie and she closed her eyes for a couple of moments and concentrated on drawing breath through the mask.

"They knocked on my door," she continued. "When I opened it they pushed me inside. One of them said to me, we run the girls in this town and you're interfering with our business."

Jackie began to wheeze. "Take a rest," Angela said kindly, "There's plenty of time."

"The wee girl was hiding in the bedroom and she made a bolt for the door when they pushed me into the lounge. She got away. 'Fuck off back to Albania', I said to them, 'and stop selling children in my country.' They were really angry."

"I'm not surprised, Jackie," Angela said. "I bet no one's ever faced up to them before."

"Look where it got me," she replied and tried to smile. "I'm too out-spoken for my own good. I think they might be the men who murdered my friends. They want to control all the girls who are working as prostitutes, Anne-Marie and Megan wouldn't have stood for that."

"I don't know if they're linked to the case, Jackie, but we'll certainly try to get them for doing this to you. Can you tell us anything about the men?"

"They were big, blonde and ugly. One had a deep red scar that ran from his eye to his mouth and from his mouth to his ear. It was very distinctive. The other had a tattoo of a cross on the back of his hand. I saw it when he waved his fist at me."

Once again Jackie drifted into unconsciousness and Angela sat patiently waiting for her to come round.

When she did she said, "Are you still here? Have I been asleep for long?"

"Just a few minutes," Angela replied. "You were telling me about the men," she prompted.

"Oh, yes, I remember. The next thing I knew Imran, my neighbour, was leaning over me, staring at me. He'd rescued me from the burning house and he laid me on the pavement. He was crying because he thought I was dead. I gave him a hell of a fright when I came to." Jackie started to laugh and her wheezing turned into a cough. "It only hurts when I laugh," she said.

"God, you're one brave lady," Bill said and his voice was full of admiration.

"You've got nice eyes," Jackie replied unable to stop herself from flirting.

"I don't believe you, Jackie," Angela said laughing. "You're lying here half dead and you still find the energy, somehow, to chat up my colleague."

"Well you said it, Hen, I'm only half dead. The other half is alive and kicking." Jackie tried to laugh but once again coughed alarmingly.

The nurse returned to the bedside, "I'm sorry Detectives, but that's enough for now. Jackie has been through a terrible ordeal and she needs to rest. You can return tomorrow and of course I'll contact you if she remembers anything else she wants to tell you."

After saying goodbye to Jackie, Angela and Bill left the hospital.

"Well, Bill," Angela said, "There's a job for you when we get back to the office. You can look at mug shots of Eastern European gangsters and see if any of them have distinctive scars or a tattoo of a cross on their hand. I don't know if either of them will be known to us but we have to start somewhere. I'm going to try and speak to a couple of people who might know the whereabouts of the girl that Jackie was hiding. We have to try and find her before the gangsters get hold of her or we might very well have another corpse on our hands."

"Do you really think they'd kill her?" Bill asked. "Surely she's worth more to them alive."

"She's worth a lot to us if she can identify them. Trust me if they find her they'll kill her. There's plenty more where she came from to replace her."

When they got back to the office Bill began the tedious trawl through the computer files. Finding either of the men that Jackie described was a long shot because these gangsters rarely got caught. Whenever a place became too hot for comfort they simply moved on and somebody else replaced them.

Angela made several calls. She contacted the heads of the local chapel, church and mosque. Because most of the women who were trafficked came from Eastern Europe it was most likely that the girl was either Moslem or Catholic. Angela thought she might try to seek sanctuary in a holy place. Angela also telephoned the contact number for the Street Pastors, an inter-denominational group of caring volunteers who policed the city streets at the weekend helping people in trouble. Jackie did a lot of work with the group. Sometimes they aided teenagers as they left the nightclubs too drunk and disorientated to look after themselves. Other times it was the homeless who needed a kind word from someone who cared that they existed. If Jackie's girl was on the streets then one of the Street Pastors might just come across her. Angela felt drained and she was relieved when eleven o'clock finally came and she could leave the office and go home. Her mind was so active from the adrenalin rush she doubted that she would get much sleep.

"Frank didn't say when he wanted me in tomorrow," Bill said. "He just said I should shadow you until he could work out a rota for me."

"My day starts at seven," Angela replied.

"But that's only eight hours away," Bill protested.

"Welcome to my world," Angela replied. "I told you it was Hell."

Chapter 37

Angela arrived in the office at five to seven only to find Bill already there and sitting at her desk. He was chatting to Paul and the two men were laughing. Angela didn't know why that image disturbed her so much, but it did. Perhaps she was jealous of the way the two men slipped easily into conversation when they'd only just met. There was no doubt in her mind that men found it much easier to be accepted in the job.

"Would you jump into my grave as quick?" Angela asked as she approached her desk.

"Sorry, just keeping the seat warm for you," Bill replied and he jumped up from the chair. He and Paul exchanged glances.

"We'll have to allocate you a desk and a computer to work at," Angela said. "Take Jack's desk, he won't need it today." She pointed to a desk at the other side of the room. "I think you should try and get through the rest of the files on the Eastern European gangsters. I make it past seven," she said looking pointedly at her watch. "If you plan to do any work today you'd better get started."

Bill looked at Paul who pursed his lips and raised his eyebrows. "I'm sorry. Did I interrupt your conversation?" Angela enquired. Paul gave a sigh and switched on his computer screen and Bill made his way to Jack's desk.

After a few minutes Paul spoke, "Tough night, eh? Bill's been telling me about Jackie."

Angela didn't answer she was in a mood because of lack of sleep.

"PMT?" Paul enquired. He was determined to get a reaction.

"I'm dead tired and I'm not in the mood for your chit-chat."

"If it's any consolation, I'm tired too because my little girl was up all night being sick."

"I'm sorry your kid was ill. How is she today?"

"Right as rain, typical, she was happily munching breakfast when I left and I'm a physical wreck."

"Serves you right for laughing at me yesterday. It's poetic justice. You deserve everything you get because you're a rotten bastard."

"And what did Bill do to deserve your wrath?"

"He sat on my chair and leaned on my desk," Angela replied tartly then she began to laugh. "I was a bitch wasn't I?"

"Yup, a class A bitch," Paul replied.

"Should I apologise?"

"Not on your life. You don't want him to think you're soft. Call over to him and have him fetch us coffees. He's now replaced you as bottom of the food chain. Enjoy it."

"Is that how it works here? Last in is the whipping boy?"

"That's how it is and that's how it's always been. You didn't think we were hard on you because you're a girl, did you? It was because you were the newby. You being a girl just made it more fun."

Paul was pleased that Angela was speaking again he hated it when she sulked because he always felt that somehow it was his fault. They worked on for a few minutes then the silence was broken by Bill.

"Eureka!" he shouted. "I've got him. I've found scar face. He's Russian not Albanian and he was deported two years ago."

Angela and Paul stood up and went over to look at Bill's computer screen.

"God he's ugly," Paul said.

"He looks dangerous," Angela added.

"He fits the description that Jackie gave us. Should I print a picture to take in and show her?"

"If he was deported how the hell was he able to return here?" Paul wondered.

"With a new identity, I guess," Angela replied.

"It's not too difficult especially if you have money and a guy like that would have shed loads of dosh," Bill added.

"Print the picture then we'll go straight to the hospital. This is a real breakthrough, good work Bill," Angela said.

Abandoning Paul to the office, Angela and Bill made their way to the car. A bit of good luck at last, Angela thought, maybe now we might actually catch one of the bad guys.

When they approached the intensive care unit they pressed the bell to be let into the ward. The sister in charge opened the door.

"We're here to see Jackie Cosgrove," Angela said. "How is she to-day?"

"You'd better come into my room," The sister replied ominously. When they were all seated she continued. "I'm very sorry to inform you that Jackie died half an hour ago. It was a pulmonary embolism, she couldn't be saved. We believe it was caused by the beating she took. She lost consciousness then died very quickly. She didn't suffer."

"But she was fine last night, she was even flirting with me," Bill replied, he was clearly shocked.

"I know it's hard to take in, but these things are almost impossible to detect. There was no way of knowing it was going to happen."

Angela felt sick to her stomach. She didn't know Jackie very well but she had gained enormous respect for her and the work she did. Now there was no witness who could identify the Russian, unless of course, they could find the missing girl, but they had no idea who she was or what she looked like. We're fucked, Angela thought, we're well and truly fucked.

Chapter 38

Jackie Cosgrove left this world the same way she came in, owning nothing. It turned out the house she lived in was rented and the fire destroyed all her worldly possessions, even the small cross and chain she wore round her neck was base metal. It was a very sad ending. The police made every effort to find her next of kin, but to no avail. Jackie Cosgrove had nothing and no one.

A week after her death over two thousand pounds had been collected by the Community Council for her funeral. It seemed there were people who cared about her after all and over a hundred of them attended her internment which was held at the Linn Cemetery. Members of her church spoke about all the wonderful work she did for the community and Angela was completely taken aback by their sentiments. She had no idea that Jackie had helped so many people.

The pavement outside her burned out home was carpeted in flowers. Dozens of bouquets began arriving within a few hours of her death and even local children left offerings. It was an amazing sight, who would have thought that a reformed prostitute would be mourned with such a genuine outpouring of affection and on such a scale? Both Angela and Liz Brown attended the funeral not just to represent the police force but also to pay their respects. After the service they stood in the gardens of the cemetery and talked.

"I want to get the bastards who did this," Liz said her voice full of outrage.

"At least we know who we're looking for," Angela replied. "If we could just find the missing girl and keep her safe. She must be absolutely terrified and she won't know who to trust. She was brave enough to go to Jackie's house so hopefully she'll turn up at a church or a hospital and ask for help. I've shown the photo of Nikolay Zhukovsky to everyone who'll look at it. He's one of the bastards who killed Jackie."

"My boss said there's to be an appeal on Crimewatch and they're going to show his photo on the 'most wanted' section of the programme. Surely someone will recognise him," Liz said.

"If he thinks he might be caught he'll simply disappear, he's done it before. The programme isn't going out for a couple of weeks, he could be anywhere by then."

"When does your uni course start?" Angela asked changing the subject.

"Not until September. You do know I'm going to be studying part-time don't you? You're not going to get rid of me that easily."

"I thought it was a full time course and I was disappointed that we wouldn't get the chance to work together again. I'm really pleased that I got it wrong because I value our friendship Liz. You're one smart cookie and you're good fun, a pain in the neck sometimes, but good fun."

"Thanks, I think," Liz answered and she laughed.

There was going to be a small tea in the church hall after the funeral but neither Angela nor Liz was inclined to attend. Instead the girls arranged to talk on the phone later then they said goodbye to each other and headed off home.

As Angela drove away from the cemetery she spoke aloud, "I promise you, Jackie, I'll catch the bastards who did this to you and I'll find the missing girl."

If every crime could be solved with steely willpower and grim determination then every criminal would be in jail and the streets would be safe.

The papers were now full of stories about Jackie Cosgrove. It's amazing how quickly things become old news. There had been nothing about the Southside Slasher for days. Instead there was outrage that asylum seekers and economic migrants were bringing crime to Glasgow and the tax payers were forced to support them financially. The murders of Margaret Deacon, Anne-Marie Connor and Megan Reece had drifted into obscurity. The threat from gangsters living on their doorstep was much more frightening to the public than a murderer who killed prostitutes. When it came down to it most people were only interested in themselves and that was good news for Thomas Malone.

Thomas loved driving the van and he went out in it every day. He'd never been to Prestwick before and now he could drive himself there and take a walk on the beach whenever he wanted. It wasn't the cleanest of beaches but he enjoyed seeing the walkers with their dogs and the waves breaking on the shore. The taste of the salt on his skin surprised him and the sounds of the gulls delighted him.

When Thomas arrived back at his street he immediately saw how dirty and shabby Govanhill was. He'd never realised that before because he'd had nothing to compare it with. Thomas parked in Alison Street outside the sweet shop because he hoped to see Nadia. He desperately wanted to show off his van to her. Her uncle Safdar was standing in the shop doorway and, as Thomas got out of the van, he stepped forward to speak to him.

"Are they your wheels?" Safdar asked.

"Yes, Safdar, I just got my van, it's great, isn't it?" Thomas said proudly.

"It looks new do you clean it every day?"

Thomas hesitated he didn't know the right answer. Safdar laughed and then Thomas realised that he was teasing him.

"Twice a day actually," he replied. "Don't you clean your van then?"

"No, ours is used for business not pleasure, I'm just happy when it starts. Mind you my car is used for pleasure and I don't clean it either" he added. "Cleaning is women's work. You need to find a woman

Thomas, I'm sure that there are lots of nice Scottish girls around," he added pointedly.

Thomas looked down the street and saw Nadia and Susan walking towards the shop.

"Well I'll say bye to you now, Thomas," Safdar said but he didn't move and Thomas realised that it was he who was expected to leave.

"Actually I've stopped outside your shop because I want to buy some sweets," Thomas replied and walked towards the door. "Is someone inside to serve me?" he asked.

Wait inside and I'll be right with you I've just got to talk to the girls first," Safdar said.

Thomas had no option but to enter the shop and wait inside. He was desperate to talk to Nadia, but when she did finally come in to the shop she and Susan went straight into the back with only a nod of acknowledgement.

Safdar walked round behind the counter, "Well, Thomas, what would you like?" he asked and a satisfied smile spread over his lips.

"Um," was all Thomas could say.

"It was sweets, you said. That was all you wanted wasn't it?"

"Um, of course," Thomas replied. "What else would I want in a sweet shop?"

"I don't know, Thomas," Safdar replied. "You tell me."

When Thomas left the shop he was raging. Safdar was going to be trouble.

'*He's got the measure of you,*' the voice said. '*You'll never get near her now. Better make a plan, can you do that? Can you? Can you take on a real man? I don't think so. You can't even get a girlfriend. You're useless, worse than useless. You're a fucking useless moron.*'

Thomas wanted to fight back to defend himself against the voice but his anger had subsided into helplessness. He felt weak and miserable and all he could do was weep.

* * *

Nadia saw Thomas standing outside the shop as she walked along the street with Susan.

"Oh no, that idiot's hanging around waiting to see me," Nadia said. "Your Dad's going to be livid."

"I told you talking to him would be trouble," Susan replied. "I don't know what you were thinking of."

"Look Susan we need a friend, someone our Dads won't suspect and he's all we've got. Oh dear, he's going into the shop and your Dad's waiting outside for us. What'll we do?"

"You're the smart one, dream something up genius."

The girls walked up to Safdar, "Hello Uncle," Nadia said. "We've got stacks of homework. You should be very proud of Susan she got top marks in a history test."

"Top marks, eh?" he replied frowning. Safdar wasn't sure if Nadia was playing him or not. He didn't think she was devious enough to lie. "Lots of homework, eh?" he said. "You girls go straight into the back shop and get your books out I've got a customer to serve. You remember your traffic warden, Nadia? The one who lets us park on a Saturday." Safdar stared pointedly at her looking for anything that would give her away.

"He's not my traffic warden, Uncle," she replied meeting his gaze. "I don't really know him."

"Aye, that's right Dad," Susan cut in. "You'd better not call him Nadia's traffic warden or people might get the wrong idea."

Safdar stared from one girl to the other and they both looked him in the eye. Maybe he was imagining things, they were good girls and he'd always been able to trust them. He wasn't so sure about Thomas though, but that wasn't any concern of the girls. Safdar walked behind Nadia and Susan and noted that they barely acknowledged Thomas as they scurried into the back shop to do their homework. Aye, he thought to himself, the problem is with him not my girls.

Chapter 39

One of Angela's colleagues had arranged a charity fundraiser for Yorkhill Children's Hospital and Angela was trying to make up a table to support the event. As it was to be held in the Stamperland Community Centre, which was only a ten minute walk from her home, she was looking forward to a night out where neither she nor Bobby had to drive. They had already asked Jake and his partner Miranda to join them but ideally they needed another couple to make up a table of six. Angela telephoned Liz who wanted to attend but she didn't have a current boyfriend to bring with her.

"I've an idea Liz," Angela said. "Leave it with me and I'll phone you later. There's someone at work I'd like to invite and he's gorgeous, trust me."

"Is he as good looking as your Bobby?" Liz asked. "I don't want just anybody and I don't want to look like a saddo who can't get a man."

"He's six foot four, muscular, gentle eyes, need I say more?"

"Why's he single then if he's so good looking? Has he got B O or Halitosis?"

"He smells great, shut up and let me ask him, I'll phone you right back."

"Oh, all right, but get a move on, the suspense is killing me. Oh, and by the way, I want a photo before Saturday night."

Angela hung up the phone, she didn't usually get involved with matchmaking but this was a perfect opportunity to introduce two people who she was sure would get on.

"Bill," she called over, "What are you doing on Saturday night?"

"Are you asking me out? I thought you were married," he replied cheekily.

"I am asking you out and yes, I am married. I'm trying to make up a table for Matt Turnbull's charity race night. It's for the children's hospital, will you come?"

"Where is it?"

"Don't worry it's at the Stamperland Community Centre so you'll be able to walk there and back."

"Just checking, Saturday night wouldn't be Saturday night if I couldn't have a pint or two. Who else is going?"

"Just me, my husband Bobby, his business partner and wife, oh and my friend Liz Brown, you'll like Liz she's cute and funny and she's a cop."

"Are you trying to arrange a blind date for me because I'm not comfortable with that?"

"Don't flatter yourself Liz doesn't need me to arrange a date for her. I'm just trying to make up the numbers that's all."

"Well if you put it like that I'd love to come. Does Liz Brown know that we're going to be the odd couple?"

"Actually she wouldn't care because she's coming out for an evening with friends, nothing more. You see not everyone's as paranoid as you."

Angela telephoned Liz immediately, "He said yes, and he's dying to meet you."

"What have you told him about me?" Liz asked suspiciously.

"Just that you're single, desperate and a saddo who can't get a man," Angela replied.

"That's okay then, I didn't want him to think he had any chance of romance."

"Anyway," Angela continued. "Come round to mine at about seven o'clock and we can walk up together, okay?"

"Yeah, yeah, I'll be there. I'll be the single, desperate saddo ringing your bell at seven o'clock. Gotta go, I'm wanted on a job, see you on Saturday."

Angela felt very pleased with herself maybe she was good at this matchmaking malarkey after all. She worked steadily and watched the hours tick by until it was ten minutes till lunch time.

"I feel as if this day will never end," she said to Paul.

"Me too, I hate paper work it's so boring. I've been willing the phone to ring for the last half hour."

No sooner were the words out of his mouth when Angela's phone rang. "That's your problem Paul, you've been willing the wrong phone," she said laughing.

When Angela answered the call she was told that a woman called Helen MacInnes was at the front desk and wanted to talk to her about Jackie Cosgrove. She immediately went out to meet her and showed her into an interview room. The two women sat down facing each other.

"I'm Detective Angela Murphy," Angela said offering the woman her hand. "How can I help you?"

"As you know my name is Helen MacIness, I'm a Street Pastor and I'm linked to Govanhill South Church. We have a drop-in centre at the church where we give people a cup of tea and a chance for company. It operates between six and eight every weekday evening. It's not open on the weekends because that's when we patrol the city centre streets through the night."

"I do know of your work and it's very commendable," Angela said.

"Anyway," Helen continued. "Last night a man came to the centre and spoke to me. He was obviously Eastern European by the look of him and his accent. He had a terrible scar on his face and I immediately thought of the man who murdered Jackie. I remembered being told the man you're looking for was badly scarred. Something about this man frightened me, he was sort of menacing although he was very polite." She paused and fished around in her handbag. "He gave me this photo and he told me he was looking for his daughter Tetiana Markin."

Angela reached out and took the photograph it was very crumpled as if it had been screwed up at some time. A waif of a creature with a child's face stared back from the photo. She looked about fourteen.

"He gave me a mobile number, I have it here," Helen said, handing Angela a scrap of paper. "He said I should phone him if Tetiana came into the centre. He said she's simple and can't look after herself. Do you think this could be the girl that Jackie was trying to help?"

Angela couldn't help grinning. "Helen, I could kiss you," she said. I'm sure this is the girl and now we have a picture of her and a name for her. The icing on the cake is the mobile phone number. If we can find this girl before he does then you may very well have saved her life."

Helen blushed, she pursed her lips, smiled and brought her hands together as if in prayer, "I hope you're right," she said. "She looks such a fragile wee thing and the man was chillingly calm. He really frightened me."

Angela didn't want to be rude but she couldn't wait to show Helen out so she could start looking for the girl. Once she'd gone Angela bounded back into the office and hugged a very startled Paul.

"Steady on," he said glancing about nervously to see if anyone had seen. "People will talk and I'm a married man."

"Stop being such a girl," Angela replied. "I've got great news. Look, here's a photo of the missing girl and this is the mobile phone number of the killer. Angela waved both items in Paul's stunned face.

"Bloody Hell, Angela, where did you get that?"

"One of the Street Pastors brought it in. She's spoken to the murderer."

"Bloody Hell," Paul repeated. "Go to the top of the class Murphy. We'd better tell the Boss, he'll be delighted. If this investigation went the way of the other murders I think he'd top himself. He couldn't cope with any more bad press."

"I'm dying to get out on the street and look for this girl now we know who we're looking for. I wonder where the hell she is. At least we know she's still alive and Nikolay Zhukovsky doesn't have her."

When Angela told Frank her news he was surprisingly reserved.

"We have to handle this very carefully," he began. "No one and I mean absolutely no one outside of this office must know where the information came from. We can't risk exposing your Street Pastor to danger. The condition of the photo is shite anyway, so I think we'll get an artist in to make a drawing of the girl and we'll get it shown on the television."

"Do you want me to phone for the artist now, Boss?"

"No thanks leave everything with me and I'll get it organised. As soon as we have the picture I want you to make copies and show it all over Govanhill. We have to be quick at locating her because the gangsters in the area will know there's a price on the wee lassie's head as soon as the picture is circulated. I think someone's hiding this girl because there's not been any sign of her. My guess is that she'll be in the company of a young man, perhaps a student from Langside College so make the college your first port of call."

"That's a good idea, Boss, I didn't think of it but it makes sense. She'd naturally be more trusting towards another young person and she's pretty, so she'd probably attract a young man."

"So we know where we are with this, yes?"

Angela nodded in agreement.

"I'm going to see if we can locate an address for the mobile phone. Now fuck off back to your desk and fill in Paul and Bill about what's happening. We've got to be ready to roll as soon as I've got the picture."

Angela turned to go out of the door.

"Oh, and Murphy," Frank said.

"Yes Boss," she said looking back.

"Nice job," he said smiling and gave her a thumbs-up.

Chapter 40

Thomas had the day off and what a horrible day it was, the icy rain fell in a deluge and the wind was gale force. Thomas didn't take holidays but his boss told him that he had to start taking days off because he was entitled to twenty six days of holidays a year. He was reluctant at first because he liked his job and, apart from his colleague Alan, there was nobody he spent time with. He'd planned to drive to the beach that day but he hadn't expected the atrocious weather so instead he got into the van and drove to the cinema complex at Springfield Quay. He'd watched two movies and had his lunch and now he was driving home.

As Thomas neared his street he drove past the private school. The bell had gone for the end of the day and pupils were pouring out of the gates. Slightly ahead of him Thomas saw Nadia but there was no sign of Susan. She was struggling with a heavy bag and trying to hold up the hood of her jacket while battling the wind and rain. Thomas drove ahead of her and pulled in at the kerb. He opened the window on the passenger side.

"Nadia, Nadia," he called as she drew level with the van. She hesitated and peered through the rain. "Nadia, it's me, Thomas, get in. You're soaked." A look of recognition passed over her face. Thomas leaned across the passenger seat and threw open the door. "Get in, Nadia before you catch your death of cold."

Nadia threw her bag onto the floor of the van and climbed in dripping water as she sat down. "Thomas, what are you doing here? Are you not working today?"

"It's my day off and I've been to the cinema. Do you want a lift to the shop?"

"No thanks, I'm going straight home, and besides, if Uncle saw me in your van I'd be grounded for life."

"Where's Susan? Why are you on your own?"

"She's gone with her Mum to visit relatives in Birmingham. It's her Mum's cousin so no relation of mine otherwise I'd have gone with her. I was just cutting through to get the bus home," Nadia explained. "I suppose I'd better get going."

"Don't go back out there it's torrential, I'll drive you home, where do you stay?"

"I can't be seen in your van. I'd get into terrible trouble."

"I'll tell you what," Thomas began. "You keep your hood up, nobody will recognise you in this rain, and I'll drive you home. I'll drop you a few doors away from your house and no one will be any the wiser."

Thomas was desperate to keep Nadia with him. He couldn't stop looking at her. Nadia's thin silky trousers were soaking wet and they clung to her shapely legs. Even with her hair dripping unflatteringly onto her face Thomas was mesmerised by her. He wanted her so badly he could taste it. Every inch of him ached for her.

Nadia really didn't want to go back into the wind and rain but she knew her father would kill her if she was seen alone in a van with a man. It just wasn't acceptable in any way. She sat contemplating her options.

Thomas restarted the engine, "I'm going to drive now Nadia, where are we heading?" he said making the decision for her.

"Newlands," she replied and she gave him her address.

As Thomas changed gear his hand brushed against Nadia's leg the feel of her was electrifying. "Sorry," he said, "The gears are a bit stiff." And that's not all that's stiff, he thought as he struggled with the accelerator.

Thomas and Nadia chatted effortlessly as he drove her home. They discussed her school and the movies he'd just seen. When they were nearly at Nadia's street Thomas pulled in and switched off the engine.

"I'd love to spend time with you, Nadia," he said. "You're such an interesting woman. You're so smart and you can talk about so many different subjects. I wish we could be friends."

"You're interesting too, Thomas," Nadia replied, flattering him. "You know how my Dad and my Uncle feel about Susan and me meeting men. Their plan is to marry us off in a couple of years time to men they approve of. Susan and I want to go to university we want to make our own choices, but in our community a father's word is law."

"But that's awful," Thomas replied. He was deeply shocked. Nadia was his girl, how could she marry someone else? "Do you know the man you're to marry? Does he live locally?"

"No and no," she replied. "But don't worry it's not going to happen because Susan and I are planning to run away."

Nadia told Thomas of their plans and her fears for the future. Now that she'd confided in him she felt better.

Thomas reached out and took her hand in his and he gently rubbed his thumb over the back of it. "Don't worry, Nadia, when the time comes for you to leave home, I'll help you. Whatever you need, I'll help you. I've got money and a job. I've got my own house and the van. I'm your friend now and I'll take care of you."

Nadia knew she was playing with fire after all Thomas was a virtual stranger. She felt a bit uncomfortable with him holding her hand but, she reasoned, he hadn't tried anything heavy he hadn't tried to kiss her. What harm could there be in a simple friendship?

"I've also got a mobile home in the country," Thomas continued. "It would be handy if you had to leave in a hurry. It's very comfortable and it's even got a cooker and a toilet. It would easily sleep two people."

"That's fabulous," she replied genuinely excited. "If we could go there it would give us time to make arrangements without being under pressure. If I can arrange some time away from the family could you show it to me?"

Nadia imagined herself and Susan as the two people sleeping in the mobile home but Thomas had other ideas.

"You let me know when you're free and I'll make the time." He lifted a scrap of paper from the glove box and wrote down his mobile phone number. He'd only received two phone calls in the past two months one from his work and one from Alan. "Put this somewhere safe," he said giving Nadia the number. "You can call me whenever you like."

The rain had died down a bit so Nadia thanked Thomas for the lift and she got out of the van. It was only a short walk to her home. She scurried away with her head covered and prayed that nobody had seen her. Thomas was so happy he could cry, Nadia was his girlfriend now, she really was his girlfriend and she wanted him to protect her. She'd chosen him over the man her father wanted her to marry, she'd let him hold her hand and she didn't complain when he touched her leg. He knew now that Nadia wanted him as much as he wanted her and he began to make plans for the future.

Chapter 41

The six o'clock news showed a picture of Nikolay Zhukovsky. The reporter asked, "Have you seen this man?" then continued, "Police are searching for Nikolay Zhukovsky in connection with the recent murder of Glasgow woman, Jackie Cosgrove. The public are warned not to approach this man who is considered to be dangerous. Nikolay has a very distinctive scar on his face which you can clearly see in the photograph shown on your screen. If you have any knowledge of the whereabouts of Nikolay Zhukovsky who may be using an alias, please contact the police immediately and I repeat, do not approach this man."

The news at ten carried the same report but also an artist's impression of Tetiana Markin. The news reader said, "Police are trying to locate a vulnerable girl, she is called Tetiana Markin. Tetiana went missing several days ago and she may be in hiding. Tetiana is not in any trouble. If you know the location of Tetiana please get in touch with your nearest police station or telephone the incident number that is being shown on your screen now. I must stress that Tetiana is not in any trouble but she may be frightened and she is considered to be vulnerable. Police are appealing to the public for help."

Nikolay Zhukovsky watched the reports with interest. So, my frightened little bird, you are still hiding, he thought to himself. Without you the police have nothing on me. His companion Alexander looked at him worriedly and asked, "What are you going to do about the police? Everyone will be looking for you. Should we leave Glasgow for a while till things settle down?"

"Alexander, Alexander, that is the difference between you and me," Nikolay said with a sigh. "That is why I am the boss and you are my employee. Without the girl there is no witness. The other woman is dead and her house burned down. We just have to find Tetiana before the police do.

"Everyone is looking for her, but she's hiding from us."

"Of course she is hiding, she wants to live, but do not worry we will find her and, when we do, I will make sure that she never talks."

"And what of you, Nikolay, will you hide from the police until we find the girl?"

"Once again Alexander you show me why I am the boss. I will not hide from the police. If they find me the worst they can do is deport me again. So I change my name and return, it costs me time and money nothing more. As long as they don't have the girl I am innocent of any crime."

After the photo of Nikolay appeared on television the police received two significant phone calls, one from a Russian grocer's and the other from a Russian restaurant. Both establishments were in the city centre. It seemed they'd received visits from Nikolay Zhukovsky and he was looking for a young woman. The owner of the restaurant was particularly disturbed by the encounter so Angela and Bill went to talk to him first.

The restaurant was in the city centre but only just. It was as far to the east of the centre as was possible, in a slightly run down area. It was constructed out of the whole ground floor of a tenement building and when Angela and Bill entered they were surprised to see that the layout was warm and inviting. A series of platforms divided the high-ceilinged space creating little booths to sit in and the whole place looked rich, decorated with fabrics of red and gold and lots of natural wood. The air smelled of cinnamon, apple and a rich meaty stew. Low lighting added to the cosiness of the surroundings. They were greeted by the proprietor who introduced himself as Sergei. He was a slightly built man, quiet spoken with small round spectacles perched on his small nose. He looked as if one good puff of wind would blow him away. Sergei invited them to sit down and, when they did, he placed a bowl of mixed nuts and dried fruit in front of them then offered them tea which they declined. He was a patient man and he waited to be invited to speak before relating his story.

"You said you were upset by a visitor to your restaurant, would you like to tell us about it?" Angela prompted.

"Two men, there were two men," Sergei began, his voice had a slight tremble in it and Angela realised that he was frightened even by the retelling of his encounter. "They came into the restaurant and they spoke to me in Russian, they were friendly at first. They ordered tea and plum cake." Sergei paused he took off his spectacles and rubbed his eyes. "I didn't know they were bad men. I didn't know I was exposing my family to danger," he said his voice rising as he became agitated.

"Take your time, please don't upset yourself, we're here to help you," Bill said kindly trying to reassure Sergei who was at risk of crying.

"I'm sorry, I'm very sorry, but I don't know if I can do this. I don't know if you can help me." Sergei stood up from the table as if to go and Angela immediately stood and placed her hand on his arm.

"If you are so frightened of these men, then telling me about them cannot make it any worse," Angela said. "If I find the men they'll be deported because they are in the country illegally, so if you talk to me the problem might go away for ever."

Sergei thought for a moment or two then he sat down again. He began, "One of the men, the one with the scarred face, asked me about my family and I told him I have a daughter. That is when he told me about Tetiana, his niece. He said that she'd run away from home and his sister was worried. He showed me a picture of a young girl and he said, 'she's a pretty little creature, what man would not want to sleep with her?' " I was shocked, she was a child.

Sergei removed his glasses and rubbed his eyes again and this time Angela was sure he was struggling not to break down. "Go on Sergei, you're doing really well," she prompted.

Sergei took a deep breath and began again. " 'Is your daughter pretty?' the man asked and I felt a chill run down my spine. 'What has my daughter to do with any of this?' I asked him. 'I am missing a teenage girl,' he continued 'and you have a daughter, perhaps your girl would like to work for me. She could replace Tetiana.' I was frozen with fear because I knew it was a threat. The man said he would return in a few days and I was to find the girl Tetiana or maybe he would take my daughter instead. I was terrified, so frightened that I sent my Ava to visit her cousin in London."

"That must have been horrible for you," Bill agreed. "What happened next?"

"Nothing, they just left, they didn't pay for their tea and cake and I didn't challenge them. I was so relieved that they were gone. Oh, there was one other thing. The man with the scar gave me a telephone number so I could get in touch if I found the girl. I have it here." Sergei produced a scrap of paper from his pocket and Angela recognised the number as the same one Helen, the street pastor, had been given. However, her excitement at getting the number from Helen had been short lived because when the phone was traced it was found on a table in a library where it had been abandoned. The owner of the phone, a young man called John Forbes, had reported it stolen when his car was broken into two weeks before.

Angela and Bill tried to reassure Sergei that everything would be all right. They told him he would probably never hear from the men again now as their pictures had appeared on television. Sergei stared at Angela when he shook her hand and she tried to hold his gaze to confirm her belief in what she'd said, but she couldn't, because the truth was she had no idea whether or not the men would return and she was pleased that Sergei's daughter was safe in London.

"That poor bugger's terrified," Bill said when they reached the car. "Can't say I blame him, Nikolay's one scary fucker and he's killed at least one person that we know about."

"It's so frustrating knowing the girl's out there and we can't find her. Where would you go if you were trying to hide from Nikolay?" Angela asked.

"I keep asking myself the same thing and the only answer I can come up with is as far away from Govanhill as possible."

They drove back to the station in silence each lost in their own thoughts. When they arrived at the office Angela updated Frank and Paul about the meeting at the restaurant then she sat at her desk with her head in her hands. She had the start of a sickening headache so she rooted about in her bag for some aspirin to nip it in the bud. Angela tried to swallow a couple with a gulp of coffee which was too hot and it burned her throat, now she had a headache and she couldn't swallow. Damn, she thought, this day just doesn't get any better. The second sip of coffee made her cough just as the phone on her desk began to ring so Paul reached over and answered it for her.

"Hello, Detective Murphy's phone, she's unavailable at the moment, can I help? It's Detective Costello here."

Paul was silent for a moment while he listened to the person who'd called. He scribbled down some notes then pushed the paper towards Angela. She glanced at it, 'girl sighted in Townhead, concierge of high rise on phone', the note read.

"I'll take the call," she croaked and reached for the receiver.

"Please put the caller through, I've got Detective Murphy here now," Paul said then he handed her the phone.

The caller introduced himself as Robin Carswell, head concierge in charge of four multi storey residential buildings in the city centre.

"I've seen the same girl every day now," he began. "I've got her on the CCTV. She waits until someone uses their security entry key then she walks into the building behind them before the door closes. The first day she took the lift and I saw her get off at the eighteenth floor. I assumed she was visiting someone but each day she's got off on a different floor. She always arrives late in the day then leaves early the next morning but I'm not sure where she goes in between. I was going to search some of the drying rooms later today because she might be spending the night in one of them. They're often unlocked and they're rarely used because most of our tenants would steal your Granny if they thought they could get a price for her. Nobody in their right mind would risk leaving their washing in them."

Angela was excited by the call, the adrenalin rush cut through her headache and after clearing her throat she spoke, albeit rather croakily.

"What time approximately does she come into the building and is it always the same building?"

"Aye, it's always the building at St Mungo Place and she usually arrives at the back of four."

Angela glanced at her watch it was two thirty. "I'm coming in to see you," she said. "It'll take me about half an hour. If the girl arrives before I get there try to ascertain which floor she gets out at but don't approach her. Thank you so much for calling Mr Carswell. I must stress the girl is not in any trouble. I'll be with you soon."

After saying goodbye Angela ended the call. "I think we've found our girl," she said to Paul. "I'm going to Townhead do you want to join me?"

"You always choose the most delightful places for our dates," Paul replied sarcastically. "If you don't mind I'll give this one a miss. Take Bill, I'm drowning under paperwork and I want to finish sharp today because I've got a hot date with my wife," he added with a wink.

"Suit yourself," Angela replied, "I'm happy to take all the praise for this and believe me there will be lots of praise."

"Knock yourself out," Paul said. "Keeping my wife happy is more than enough for me at the moment.

Angela and Bill arrived at Townhead at three-thirty, traffic had been hell and parking was impossible. It was going to be another long day but if she found the girl, it would be worth it. After driving round the estate twice and finding none of the parking bollards open Angela finally resorted to phoning Robin Carswell, she asked him to unlock one of them and he was only too happy to oblige.

"Anything for the police," he said. "You're always quick to respond when I need you."

He explained that lockable bollards were introduced because local residents often couldn't get parked on the estate because workers and shoppers had taken all the spaces.

"It's just a two minute walk from the city centre shops, universities and the Royal Infirmary," he said. "But the majority of the residents of Townhead don't own cars that's why so many bollards are locked at empty spaces," he added. Which kind of defeated the purpose, Angela thought.

They arrived at the concierge's office which was little more than a cupboard with television screens for the CCTV. It had a sliding glass window so the public could speak to the concierge. Angela noticed that the glass was reinforced and the door of the entrance was heavy and had an impressive locking system.

"You can't be too careful round here," Robin explained. "We get our fair share of junkies needing money for their drugs not to mention a never ending stream of aggressive drunks. Disneyland, it ain't," he said with a wry smile.

They squeezed themselves into the small space and Robin introduced Angela and Bill to his colleague Simon. There was hardly room to swing a cat but somehow Simon had managed to fit four plastic chairs into the space and they all sat shoulder to shoulder.

"I've got the first day's film on screen," Simon said. "It's got the clearest image of the girl because when she gets into the lift she stares straight at the camera."

They all peered at the screen and sure enough the image was that of Tetiana Markin.

"Oh, fantastic, that's our girl," Bill said enthusiastically.

"She's not come into the building yet, has she Simon?" Angela asked. "We're later than we intended to be because of the traffic."

"No, not yet and I've been watching the screen closely."

"You said she's done nothing wrong," Robin stated. "Has this got something to do with that Russian gangster who murdered the preacher?"

"We think he might be looking for her because she's from Eastern Europe and Jackie Cosgrove knew her." Angela replied. "She didn't want to tell him that Tetiana almost certainly saw the killers, but she was happy to give him something to satisfy his curiosity."

"Poor wee lassie must be awfully frightened," Simon said. "I wouldn't want to spend a night in one of those drying rooms. Sometimes we get rats in them because of the bin hatches. You're never more than three feet away from a rat you know."

"I guess she's more worried about the big rat that's looking for her," Robin answered and laughed at his own witticism.

They spent a very uncomfortable hour and a half in the stuffy little room drinking mugs of stewed tea and listening to Robin's tales of life in a high rise building. Angela was at breaking point, she couldn't stand Simon's body odour a moment longer and she was ready to give up and go home. It was now after five and there was still no sign of Tetiana. It would just be typical if after hiding out here for all this time she now decided to move and go somewhere else. Five- thirty came and went and Angela exchanged a worried glance with Bill. She was about to say something to the concierges and she was just about to put a limit on their vigil, when Robin spoke.

"There she is," he said excitedly pointing to the screen. "Can you see her? She's the girl with the carrier bag walking in behind that old couple."

"Yes, yes, I see her," Angela replied.

"She's going to get into the lift but how will we know what floor she gets out at?" Bill asked.

"Easy," Simon said, "Watch this."

Simon pressed a switch on the console and the screen changed to a picture of the inside of the lift. He fiddled about with another button and the camera turned to the panel in the lift that showed the floor numbers. The girl got out on the seventh floor.

"I think we should give her a couple of minutes to get settled then we'll go and look for her," Angela said. "Is there anything we should know about the drying rooms?"

"They're just big empty shells," Robin replied. "Most of them don't even have washing lines any more. We clear out rubbish from them every month because people are too lazy to take big items to the bin room. Sometimes you'll find a sofa or an old bed, perhaps that's what your wee girl's using. I'd better come with you though because without some kind of warrant, I can't let you wander about yourselves, health and safety," he explained.

Angela and Bill thought that was a load of rubbish and he just wanted in on the excitement, but there was no point in making an issue out of it. They waited another couple of minutes then all three headed for the drying room on the seventh floor. The concierge's room was in a different building to St Mungo Place but it took them only a couple of minutes to reach their destination. Angela was surprised at how warm and safe the lobby of the building felt and the lifts were clean and well maintained. She felt a jag of excitement as the elevator carried them to the seventh floor and her heart was pounding in her chest. Robin led them to the drying room.

"There's only one door in and out," he said, "So there's nowhere for her to run."

Angela pushed the door gently and it swung open revealing a dismal grey area. There was an old mattress on the floor in the corner of the room along with empty cardboard boxes which at one time had held appliances. At first there was no sign of Tetiana but Bill walked over to the boxes then turned to nod at Angela. He signalled for her to come to him.

"Her carrier bag is on the mattress," he whispered. "I think she's hiding in one of those empty boxes. My money's on the fridge freezer box because it looks big enough and it's complete."

Angela moved closer to the box but didn't touch it. "Tetiana," she said softly. "My name is Angela and I'm from the police. I'm here to help you. You're safe now Tetiana. Nikolay can't get you now. Please come out of your hiding place."

There was silence and no movement from the box. "Tetiana I'm not leaving without you. I promise you're safe now. I'm with the police and I was a friend of Jackie's."

The lid was lifted and a slightly built, skinny girl with dirty-blonde hair rose from the box. Angela offered her a hand and she took it and climbed out.

"Fantastic," Robin said. "Wait till I tell the wife, we'll be dining out on this for weeks."

Tetiana glanced about nervously then she said, "Nikolay and Alexander hurt Jackie. I saw them. They were going to hurt me so I ran away. I left Jackie and they killed her. She was my friend and I left her." Tetiana broke down in great gasping sobs, she was distraught. It was as if she'd kept her emotions in check for all the time she was hiding and now the dam had burst.

Angela placed her arm gently round the sobbing girl's shoulders. "There was nothing you could have done to save Jackie," she said kindly. "If you hadn't run away you too would be dead. I spoke to Jackie before she died and she was pleased that you got away."

The girl took some comfort from Angela's words but she was very sad. Bill and Angela thanked Robin for all his help then they led the exhausted girl to the car. When she was settled in the back seat they headed back to the station. They had only been driving for about ten minutes when the girl fell sound asleep.

"Now that we've got her how do we keep her safe?" Bill asked.

Angela had been thinking exactly the same thing. "The first thing we do is make an announcement to the media that she's been found and is in police custody. With a bit of luck Nikolay will have more to worry about then. I think he'll probably bolt."

"That still doesn't answer my question," Bill said. "She's not a prisoner so we can't keep her in a cell and she's not a child so we can't put her in a Children's Home."

"Looks like the Woman's Refuge would be the best place for her," Angela replied, "But first things first, let's find out what she knows and get the Boss to make that press release.

"I hope he doesn't try to steal your thunder, you deserve the kudos for this," Bill said.

"Either way he'll owe me," Angela replied. "As far as I'm concerned it's a win, win situation. Finding this girl is going to save his arse, he'll know it and I won't let him forget it."

"I must make sure never to cross you," Bill replied smiling, "You're much tougher than you look."

When they managed to question Tetiana she actually knew very little. She told them she'd expected to work as an au pair in London but instead she found herself in a dirty apartment in Glasgow where she was drugged and raped. She met Jackie when the older woman came to pay for another girl called Anya. Angela was pretty sure that it was the same Anya she'd seen at Jackie's house. Tetiana told them that Jackie had slipped her a piece of paper with an address on it when they passed each other in the hallway. One day Tetiana simply left the apartment, she just walked out the door and nobody stopped her then she made her way to the address she'd been given which turned out to be Jackie's home. The rest was history.

The discovery of Tetania made the 'News at Ten' and by midnight Nikolay and his associate, Alexander were in a Mercedes heading south. They would probably never be caught and Angela had resigned herself to that, but at least they would no longer be around to terrorise the people of Govanhill.

Chapter 42

It was Saturday morning and Thomas had the day off. He was on a mission and as usual he was meticulous about every detail. Later that day he was going to visit Alan's caravan and he had a checklist of supplies that he wanted to take with him. Everything had to be perfect before he brought Nadia to stay. He'd thought of every eventuality and had stocked up with a wide range of products from bottled water and Pot Noodle to toothpaste and toilet rolls. Once he took Nadia to the caravan she might be there for months so he had to have a week's worth of stuff at the very least, there was no point in taking just one of everything because that would never do. He also packed bed linen and cleaning supplies because he couldn't expect a girl of Nadia's class to stay in a dirty place or sleep on someone else's sheets.

By lunchtime the van was packed and Thomas was on his way. His face felt hot and his penis stiffened between his legs at the very thought of Nadia living with him in the caravan. Thomas was sure she'd be as excited as he was about the plan, after all, she was his girlfriend and girlfriends wanted to become wives. Thomas wondered if Nadia dreamt about him. He certainly dreamt of her and in his dreams she was always naked and he was making passionate love to her.

When Thomas arrived at the caravan he made himself a bite of lunch then he set about tidying and cleaning. It had to be of a much higher standard than Alan required. After a couple of hours all he had left to sort out was the box of Alan's fishing gear. He carefully tidied the flies and lures and put them into a plastic box then he went to place the box in a canvas fishing bag. As Thomas lifted the bag a bundle of magazines caught his eye and when Thomas lifted them he saw that they had nothing to do with fishing. The magazines were full of pictures of naked girls in seductive poses. Thomas was shocked and fascinated at the same time, surely these couldn't be Alan's he thought, but of course they had to be.

Thomas was intrigued by the magazines there was something deliciously dirty about them. He felt like a naughty schoolboy as he flicked through the pages but he couldn't put them down. Thomas's hand slipped inside his trousers and into his underpants and he massaged his genitals. He imagined Nadia's face on the bodies of the girls pictured pinching their nipples or fingering their crotches. After only fifteen minutes he'd climaxed twice and was so spent that he fell asleep. When he woke he felt rather alarmed by the unfamiliar surroundings and it took him a moment or two to remember where he was. Then he saw the 'Hot Babes' magazine beside him on the bed and it all came flooding back to him.

Thomas decided to stay longer at the caravan than he'd first intended. All the work he'd wanted to do was complete so he carried a deck chair outside and set it down in a spot that was sheltered from the wind. He lifted a magazine called 'Bondage' with him. He'd noticed an article called 'Wife in Chains' and he wanted to read it because it mentioned the word 'wife'. Perhaps it would teach him something about how to look after his wife he thought.

The story began by telling the readers about Marvin and Hank. They were mountain men living in a remote region of America. Marvin had a wife and seven kids, five of them girls but Hank had nobody. It turned out that Marvin owed his friend Hank a lot of money but he couldn't pay him so instead he offered to give him one of his daughters to take for a wife. They arranged that Marvin would bring the girl to Hank's cabin high up in the mountains so Hank could have sex with her and see if he wanted to keep her. When the girl realised what was about to happen she tried to run away but her father held her down. 'As soon as my cock was in that hot little hole I knew she was the girl for me,' Hank said. The two men struck a bargain and Marvin headed for home leaving his daughter behind. The girl cried and cried for her Mama and tried to escape at every opportunity so Hank chained her to a tree. When the girl realised that she could no longer run away she became subdued and she was easier for Hank to manage. Hank attached a heavy metal ring to the inside of the cabin so he could keep his wife chained up inside. 'Once she knew who was boss she was real nice to me,' Hank said. He went on to describe various sexual acts he made his wife perform and he told the reader that the best sex is when a woman is in chains and controlled by her man. Thomas was really turned on by what he'd read and once again his thoughts focused on him having sex with Nadia.

'*The only way you'll stick your dick in her cunt is if you tie her down,*' the voice said nastily. '*She won't want a weak little fucker like you.*'

"You're wrong she loves me," Thomas replied.

'*She doesn't love you. She hardly knows you. Do you think she'd choose this poxy caravan over her home in Newlands? I don't think so,*' the voice taunted cruelly.

"Once she's here for a while she'll realise that I'm the only man for her, she'll love me and she'll want to stay with me."

'*After a while maybe, if you're her only option. But what about when you first bring her here, what then? She won't want a useless fucking moron like you. She'll run away home to* her *mother. The main road's just a couple of minute's walk away it's not like being stuck in a remote cabin in the mountains.*'

She won't run away, I won't let her, Thomas thought. She can't escape if she's chained to the caravan. She'll have no one else to look after her. She'll have to love me or I won't give her food, she won't want to starve to death. She'll have to make me happy and do as she's told, just like Hank's wife.

* * *

Bobby had brought Angela breakfast in bed and they sat munching toast and reading the Saturday papers. For once the paper boy had managed to get all the papers through their letter box without ripping any of them. Angela was still on a high from the discovery of Tetiana Markin. The girl couldn't tell them much when they found her on Thursday because she was so exhausted, but Friday was an entirely different matter. When shown mug shots of known Eastern European criminals she not only picked out Nikolay and his accomplice Alexander but she also identified a man called Boris Kinsky who she said was a polite man with an educated voice. He met her and three other girls at the airport in London. It was Kinsky who told them that he was taking them to their hotel but instead drove them to a disused warehouse building where they were drugged and raped repeatedly by him and several other men. It was a real breakthrough because now they had a name and photograph of one of the London gangsters who made up the chain.

When Frank realised just how much Tetiana knew he moved her from the Women's Refuge to a safe house in East Kilbride, a small town south of Glasgow. The London boys were going to keep an eye on Boris Kinsky in case Nikolay and Alexander showed up and, in the meantime, Frank couldn't risk someone getting to Tetiana as she was their only real witness. Frank was so happy with the turn of events that he bought cream cakes for the entire office. He even fetched Angela a cup of coffee and bowed as he placed it on her desk.

Now it was Saturday and she was sitting up in bed having been given the day off. She was eating breakfast prepared by her husband and reading a newspaper that hadn't been ripped. It didn't get much better than this. Angela was looking forward to the race night and Jake, Miranda and Liz were coming round at seven so they could all walk up to the Stamperland Club together. Bill was meeting them there because Angela didn't want to force him and Liz into each other's company too soon. If they all walked up together it might seem like they were expected to be a couple instead of two individuals who were simply part of the same group. Angela enjoyed Miranda's company and she was happy to have the opportunity of socialising with her. It would be their first proper evening out together since Bobby and Jake formed their partnership and Angela was anxious to know if Miranda was as happy about it as they were.

Angela and Bobby had a very lazy day. They didn't get out of bed till two o'clock and they only rose then to search for food because they were hungry. It was to be the first full day off they'd shared together in weeks and they were going to enjoy every minute of it. Unable to find any food in the house that they fancied, Angela and Bobby strolled down the main road till they reached a local tearoom where they ordered soup and a sandwich. On the way back Bobby bought a bunch of spring flowers from the florist and presented them to his delighted wife.

"I just wanted to say thanks, Darling," he said. "I know the last few months have been Hell but everything will be fine now. Business is booming and I'm so well organised that I can even take a whole day off. Thanks to you my life has completely changed. I wouldn't have risked it if you hadn't supported me."

Angela didn't know what to say. So instead she smiled at Bobby, took his arm and squeezed it and they headed for home. The truth was she'd hated the change in circumstances so much in the beginning and she'd been so selfish and spoilt that it practically cost them their marriage. Now the sweet man was buying her flowers she didn't deserve. Angela's job with the police had certainly changed her in the last few months, she'd grown up a lot and she much preferred the person she'd now become.

Even though she'd had all day to prepare, at five to seven Angela was still fiddling about with her hair straighteners and when the doorbell rang heralding Liz's arrival she screamed for Bobby to answer it. Liz had only met Bobby once before but he immediately put her at her ease by offering her a glass of white wine which she accepted. She'd just taken the glass when the bell rang again and Bobby disappeared to let Jake and Miranda in. They too accepted wine and then all four

Elly Grant

stood in the kitchen chatting until Angela came downstairs. They were surprised to discover that Jake went to school with Liz's older brother.

"It's a small world isn't it?" Miranda said.

"So sorry I'm late," Angela said as she entered the room. "I've been having a bad hair day," she explained. "Have you all been talking about me?"

"Don't flatter yourself, Murphy," Liz cut in. "We didn't even miss you," she said teasingly.

"Thanks a lot Brown," Angela replied. "It's so nice to be appreciated."

The conversation and banter continued for another ten minutes then they all thought they'd better be on their way.

"If we don't get a move on Bill will think we're not coming," Angela said.

"And we can't have poor Bill fretting there on his own," Liz added. The truth was that she felt quite anxious and excited about meeting him. She'd asked around her colleagues and those of them who'd met Bill had a high opinion of him.

On the walk to Stamperland the group bumped into another two girls who were colleagues of Liz and after introductions they continued the journey together. Liz liked the other girls but she didn't really want to hang around with them and she hoped they were at a table as far away from her as possible. Like her, the other girls were single, and she didn't want either of them to get their hands on Bill before she'd had a chance to get to know him.

When they reached the club house Bill was pacing about outside, "I thought you said seven," he said showing his watch to Angela. "It's now gone seven-twenty-five, nearly seven-thirty, did I get it wrong?"

"Sorry Bill, you got it right, we're late because of me. "Let me introduce you to everyone then we'll get inside."

Liz's colleagues didn't hang around for the introductions but instead they hurried inside. Angela quickly introduced her group to Bill then they too entered the Club and went to find their table. From their first tentative 'hello' Liz and Bill fell into an easy conversation helped by their exchange of stories about what it's like to work with Angela.

"You two better say nice things about me," Angela said shaking her finger at them as a warning. "Remember, I'm the Boss," she joked.

"Ooh, I'm frightened," Liz quipped.

"Tremblin'," Bill added and the pair clutched each other in mock fear.

The evening went well and their table made some good choices in their betting, but on the whole, the charity made quite a lot of money out of them. At the end of the races the bar stayed open and people were encouraged to linger a while and spend more of their money. Angela had enjoyed her evening chatting to Miranda. It was clear that Jake had needed Bobby because he could no longer cope with the vast amount of work and, of course, Bobby had brought to the table the opportunity of extending the electronics sales.

"I got quite a surprise when I came home early last Wednesday to find the secretary in my house," Miranda said. "I didn't even know that the boys had hired Olivia. But Jake explained that she works a half day at our place and the other half day at yours to help with the paperwork. I was a bit annoyed that she'd used our en-suite bathroom but she explained she didn't see the door to the main one and she was desperate."

Angela was stunned, she'd never heard of Olivia and Bobby was always moaning about his paperwork surely he'd have told her if he'd hired someone.

"Well what do you think of her? I think she's very young and very pretty, I just hope she's good at the job," Miranda added.

"What do you think of your new secretary?" Miranda said turning to Bobby. The conversation between Jake and Bobby stopped and a sick look passed over Jake's face, before he could say anything Bobby answered.

"You didn't tell me you'd hired us a secretary, that's great. When does she start and how many days will she work?"

Jake looked helplessly at Miranda. Her face twisted with rage and she threw him a look that could kill.

"You brought a whore into our house, into our bedroom. She used the en-suite for God's sake."

The whole room went silent.

"Shush, Miranda, you're making a scene, we'll talk about this at home," Jake replied in a loud whisper.

"Making a scene," Miranda shouted. "No, this is making a scene," she said standing up and slapping Jake hard across the face. There was a murmur from other tables. "Have you seen enough," Miranda shouted swinging round and the room fell silent again. "Don't worry, I'm leaving now. You can all talk about me when I've gone." She grabbed her bag and jacket from the back of the chair and with tears streaming down her face she ran to the door.

"Sorry, I'm very sorry. I'd better go after her. I'll phone you tomorrow, Bobby," Jake said and he raced after Miranda."

"The lying cheat," Liz said. "That was awful, poor Miranda."

"Did you know anything about that?" Angela asked Bobby angrily.

"N no, nothing," Bobby answered. "I've always known Jake had an eye for the girls. He's always flirted, but I knew nothing about this. I promise you."

"He took a stranger into their home and had sex with her in their bedroom. It's a terrible betrayal. I don't know if their marriage can survive this," Angela said. "I don't think I could forgive a stunt like that."

"Lucky you'll never have to," Bobby replied. "I'm not like Jake."

"I don't know about you guys, but I'm ready to leave," Bill said. "I'm feeling a bit uncomfortable being the centre of everyone's attention."

"Yeah, me too," Liz said. "The people at the other tables keep looking over and talking. Let's get out of here."

They stood, gathered their belongings and walked towards the door. Bill invited everyone back to his for coffee but only Liz accepted. Angela and Bobby just wanted to get home.

"Bill and Liz seemed to hit it off," Angela said as they sat unwinding and sipping coffee in their lounge.

"As one relationship ends another begins," Bobby answered philosophically.

I hope Jake and Miranda can get over this because I don't want anything to harm Bobby's business Angela thought selfishly. I don't want us to lose everything Bobby's worked for just because Jake can't keep it in his pants.

Chapter 43

Angela tossed and turned all night, she just couldn't sleep. She was really shocked by Jake's betrayal of Miranda and also by the way he'd included Bobby in his lie without even forewarning him. Not that Bobby would have supported him, but at least the scene at the Club could have been avoided. She felt sick for Miranda. Imagine being put in that position by someone who's meant to love you. Angela used to like Jake, but now she'd lost all respect for him and she definitely didn't want to have anything more to do with him. But there posed the problem, with Bobby being in business with Jake they couldn't avoid having some contact. At six o'clock Angela gave up trying to sleep and she went downstairs to make herself some coffee and toast. Within ten minutes Bobby had joined her.

"I see you can't sleep either," he said, "It's a bloody mess this business with Jake. I'm not sure what to do."

After a few moments of thought Angela replied, "I think you should just carry on as normal. There's no problem with the business and it's not like you have to go round to their house very often, you said yourself that everything's done by computer. Leave Jake and Miranda to sort it out, I'm sure this isn't the first time they've had problems. He's probably cheated on her before."

"You're absolutely right, I'll ignore it and hope it goes away and with a bit of luck Miranda will do the same thing. I just want things to get back to the way they were before, I know I'm being selfish and

I should be thinking about poor Miranda, but the truth is, I don't care about anyone else but us."

At seven o'clock they both went back to bed and within minutes they were sound asleep. Angela stirred at eleven feeling groggy, second sleep often made her feel that way and she struggled to fully wake up. The phone beside her bed began to ring at eleven-fifteen and she was dragged back to consciousness. She fumbled for the receiver dropping it onto the carpet, "Just a minute," she called as she reached to retrieve it.

"Hello, hello, Angela. It's Liz."

"Just a minute I dropped the phone, I'm here now Liz. I didn't sleep well last night so I'm still in bed. What's new?"

"I've loads to tell you about Bill, can we get together for a chat later?" Liz asked excitedly.

Angela didn't really want to leave the house and she didn't want to ask Liz round in case she stayed too long. She was tired and she wanted the day to herself.

"Bobby's working from home and I'm helping him with paperwork," she lied. "Because as we both know, he doesn't have a secretary."

"Wasn't that awful last night?" Liz asked. "How shocking for you and Bobby, not to mention Miranda, Bill and I were chatting about it when we got home. Could you manage to meet me at the Derby cafe for a cup of coffee, just for an hour? It's only a couple of minutes walk from your place and I'll even buy you some Pavlova and ice-cream. I've so much to tell you."

"Oh go on then, you've twisted my arm." Angela looked at the clock on the bedside table, "How about twelve-thirty? That will give me time to shower. The coffee and Pavlova can be my lunch. You'd better have some tasty gossip because I really didn't want to leave the house today."

"Trust me, I won't let you down," Liz replied. "See you soon, prepare to be surprised, bye now."

The phone went dead and Angela dragged herself out of bed. She was now fully awake and she wondered what news Liz had to tell."

The walk to the local bistro in the cool fresh air made Angela feel much better. The road was practically empty as she walked along, Sundays were often like that. Angela was looking forward to hearing Liz's news. She'd hoped that Liz and Bill would hit it off. When she entered the Derby it was surprisingly busy but luckily Liz was already there, seated at a table by the window

"Would you like something more solid to eat for lunch?" Liz asked. "I'm going to have a croissant and bacon before the Pavlova."

Realising that she hadn't eaten anything since six that morning Angela accepted Liz's suggestion.

When the coffees arrived Angela said, "Right Liz, you've bribed me to get me out of my comfy pit, now spill, tell me everything that happened last night and spare nothing, I'm not easily shocked."

"Well," Liz began, "when we got back to his house he made us some food, he's quite handy in the kitchen. He told me all about his career and his ex-wife. They married too young you know."

"Yes, yes, I know all this," Angela said impatiently. "Tell me something I don't know."

"I phoned my brother Michael this morning, he told me he knew Jake quite well and they were much closer than Jake let on," Liz began. "Michael not only went to school with him but they were actually quite good friends until two years ago. It seems that Jake and his girlfriend were out for a drink with Michael and his wife Barbara when Miranda turned up at the same bar with her work colleagues. Jake tried to pass off the girlfriend as an associate but Michael said Miranda saw right through him and she was livid. Michael and Barbara were very embarrassed by the whole thing. They'd never met Jake's wife only a series of girlfriends. Michael stopped seeing Jake after that, the truth is Barbara wouldn't let him go near Jake again she was disgusted by his behaviour. So you see this isn't the first time it's kicked off like that. Jake is a serial womaniser and Miranda puts up with it."

"I don't know whether I feel better or worse knowing that," Angela replied. "On the one hand I'm so sorry for Miranda. Jake really is a shit. But on the other hand if this happens all the time then it shouldn't affect Bobby's business." Angela bit into her croissant and chewed slowly.

"Bill kissed me, I spent the night on his sofa and we're going out tonight for dinner and a movie."

"What? What did you say?" Angela responded, once again giving Liz her full attention.

"Bill kissed me, I spent the night on his sofa and we're going out tonight for dinner and a movie," Liz repeated.

"That's great news I knew you two would get on. When's the wedding?"

"Hold your horses, Murphy, it's just a first date don't let your imagination run wild.

"But you like him, you like him a lot?"

"What's not to like?" Liz said. "He's gorgeous."

The girls chatted about this and that and after the food was finished Angela brought the get-together to an end as she was in a hurry to get home to Bobby. Angela was concerned by what Liz had told her about Jake because he and Bobby were very good friends, surely if Michael had known what he was like so must have Bobby. If Bobby did know more than he let on did he condone that kind of behaviour? Angela wracked her brain trying to remember all the times Bobby and Jake had gone out together for a drink. Did Bobby have a string of girlfriends too? Angela felt unsettled she didn't know what to believe. When she returned home Bobby was getting ready to watch Formula One on television, he had the essential supplies set out on the coffee table, beers, crisps, chocolate biscuits and more beers.

"Hi, Darling," he said as Angela entered the room. She slouched into an armchair. "Nice chat with Liz?"

Angela didn't want to get into a discussion about Jake because she was tired but she couldn't help herself.

"Funny you should ask," she began. "Liz had quite a lot to say about Jake."

"No wonder, that was quite a scene last night," Bobby replied.

"She wasn't only talking about last night. It seems her brother Michael and Jake were rather good friends until a couple of years ago. I was quite surprised to hear that because you and Jake are good friends and you never mentioned a Michael."

Jake sat in silence his face became serious.

"Liz also said the reason Michael and Jake are no longer friends is because of Jake's appalling behaviour. Michael didn't want to be associated with a lying, cheating bastard and that made me wonder why you are still Jake's friend."

"Okay, okay, you're right," Bobby said holding his hands in front of him in a placatory fashion. "I knew all about Jake's womanising. Why do you think it took me so long to agree to work with him? I was so desperate to get out of teaching if the devil offered me a job I'd have taken it."

"And all the times you went for a drink together," Angela couldn't finish the sentence but the implication was clear enough.

"It was just a drink, I promise you, nothing more."

"Then why did you hide it? Why did I have to find out for myself? I thought we didn't have any secrets."

"Look, Angela," Bobby said becoming annoyed. "I've done nothing wrong. I didn't lie to you. Jake's behaviour was his own business it had nothing to do with me. We're no longer close friends I simply work with the guy. Can we drop it now, please?"

Angela was too upset to talk any more so she left Bobby to the Grand Prix and his beers. She went upstairs to their room and lay down on the bed to think. There was nothing she could do about the past, but she'd make damn sure Bobby and Jake never socialised alone again, and in the future, if Bobby went out for a drink with his friends, Angela would want to know every tiny detail.

Chapter 44

Saturday had been a wonderful day for Thomas and he'd enjoyed every minute of it. When he left the caravan he brought Alan's magazines home with him and they'd opened up a whole new world to him. He spent Saturday night reading the articles stopping only to masturbate and sleep. Thomas hadn't realised that God created women to care for men. Thanks to the magazines he now knew that women liked to be dominated by a strong man and they enjoyed serving their partners sexually at all times of the day and night. One man even wrote that he sometimes shared his wife with his friends when they were having a social evening drinking and playing cards. Thomas would never share Nadia. He'd kill her before he'd let another man touch her. She was his and his alone.

Thomas was angry at his mother for denying him his father while he was growing up because he had no one who could teach him about sex or about how to look after a woman. At least Alan had helped him by leaving the magazines for him. Thomas felt he should be doing something to thank Alan and his wife Ann for giving him the van and the caravan, especially with Ann now being ill. He hadn't even been to see them even though Alan had invited him several times. He always made excuses.

Thomas was planning to go to the Barras market to pick up a couple of things for the caravan but he reckoned that a half hour detour would be possible first. Armed with flowers and chocolates he'd bought in ASDA, Thomas rang the bell of his friend's house.

"Thomas, you're a sight for sore eyes. Alan, it's Thomas," Ann called when she opened the door to find him on the front step proffering his gifts. "Come in, come in, you must have smelled the coffee. You'll have a cup won't you? And a wee sandwich?"

Thomas was led into the front room where Alan was fiddling with the television.

"Hi Thomas, nice to see you, I'm planning to watch the Grand Prix later and I'm just checking when it starts," he explained. "Do you want to stay for lunch and watch it with me?"

"Sorry Alan, I can't, I'm meeting Mary later. I'm driving her to see her aunt. Mary wants me to meet the old Dear." The lie slipped easily off Thomas's tongue.

"I see, meeting the family now. Next thing you'll be getting engaged. Won't he Ann? I said next thing he'll be getting engaged."

Thomas's face flushed red, the very thought of getting engaged to Nadia thrilled him.

"Now look what you've done Alan, you've embarrassed the lad. Take no notice of him Thomas he's just teasing you," Ann said kindly. "Anyone who's as thoughtful as you deserves a kind girl like your Mary. And by the way, you can drop in to see us any time, you don't need to bring flowers and chocolates, but it was very nice of you to do it. Now, what would you like in your sandwich, ham or cheese?"

It took Thomas over an hour to escape from Alan and Ann and when he eventually stepped out of their house he inhaled deeply. The cool fresh air filled his lungs and relaxed him. He'd been wound tight as a spring in the claustrophobic atmosphere of their home. Between Ann's fussing, their little dogs yapping and Alan's jokes, he would have exploded had he been stuck there any longer.

Sitting in his van Thomas felt free as he drove towards the east end of the city and the Barras market. He'd always loved the Barras because it opened at the weekend and sold everything from butcher meat to double beds. In its heyday you'd find half of Glasgow there on a Sunday, it was a cheap day out and very entertaining. The stall holders each had a spiel and 'Glasgow Harry' put on nothing short of a show with his banter. Sadly now, things had changed. Sunday television and out of town shopping centres kept the people away and more and more stallholders retired without being replaced. However, to Thomas, it was still a magical place and as he climbed out of the van the familiar acrid smell of mussels and vinegar filled his nostrils. He felt more comfortable walking these dirty streets and shopping at the mish-mash of stalls than anything the high street had to offer.

Thomas made his way to the large hardware store on the corner. It was a wonderful place that seemed to sell everything. The shop was very old fashioned and probably hadn't changed much in over seventy years. He was served by a slim middle-aged man wearing a brown overall. Thomas explained that he wanted a length of chain to use as a gate and the man suggested a length of ten feet. He also sold Thomas two sturdy metal poles to sink into the ground and two metal rings to attach to the chain. The items weighed too much for him to carry any distance so he told the man that he'd be back in a couple of minutes with his van.

As he left the shop Thomas felt elated because he'd been able to buy exactly what he'd come out for and, even better, the man had explained how to fit everything together. All he needed now was the handcuffs and he knew that he could buy them in Tam Shepherds the joke shop.

When Thomas returned to the hardware store he also bought tools, screws, nails and some pieces of wood. He would have to make a hole in the caravan wall for the chain to fit through and he'd also have to board up the window. He didn't want Nadia to be able to run away or call for help. After a while she'd get used to being there and she'd love him just like the woman in the story, 'wife in chains'.

All through Sunday night thunder crashed, lightning flashed and the rain came down in torrents. Wind howled through the streets rattling roof tiles and windows in their frames. This was not a normal April shower but a full blown storm and Thomas slept right through it. By the time he arose on Monday morning after a good night's rest the weather had improved and only a slight smur of rain remained. When Thomas met Alan on the street corner to begin their shift the older man was in a jocular mood.

"It was really nice to see you yesterday, Son," he said. "My Ann was delighted with the flowers and chocolates. How was your day with Mary?"

"Great, it was great," Thomas said. "Her auntie was nice," Thomas said unable to think of anything else to say.

"I don't know why the streets are so busy today," Alan continued. "We'll have no bother filling our quotas."

"I was going to ask a wee favour," Thomas said. An idea had just popped into his head.

"Ask away, I might say no, but if you don't ask you don't get."

"I'd like to finish early today I've an errand to run for Mary. Could you cover for me? I'll make it up tomorrow or I could cover for you another day if you'd like."

"No problem Son, how early do you need away? We're due to finish at four today."

"Three would be great I just need an hour off."

Thomas had a plan and he wanted to see Nadia when she got out of school. If he parked the van outside the school gates he'd see her as she left and they'd be safely out of sight of the shop and her uncle Safdar.

All day long Thomas kept one eye on the job and one eye on his watch, the minutes ticked by interminably. Eventually three o'clock came and he said bye to Alan then raced home for his van. By three-twenty he was parked across from the school gate and at three-thirty he heard the bell ring. Pupils piled out of the school and the small gate created a bottleneck of bodies and bags. Thomas saw Nadia as she exited the playground, she was beautiful. As he stared at her he saw a shorter, plumper girl with a skirt so small that it barely covered her behind run up to Nadia and push her in the back causing her to stumble. Thomas leapt from the van he was outraged. The girl was screaming at Nadia who'd risen to her feet. Thomas could see that her knee was hurt and she limped slightly as she tried to get away from the girl. Thomas rushed over to Nadia and grabbed her arm.

"Are you all right," he asked her ignoring the red-faced screaming banshee who was still shouting abuse.

"Oh, it's you Thomas," Nadia replied, clearly still shocked by the attack. "I'm okay thanks."

"Is this your boyfriend, Nadia?" The girl asked looking pointedly at Thomas. "Wait till your Dad hears about this," she added nastily.

"Get lost, Brenda," Nadia replied. "I don't want anything to do with you or your horrible friends and I certainly didn't look at your poxy boyfriend. Now go away and leave me alone."

The girl turned to Thomas, "I'll remember you," she said with a sneer. Your secret's not safe with me. Wait till Nadia's Dad or better still her uncle hears about you. Your life won't be worth living. And as for you, you bitch," she said once again addressing Nadia, "You don't have your cousin to protect you so watch your back, I'm gunning for you and I'll get you, you stuck up cow."

Thomas saw that the girl had some friends waiting for her on the sidelines so he led Nadia to the van and opened the door for her.

"You'd better get in and let me drive you home," he offered. "You'll be much safer with me in the van than risking them following you and attacking you again."

Nadia nodded her head docilely she was rather upset and Thomas saw tears well up in her eyes. As he drove she began to calm down and after a few minutes he began to speak.

"I came to talk to you because I wanted to arrange a suitable date and time for me to show you my caravan in the country," he said. "Will it be possible for you to come with me?"

With Susan still away with her Mum, Nadia was bored to death because she was either stuck at school or stuck in the house. She thought about a trip to the country and she really wanted to go. Nadia hadn't ever been anywhere on her own, it would be an adventure, she thought. She felt safe with Thomas because he obviously liked her and he was in an official job so he must be trustworthy, and besides, being a traffic warden meant he'd probably be a good driver.

After thinking about the logistics, finally she spoke, "I can't do anything this weekend because it's far too soon. I'll tell my folks that I've an art project to do and I'll ask my Dad to drop me at the Kelvingrove Gallery a week on Sunday. I've done that before so it should be alright. He'll leave me at about one and he won't come back for me until five o'clock so we'll have about four hours, will that be long enough?"

Thomas felt a surge of excitement, his heart pounded and his face felt hot. He was thrilled by her reply. "That'll be perfect, absolutely perfect," he said, "The land is only an hour's drive away so we'll have plenty of time."

"You must promise me you won't mention this to a single soul," Nadia said, her voice stern and serious.

"You don't have to worry about a thing," Thomas replied. "I've no intention of anyone finding out."

Who's the fucking moron now? He thought to himself, who's the useless little prick?

For once the voice in his head was silent.

Chapter 45

When Angela pulled into the car park on Monday morning, Paul parked in the space beside her and they walked into the building together.

"Good weekend?" Paul asked. "I've spent the whole time running my kids to various activities," he continued. "I'm so exhausted I've come to work for a rest."

"My weekend was up and down, some of it good, some of it not so good. I must say I'm quite glad to be at work too."

"What a pair of sad losers we are," Paul said and they both laughed.

"At least we're both early, time for a hit of caffeine before the Boss gets in," Angela replied.

When they entered their office they were surprised to see Frank was already in his room, another man was with him and the door was closed.

"Why is the Boss in so early and who's he with?" Angela asked Gordon Mckay, who was just finishing his shift.

"The Boss is with his boss and Frank is not a laughing policeman. His boss never comes here unless there's a problem so I'd say Frankie Boy's in big trouble. I'm pleased to say I'm going home and leaving the problem with you. Goodbye and good luck." Gordon headed for the door and as he left the office he turned and gave a V sign to Angela and Paul.

"Oh shit, I wonder what's going on. If Frank's in trouble then we're in trouble," Paul said.

"Let's not fret over it until it happens," Angela replied, "I, for one, plan to keep my head down and avoid the Boss at all costs."

"Spoken like a true coward," Paul said, "And being a big fearty myself, I'll follow your lead."

After half an hour Frank's door opened and he walked with his boss to the exit. Angela could see they were talking but she couldn't make out what they were saying. They both looked serious and that wasn't a good sign. They formally shook hands and Frank returned to his room and pointedly shut the door.

"Do you think he'll call for one of us?" Angela asked Paul.

"If he does I hope it's you he wants," Paul replied. "I don't think he's going to be in a good mood."

"The age of chivalry is indeed, dead," Angela replied.

"I've never pretended to be chivalrous or brave for that matter."

The next two hours dragged on without a peep from Frank. Angela and Paul were hoping he'd stay in his office until the end of their shift but they were to be disappointed. Suddenly his door was thrown open.

"Murphy, Costello, my room, now."

"Oh, Oh, here we go, into the valley of death."

"Shut up Paul, he'll hear you and he's probably looking for a victim to yell at."

When they entered Frank's room the smell of whisky nearly knocked them out. Frank was slumped over his desk and he raised his head and squinted at Angela trying to focus on her face. The empty whisky bottle stood like a trophy on top of a telephone book. Frank was clearly inebriated.

"Boris Kinsky's been arrested by the Met boys. One of you'll have to arrange to send Tetiana Markin to them," he slurred.

"That's great news, Boss," Angela said trying to sound enthusiastic.

"Aye, that's okay," Frank agreed. "The bad news is we haven't got any results for the Shlasher murders and my boss isn't happy. In fact if we don't come up with something positive in the next month he's going to replace me as head of the inveshtigation."

Angela and Paul looked at each other, they weren't sure what to say or do.

Finally Paul spoke, "I think you should go home, Frank. You've had a wee dram or six and you're going to get into trouble if anyone else finds out. Angela and I won't say anything but you need to get out of here."

Frank looked as if he might protest then he hung his head in resignation.

"I'm sorry, I'm sorry, I just needed a wee drink. There was only a bit in the end of the bottle so I finished it. I've not had breakfast so it's gone shtraight to my head. I'll go home and get something to eat now and I'll come back in a wee while. Now where did I put my keys?" he said searching his jacket pockets and lifting papers on his desk.

"You're not driving Boss," Paul said vehemently. "You're in no state to drive. I'll take you home."

"But my car's in the car park," Frank protested.

"And that's where it's staying until you sober up. Now let me help you to stand and we'll get you out of here before anyone else sees the state you're in."

Angela's loyalties were strained. Frank had obviously developed a drink problem and if they continued to ignore it he wouldn't get the help he needed. On the other hand maybe he was just going through a difficult patch and he'd pull himself together soon. Paul went over to his boss and hooked his arm under Frank's. He tried to raise the heavy man from the seat but struggled with the task. Finally Frank stood up. Paul was red-faced from his exertions.

"Stop daydreaming Angela and help me get him to my car," Paul hissed. "He's all over the place and he weighs a ton. Grab him under the arm and help me steer him to the door."

Angela did as she was told and between them they managed to get Frank out of the station and into the car park. They pushed and shoved and eventually managed to manoeuvre Frank's large frame into the passenger seat of Paul's car where he promptly fell asleep.

"You sort out Tetiana Markin and I'll get this drunken sod home," Paul said. "I hope to God he doesn't throw up in my car or I'll never hear the end of it from the wife."

"Didn't your parents teach you never to volunteer?" Angela quipped.

"Funny, very funny Murphy," Paul replied scowling.

As Paul drove off Angela went back to the office. I'd better clean up the mess in Frank's room, she thought. If anyone sees the state of the place and reports him he'll be out the door before he can draw breath. Why does life have to be so damned complicated, first the problem with Jake and now this, why can't life be simple?

Chapter 46

The altercation between Nadia and the girl called Brenda preyed on Thomas's mind. She saw me he thought to himself, she can identify me.

'*Now you're in trouble you fucking little pervert. If you take Nadia, fat Brenda will shop you. She'll tell Nadia's Dad, she'll tell her Uncle Safdar. Then you'll be in trouble, won't you? Won't you?*' The voice shouted in his head. '*You're fucking useless,*' it taunted.

"What'll I do? What'll I do?" Thomas said aloud. He slapped his head with his hands, slap, slap, slap, over and over again until his ears rang. Thomas paced the floor of his flat. He didn't want his plans to fall apart when he was so close.

'*So near and yet so far,*' the voice said mockingly. '*Why don't you stop her? Cut her down before she tells. Get rid of the problem. Get rid of her.*'

Thomas didn't want to go to work he wanted to stay home and think but he had no choice. He had to carry on as if everything was okay or Alan would ask questions. So he washed his face, buttoned his uniform jacket and left his apartment. He hurried past the sweet shop without giving it a second glance because he knew Nadia would be at school and he wanted to distance himself from her family. When he reached the corner where he'd arranged to meet Alan, he saw that he was looking at his watch.

"I was beginning to think you weren't coming, you're ten minutes late. Are you okay, Son?"

"Yes, yes I'm fine, I didn't realise I was late my clock must be wrong."

"Oh well, better late than never," he replied.

Alan's trite sayings were beginning to annoy Thomas, familiarity breeds contempt. Thomas had learnt all he could from Alan and the older man was really getting on his nerves. If it hadn't been for the van and caravan Thomas would have no more need of him. However he had no choice at the moment because if anything happened to Alan and his wife he would certainly lose the vehicles and then he would lose Nadia.

"I've a bit of news for you, Son," Alan said. "I'm going to be leaving you."

"Wwwhat," Thomas stammered, had Alan read his mind, "When?"

"Got ya," Alan replied laughing. "It's only for a few days. I'm taking Ann for a wee break. I've booked that posh hotel at Loch Lomond for a four night stay. We leave on Thursday night and return on Monday. Will you miss me?"

"Of course I will," Thomas lied his mind was working overtime. With Alan gone he'll be able to find out more about fat Brenda because they'll be nobody to check on his timetable.

"I just thought my Ann could do with a holiday. She's become a slave to the hospital with all her tests so I wanted to give her a treat. She was cheered up by your visit, by the way. All her friends think she's got a son because she talks about you all the time just like they chat about their children. When you came round it was a real tonic for her."

"Will you take the dogs when you go on holiday?"

"No, no, they'll go into the kennels for the weekend we don't want any responsibilities while we're away. There was just one thing Thomas, could you keep a set of our keys in case of an emergency? Ann's sister would do it but she's going to be away as well."

"Of course Alan, no problem," he said. Thomas welcomed the opportunity to go into Alan's house while he was away so he could look for more magazines.

* * *

Nadia was nervous about going to school as she didn't want another run in with Brenda. If Susan had been around there wouldn't be a problem because she could handle the bullies. However, Nadia had just heard that she was staying down south with her mother until a week on Monday, so as well as today that meant another eight school-days avoiding Brenda and her gang. On the plus side it meant that she didn't have to tell Susan anything about her trip with Thomas to the countryside. Susan would definitely not understand it and, truth be told, Nadia hardly understood it herself. Her father would kill her if he ever found out. She hurried through the school gate looking around nervously for Brenda but she was nowhere to be seen. Relieved Nadia ran through the playground towards the entrance door, but as she rounded the corner with her goal in sight, Brenda stepped in front of her.

"Where's your boyfriend, bitch?" she said grabbing Nadia's jacket and spinning her around. "Oh, I forgot, he's much too old for school isn't he," she added spitefully. "He's much too old for you."

"Leave me alone," Nadia begged. "He's not my boyfriend he's a friend of my uncle's."

"Yeah, yeah, and Moslems eat pig," Brenda replied with a snarl.

"Let me go, leave me alone I'm going to be late for my class," Nadia pleaded.

"What's going on here girls?" A voice boomed. "Haven't you lessons to go to?"

"Sorry, Mr Murray," Brenda replied, "We were just having some fun."

Nadia breathed a sigh of relief her saviour had arrived in the shape of the Head of English.

"You're not here to have fun. You're here to learn. Now get going and stop carrying on."

Brenda released her grip of Nadia's jacket and they both raced for the entrance. "I'm not done with you yet," she hissed. "Don't think this is over."

At least one of Brenda's cronies was in each of Nadia's classes and they stared at her with narrowed eyes or made vulgar signs whenever she glanced their way making her feel very uncomfortable. She couldn't concentrate on her work and on two occasions she was pulled up by her teachers for not paying attention. As the minutes ticked away towards three-thirty and the close of day Nadia prepared her bag ready to leave as soon as the bell rang. She glanced over to Brenda attempting to gauge her mood without being noticed, but Brenda saw her. She stared straight into her eyes and, with her forefinger, drew an imaginary slash across her own throat then with the same finger pointed to Nadia. Brenda nodded slowly, smiling in a most menacing way. Nadia was terrified.

When the bell rang Nadia grabbed her bag and jacket and bolted from the room before the teacher had finished dismissing the class. She sprinted out of the school and across the playground without stopping and was the first pupil through the school gate. With tears in her eyes she looked ahead and saw her mother waiting in her car to pick her up. Nadia had completely forgotten she had a dental appointment and her mother was going to drive her to the surgery. For the first time ever she was actually pleased to be going for a check-up and she threw herself in the car and sighed with relief.

"Have you been crying?" Nadia's mother questioned looking closely at her daughter.

Nadia turned away she'd never been very good at hiding her feelings.

"Let's just go, Mum," she replied looking nervously at the school gate. "I don't want to be late for my appointment.

"Now I know something is wrong," her mother replied. "You've always hated going to the dentist. Tell me, I'm not moving 'til you do. Have you got into trouble with one of the teachers?"

"No, Mum, nothing like that."

"Then what is it? Tell me now or I'll have to ask your father to talk to you."

"No, Mum, don't tell Dad, it's one of the girls at school she's been annoying me."

"Annoying you how?"

"She accused me of looking at her boyfriend, but I didn't, he's horrible and you know I'm not interested in boys. Brenda just wanted an excuse to start with me while Susan's away."

"So has she been calling you names? Talk to me, Nadia, I'm your Mum, I'll help you."

Now that Nadia had confided in her mother the words came pouring out. "She does more than call me names, Mum. I could handle it if it was just name calling, but yesterday she pushed me over and today she grabbed me and threatened me. She's got a gang of friends, Mum and at least one of them is in every one of my classes. I'm scared of them, Mum."

"And this girl's friends are any of them Moslems?"

"No, they're all Scottish," Nadia replied miserably.

"Right, get out of the car we're going to talk to the Headmaster. This is racially motivated bullying and I'm going to put a stop to it. If the school don't act immediately I'll talk to your uncle, Councillor Ahmed." Nadia's mother was already climbing out of the car with a determined look on her face. Nadia hesitated. "Get out of the car, now, Nadia," her mother insisted. "I want this girl and her friends suspended."

"Mum, if you make a fuss and get them suspended, they'll wait for me after school. I still won't be safe."

"I'll get my lawyer to take out an interdict stopping them from coming near you. To attend this school their parents must have money. Trust me they won't ignore that."

Nadia allowed her mother to take her back into school. She was relieved that she'd been able to unburden herself and secretly rather pleased to have the ammunition to fight back. Let's see how brave Brenda is now, she thought. Bullies don't like to be exposed for the cowards they are.

Chapter 47

Frank came into the office on time every morning and functioned, somehow. He was grateful to Angela and Paul for their loyalty and for throwing him the lifeline that undeniably saved him from deep shit. He knew he looked terrible, his face was puffy, his eyes were red and he felt awful too. His head was sore, he was nauseous and his hands shook alarmingly. In his career Frank had come into contact with many drunks, but he never dreamt he'd become one of them. He still didn't know how it happened. Frank always had a bottle of whisky in his desk drawer for medicinal purposes, but when did his 'medicine' become his water of life? He knew his only option was to tackle the problem cold turkey, but it was difficult especially given the strain he was under.

The amount of work that Frank was coping with would have caused most men to crack. He was foolish to lead all the murder enquiries himself but he thought he could manage it besides he didn't want to admit he was under pressure. Staff shortages and the recent Easter holidays exacerbated the problem and instead of delegating some of the responsibility he turned to the bottle and, like a thief in the night, it crept up on him and bit by bit stole his ability to cope.

When Frank had returned to work after Monday's incident his office was clean and tidy and he couldn't remember the last time it looked so good, he was not known for his housekeeping skills. Frank quickly searched the box file which stood on the cabinet but it was empty. His secret stash of a half bottle of whisky was gone and he was pleased not to have to face his demons. He probably should thank Angela for this he thought, but he couldn't bring himself to yet, so instead, he remained in his office and drank copious amounts of very black coffee and watched the clock as each minute ticked by bringing him ever closer to the end of the working day.

Angela and Paul felt as if they were walking on egg shells. They had work to be getting on with but only the Boss could tell them the order of importance of these tasks and he was incapable of instructing them. Angela set out some things for Bill to be getting on with so he didn't find himself twiddling his thumbs. Paul dealt with the Russian case leaving Angela free to re-read the paperwork on Megan Reece and Anne-Marie Connor. Angela hoped that by reviewing the mountain of interviews, telephone calls, forensic notes and police reports, she would find something new. Some piece of vital information that had been missed, the piece of the jigsaw, the magic talisman which opened the door and allowed her to solve the crimes. Late Thursday morning the Boss finally emerged from his room. He headed over to where Angela and Paul sat.

"I just want to say thanks," he said awkwardly. "I know what you did for me and I appreciate it. I've been a useless bastard these last few days but I'm getting better now. That's all I wanted to say." Without waiting for a response Frank turned and walked back to his room.

"I'm surprised. Are you surprised Angela?" Paul asked. "I never thought I'd see the day that Frank Martin apologised for anything."

"He didn't actually apologise," Angela pointed out. "He said thanks."

"It amounts to the same thing in my book. We did good kid," Paul added and a wide grim spread over his face. "Do you think this would be a good time to ask for a raise?"

"Only if you're a masochist, the Boss's weak moment is over. Trust me you don't want to go there."

In the early afternoon Angela received a call from the warden of the Govanhill South Church. He quickly introduced himself as Derek Mulgrew before telling her the purpose of the call.

"The united religious groups are holding a memorial service in our church on Sunday afternoon. The service is for the three murdered prostitutes and also for Jackie Cosgrove who, as you know, was a preacher who helped the girls. We want to show the community that we are united in our sadness at the loss of these women. It was suggested the police might want to send a representative to attend the service and pay their respects."

Angela was sure the police would want to attend but not for the reason Mr Mulgrew imagined. There was every chance that the killer would turn up. Maybe he would feel some remorse and want to unburden himself in the church or perhaps he might get some sick pleasure from being amongst the mourners. Either way someone had to attend and Angela was prepared to volunteer.

"Thank you for informing us Mr Mulgrew. Someone will attend the service just give me the exact address and time."

The church warden gave Angela all the information she required and thanked her.

"The families of the dead women will be pleased with your support," he said before ending the call.

Yeah, that'll be right, Angela thought, she didn't expect anyone would turn up for Megan or Anne-Marie and Jackie had no family to mourn her. Normally Angela would shy away from working on a Sunday but she would be glad to be out of the house. Since the revelations about Jake, she and Bobby had come to an awkward truce, but she was still angry at him for keeping her in the dark.

Angela went to Frank's office clutching the cup of coffee she'd had the foresight to pour for him. She had to clear the overtime with him before she attended the service. Angela knocked on the door and entered without waiting for a reply.

"Brought you a coffee, Boss," she said. "How're you doing?"

"Fine, fine, yeah I'm okay, Angela. Thanks for the coffee, although I've had so much caffeine my eyes are out on stalks. What can I do for you or was this just a social visit?"

Angela quickly told Frank about the church service.

"Bloody do-gooders," Frank replied. "They've always got to make everything about religion. But as you so rightly pointed out, our psycho might turn up. The overtime is no problem, I'm happy to authorise it, but I don't want you going there alone. Either Bill or Paul will have to accompany you and I don't care which one of them it is. You choose or let them fight it out between themselves. Obviously, they'll get the overtime too."

"Thanks Boss," Angela replied. "I'm glad you're back," she added with a smile.

"Me too, Murphy, now fuck off out of my office and get some work done."

"Fucking off right now, Boss," Angela answered laughing and she shut the door as she left.

Finding a volunteer was easy because Bill immediately said he'd attend. Liz was working on Sunday and he was pleased to have something to do. Paul was barely coping already with his working week because his four children were very demanding and his wife was becoming more and more tired as her pregnancy progressed, so he was relieved to be let off.

"I'll pick you up and we'll travel together there's no point taking two cars," Angela said. "Besides I'm going on somewhere else after the service so I'll need my car," she explained.

The truth was she didn't have any plans she just wanted time out from Bobby.

Chapter 48

Thomas was in a great mood even though Mrs Anderson's elderly mongrel had peed in the close again making it stink of ammonia. He actually found himself whistling on his way to work knowing that Alan was on holiday. He would now choose his own route and make his own timetable. It had always been Alan's way or no way, but not today. As he walked past the Asian fruit shop, he helped himself to an apple from one of the boxes displayed outside and pocketed it without paying. He knew he wouldn't be caught. Today he felt invincible, he could do anything. He was in control.

His plan was simple he would work hard all morning and early afternoon gaining, if possible, enough bookings to satisfy his bosses. Then at about three o'clock he would return to his flat, change his clothes and position himself outside the school so he could spy on Brenda and see where she lived.

'Don't let Nadia see you,' the voice warned. 'Don't talk to her before your date or she might change her mind and cancel.'

"Don't worry," he said aloud, reassuring himself. "Nadia always turns left as she leaves the school, I'll be hiding round the corner on the right. She'll never spot me."

* * *

Nadia was pleased she'd told her mum about Brenda even though at first it felt wrong to tell tales. Now that Brenda and her gang had been given a two week suspension Nadia felt safe, particularly as Brenda's father had phoned to apologise. He said he was shocked by his daughter's behaviour and he assured Nadia's dad that neither she nor any of her gang would threaten Nadia again. He also offered to make Brenda apologise in front of the whole school assembly but Nadia declined the offer as it would have been excruciatingly embarrassing.

After her parents had been so understanding and supportive Nadia felt a bit guilty by deceiving them over Thomas. But, she reasoned, they would never find out as she'd be back at the gallery in time to be picked up. Besides, they had no qualms about deceiving her and Susan. She was hardly ever allowed to go anywhere by herself, so she had to grab her opportunities where she could.

* * *

Thomas had a very good day ticketing cars. There was a special event being held in Victoria Road to herald the opening of a new supermarket and people had been abandoning their cars anywhere and everywhere to try to be first in line for some free hand outs. Thomas had collected well over his daily target by two o'clock. After quickly checking that no one was around to see him he slipped away and went home.

The extra hours he'd saved allowed Thomas the luxury of spending time sitting on his sofa and day-dreaming about Nadia. He imagined her in his caravan wearing her flimsy, silky clothes. He wondered what it would be like to slip his hand between her legs and feel her nakedness through the fine fabric. Thomas unzipped his trousers, he wet his hand, slowly licking it with his tongue then he reached inside his underpants closing his fingers round his throbbing penis. He imagined himself pulling down Nadia's trousers, touching her hot wetness, lying between her legs and easing himself into her making her moan with pain and pleasure. Thomas was overwhelmed with excitement.

He came to a shuddering climax then lay down and curled into a foetal position on the sofa. He was in danger of drifting off to sleep but he forced himself to get up and take a cold shower which jolted him awake. Then he carefully dressed in blue jeans, a sweatshirt and a dark coloured, hooded waterproof and set off for the school.

When Thomas reached his destination he saw that a large van was parked at the side of the road. Perfect, he thought I don't even need to go round the corner I can hide behind this van and no one will see me. It was only ten past three, Thomas had twenty minutes to kill before the bell rang and he was feeling peckish because he hadn't eaten lunch. Feeling confident that he'd plenty of time, he went to the newsagent on the corner of the street and bought a bag of smoky bacon crisps and a Kit Kat. He wondered if Moslems ate smoky bacon crisps, maybe Nadia would like to try them when she was living at the caravan. Of course, once she was his wife she wouldn't be Moslem any more, she'd be just like him, whatever that was.

Thomas quickly wolfed down his food then returned and stood behind the van. He felt a surge of excitement when he heard the bell ring. I'll get you now you fat little cow, he thought, and a feeling of sweet anticipation swept over him.

* * *

Nadia sauntered out of the school gate and saw her mother parked immediately outside. She didn't really need to be collected but she was happy to get the lift. With Susan away Nadia enjoyed spending time with her Mum. Their lives were very isolating and it was difficult for them because, being devout Moslem women, they were expected to behave as if they resided in some remote village in Pakistan. All around them were examples of the modern western world where women had the freedom to act as they pleased. Not that Nadia approved of the way most of her school friends behaved, but it would be nice to be able to come and go without always asking for permission.

"I came to collect you so you could get home quicker," Nadia's mum said. "Your father and your uncle are having a business meeting at home tonight and we've a lot of cooking and preparing to do. We won't be allowed in the family room or the hallway once everyone arrives so make sure you have everything you need in your bedroom before six-thirty, acha?"

Great, Nadia thought, that's all I need. Her father would not let any of the women in the household be seen by any male visitors who were not relatives. They were to be shut away out of sight and out of mind like chattels not people in their own right.

* * *

Thomas watched the throng of pupils as they poured through the gate. He could see their faces clearly and his heart missed a beat when Nadia walked out. He saw her get into a car driven by an older Asian woman, probably her mum, he thought.

The stream of people kept coming and Thomas's eyes were sore from staring. Where is she? He wondered. He knew he hadn't missed her but as the last stragglers exited she was nowhere to be seen. Perhaps she's been kept in late because of her behaviour, he speculated, I'll wait another ten minutes.

As Thomas waited he got more and more annoyed, "Fat bitch," he said aloud, pacing angrily. People moved out of his way, they crossed the road because his odd behaviour frightened them. He placed his hands on his knees and bent over slightly. "Fat bitch," he yelled at the road. "I'll find you, I'll find you and I'll cut you down."

Chapter 49

Angela was happy to be working on Sunday, it was a lovely sunny day and she felt a sense of freedom leaving the house. She'd arranged to pick Bill up at ten o'clock so they could arrive at the church for the regular Sunday service. The memorial service was scheduled to begin when the children went to the Sunday school at eleven-thirty. Angela wasn't religious but she felt they should be at the church for the start of the service so they could observe the congregation.

When she arrived at Bill's she was surprised to see how handsome he looked in a suit. He had the stature and presence of a fashion model with his fine features and large lean frame. No wonder Liz was smitten, she thought. She was actually rather jealous of the love affair Bill and Liz seemed to be having. Angela wished that she and Bobby could get back to where they'd been before the fateful race night. Their relationship was strained and neither of them could bring themselves to talk about Jake. Miranda had called Angela a few days after the event to apologise for making a scene when she and Jake were her guests, but Angela told her not to upset herself over it. It might have meant something if it was Jake who had phoned. But the snivelling coward acted as if he'd done nothing wrong and ignored the incident completely.

"I'm not sure what we're supposed to do at the church," Bill said. "What have we to look for?"

"Anyone acting strangely or any unusual incident," Angela replied. "The truth is, this is probably a complete waste of time, but we're being paid overtime so let's make the most of it."

"Liz is policing a football match at Hampden," Bill said. "It's my team that are playing and I'd love to be at the match. I wish I could have swapped her jobs. No offence meant, you understand, it's nothing to do with you, I like working with you, but it's my team," he whined.

"Who's playing? Who do you support?"

"I support Queens Park and we're playing Forfar."

"Trust me, you don't need to attend the game," Angela said laughing. "I can tell you you're going to get beat."

"That just shows me how little you know about the beautiful game," Bill replied huffing. He was affronted.

"So are you and Liz going out tonight?" Angela asked changing the subject. She hated football and didn't want to get drawn into a conversation about it.

"We're seeing each other but we're not going out. I've planned a romantic evening in with candles, soft music and a bottle of wine. I've even cleaned the house and changed the sheets."

"Stop right there Bill, don't say another word, too much information, I'm sorry I asked."

Angela turned into the street where Govanhill South Church was situated.

"Bloody Hell," she said. "Would you look at all those cars we might have to park a distance away. That's a BBC outside broadcast vehicle. I didn't know the media would be here."

"Glad I wore a suit," Bill replied. "Look Angela," he said pointing to a space just ahead of them. "That car's just pulled out. Quick put your foot down before someone else sees the space."

Angela quickly manoeuvred her car into the space and grinned at Bill, "Well done," she said. "Don't look now but the guy in the blue car over there was waiting for this space but he was in the wrong position to pull into it. Let's get going before he comes over to complain. He doesn't look too happy."

They climbed out of the car and hurried towards the church without a backward glance at the other driver whose eyes burned into the back of Angela's head. When they reached the door Angela introduced herself and Bill to Mr Mulgrew, the church warden, who was waiting to greet the congregation. He indicated to a row of seats at the back that had been reserved and the pair sat down. The church was not very large but it had a magnificent high ceiling. It was built in the Victorian era, constructed from the sandstone that Glasgow is famous for. Although the building was austere the atmosphere was very welcoming. Some members of the congregation came over and introduced themselves to Bill and Angela because they didn't recognise them and they wanted to make sure newcomers to the church felt welcome.

The memorial service was packed, every seat was taken and some people stood at the back. None of the dead girls' relatives attended. The church was mostly filled with the same sort of people who telephoned the incident line. People who empathised with the victims and wanted to help and those who wanted to be associated with the crimes so they could talk about them knowledgeably with their friends. Then there were others who hoped the TV cameras would find their face in the crowd and afford them five seconds of fame.

The memorial service was led by religious leaders from the Protestant Church, the Catholic Church and the local Mosque with other groups being represented. Bill sat and munched M&M's throughout the entire service and Angela was desperate for it to end because her bum was numb from sitting on the hard wooden seat. At last, after an hour, the congregation recited the Lord's Prayer and it was over. Being at the back Angela and Bill were amongst the first to leave. They stood outside and watched as everyone piled out and, within the next hour, the crowd had dispersed.

"That was a waste of time," Angela said stating the obvious. "You've still got time to get to your football match. If you show your warrant card at the gate they'll let you in."

"But we're not meant to do that," Bill protested.

"Tell them you've to give Constable Brown a message from Detective Murphy and I'll back you up. Liz worked for me on the Margaret Deacon case so nobody will question that."

"But what if a senior officer asks me what the question is?"

"Tell them you're not at liberty to say and refer them to me. Trust me, no one will bat an eyelid and you'll get to see your game. Now do you want to go or don't you?"

"Well, yeah, thanks very much. It's a two o'clock kick off so instead of taking me home could you drop me at Hampden, please? I'll just make it then."

"Your wish is my command," Angela replied. "Now in the words of the Boss, let's fuck off out of here."

Chapter 50

It was Sunday night and Thomas was livid. He'd been to the school on Thursday and Friday but there was no sign of Brenda. By Saturday he'd become annoyed but now he was enraged. "Fucking little cow, where are you?" he said aloud.

'*She said she'll remember you and she will, she will, your secret's not safe with her, she told you that,*' the voice goaded.

"Gotta find her, gotta stop her," Thomas began to chant slapping his forehead with his open palm.

His head felt as if it was being crushed in a vise and he couldn't breathe in the house. A week today and Nadia would be his, just one week today, if Brenda didn't tell. "Fucking little cow, where are you? Where, the Hell, are you?"

He had to get out of the apartment he had to get some air or his head would explode. It was ten-thirty on Sunday night, the park would be empty. Thomas made his way through the streets of Govanhill until he reached Queen's Park. He took his usual route slipping through a break in the metal railings. It was very dark as there was cloud cover so no moonlight shone through. Thomas liked the dark it made him feel anonymous and safe. He walked silently across the length of the park taking the route past the duck pond towards the swings.

As Thomas neared the children's play area he heard voices and it surprised him because the park was usually empty at this time on a Sunday. He cut through a shrubbery so he could keep out of sight but be able see who the voices belonged to. There was a lamp standard on the road behind the park which provided some limited illumination and Thomas's heart skipped a beat when he saw Brenda and her friends smoking and drinking cans of beer while sitting on the swings.

'*Well, what do you know? That's a sign,*' the voice said. '*Some things are just meant to be.*'

Thomas hid in the bushes the earth was muddy under his feet. Brenda looked like a whore dressed as she was in a tight see-through blouse and a micro mini-skirt which left nothing to the imagination. As she bent to pick up her can of beer from the ground, Thomas could see her buttocks, fat, pink buttocks, on the blue plastic seat of the swing. He licked his lips.

Thomas didn't know how long he'd been standing watching them, but after some time, Brenda and her friends said their goodbyes and then they walked off in different directions. Brenda made her way through the park in the same direction that Thomas had come from. She must live in one of the expensive apartments in Queens Drive or thereabouts, he thought.

Brenda walked slowly. She was in no hurry to get home. She had no fear of walking through the park at night because she'd come this way several times before on a Sunday and it had always been empty in the past. She had no idea, that on this night, Thomas was stalking her.

Brenda sat on a bench and lit a cigarette. She'd had several puffs before Thomas, armed with a tree branch, hit her over the head. She fell forward onto the pathway. Thomas watched fascinated like a cat playing with a mouse as, in her dazed state, Brenda crawled over the grass towards a shrubbery. Thomas hit her again knocking her over. She tumbled forward onto the wet earth her skirt riding up to reveal her fat buttocks covered only by a thin nylon thong. As she lay face down on the ground, Thomas fell on her sliding his hand between her legs. He felt her hot wetness. Brenda moaned as the sharp pain of Thomas' fingers penetrating her vagina cut through her dazed state. Thomas unzipped his trousers he took out his penis and pushed it clumsily into the semi-conscious girl.

"Noooo," she said. "Get off me."

Thomas held onto one of her legs as he pounded into her. "Fuck, fuck, fuck, fuck," he chanted with every thrust. The feel of her soft flesh in his hand drove him crazy with lust.

"Brenda's cries got louder as she struggled to get free. Using his free hand, Thomas pushed her face down into the soft earth and held it there until she stopped thrashing about. Then he came, a great pulsating climax so powerful he let out a primal howl that echoed through the park.

Thomas rolled off Brenda, his trousers and shoes were covered in mud. He carefully placed his fingertips on Brenda's neck to check for a pulse then, satisfied that she was dead, he stood up, straightened his clothes, brushed himself down with his hands and headed for home. Thomas was pleased with himself. I did it, he thought, now I'll know how to make love to Nadia. Now I'm a real man.

Brenda's corpse lay face down in the shrubbery. Blood and semen oozed from her vagina and a black bruise of Thomas' thumb print showed vividly on the pink flesh of her thigh. Wet earth filled her nose and mouth and a large patch of congealing blood matted her hair where she'd been hit with the branch. At seven-thirty on Monday morning the incessant barking of a German Shepherd dog led his horrified female owner to Brenda's corpse and, after throwing up and contaminating the crime scene, with shaking hands, she called the police from her mobile phone.

Chapter 51

Blue screens had been placed around the body of Brenda Eadie and by the time Frank and Angela arrived at the scene a sizeable number of people were milling about all with jobs to do. A murder always required input from several departments ranging from forensics to uniformed police who dealt with crowd control. Frank had chosen Angela to accompany him over Paul Costello because he felt the expectant father would be too emotional to deal with a child's death at this particular time.

Frank learned from a uniformed officer that Brenda's father had phoned them at three o'clock in the morning to inform them that his daughter hadn't come home. He'd been out searching for a couple of hours by then crossing the park several times. Because her body was hidden in the shrubbery he didn't find her even though he must have passed only feet away.

"Poor bugger," Frank said. "Where is he now?"

"A doctor's attending him and his wife at their home," the officer replied.

"We'll have to get him in for questioning," Frank said to Angela. "The wee lassie's been raped."

"You don't think her father had anything to do with this, do you?"

"No, I don't, but we must follow procedure and more often than not a family member is involved in murder cases. Besides, this wee lassie is still under sixteen, what the hell was she doing out so late on a Sunday and why didn't her father phone us until three this morning? We can't let ourselves get too emotional. We've got to look at everything and everyone is a suspect."

One of the medical team emerged from the screens and walked over to them.

"What have we got here Doc?" Frank asked.

"Fifteen year old girl, raped, entered from behind, nasty bash on the head but that didn't kill her, asphyxiation from her face being pushed into the earth. She died at the scene the body hasn't been moved. Lots of evidence for forensics, there's a bruise like a thumb print on her thigh and what looks like semen and blood surrounding the vagina. Why do the parents of these children let them out of the house at night dressed like tarts?" he said, the frustration evident in his voice. "They're bound to attract perverts."

"Do you think the attack was purely sexual and the murderer accidentally killed her given the mode of death?"

"I'm just not sure. How can any of us understand these psychos? Anyway I'm pleased to say I'm done for today. I'm going home for a shower and a cooked breakfast. Good luck with this one, I don't fancy your job."

"I don't fancy my job either," Frank said with a wry look, "But the only fucking person I could hand it over to, has gone on a bloody course."

It was nearly lunch time when Frank and Angela were finished at the scene and Angela thought Frank looked exhausted. His face had a strained, wan look and his hands were trembling and she knew that this is when he would have reached for the bottle of whisky.

"Do you want me to get us something to eat before we go and talk to the parents?" she asked.

Frank looked at his watch, "Christ is it that time already," he said. "No, we'll take a break and go and get some food. The Battlefield Rest is only a few minutes away and they do a great deal, pasta and a drink for five pounds fifty. You drive and I'll pay. You do like pasta, don't you, because otherwise you can get Minestrone soup and a piece of Italian bread."

"That sound great, Boss. Are you ready now?"

During lunch neither of them felt inclined to discuss the case but they couldn't help hearing a news report from the radio that was playing behind the serving counter. 'Teenage girl found dead in a Glasgow park. Could this be another victim of the Southside Slasher?' the reporter said.

"Bloody Hell, that's all we need. Why do the media do that? They won't be happy until there's panic in the streets. It doesn't make our job any easier," Frank said keeping his voice low.

"People love to talk and they love a bit of sensationalism. Good news doesn't sell papers," Angela pointed out.

After their lunch Frank and Angela went to the Eadie residence to talk to Brenda's parents. They were shown into a large bright lounge by the family liaison officer. The room was huge 'big enough to hold a dance in', Frank observed. After a couple of minutes a slim, bald man of about fifty entered the room and introduced himself as Dr. Colin Paterson, Brenda's uncle.

"I'm very sorry," he said, "But my brother-in-law, Peter, has been taken to the Victoria Infirmary with a suspected heart attack and my sister Janice is being treated for shock. She's in bed and she's heavily sedated. My Mum and Dad are travelling down from Aberdeen. I can't imagine what they're going through."

Colin was barely managing to keep his emotions in check, his face twitched and his lips trembled as he spoke.

"We really are so very sorry for your loss, Dr Patterson," Frank said. "I can assure you we are doing everything in our power to catch the person who did this."

"What kind of sick degenerate attacks and murders a fifteen year old girl?" Colin Patterson said to no one in particular. "Brenda was a child, for God's sake."

There was no point in Frank and Angela waiting around any longer. Colin was able to tell them that Brenda had been suspended from school, but he assured them it was over a minor incident with another girl and the matter had been resolved. Before they left he gave them the name of the school and begged Frank to keep the media away from his family.

"My poor brother-in-law is in a bad enough state as it is without being hounded by the press," he explained.

"The family liaison officer is here to shield your family from any harassment and he'll be able to stay with you twenty-four/seven if you need him," Frank assured.

They left the flat and headed back to Angela's car. Frank hadn't been driving his car since the incident when he was drunk. He told everyone that is was in being repaired and only Angela and Paul knew the real truth. He was being very cautious as the withdrawal symptoms he was experiencing affected his concentration and sometimes made his behaviour erratic.

"Let's go to the school," Frank suggested. "I'd like to know why Brenda was suspended. It must have been something serious because they like to keep kids in school if they can."

"Do you think her murder has something to do with her suspension? Do you think she's upset someone dangerous?"

"I can't be sure, but I do think it's a line of investigation worth following. I'd also like to advise the Headmaster how to handle the murder of one of his pupils. The press will be hovering and he'll need to prepare a statement about Brenda. You know the usual sort of thing, 'she was a popular and bright student, yadda, yadda, yadda.' He'll need to be ready when they ask why she was suspended."

When they reached the school reception office the girl at the desk led them to the Headmaster's room and offered them a seat. They were soon joined by the Headmaster and his secretary. He informed them that Brenda had been suspended along with others for bullying and assaulting an Asian girl called Nadia Sarwar.

"We take bullying very seriously in this school," the headmaster said. "Particularly where there is a racial element."

He gave Frank the address of the Sarwar home. The meeting was brief and after only a few minutes they were shown out by the secretary.

"He was a posh git," Frank observed, "And his secretary was a stuck up cow. She looked at us as if we were dirt under her feet."

"They were probably just nervous. I shouldn't imagine they've ever had to deal with something like this before," Angela replied trying to placate her boss.

Frank instructed Angela to drive to the girl's home. It was only a fifteen minute journey from the school to Newlands. They were surprised when they arrived because they hadn't expected such a grand residence. The house took up a large part of the street and as Angela pulled up outside she was surprised to see impressive gateposts topped by stone lions.

"Fucking hell, it's a bloody mansion. They must be fucking millionaires," Frank said.

They climbed out of the car and walked to the entrance. When they arrived at the ornamental wrought iron gates Frank saw they were controlled by a security entry system which meant they had to press a button on a panel on the gatepost to be admitted.

After pressing the button several times there was a crackling sound and a voice said, "Who is it? Who's there?"

"Police," Frank said, "We're looking for the Sarwar family can we come in?"

"They're all out," the voice replied. "Mrs Sarwar is down south with her daughter Susan, the other Mrs Sarwar is out in her car, all the children are at school and the two Mr Sarwars are at their shop in Allison Street. I'm the cleaner and I'm sorry but I can't let you in."

"And your name is?" Frank asked.

There was another crackling and then silence.

"She's probably claiming benefit and working on the black," Frank surmised. "We're not going to get anything out of her. We might as well go to Allison Street and see if we can corner the two Mr Sarwars there."

When they arrived at the shop in Allison Street Frank was once again surprised.

"There's no way this shitey wee shop makes the sort of money that would buy the mansion we've just left," he said. I think the serious crime squad might want to take a closer look at the Sarwar brothers' business and I bet they'll find more than sweeties."

When they entered the shop several of the customers left and the man behind the counter looked around shiftily.

"I should have put on deodorant before I came in here," Frank said. "I think I must have BO."

"Can I help you?" the shop assistant asked.

"We're looking for Mr Sarwar," Angela said.

"Which one do you want, Zaffer or Safdar?"

"I tell you what," Frank suggested. "You tell me which one of them I'm hearing in the back shop and then I'll tell you who I want."

The curtain leading to the back shop parted and two men came through the opening.

"I'm Zaffer Sarwar," the taller of the men said. "This is my brother Safdar," he added pointing to the other man.

Safdar said something to the assistant in Urdu and the man picked up his jacket from a chair behind the counter and scurried out of the shop.

"He didn't have to leave on our account," Frank quipped.

"Why are you here? Who do you want to talk to?" Safdar asked.

"Which one of you is the father of Nadia," Angela asked.

"I'm Nadia's father," Zaffer said and a worried expression crossed his face. "Is she in trouble? Has something happened to her? My wife picks her up from school."

"Nothing's wrong and she's not in any trouble. I just want to ask you a few questions about a class mate of hers called Brenda Eadie," Frank said.

"That's the girl who was suspended for hitting Nadia," Zaffer stated. "She's a bad girl. Nadia says she dresses very inappropriately and she hangs around with boys and drinks alcohol. What do you want to know about her?"

"When did you last see Brenda?"

Zaffer thought for a moment, "The week before Christmas at the school Fair," he replied.

"And you haven't seen her since?"

"It's possible but I probably wouldn't recognise her. I've only been introduced to her and her parents once and that was at the Christmas Fair. What's this all about? Why are you asking all these questions about Brenda?"

Sometime last night she was assaulted and murdered in Queen's Park. Your family had a grievance against her so we have to ask you about her," Frank replied staring hard into Zaffer's eyes to look for any reaction.

"Oh, my God, oh my God, how awful," Zaffer said leaning on the counter for support. "I spoke to her Dad a few days ago he phoned me to apologise for Brenda's behaviour. He seemed such a nice man, how awful."

"Yes, it's terrible news," Safdar agreed. "But as you can see my brother is very upset. He had nothing to do with this girl's murder."

"I don't suppose you know anything about the girl either?" Frank asked Safdar.

"Of course not, what kind of men do you think we are?" he replied.

Angela could see that Safdar was getting annoyed and she didn't want Frank being accused of racial discrimination so she quickly jumped in, thanked the brothers for their help and gave her card to Zaffer, then before Frank could protest, she left the shop. Frank followed closely behind her.

"I wasn't ready to leave," he protested. "What are you up to?"

"Saving your arse before one of them kicked it," she answered. "Now get in the car if you want a lift or you can make your own way back."

Frank frowned at her for a moment then he burst out laughing, "I've created a monster," he said then he did as he was told and climbed into the passenger seat.

Chapter 52

Nadia was very upset when she'd heard about Brenda, she disliked the girl intensely but she didn't wish her dead. When the announcement was made by the Headmaster, Nadia broke down and had to be escorted to the school nurse's room and when her mother collected her from school, she cried all the way home in the car. She felt even worse when her father came home. He was very angry that the police had questioned him and kept pointing out to Nadia the differences between them and Scottish people. As if she didn't already know. Zaffer went on and on about Brenda's behaviour and the shortcomings of her parents when all Nadia wanted to do was put today's awful news out of her head. By nine o'clock the family had eaten and the children were either in bed or getting ready for bed. Zaffer had finished speaking ill of the dead and finally noticed how upset his daughter was.

"What's happening at school this week?" he asked. "What are you studying?"

Nadia was so desperate to be out of the house and have some time away from her family that the lie slid easily off her tongue.

"I've an art project due next week Dad and I really need to go to the Kelvingrove Gallery to do some drawings. If it's all right with you I've arranged to meet one of the girls from my class on Sunday so we can make some sketches and take some notes."

"Who is this girl? Is she someone I know?"

"I don't think so Dad. She's a nice girl from a good home and she's only allowed to go after church on Sunday so her family are decent people." The lie was growing legs.

Zaffer would normally have given his daughter a much harder time but as she'd been so upset today he relented. What harm could she come to in a museum on a Sunday afternoon he reasoned?

"Okay," he said, "But I will drive you there and I will come and collect you at five o'clock. I don't want you to leave the building. I'll park the car and come in and get you. Make sure you're ready and waiting inside the main door for me."

"Thanks, Dad. I love the museum and I'll do a really good project," she promised. "I'm so tired I think I'll go to bed now."

Nadia kissed her father dutifully on the cheek and went up to her room. She had mixed feelings about lying to him and she was very unsure about meeting Thomas, but she was caught up in the deception now and there was no turning back.

* * *

When Thomas met Alan for the start of their shift on Tuesday morning his colleague was very happy to see him.

"What've I missed? What's been happening while I've been away?" Alan asked.

"Nothing much," Thomas replied. "I filled the daily quotas with no problems except for one woman who called me a useless piece of crud when I gave her the ticket."

"So you didn't see the news yesterday? A girl was murdered in Queen's Park and you know nothing about it?"

Thomas stared blankly at Alan, he'd forgotten about Brenda.

Alan started to laugh, "I suppose your mind is full of Mary and you've no time for anything else."

Thomas smiled slowly as he envisaged Nadia, "She's wonderful, beautiful," he said.

"Good lad, you keep those lovely thoughts. The world is a horrible place but your world is beautiful. Good on you, Son."

Alan rabbited on and on about his holiday, about Ann, about the weather, Thomas was bored out of his mind. He didn't know how he was going to keep working with the man. Thomas had to think of a plan to keep the van and the caravan but get rid of Alan. But he had other more immediate things to think about first. He had to do the final work on the caravan before he took Nadia there. He still had to plant the metal pole in the ground and attach the metal ring to it. Then he had to make a hole in the caravan wall to feed the chain through, attach the handcuffs to the chain and board up the window. He needed a day off or he'd not have enough time. It wasn't a job he could do after work when it was dark.

"Alan," he began, "How do I get a day off when it's not my summer holidays?"

"You tell me the day you want and I put in a holiday sheet for you. Do you want a day off? Because, you've lots of holidays left if you need one."

"I'd like Thursday off so I can take Mary out. She's not working on Thursday you see."

"You should take her to the caravan, Son. It's lovely down there and it could be very romantic," Alan winked conspiratorially.

"I'll do that, Alan, I'll take Mary there and I'm sure once she sees the place she'll never want to leave."

Chapter 53

The murder of three prostitutes in Govanhill naturally upset the people of Glasgow so too did the death of Jackie Cosgrove. However the general public were fickle creatures and within a very short time they had reasoned that whoever killed the prostitutes wasn't interested in them and neither were the Eastern European gangsters who murdered Jackie Cosgrove. So they went about their business as usual visiting the Asian owned fruit shops to purchase the strange fruits and vegetables that they couldn't buy in ASDA, or they made appointments at the Turkish barber for a close shave with an open razor. In a very short time people stopped talking about the deaths. The posters declaring 'have you seen this woman' featuring photos of Kelly Jamieson, became faded and curled and were torn from lampposts, nobody cared about a heroin addict who'd overdosed. News is only interesting when it's fresh.

Angela and Paul were in the office working on the Brenda Eadie case but they had little to go on. All the friends she'd been with on the night she was murdered had seen nothing and knew even less about what happened to her after she'd left their company. The interviews with the young people were traumatic and distressing. Teenagers don't expect their friends to die. The media was making a meal of her death and the newspapers and television reports either implied she was a saint or suggested that she and her friends were delinquents who were allowed to run wild. Neither, of course, was true, but it made good press and sold newspapers and who really cared about the truth?

As they ploughed through the various pieces of information Angela was rather subdued. Her mind was on other things. Her mother had telephoned the previous evening to tell her that her Uncle Larry, a confirmed bachelor, had finally made a will leaving Angela everything he owned. She'd known she was Uncle Larry's favourite relative, because apart from her mother, she was the only one who telephoned or visited him regularly. He didn't really have very much to leave anyone but somehow learning that he'd made a will favouring her, made Angela think about how old and frail he'd become and it saddened her. She was deep in thought and had decided to visit the old man at the earliest convenient time when Frank came out of his office.

"Can I have your attention please," he said formally and everyone looked up. Bill glanced at Angela frowning but she just shrugged because she had no idea what this was about.

"We've had a breakthrough in the Eadie case but it's a mixed blessing," Frank began. "I've got the DNA report." Frank held his hand to his forehead and massaged his brow with his thumb. "The DNA found on Brenda Eadie matches exactly to the DNA of the hair found on the skirt of Megan Reece." Frank paused for a moment to let the news sink in. "I'm afraid we're now dealing with a serial killer and his crimes are escalating. He's moved from prostitutes to a teenage girl and we have no idea where he'll strike next. This will hit the lunchtime news and it's going to cause absolute bloody mayhem."

There was silence in the room, everyone was stunned. Finally Angela found her voice.

"So that means we'll be hanging on to this case because it's connected to the others."

"Yes, Murphy, I'm afraid so," Frank replied. "We're short staffed due to sickness and holidays and our budget is strained to the limit, but I can't pass it on because, as you rightly pointed out, the murders are linked."

"What do we do now, Boss?" Paul asked. "How do we use this news?"

"Well Costello, that's the problem. This DNA evidence doesn't get us any further on with the enquiries. All it tells us is not to waste our time looking for a separate murderer. It doesn't tell us where to find the fucker."

"Anyway people, I've got to go and speak to my boss now. I should be back in the afternoon if he doesn't fire me. I'd like you to drive me Bill, please. We're meeting in the city centre."

Bill and Frank headed out the door leaving a stunned Angela and Paul in their wake.

"I'm dreading this hitting the news," Paul said. "And I'm not letting my wife visit Govanhill until this maniac's caught," he added.

"I know exactly how you feel," Angela replied. "I'd be nervous about going there alone and I'm a cop. No woman will be safe till we get this man. He could strike anywhere, anytime."

"And more to the point, he could attack anyone now he's moved from prostitutes to children," Paul added grimly.

As expected, Govanhill became a no-go area practically overnight and people were afraid to leave their houses. The streets were empty after seven o'clock as everyone wanted to get home and stay home before it got dark. Local businesses suffered and the female population living in the area felt isolated. The news advised women not to walk alone and not to let anyone into their homes. There were warnings from the local gas and electricity suppliers advising that their repairmen would not call without a prior telephone arrangement and that all their employees carried photo ID. It was as if the whole area had shut down. Thomas and Alan were struggling they just couldn't get enough illegally parked cars for their daily quota.

"I'm not sure what's going to happen, Son," Alan said. "The gaffer might move one of us to a different area because there's not enough work for two of us at the moment. How would you feel about it if they moved me away?"

Thomas thought about what Alan had said and the truth was he'd be ecstatic. He was sick of Alan.

"Where would they move you to?" he asked.

"I'm not sure, Thomas, but it would only be temporary you understand, just till things got back to normal here."

"And they'd move you and not me?"

"Yes, I think that would be for the best because I'm more senior and I've worked in different areas. You're happy here because you're familiar with the streets."

'*He has to go, one way or another you've got to get shot of him,*' the voice said.

"Yes," Thomas agreed, "But not yet, not now."

"No, Thomas," Alan said thinking Thomas was speaking to him. "It's not happening yet I'm just warning you that it might."

Thomas didn't care where Alan went as long as he didn't have to put up with him. All he could think about was Nadia and he was counting down the days until Sunday. He'd gone to the caravan the previous day and it was now ready for her. It had taken Thomas all day to make fast the chain and thread it through the hole he'd made in the wall of the vehicle but he was happy with the outcome. He just had to get through the rest of today then Saturday. On Sunday he'd be with her and then Nadia would be his forever.

Chapter 54

Angela had the office practically to herself on Sunday. There was, of course, typists and admin staff but Frank was somewhere else in the building doing God knows what, Paul had the day off and Bill had been loaned to another department. Her head hurt with trying to remember all the different bits of information she'd gathered on the murders, so she decided to review all the files from the beginning, to try to make some sense of them. After four hours of staring at her computer she was no further forward.

She was hungry and fed up, hours of work and nothing to show for it. Angela made herself a cup of coffee and took a chocolate biscuit from her bag. A glucose fix might help, it certainly couldn't do any harm, well not much because fortunately she could eat what she liked and never gained an ounce. As she sipped the hot, slightly metallic tasting liquid she thought back to the first case of Margaret Deacon. Angela remembered Frank saying the scene looked as if it had been staged. He referred to a cold case of ten years before. He said a boy had been found at his dead mother's side and she remembered he'd told her later that day the victim was called Clare Malone and her son was Thomas, a skinny wee boy, he'd said. Her death occurred in winter, January in fact, when Frank was a junior officer. Frank dismissed Angela's suggestion that there might be a connection between the cases even though there were similarities. Where had the killer been for the last ten years and why hadn't he killed until now? Nevertheless she had nowhere else to look and nothing else to do, so Angela called up the file on her computer and in seconds she was looking at a picture of Clare Malone.

She looked so young and fragile, too young to be a mum, Angela thought and she wondered what happened to her son? She sifted through the pages of reports and evidence and was almost about to give up when she saw that DNA evidence had been gathered at the scene. As she read the report she saw that initial testing had been done on skin samples found under the victim's fingernails but some of it had been contaminated with her own blood. Further tests were taken of the victims DNA to avoid confusion.

Angela didn't know what drove her to call up the DNA records to compare with those of the Southside Slasher but when she did her heart pounded in her chest. It wasn't an exact match but so near that only a very close relative, like a father, mother, sibling or child could have this DNA. Feeling dazed, she looked again. Angela had to be absolutely sure before she called the Boss on his mobile. She stared and stared it was almost an exact match. Angela was about to reach for her phone when she realised she'd made one subtle mistake. It was the victim's DNA that matched with the Slasher not her attacker's.

"Oh my God," she said aloud. "Our killer is a relative of Clare Malone."

Angela leaned her elbow on the desk and covered her mouth with her hand. According to the records, at the time of her death, Clare had two siblings and her parents were both alive. It also said that her son Thomas became a ward of court. So he wasn't raised by the family, how strange, she thought. Angela typed in the name Thomas Malone in the off chance there was some information on him, and bingo, up he popped. When he was sixteen Thomas was given a formal warning for kicking a dog. He said it tried to bite him but witnesses disagreed. He also had a police check when he became a traffic warden.

"Oh sweet Jesus," she said. "He's a traffic warden."

Mr Anwar's words came flooding back he'd said the man he saw wore a uniform. Angela felt as if she might faint and tears of emotion streamed down her face. I've got him she said to herself, if Frank hadn't written off her question about the son as stupid when they were at Margaret Deacon's flat, the other girls might still be alive.

* * *

Thomas arrived at the Kelvingrove gallery at twelve-thirty and parked across the road from the building. He wanted to have a good view of the main entrance because he didn't want to miss seeing Nadia when she turned up. By one o'clock there was no sign of her and he began to get nervous.

'*She's not coming,*' the voice said. '*Did you really think she would?*'

"She'll be here soon, she will," Thomas said aloud trying to convince himself. "She loves me."

'*Why would she love a useless prick like you?*'

"I'm not useless I'm a man, a real man. Shut up and leave me alone."

'*Shut up and leave me alone,*' the voice mimicked.

One-fifteen and still no sign of Nadia, Thomas was about to get out of the van and walk across the road to the gallery. Perhaps he'd missed her somehow, he thought. Perhaps she'd come in the other entrance. Just as he reached for the door handle a car pulled up and parked behind him and he looked round to see Nadia sitting in the passenger seat. He turned and faced the front quickly so as not to be recognised and watched as she stepped out of the car and crossed the road. Thomas waited for the driver to move off but he didn't seem to be leaving. He risked another glance and saw that the man was talking on his mobile phone. Thomas didn't want the man to see him so he waited an agonising five minutes until the man finished his call and drove off. As soon as the coast was clear Thomas leapt out of his van and sprinted to the gallery.

When he entered the vast hall that was the main body of the building, he crossed the magnificent tiled floor and stood in the middle of the room facing the back. He'd arranged to meet Nadia in front of the grand organ that was at the rear of the building. The huge musical instrument drew people to this place most afternoons so they could hear its amazing sound fill the hall. It was a very popular feature of the gallery. Thomas studied the milling crowd and even though it was early in the year the place was very busy. Thomas searched the faces before him and he saw Nadia almost immediately, standing dutifully, close to the rear door as arranged. She looked beautiful. She was wearing an emerald green three piece suit with the scarf draped demurely over her hair. Thomas's heart melted. She was here, she hadn't let him down he felt a familiar stirring in his loins. She'd soon be his forever.

As he walked towards Nadia she looked up and saw him. She smiled. Thomas stood before her and slowly returned the smile then he dropped his head and stared at the ground. He unconsciously moved his right foot as if rubbing something on the tiled floor. When Nadia saw Thomas he looked thinner out of his uniform and he was so shy he couldn't meet her eyes. How could she ever have doubted him she wondered? This gentle, shy, young man couldn't say boo to a goose. Now she could relax and have a lovely day in the country and her father would be none the wiser. Nadia looked forward to telling Susan all about her adventure.

They exchanged 'hellos' and chatted for a moment or two about Nadia's family and Thomas's work then Nadia asked, "Did you hear about Brenda?"

Thomas nodded but said nothing.

"Sorry, sorry," Nadia replied. "We'll just talk about nice things today."

"I think we'd better get going," he said, finding his voice. "We don't have very much time."

'*Liar, liar,*' the voice said. '*You've got all the time in the world.*'

The pair walked out of the gallery and crossed the road to the van. Thomas opened the passenger door for Nadia.

"You're such a gentleman," she said climbing in.

It was lucky that the country roads were quiet as they travelled to the caravan because Thomas found it hard to concentrate on his driving. He couldn't take his eyes of Nadia's legs. The fine fabric of her trousers left little to the imagination as it clung tantalisingly to her shapely limbs. Thomas turned on the radio and searched for a station playing easy listening music to try to distract him from his erotic thoughts. He didn't want to spoil things now. He didn't want to blow it when he was so close.

Chapter 55

The shock of her discovery completely overwhelmed Angela and it took her a few minutes to compose herself. She wasn't sure what to do next. It was now obvious, that due to Frank's dismissal of there being any connection to the earlier case, a terrible oversight had taken place. Angela didn't know how he would take the news and she was frightened to call him. She sat toying with the telephone for a few moments then she dialled her home number and prayed that Bobby wouldn't be too immersed in his work to pick up. On the fifth ring he answered.

"Hello," he said. "Who's speaking please?"

"Hi Bobby, it's me," Angela replied. "I've discovered something and I need to talk to a friendly voice before I call my boss."

"What's wrong, Darling, is there a problem? Are you okay?" Bobby sounded genuinely concerned for her. Their relationship was gradually getting back to normal after all the problems over Jake.

"I'm fine, everything is all right. I just wanted to talk, that's all. I might be late home today because when I tell the boss what I've discovered, all hell will break loose. So don't worry if I'm late, I'll see you when I see you."

"Okay, Darling. It all sounds very mysterious, but as long as you're okay. Can you tell me anything or is it a secret?"

"I can't really say anything at the moment, but we'll talk when I get home, whenever that may be."

They said their goodbyes and Angela hung up. She was now ready to phone Frank and she hoped he was still somewhere in the building and could get across to the office quickly. Her discovery was like a hot potato and she was desperate to place it in someone else's hands.

Within five minutes Frank was at her side.

"This better be good, Murphy," he said clearly annoyed. "I was in the middle of a meeting. What's so important it couldn't keep for half an hour?"

"I know the identity of our killer. I know who the Southside Slasher is," she replied flatly.

"What? What, how do you know?"

"DNA evidence, it shows that the murder of Clare Malone ten years ago is linked to our cases. Our killer has almost identical DNA to Clare Malone. So it has to be a close relative of hers who murdered the women in Govanhill."

Frank's face flushed deep red he looked as if he might have a stroke. "You're absolutely sure of this. No doubts?"

"Absolutely," Angela replied. "And there's more, I interviewed a Mr Anwar about Margaret Deacon's murder. He came to the incident room and told me that he'd seen a man in uniform, remember?"

"Yes, yes, I do remember that."

"Well it turns out Clare Malone's son is a traffic warden and he lives and works in Govanhill."

Frank sank into a chair, "Fucking hell, fucking hell, Angela. So he's our killer? That skinny wee boy I carried out of the flat over ten years ago is the Southside Slasher?"

"It looks like it, Boss."

Frank stared at Angela he looked beaten and bereft, in that instant Angela knew he remembered their conversation at Margaret Deacon's flat. There was no need to mention it again. Frank had to live with his own demons. Frank made a brief telephone call to his colleagues to say he wouldn't be returning to the meeting. Although there were important issues on the agenda he now had bigger fish to fry.

"Have you got a note of Malone's current address," he asked Angela and she assured him she had. "We'll head there now and see if we can nab the fucker. Have you got your car today?"

"It's in the car park, Boss."

Frank seemed edgy his face twitched and his hands couldn't stop moving. "I could do with a whisky right now," he said and gave Angela a wry look. "That's how it starts, Murphy, with one drink."

Angela didn't reply, what could she say that Frank didn't already know? Within a couple of minutes they were in her car and within fifteen they were pulling up outside Thomas Malone's apartment. Frank pressed the security entry button then they waited, but there was no reply. He then pressed the other buttons on the pad and a resident of one of the apartments buzzed them into the close. Thomas lived on the second floor. Frank peered through the letter box but there was no sign of anybody being home. As they descended the stairs the neighbour on the first floor who'd let them in was standing at his door.

"He's gone out," the man said. "I saw him leave about lunchtime. Can I give him a message for you?"

"Do you know Mr Malone?" Frank asked.

"Not really," the man replied. "He keeps himself to himself."

"Oh well, I'll catch him later," Frank replied the ambiguity of his statement not being lost on Angela.

When they were back seated in the car Angela asked, "What do we do now, Boss?"

"I'll telephone and arrange for a warrant to search the apartment and in the meantime we wait. Hopefully he'll come home later today. Paul and Bill will have to be on call to relieve us if he doesn't come home soon and we need a break. Now be a good girl and nip round to the cafe for some sandwiches and tea before I faint from hunger and I'll have a custard doughnut as well."

Angela did as she was told and walked to the cafe while Frank made some calls. She wasn't sure if she was hungry because her stomach was tied in knots from the tension and excitement of it all. However, she thought she'd better buy something, just in case she was stuck there for a long time. As she walked along the street she realised that any of the men she passed could be Thomas Malone and she began to search their faces. It had suddenly become very real.

* * *

Thomas and Nadia arrived at the land where the caravan was parked at two-fifteen and they stepped out of the van into the sunshine. It wasn't a warm day but at least it was dry and bright.

Nadia looked around, "Where's this caravan then? I don't see anything."

Thomas chuckled to himself, "I couldn't see it the first time I came here, but I can assure you it is still there, it hasn't been moved or stolen. Look over towards the small group of trees on your left. Can you see it now?"

Nadia stared and stared, "No," she stated, "I can't see anything."

"Walk with me and I'll show you. You'll see it when we get closer."

They walked towards the trees and as they neared them Nadia exclaimed, "Oh, I see it, I see it now. It's so well hidden that unless you knew about it you'd never find it."

Thomas led Nadia to the door, unlocked it then ushered her inside. He switched on a light because with the window boarded up it was very dark.

"You see what I mean about this place. You could live here very easily for quite a long time and be very comfortable."

Nadia looked around as Thomas showed her the toilet, the cooking rings, the long seat and the table. "But where would you sleep?" she asked. "I don't see a bed."

"There is a bed and it's very comfortable," Thomas said. "Stand back and I'll show you how it works."

Nadia did as she was told and stood aside. Thomas lifted the table top out of the supports and placed it to one side then he unfolded the long seat to reveal a double bed.

"There you are," he said triumphantly. "It's comfortable, try it."

Nadia stepped forward and sat on the bed, "It is comfortable," she agreed.

Thomas stood opposite her facing her. His heart was thumping so loud he could hear it. Nadia made to stand up.

"Wait just a minute," Thomas said, "Stay in your seat I've something to show you."

He reached down and rooted around at the side of the bed then without warning he grabbed Nadia's wrist and snapped on the handcuff. She sat startled staring at her wrist.

"What is this, what's going on, let me go," she said pulling at the cuff, panic rising in her throat.

Thomas went to the other end of the caravan and squatted down leaning against the wall. He stared at Nadia as she wrenched at the chain and tried to get free. He was filled with a mixture of fear and lust as Nadia shouted and pleaded and cried. Her eyes were wide with terror and she looked like a frightened deer.

Thomas reached inside the waistband of his trousers and massaged his genitals. Nadia stared in horror as he unzipped his trousers and took out his penis, it looked hard and huge, she'd never seen a naked man before and she was petrified. Thomas rubbed and caressed himself to a shuddering climax then leaned back and shut his eyes. Nadia curled herself into a tight ball and cowered in the corner of the bed. After a few moments Thomas regained his composure, cleaned himself up and tucked himself back into his trousers. He walked over to where Nadia lay.

"Next time I'll make love to you. Did you like how I looked? Did you see how big I got? Women love big cocks," he said to the terrified girl. "I read that in a magazine. Next time I'll put it inside you and turn you into a real woman. I know how to do it and it won't hurt much. I'm sorry you won't be my first, Brenda was my first but she doesn't count because I didn't love her."

Nadia couldn't speak, raw terror silenced her.

"I'm going to go now," Thomas said looking at his watch, "I want to be home for dinnertime. You can reach the toilet and there's bottled water in the little cupboard beside the bed. I'll feed you in a couple of days when I come back. You'll be hungry and tired but that'll make it easier for me to make love to you. After the first time it won't hurt you and you'll beg me to fuck you again and again. I promise you Nadia, you'll see, you'll love it. I know all about sex thanks to my magazines."

Thomas leaned over and kissed Nadia on the top of her head. Her face was frozen with fear and she was shaking uncontrollably. "You might want to ration the light, there's a switch beside the bed," he added before leaving. "The battery won't last forever and you'll need it to find your way to the toilet."

Thomas left the caravan and locked the door behind him. Everything had gone exactly to plan and he was feeling elated, and as he drove home in the van he couldn't help whistling. He couldn't wait for Tuesday because he'd booked the afternoon off and he planned to spend the whole of it with Nadia.

Chapter 56

It was nearly ten to six and Angela and Frank had practically exhausted 'I spy with my little eye' when a small white van pulled up and parked in front of Angela's BMW. Angela was feeling grubby and tired after working for eleven hours, but an adrenalin surge drew her fully awake when she saw Thomas Malone step from the van carrying shopping bags from Morrison's.

"That's him, that's our man," she said excitedly and her hand reached for the door handle.

"Whoa, stop right there, hold your horses, where do you think you're going?" Frank asked.

"I'm going in there to get him," Angela replied pointing a thumb towards Thomas's apartment.

"Just think for a minute will you Murphy. A few hours ago I phoned for a warrant, we'll have it by now. Mr Malone is probably home for the night and if the shopping bags he was carrying are anything to go by, he's about to make his dinner. We know we're going to bring him in but do you really want a crazed killer loose in the back of this nice car?"

Angela stared blankly at Frank, "What should we do then?" she asked.

"I'm going to make a telephone call for a van to be sent to transport him and I'm also going to ask them to collect the warrant. When they arrive and only when they arrive, you and I will pay Mr Malone a wee visit. In the meantime we sit here and observe. It's my turn, I believe, I spy with my little eye...."

The next twenty minutes were excruciating for Angela, her patience was strained to the limit. How could the Boss be so calm when their killer was only a few yards away? Finally the van arrived with two uniformed officers. They parked in front of Thomas' white van and then they sauntered over to Frank's side of the car. He wound down the window.

"Hi lads," he said. "Have you got my warrant?"

One of them produced a folded paper from his pocket and handed it to Frank.

"Have we really got the Southside Slasher?" he asked.

"Looks like it," Frank replied. "Detective Murphy and I are going to get him right now. If you boys wait here we shouldn't be too long."

Angela and Frank ascended the stairs. They'd already left the lock of the front security door in the open position, so they didn't have to be buzzed in this time. Angela's heart was in her mouth and her ears pounded with rising blood pressure. She was scared and excited all at the same time. Frank pressed the bell and after only a moment, a tall, slim, fragile looking, young man opened the door. He had gentle eyes with heavy lids and his expression didn't change when Frank identified himself and Angela.

"Do you want to come in?" Thomas invited and they stepped through the door.

The apartment was immaculate and uncluttered. There was just one armchair in the room and one wooden chair at the table. Thomas sat at the table leaving Angela and Frank to stand.

"We'd like to ask you a few questions about the recent murders Mr Malone. Did you know Margaret Deacon?"

Thomas heard the name Margaret Deacon but in his mind he saw his mother. She was lying on the floor in a pool of blood and he was kneeling beside her.

'*It's all right Thomas, I'm with you now and I'll help you,*' the voice said. '*Don't be frightened, go with the policeman. Someone else will sort out this mess. It's not your problem. Forget about it.*'

Frank realised by the blank look on his face that Thomas Malone had retreated to another place and time. He gently held Thomas's arm and eased him out of the chair then grabbed the jacket that was hanging on a hook by the door as he led him out of the apartment.

"Thank you," Thomas mouthed but no sound came out.

* * *

It was nearly seven o'clock and Zaffer was frantic, where was she? It was nearly two hours since they should have met up and Nadia had never been late before. He'd searched all over the Gallery but she wasn't there. He'd even had the gallery staff help him but they'd found no trace of her. If she's gone off gallivanting with her friend she'll be grounded for the rest of her life, he thought. Zaffer phoned the house again but she still hadn't come home. He didn't know what to do. Then all he could think about was Brenda Eadie and he began to panic. What if someone had taken his Nadia?

Zaffer phoned the police. The officer taking the call had tried to placate him by telling him that wandering off and lying to their parents about where they were going was normal teenage behaviour. But when Zaffer mentioned Brenda Eadie and the fact that they had been in the same year at the same school, the officer's attitude changed and he had him put through to a Detective Gordon McKay.

Gordon hadn't been doing much work on the Eadie case but he knew that the Sarwar family were somehow connected to it so he quickly called up the files and read the notes on his computer screen as Zaffer was patched through. After a few minutes of conversation with Zaffer he realised that they might have a genuine problem. Nadia Sarwar had led a very sheltered and protected life, going missing like this was completely out of character for her. Gordon McKay told Zaffer to go home and wait there and a police officer would call to take his statement. He asked the distraught man to look out a recent photograph of his daughter. Then he called Frank's mobile phone because he needed advice about what to do next.

Frank and Angela were in an interview room with Thomas Malone. The young man was calm but unresponsive. So far he hadn't even acknowledged where he was never mind answering questions. Frank's mobile began to ring and he answered it then listened intently to what Gordon McKay had to say.

"Nadia Sarwar's missing? You're sure she not just gone away with a friend?"

A flash of recognition crossed Thomas's face and Frank noticed it.

"Hold on a moment Gordon," he said. "Nadia Sarwar is missing. Do you know where Nadia is Thomas," Frank asked.

Thomas stared at Frank. His eyes were like hard little stones. "She's safe, my Nadia's safe. I've got her and they'll never find her. They wanted to send her away. She loves me and I love her. She's going to be my wife."

"I'll call you back Gordon," Frank said and hung up. He felt sick. He wondered if Nadia Sarwar was still alive and, if she was, then where the hell was she? He looked at Angela for inspiration because this was all new ground for him.

Taking his cue Angela spoke gently to Thomas. "Have you got a house for Nadia, have you got somewhere to live?"

Thomas turned to Angela she had a nice smile and a gentle voice. "I've got a wee house in the country," he replied.

"Whereabouts in the country? Is it somewhere nearby?" Angela probed.

'*Shut up you fool,*' the voice said. '*Do you want her to be found? Fucking idiot, you nearly gave the game away. If they find her she'll be shipped to Pakistan and married off. Is that what you want? Idiot, you're a fucking idiot.*'

Thomas's face resumed its blank expression and it was clear he wasn't going to talk anymore. Frank had arranged for a psychiatrist to assess him but he already knew what he'd find. The young man was off his head, his brain was fried and he was definitely headed for the mental hospital at Carstairs.

Angela and Frank left the interview room to talk.

"Oh Frank, he's got that young girl," Angela said with a catch in her voice. "Do you think he's killed her?"

"I just don't know and I don't know how to find her. Laughing boy in there's not talking."

"Why don't we put their pictures on the telly and ask the public for help. Someone might just have seen them together."

"I hate involving the public because we get so many loonies calling in but I can't think of anything else to do. The minutes are ticking away and she might be lying injured somewhere. I'll phone Gordon Mckay back, he took the call from Zaffer Sarwar. Your shift was over hours ago Murphy but you can work on if you want."

"Thanks, Boss, I'll stay," Angela replied. Wild horses couldn't have dragged her away.

By the time the police secured a photo of Nadia and discussed their plans with her family it was nearly ten o'clock. The parents were understandably horrified that their daughter had been taken by the man responsible for four murders.

"Please find her, please bring her home," Nadia's mother pleaded with Angela. She held Angela's hand in a tight grip as if by letting her go, she was also somehow, letting go of her daughter.

"We're doing everything we can, Mrs Sarwar," Angela assured her. "Mr Malone is being questioned by a psychiatrist and we're hopeful that he'll tell him where Nadia is. There's shortly going to be a news-flash on the television asking for the public's help. Stay strong we'll find her."

Angela gently extricated her hand from Mrs Sarwar and passed her over to the care of a family liaison officer. Then she went to join Frank.

"We can't do any more tonight," he said. "Go home and get some sleep, we'll be called if anything happens otherwise I'll see you at seven tomorrow morning." Frank looked sick with exhaustion and Angela felt the same way. The initial adrenalin rush had dissipated and she was shattered.

"Do you want a lift home, Frank?" she asked.

"No, you just get yourself home," he answered. "At least you've not got far to go. A uniformed officer is taking me. Are you okay to drive or do you want a lift? You could pick your car up tomorrow if you want."

"Thanks Frank, but I'm fine. I'll see you tomorrow."

Angela drove home in a daze. When she got inside her house she couldn't even remember the journey because she was so tired. Her arms and legs felt leaden and she let Bobby help her to undress and put her to bed. Angela was asleep as soon as her head hit the pillow and thankfully her sleep was dreamless.

Chapter 57

When Thomas left the caravan without hurting her, Nadia was very relieved. She waited, listening intently for any sounds of him moving about outside before exhaling her bated breath and taking stock of her situation. He said he'd return in two days. Surely by that time she'd be able to free herself and make her escape, she thought. Nadia looked around for something to pry open the handcuffs but found nothing. She pulled at the chain to try and loosen it but it was securely anchored somewhere outside the caravan. Because the window was boarded up she had no idea whether it was day or night or how long she'd been there. Her bag containing her drawing pad, purse and mobile phone were tantalisingly out of reach. Nadia pulled and pushed at the handcuff trying to force it over her hand. She worked and worked at it but only managed to rub the skin raw on her wrist.

Realising that she couldn't escape Nadia sat on the bed and wept with despair. She cried for her poor mother who'd be distraught and she wondered if her father was looking for her. He'd be so angry that she'd been alone with a man, she wasn't even allowed to talk to men from her community unless chaperoned and now she'd trusted someone she hardly knew.

Nadia was overwhelmed with feelings of claustrophobia, what if the caravan caught fire and she was trapped? She didn't want to sit in the dark but she was scared that the electric light might somehow set fire to the wood of the structure. She switched off the light but immediately felt crushed by the darkness, imagining spiders and ants running all over her body, she flicked on the switch again and cried with frustration at her weakness.

An arranged marriage didn't seem so bad now because at least it was planned with love and with her best interests at heart. The man's family would never want her now, no one would. After this, she'd be damaged goods. If someone didn't find her and save her, Thomas would return to rape her. He'd raped and murdered Brenda maybe he'd kill her too.

Nadia knelt on the floor, cupped her hands over her face and began to pray.

* * *

The newsflash hadn't been shown until after Alan and Ann had gone to bed, then he'd left for work in the morning without switching on the television set. It was nearly ten-thirty when Ann got up, her MS was playing up and she couldn't summon the energy to rise before then. She listened to her favourite CD as she ate her breakfast and only then switched on the television for the lunchtime news at one. Fortunately she was sitting on the sofa in the lounge when the photos of Thomas and Nadia were flashed onto the screen because she passed out from the shock. When she'd recovered sufficiently she telephoned Alan. She was almost incoherent. Fearing she was seriously ill he raced home where he found Ann still sitting on the sofa, she was distraught and her eyes were red from crying.

"What's happened Ann? Are you ill?" Alan asked. He was very worried about her.

"It's Thomas," was all she could manage to say.

"I'm not working with Thomas this week," Alan replied. "You know I'm working different streets at the moment."

"Thomas's picture was on the news," Ann spluttered. "He's the murderer. Thomas is the Southside Slasher."

Alan stared at his wife as if she'd spoken in a foreign language. He couldn't comprehend what she was saying.

"What are you talking about, Ann? Where has all this come from? Are you Ill? Do you need a doctor?"

"Oh, for God's sake Alan, listen to me," she protested. "It's all over the news. Thomas is the Southside Slasher and he's kidnapped a young girl. He's holding her somewhere. You need to call the police."

Ann's words finally sank in. Alan sat on a chair, rested his elbows on his knees and held his head in his hands.

"Oh my God, oh my dear God," he said. "He's kidnapped a girl you say?"

Ann nodded, "He's hidden her somewhere. The police think she's being held in a house in the country. They've asked the public for help. Do you think he's taken her to the caravan?"

Alan felt a wave of nausea sweep over him and he could taste sick in his mouth. Of course that's where he'd take her, he thought. "Did they mention the girl's name?" he asked.

"It's all right it's not Mary," Ann replied. "The girl's name is Nadia."

"Oh sweet Jesus, that's the name of the Asian lassie he fancied, her name's Nadia. I'd better phone the police," Alan said.

With shaking hands he dialled 999 and told his story to the girl who answered the call and within a couple of minutes he was put through to Angela. Alan explained that the mobile home was hard to find and Angela arranged for a police car to pick him up.

Within two hours Angela and Frank, two patrol cars, one of them transporting Alan, and an ambulance raced down the narrow country roads towards Alan's mobile home. As two uniformed officers broke down the door Nadia started screaming, she thought Thomas had returned. It took a couple of minutes and a pair of bolt cutters to release her from the handcuff then the exhausted girl was taken to the ambulance and driven away.

"He hadn't touched her yet, thank God," Frank said. "It could have been so much worse."

"He's done so many terrible things, he's damaged so many lives," Angela replied. "Even that Alan and his wife have been hurt. They'll never get over this you know."

Frank put in a call to Nadia's parents then arranged for a car to take them to the hospital to be reunited with her. They were overjoyed, although once he knew she was safe, Zaffer was particularly interested to make sure that no man had touched his daughter.

"That's her school days over," Frank said. "That wee lassie will be on the first plane to Pakistan to marry some old grandfather."

* * *

Within a week Thomas Malone was old news, but it would be months before Angela could shut the book on the case. One thing was sure though, she'd never forget the frightening, dangerous, young man and she hoped he'd spend the rest of his life locked away.

Thomas didn't mind being in the hospital although he wondered why he was there. He didn't feel ill but he dutifully took his medication nevertheless. As he sat on the chair in his psychiatrist's room he was calm and coherent. He was happy to answer questions but he simply didn't know the answers. He'd never heard of Margaret Deacon, Anne-Marie Connor, Megan Reece or Brenda Eadie. He was desperate to get back home to Nadia, he was sure she'd be worried that he'd been away for so long.

"Nadia loves me," he told his doctor. "She's waiting for me to come home. Will you phone her and tell her I'll be back as soon as I can?"

'*Fucking idiot,*' the voice said. '*They're not going to send you home. You'll have to make your own plans and be ready to leave here when you get the chance.*'

The psychiatrist was frustrated with Thomas he just couldn't get through to him. He stood up from his chair and paced the room and, as he did, Thomas reached out and helped himself to his very well sharpened pencil.

Also by Elly Grant

The Coming of the Lord
Breaking the Thomas Malone case was an achievement but nothing could prepare DC Angela Murphy or her colleagues for the challenge ahead.

Escaped psychopathic sociopath John Baptiste is big, powerful and totally out of control. Guided by his perverse religious interpretation of morality, he wreaks havoc.

An under-resourced police department struggles to cope, not only with this new threat, but also the ruthless antics of ganglord, Jackie McGeachy.

Pressure mounts along with the body count.

Glasgow has never felt more dangerous.

Read the whole book; buy your copy from http://author.to/ellygrant

Death in the Pyrenees Series

Book 1- **Palm Trees in the Pyrenees**
   Take one rooky female cop
   Add a dash or two of mysterious death
   And a heap of prejudice and suspicion
   Place all in a small French spa town
   And stir well
   Turn up the heat
   And simmer until thoroughly cooked
   The result will be surprising

Palm Trees in the Pyrenees gives you an insight into the workings and atmosphere of small town France against a background of gender, sexual, racial and religious prejudice.

The story unfolds, told by Danielle a single, downtrodden , thirty year old, who is the only cop in the small Pyrenean town. She feels unappreciated and unnoticed, having been passed over for promotion in favour of her male colleagues working in the region. But everything is about to change. The sudden and mysterious death of a much hated locally based Englishman will have far reaching affects.

sample - CHAPTER 1

His death occurred quickly and almost silently. It took only seconds of tumbling and clawing at air before the inevitable thud as he hit the ground. He landed in the space in front of the bedroom window of the basement apartment. As no-one was home at the time, and as the flat was actually below ground level, he may have gone unnoticed but for the insistent yapping of the scrawny, aged poodle belonging to the equally scrawny and aged Madame Laurent.

Indeed, everything in the town continued as normal for a few moments. The husbands who'd been sent to collect the baguettes for breakfast had stopped, as usual, at the bar to enjoy a customary glass of pastis and a chat with the patrone and other customers. Women gathered in the little square beside the river, where the daily produce market took place, to haggle for fruit, vegetables and honey before moving the queue to the boucherie to choose the meat for their evening meals.

Yes, that day began like any other. It was a cold, crisp February morning and the sky was a bright, clear blue just as it had been every morning since the start of the year. The yellow Mimosa shone out luminously in the morning sunshine from the dark green of the Pyrenees.

Gradually, word filtered out of the boucherie and down the line of waiting women that the first spring lamb of the season had made its way onto the butcher's counter and everyone wanted some. Conversation switched from whether Madame Portes actually grew the Brussels sprouts she sold on her stall, or simply bought them at the supermarket in Perpignan then resold them at a higher price, to speculating whether or not there would be sufficient lamb to go round. A notable panic rippled down the queue at the very thought of there not being enough as none of the women wanted to disappoint her family. That would be unacceptable in this small Pyrenean spa town, as in this small town, like many others in the region a woman's place as housewife and mother was esteemed and revered. Even though many held jobs outside the home, their responsibility to their family was paramount.

Yes, everyone followed their usual routine until the siren blared out – twice. The siren was a wartime relic that had never been decommissioned even though the war had ended over half a century before. It was retained as a means of summoning the pompiers, who were not only the local firemen but also paramedics. One blast of the siren was used when there was a minor road accident or if someone took unwell at the spa but two blasts was for something extremely serious.

The last time there were two blasts was when a very drunken Jean-Claude accidentally shot Monsieur Reynard while mistaking him for a boar. Fortunately Monsieur Reynard recovered but he still had a piece of shot lodged in his head which caused his eye to squint when he was tired. This served as a constant reminder to Jean-Claude of what he'd done as he had to see Monsieur Reynard every day in the cherry orchard where they both worked.

On hearing two blasts of the siren everyone stopped in their tracks and everything seemed to stand still. A hush fell over the town as people strained to listen for the shrill sounds of the approaching emergency vehicles. Some craned their necks skyward hoping to see the police helicopter arrive from Perpignan and, whilst all were shocked that something serious had occurred, they were also thrilled by the prospect of exciting, breaking news. Gradually, the chattering restarted. Shopping was forgotten and the market abandoned. The boucherie was left unattended as its patrone followed the crowd of women making their way to the main street. In the bar the glasses of pastis were hastily swallowed instead of being leisurely sipped as everyone rushed to see what had happened.

As well as police and pompiers, a large and rather confused group of onlookers arrived outside an apartment building owned by an English couple called Carter. They arrived on foot and on bicycles. They brought ageing relatives, pre-school children, prams and shopping. Some even brought their dogs. Everyone peered and stared and chatted to each other. It was like a party without the balloons or streamers.

There was a buzz of nervous excitement as the police from the neighbouring larger town began to cordon off the area around the apartment block with tape. Monsieur Brune was told in no uncertain terms to restrain his dog, as it kept running over to where the body lay, and was contaminating the area in more ways than one.

A slim woman wearing a crumpled linen dress was sitting on a chair in the paved garden of the apartment block, just inside the police line. Her elbows rested on her knees and she held her head in her hands. Her limp, brown hair hung over her face. Every so often she lifted her chin, opened her eyes and took in great, gasping breaths of air as if she was in danger of suffocating. Her whole body shook. Madame Carter, Belinda, hadn't actually fainted but she was close to it. Her skin was clammy and her pallor grey. Her eyes threatened at any moment to roll back in their sockets and blot out the horror of what she'd just seen.

She was being supported by her husband, David, who was visibly shocked. His tall frame sagged as if his thin legs could no longer support his weight and he kept swiping away tears from his face with the backs of his hands. He looked dazed and, from time to time, he covered his mouth with his hand as if trying to hold in his emotions but he was completely overcome.

The noise from the crowd became louder and more excitable and words like accident, suicide and even murder abounded. Claudette, the owner of the bar that stood across the street from the incident, supplied the chair on which Belinda now sat. She realized that she was in a very privileged position, being inside the police line, so Claudette stayed close to the chair and Belinda. She patted the back of Belinda's hand distractedly, while endeavouring to overhear tasty morsels of conversation to pass on to her rapt audience. The day was turning into a circus and everyone wanted to be part of the show.

Finally, a specialist team arrived. There were detectives, uniformed officers, secretaries, people who dealt with forensics and even a dog handler. The tiny police office was not big enough to hold them all so they commandeered a room at the Mairie, which is our town hall.

It took the detectives three days to take statements and talk to the people who were present in the building when the man, named Steven Gold, fell. Three days of eating in local restaurants and drinking in the bars much to the delight of the proprietors. I presumed these privileged few had expense accounts, a facility we local police did not enjoy. I assumed that my hard earned taxes paid for these expense accounts yet none of my so called colleagues asked me to join them.

They were constantly being accosted by members of the public and pumped for information. Indeed everyone in the town wanted to be their friend and be a party to a secret they could pass on to someone else. There was a buzz of excitement about the place that I hadn't experienced for a very long time. People who hadn't attended church for years suddenly wanted to speak to the priest. The doctor who'd attended the corpse had a full appointment book. And everyone wanted to buy me a drink so they could ask me questions. I thought it would never end. But it did. As quickly as it had started, everybody packed up, and then they were gone.

Read the whole book; buy your copy from http://author.to/ellygrant

Book 2 - **Grass Grows in the Pyrenees**

Take one female cop and add a dash of power
Throw in a dangerous gangster
Some violent men
And a whole bunch of cannabis
Sprinkle around a small French spa town
And mix thoroughly
Cook on a hot grill until the truth is revealed
The result will be scorching.

Grass Grows in the Pyrenees, second book in the series "Death in the Pyrenees," gives an insight into the workings and atmosphere of a small French town and the surrounding mountains, in the Eastern Pyrenees.

The story unfolds told by Danielle, a single, thirty-year-old, recently promoted cop. The sudden and mysterious death of a local farmer suspected of growing cannabis, opens a 'Pandora's' box of trouble. It's a race against time to stop the gangsters before the town, and everyone in it, is damaged beyond repair.

Book 3 - **Red Light in the Pyrenees**

Take one respected female cop
Add two or three drops of violent death
Some ladies of the night
And a bucket full of blood
Place all in, and around, a small French spa town
Stir constantly with money and greed
Until all becomes clear
The result will be very satisfying

Red light in the Pyrenees, third in the series Death in the Pyrenees, gives you an insight into the workings and atmosphere of a small French town in the Eastern Pyrenees. The story unfolds, told by Danielle, a single, thirty-something, female cop. The sudden and violent death of a local Madam brings fear to her working girls and unsettles the town. But doesn't every cloud have a silver lining? Danielle follows the twists and turns of events until a surprising truth is revealed. Hold your breath, it's a bumpy ride.

Book 4 – Dead End in the Pyrenees

Take a highly-respected female cop
Add a bunch of greedy people
And place all in a small French town
Throw in a large helping of opportunity, lies and deceit
Add a pinch in prejudice
A twist of resentment
And dot with death and despair.
Be prepared for some shocking revelations
Dangerous predators are everywhere
Then sit down, relax and enjoy
With a dash or two of humour
And plenty of curiosity

'Dead End in the Pyrenees' is the fourth book in Elly Grant's 'Death in the Pyrenees' series. Follow Danielle, a female cop located in a small town on the French side of the Pyrenees as she tries to solve a murder at the local spa. This story is about life in a small French town, local events, colourful characters, prejudice and of course death.

Book 5 - Deadly Degrees in the Pyrenees

The ghastly murder of a local estate agent reveals unscrupulous business deals which have the whole town talking. Michelle Moliner was not liked, but why would someone want to kill her? The story unfolds, told by Danielle, a single, thirty-something, female cop based in a small French town in the Eastern Pyrenees. Danielle's friends may be in danger and she must discover who the killer is before anyone else is harmed.

Deadly Degrees in the Pyrenees is the 5th book in the Death in the Pyrenees series. It's about life, local events, colourful characters, prejudice and of course death in a small French town

Read the whole books; buy your copies from http://author.to/ellygrant

Never Ever Leave Me

'Never Ever Leave Me' is a modern christmas romance

Katy Bradley had a perfect life, or so she thought. Perfect husband, perfect job and a perfect home until one day, one awful day when everything fell apart.

Full of fear and dread, Katy had no choice but to run, but would her split-second decision carry her forward to safety or back to the depths of despair? A chance encounter with a handsome stranger gives her hope.

Never ever leave me, sees Katy trapped between two worlds, her future and her past. Will she have the strength to survive? Will she ever find happiness again?

Read the whole book; buy your copy from http://author.to/ellygrant

Death at Presley Park

In the center of a leafy suburb, everyone is having fun until the unthinkable happens. The man walks into the middle of the picnic ground seemingly unnoticed and without warning, opens fire indiscriminately into the startled crowd. People collapse, wounded, and dying. Those who can, flee for their lives.

Who is this madman and why is he here? And when stakes are high, who will become a hero and who will abandon their friends?

Elly Grant's 'Death At Presley Park' is a convincing psychological thriller.

Read the whole book; buy your copy from http://author.to/ellygrant

But Billy Can't Fly (released by Elly Grant together with Angi Fox)

At over six feet tall, blonde and blue-eyed, Billy looks like an Adonis, but he is simple minded, not the full shilling, one slice less than a sandwich, not quite right in the head. When you meet him, you might not notice at first, but after a couple of minutes it becomes apparent. The lights are on but nobody's home. In Billy's mind, he's Superman, a righter of wrongs, a saver of souls and that's where it all goes wrong. He interacts with the people he meets at a bus stop; Jez, a rich public schoolboy; Melanie, the office slut; Bella Worthington, the leader of the local W.I. and David, a gay, Jewish teacher. This book moves along quickly as each character tells their part of the tale. Billy's story is darkly funny, poignant, and tragic. Full of stereotypical prejudices, it offends on every level, but is difficult to put down.

Read the whole book; buy your copy from http://author.to/ellygrant

Twists and Turns (Released by Elly Grant together with Zach Abrams)

With fear, horror, death and despair, these stories will surprise you, scare you and occasionally make you smile. Twists & Turns offer the reader thought provoking tales. Whether you have a minute to spare or an hour or more, open 'Twists & Turns' for a world full of mystery, murder, revenge and intrigue. A unique collaboration from the authors Elly Grant and Zach Abrams

Here's the index of Twists and Turns -

TABLE OF CONTENTS

A selection of stories by Elly Grant and Zach Abrams ranging in length across flash fiction (under 250 words), short (under 1000 words) medium (under 5000 words) and long (approx. 16,000 words)

About the author

Hi, my name is Elly Grant and I like to kill people. I use a variety of methods. Some I drop from a great height, others I drown, but I've nothing against suffocation, poisoning or simply battering a person to death. As long as it grabs my reader's attention, I'm satisfied.

I've written several novels and short stories. My first novel, 'Palm Trees in the Pyrenees' is set in a small town in France. It is published by Author Way Limited. Author Way has already published the next three novels in the series, 'Grass Grows in the Pyrenees,' 'Red Light in the Pyrenees' and 'Dead End in the Pyrenees' as well as a collaboration of short stories called 'Twists and Turns'.

As I live in a small French town in the Eastern Pyrenees, I get inspiration from the way of life and the colourful characters I come across. I don't have to search very hard to find things to write about and living in the most prolific wine producing region in France makes the task so much more delightful.

When I first arrived in this region I was lulled by the gentle pace of life, the friendliness of the people and the simple charm of the place. But dig below the surface and, like people and places the world over, the truth begins to emerge. Petty squabbles, prejudice, jealousy and greed are all there waiting to be discovered. Oh, and what joy in that discovery. So, as I sit in a café, or stroll by the riverside, or walk high into the mountains in the sunshine I greet everyone I meet with a smile and a 'Bonjour' and, being a friendly place, they return the greeting. I people watch as I sip my wine or when I go to buy my baguette. I discover quirkiness and quaintness around every corner. I try to imagine whether the subjects of my scrutiny are nice or nasty and, once I've decided, some of those unsuspecting people, a very select few, I kill.

Perhaps you will visit my town one day. Perhaps you will sit near me in a café or return my smile as I walk past you in the street. Perhaps you will hold my interest for a while, and maybe, just maybe, you will be my next victim. But don't concern yourself too much, because, at least for the time being, I always manage to confine my murderous ways to paper.

Read books from the 'Death in the Pyrenees' series, enter my small French town and meet some of the people who live there – and die there.

To contact the author mailto:ellygrant@authorway.net

To purchase books by Elly Grant link to http://author.to/ellygrant

Printed in Great Britain
by Amazon

31656199R00180